The Peacock Butterfly: Redux
Second Chances

A novel by J.V. Lamotte

The Peacock Butterfly: Redux
Second Chances

Published by bent spoon Media, LLC
19595 Waterford Place, Shorewood, MN, 55331
editor@bentspoonmedia.com
Phone: (925) 588-1983

www.thepeacockbutterfly.com

bent spoon
Media

Dedication

This book is dedicated to the readers of *The Peacock Butterfly*, who encouraged me to write a sequel when there was never a thought of writing one.

Acknowledgements

My gratitude to Abir Tebbo, executive director at Towers of The Waldorf Astoria, New York, New York, for her contributions, allowing me to write the scenes of Room 42H3 with authenticity. And for graciously taking time from their busy work schedules to assist with my research of the Hotel Cipriani, I recognize; Sarah Winters, Kara Hoffman, Ulku Erucar, Alison Peters, and Kristen Fattizzi. I also want to thank, Tracey Clinton, director of marketing and communications at Le Manoir Aux Quat'Saison, Great Milton Oxfordshire UK; Sawan Thakkar, regional manager of operations (north east) for Morton's The Steakhouse; Bethany Landa, marketing executive at Chewton Glen Hotel & Spa, New Forest, Hampshire UK; Judith Curthoys, archivist; Jim Godfrey, verger at Christ Church Oxford England; Chris McDowell, head of content for the Oxford Mail/The Oxford Times (Newsquest Oxfordshire), and Rob Archer for his military expertise in explaining the operations of an aircraft carrier in layman's terms.

I want to thank each and every one of you for your invaluable insights, which enhanced the writing of this book.

The following is a sequel to J.V. Lamotte's
"The Peacock Butterfly."

Table of Contents

FAMILY GENEALOGY

FOR THE MEYER – STEWART – HICKS – STARK FAMILIES

THE MEYER FAMILY

Grandma and Grandpa Meyer

Son – Peter

~~~~~~~~~~~~~~~~~~~~~~~~~~~~

THE STEWART FAMILY

Grandma and Grandpa Stewart

Daughter – Ruth

**

Peter Meyer married Ruth Stewart

Daughter – Nena (Rena) – ex-husband Ben (Benedict – Benny) Hicks, fiancé Sam (Samuel) Katz

Son – Josh (wife Gabby)

Son – Danny (Daniel) and Daughter – Rachael

~~~~~~~~~~~~~~~~~~~~~~~~~~~~

THE HICKS FAMILY

Jack (John) Hicks

Brother – Buddy

**

Jack married Helen O'Malley

Son – Benedict (Benny – Ben)

Son – John Jr. (Jackie)

**

Ben Hicks married Nena (Rena) Meyer

Daughter – Becky (Rebecca)

~~~~~~~~~~~~~~~~~~~~~~~~~~~~~~~~~~~

THE STARK FAMILY

Jason Robinson Stark II (Jay)

Wife – Trudi

Son – Jason Robinson Stark III (Robbie) (J.R.)

**

J.R. (Jason Robinson Stark III) married Becky (Rebecca) Hicks

Twin sons – Marc John (M. J.) and Daniel Peter Samuel (Daniel)

Reflections

From her living room window, she could see gondolas silently gliding along the Venetian canal. Gondoliers serenaded their passengers, and the picturesque scene reminded her of a Canaletto painting. Flooded with memories, she thought about life's second chances.

PART I

1992–1994

Chapter 1

"Come on Ben, hurry up or we'll miss the plane."

"We have plenty of time; we're not going to miss our plane, Uncle Buddy. You're more nervous than I am, and I'm her father."

Ben jumped into the back seat of the limo where Buddy was already seated, clutching the plane tickets for dear life. They were flying to England to attend Becky's graduation from Oxford University. Buddy had been looking forward to this trip for months, excited the family would be together for the first time in years.

**

While Ben struggled to reconcile the shambles of his life, and his divorce from Nena, he had joined Buddy in the family oil business. Working alongside his uncle brought Ben more satisfaction than he could have imagined. He had assumed most of the office duties, hired additional employees, and expanded the company by adding a heating and air-conditioning service.

With Ben at the helm, Buddy was finally able to slow down. The business his father had begun, and he and his brother Jack had inherited, would live on with Jack's son — his nephew Ben, giving Buddy a sense of continuity and comfort he never envisioned. With Buddy enjoying a more leisurely workweek, the office had become a community drop-in spot, and by default he became the town historian and raconteur — a role he never contemplated, yet thoroughly embraced.

**

Arriving at John F. Kennedy International Airport, they checked their baggage and walked into the Delta lounge. Looking around the lounge, Ben turned to his uncle, "As many flights as I've taken over the years from this airport, the one I recall most vividly was my first with Mom, Jackie, and you."

That was a half-truth because he remembered the last flight — his last flight to Paris, when it was obvious he had been a fool. How naive he must have seemed to Franck, Franck's boss, and the consortium in Brussels. Regrettably the past was not completely behind him; demons remained he needed to face, but not tonight.

Ben located his seat on the plane. Sitting down, his brother Jackie's presence surrounded him. He had not relived the excitement of that first trip in years. He wanted to reminisce, with Buddy. The two men relaxed over dinner and recalled the summer of 1960 when the four of them — his mother Helen, Ben, brother Jackie, and Buddy — went to England to bring home Jack's remains, a beloved husband, father, and brother.

With trays cleared, memories tucked away, lights in the cabin dimmed, pillows and blankets distributed, the plane flew through the dark of night heading toward the dawn of a new day. Ben and Buddy put their seats back and drifted into a sweet sleep.

~~~~~~~~~~~~

Ben had arranged to meet Becky at the Ritz Hotel in London. He decided before leaving for Oxford and Becky's graduation to spend a few days in the city where he and Nena had lived during the early years of their marriage, and where Ben began his career. This city was also where Helen had spent the last days of her life, and where she and Nena found common ground. During the years Ben lived and did business in England, his ambition to succeed drove his every waking moment. While he was constructing this new life, he never took the time to question his unbridled drive, or consider the direction he was heading.

Being back in London, Ben was ready to confront his past. How different their daughter's graduation could have been; there were always those nagging what-ifs. Those nagging woulda, coulda, shouldas of life.

**

Ben spotted his daughter sitting in the hotel lobby. Her chestnut hair, hazel eyes and stature, often caused people to remark how much she looked like her mother. No one could doubt the resemblance, but as Becky matured, her fair hair had turned darker, accentuating her cheekbones, features of her father. Nonetheless, she was more Nena than Ben.

Becky scrutinized her father and great uncle as they approached her. "You two look wonderful." Both men did look well; neither man was showing his age. "How was your flight?" Becky inquired. "Tell me your plans? Are you going to Paris after my graduation?"

"Let's check in, put away our bags, and talk plans over a grand English breakfast," the ever-practical Buddy quickly interjected.

Once they registered and inspected their room, they walked to Fortnum and Mason, finding three seats at the counter in the fountain room and ordered breakfast.

With breakfast ordered, the conversation turned to plans. "Becky...about Paris," Ben paused, then continued, "yes, we're going; want to come?"

"I'll think it over Daddy, a few days in Paris might be nice. How about you, Uncle Buddy? Are you excited about Paris?"

"Never dreamt I'd get to England, and now look at how many times I've been here. Will a trip to Paris qualify me as a world traveler?"

Buddy had the most infectious attitude toward life. With the all sorrows and hardships he had endured — from losing his brother Jack in World War II, helping Helen raise Jackie and Ben, trying to shield the boys from Helen and her drinking, losing Jackie like he lost Jack in another war, Vietnam, and then to have Ben return to him a broken man — Buddy was the glue that held their little family together.

"Dad, when was the last time you saw Mum?" Becky asked as they were finishing breakfast, hoping her parents had reached a détente.

"I haven't seen your mother since your grandparents' anniversary."

Becky lamented, "I wish my final exams had been at a different time."

"I almost didn't go," Ben added, "but not too many couples make it to their fiftieth wedding anniversary, and your grandparents have never been anything but gracious towards me. There must have been over a hundred people in attendance. I was treated well, probably because Buddy was with me; everyone loves Uncle Buddy." Ben affectionately patted his uncle's back.

Ben could see his daughter had reservations regarding him and Nena being together in an intimate family gathering. Reassuring her that nothing would spoil her graduation, he changed the subject.

"What do you plan on doing with this new degree in archaeology?"

Upon graduating from Harvard University with a degree in history, Becky had considered law school, but instead accepted an offer at the Boston

Museum of Fine Arts, where she was assigned to the Egyptology department to classify artifacts. Her childhood curiosity in ancient Egypt soon turned into a serious interest, which then led to graduate studies at Oxford.

Becky shared that she planned to stay in England. She had been offered an assistant teaching post at Oxford. "And don't worry; I'll earn enough money to keep me afloat," she promised, wanting her father not to fret.

"What does your mother think?"

"She's given me her approval."

Ben agreed with Nena. Becky was glad her father approved, eliminating further discussion regarding her career choice, since she had already accepted the university's offer.

**

For millennia in China, where tea originated, to the ritual of afternoon tea brought into favor during the reign of England's Queen Victoria, taking time for tea had become a British custom, a respite from the activities of daily life.

The Ritz was world renowned for its afternoon tea. When Buddy sat at the table and looked around the room, he remembered his first time here with Helen and the boys. Nostalgia filled him to the core. Speaking to Ben and Becky, he told them how much Helen loved coming here, first with her sons and then with Nena and Becky. Buddy hoped she knew they had not forgotten. In truth it was Buddy who did not want to forget.

"Here's to Grandma," Becky said as she lifted her teacup. "I wish I could remember coming here with her and Mummy."

Ben and Buddy joined in on Becky's toast.

"Helen would have been in her glory being with us today, and she would have been very proud of her granddaughter who has grown into an intelligent, lovely young woman." Emotion crept into Buddy's voice as he spoke. "Becky, you filled the last months of your grandmother's life with sheer happiness. I wish you could remember her."

Becky had often wondered about the relationship between her mother, father and grandmother. She did not learn everything she wondered about them, but Buddy's reminiscing filled in many gaps, and while they drank their tea, perhaps influenced by its healing properties, Helen's presence visibly filled the Ritz tearoom that afternoon.

**

The following morning Ben and Buddy took Becky to Paddington train station. They waited on the platform until she boarded the train to Oxford.

"See you next week," she shouted, leaning out the window as the train pulled away.

The train out of sight, Ben turned to his uncle, "Well old man, what's on our agenda for the day?"

"Let's go to Stonehenge. I've never been, and I'm curious to see what the fuss is about."

"I've never been either. Let's do it."

They returned to the Ritz, rented a car, and made dinner reservations at Chewton Glen, a stately manor house that now served as a hotel with a coveted restaurant about thirty miles from Stonehenge.

Exiting onto the M4, they headed to Salisbury – about a two-hour drive – with Ben driving and Buddy navigating as he read from the guidebook given to them by the hotel. Once out of the London traffic and beyond the city limits, they traveled through the lush rolling green countryside of Wiltshire. Approaching Stonehenge, they were awed by the imposing, mammoth, prehistoric monument set onto an open plain.

"So this is what the fuss is about," Buddy marveled as Ben parked the car. "It's hard to imagine that humans were roaming this site eight thousand years ago, at least four thousand years before these stones were erected. How on earth did they ever move the stones here, never mind stand them upright?"

"That's the mystery and age-old question pondered by minds greater than ours, Uncle."

Walking through the grassy field toward the circle, the thought occurred to both men, what an impressive view this must have been before the two nearby major highways existed, because even with the intrusion of modern civilization, this was a sight to behold.

The Ritz had arranged for a guide to meet them. He was a retired professor, and amateur archaeologist, with a plethora of information. Among other things, they learned that the original ditches for Stonehenge were dug using deer antlers as picks, the bluestones came from South Wales 240 miles away, and the stones were raised sometime between 3,000 and 2,000 BC.

The closer they approached the stones, the more imposing the scale and structure became. The fact that any stones were standing inspired them as they tried to drink in the majesty of it all.

They lingered until the sunset, and as they were about to leave, a dark cloud passed overhead, releasing raindrops the size of pennies. When the rain stopped, a rainbow peeked through the clouds as the sun began to sink behind the horizon. Muted colors of yellow, red, pink, and blue filled the sky. The once-dark clouds became fluffy, reflecting the rainbow's dazzling kaleidoscope of colors. Ben and Buddy were mesmerized by the beauty of Mother Nature on display.

"We might not have been here for the summer solstice, but I wonder if the solstice could rival this display," Buddy said, hardly able to contain his ebullience.

Ben confirmed Buddy's sentiments as they stood in reverence and respect on the sacred grounds.

**

The gravel driveway crunched under the car's tires. A pond, nestled in the landscape and surrounded by flowers, caught their eye. The surface of the pond sparkled in the twilight as spray, in the shape of a fan from a fountain in the center of the water, reached towards the sky. Everything about the drive to Chewton Glen, the luxury hotel, formerly a country estate, said "Welcome."

They sat on the terrace overlooking the sprawling lawn that rolled toward a forest dotted with stately trees. Showy rhododendron blooms dazzled the landscape, while the fragrance of columbine and jasmine permeated the air and their senses. Ben ordered cocktails, two Pimm's Cups (a gin-based spirit added to lemonade) made from a closely guarded family recipe from the late nineteenth century.

"No ale for you tonight Buddy," Ben told his uncle as the server placed the traditional summer drink of England on the table. Ice cubes swirled around the liquid in tall slender glasses decorated with a slice of cucumber, a strawberry, and a sprig of mint.

They sat sipping the cool refreshing Pimms, watching the sky turn from twilight to dusk as they enjoyed Scottish Salmon served three ways; thin slices of smoked salmon on freshly baked black bread, mini steamed salmon wantons, and a creamy salmon pâté.

"Can't wait for dinner," Buddy said as they entered the dining room. Spring pea soup, with crème fraiche followed by an entrée of perfectly cooked herb coated baby lamb chops, nutty wild rice, and delicate sweet fresh asparagus from the hotel's garden could not have been a better choice. The meal ended with a favorite English summer dessert — rhubarb fool — rhubarb compote folded into mounds of whipped cream with candied rhubarb strips sprinkled on top and served in an elegant glass cup. Melt in your mouth shortbread cookies added an element of crispiness to the smooth dessert. The meal was nothing short of perfection.

They adjourned to the 'Tinker's Bar' to end the evening. The room's oak paneling, deep burgundy painted walls and built in bookcases, resembled a library in an elegant manor house. A fireplace and inviting classic furniture added a sophisticated but cozy feel to the bar. Sinking into the comfortable wingback leather chairs, Ben suggested they have a glass of port from the Douro Valley in Portugal. Sipping the ruby red liquid while eating handmade chocolates, the day could not have been more perfect.

On the drive back to London, a quarter moon hung in the June sky sprinkled with stars. A spur-of-the-moment decision on how to spend the day turned into a lifetime memory.

**

The day before they were to leave for Oxford, Ben received a telephone message at the hotel. Nena and her parents, Ruth and Peter, were in town and wanted to meet for dinner. Hanging up the phone, Ben sat on the edge of the bed, reflecting.

Buddy came out of the shower wanting to know who had called.

"It was Nena," Ben told him. "They're in town and want to get together tonight for dinner. Should we say yes?"

"Certainly, it'll break the ice, before the big day tomorrow."

Ben picked up the phone. His stomach was in turmoil as he waited for the hotel to make the connection.

"Hello?" The voice on the other end had an earthy quality that made his heart race.

"Hi Nena, it's Ben. I got your message. Buddy and I would enjoy having dinner with the three of you. How does the River Café sound?"

"Excellent suggestion — I've heard the food is marvelous."

"About seven?"

"Seven is fine, see you then." Ben hung up the phone glad that at least some things had not changed. Even now, Nena liked to dine at seven.

**

Ben and Buddy were already at River Café when Peter, Ruth, and Nena stepped out of the cab. Still attractive at fifty-plus, Ben could not keep his eyes off Nena. They shared polite kisses on the cheek before entering the restaurant.

Nena could not contain her enthusiasm as the host showed them to their window table. "I've read excellent reviews about the owners, Rose and Ruth; I can't wait to taste their food."

A platter of char-grilled eggplant; thin slices of sweet, mildly salty prosciutto di Parma; shaved Parmesan cheese; and toasted bruschetta tempted their palates while they ordered dinner. Nena decided on wild mushroom risotto — creamy rice infused with white wine, vermouth, leeks, and overflowing with porcini, hen of the woods, and a variety of chanterelle mushrooms. Ben and Peter settled on Dover sole, a succulent firm fish wood-roasted on the bone and dressed with lemon and olive oil. The fish was served alongside vibrant green haricot verts, and new potatoes. For Buddy and Ruth, the specialty of the evening tempted them

— a rolled veal loin bursting with rosemary, fennel, and sage on a plate with ricotta-stuffed zucchini blossoms. During dinner there were not enough superlatives to do justice to the feast set before them. Espresso and individual mouth-watering lemon-raspberry tarts followed dinner. Peter insisted they end the meal with Frangelico, a nutty liqueur made from herbs and wild hazelnuts, keeping with the Italian theme of the meal. Throughout the evening, conversation was lively and full of lighthearted banter.

What could have been a socially awkward meeting turned into a lovely evening, and tomorrow a certain young lady who had brought them together would be celebrated minus an atmosphere of tension.

Returning to the hotel, Ben was not ready to go to the room, still basking in the glow of the night.

"Come on Buddy, let's have a nightcap."

"Good idea. I'm not quite ready to have this day end either."

Sitting with their drinks Buddy was looking intently at his nephew. "Tell me Ben, what's going through that head of yours?"

"I'm full of remorse for what I did, especially to those I loved and who loved me. Will this feeling ever completely go away, Uncle Buddy? Does time erase betrayal?" Ben felt like a young boy who needed his uncle to reassure him everything would be fine.

"Ben, both you and Nena have come a long way. Give it some more time. You may always feel regret, but look at the progress you've made putting your life back together. Everyone sees you are no longer that man who was chasing windmills."

Buddy's comment amused Ben. "Where did you come up with that? Chasing windmills?"

"I read!" Buddy laughed, referring to the classic story of Don Quixote.

Drinks finished, they walked to the elevator, Ben with his arm around Buddy.

~~~~~~~~~~~~~~~

Stepping off the train in Oxford bought back a world of memories for Peter. Ruth squeezed his hand, reading his mind, as they both remembered the summer of 1960 when the family spent time in England, while Peter lectured at Oxford.

"How does it feel to be back, Dad, this time to see your granddaughter graduate?" Nena asked her father.

"Inconceivable. Truly inconceivable."

"Hi there!" Becky shouted as she ran toward them. "Daddy and Uncle Buddy are already at the hotel. Let's get you settled in and have some tea. Do I dare ask how your dinner went last night?"

"What did your father say?" Nena asked.

"No, you tell me, Mum, then I'll tell you."

Not one to pass up an opportunity, Nena teased, "Well, no one used the wrong fork, and everyone said 'please' and 'thank you'."

Peter and Ruth burst into laughter, even Becky joined in.

"Come on Mum, you know what I meant."

Nena smiled. "I would have to say the evening was a success. I enjoyed myself, but I wouldn't be honest if I didn't say there was a tinge of sadness for the might have been. Your father and I are working at moving on." Nena looked to her parents for confirmation.

"Your mother and I agree, yes, the evening went smoothly. We know you are both trying. We believe Ben has accepted the responsibility for what he did, and is attempting to make amends. Something of the magnitude of his lapses in judgment takes time for resolution, but time is on his side, and we are a very forgiving clan."

"Well said Granddad, well said."

"Okay what did your father say?" Nena was curious.

"Same as you. Dad enjoyed the evening as well: no faux pas, and he used his best table manners."

"Smarty pants!" Nena pulled her daughter aside and hugged her tightly.

**

Ben and Buddy were waiting in the lobby of the hotel.

"How was the train ride from London?" Ben inquired of Nena and her parents. Everyone agreed the train service in England beat any system back home.

"Settle in and we'll meet for tea in the drawing room," Buddy added. Ever since his first experience of tea at the Ritz with Helen and the boys, Buddy had taken to having a cup of tea in the late afternoon, a welcome break in the day, and being here in England he felt right at home with the ritual.

They were staying at the venerable Randolph Hotel. The central location meant they would not have to rent a car, and walking in Oxford was part of the city's charm. The hotel was full of history, including the recent BBC filming of the beloved *Inspector Morse* television series.

Entering the drawing room, Buddy had arranged for the hotel to serve its Celebration Tea for this special occasion. The table was laden with warm homemade scones, clotted cream, and preserves, along with a selection of finger sandwiches, tempting slices of cake, a variety of teas, and chilled glasses of champagne.

"Uncle Buddy, this is lovely," Becky gushed.

Ben proposed a toast. "To Becky for realizing a goal, and stepping into her future."

With their glasses raised, the room filled with "Cheers!"

**

After tea, Becky planned a visit for the family to the Ashmolean Museum. The museum, located across the street from the hotel, was the first university museum in the world, and home to Oxford University's outstanding art and archaeology collections.

While Becky took her grandparents and Buddy on a personal tour to view the Egyptian artifacts, Nena wandered through the museum, alone, when she suddenly came upon Ben in the French Impressionist gallery.

In the doorway of the gallery, Nena stood silently for a few moments watching Ben and wondering how different life might have been before approaching him and asking, "A penny for your thoughts?"

Startled, Ben looked up to see Nena. "I was remembering the trip we took to pay homage at the Van Gogh brothers' graves in Auvers-sur-Oise before Becky was born."

"Ah yes, remember the tiny shop where we bought those delicious jambon sandwiches, the kind you can only buy in France? That was a lovely day, sitting by the River Oise, eating our picnic lunch."

Their unexpected encounter was a reminder of happier times. However, as they strolled through the museum, neither one could forget where they were now.

**

"Could we have crammed any more into a day?" Ruth asked as they returned to the hotel after having dinner and attending a performance of the University Oxford Student Company.

"It's still early," Becky replied, "Let's go to the bar."

The bar, named to pay tribute to *Inspector Morse*, oozed with charm. They ordered the house drink, a champagne cocktail: champagne combined with Calvados, orange bitters, and vanilla essence in a tall-fluted glass.

"Here's to decadence!" Buddy exclaimed.

"To decadence!"

**

Graduation activities dominated the next day. The head of the archaeology department, and Becky's new boss, hosted a lunch, a lovely English garden affair.

"I'll see you in a week," Becky reminded the dean as they were leaving. She had accepted her father's offer of Paris, and Ben was glad she had decided to tag along.

At the hotel, the family made their rounds saying good-bye.

"Ben, it really has been good to see you. I'm glad you're doing well."

"Thanks Nena, this trip has done me a world of good. I hope we can keep in touch. Would you consider it?"

She nodded her head. It was not an enthusiastic response, but he would take it.

"Enjoy Paris."

"I don't want my last trip there to be my final memory of a city I love, we both loved," he responded with a tinge of sadness in his voice.

Ben was hoping Nena would acknowledge his comment, but she did not respond.

Becky broke the silence. "Come on, Dad. We need to catch the train if we want to make the last ferry crossing to France."

A taxi arrived for Nena, Peter, and Ruth. As the taxi pulled away, Ben's heart went with it.

Chapter 2

Paris, the "City of Light." A city that represented happy times with Nena, meetings with Franck, and building what Ben thought was a business relationship that would catapult his career and solidify his position with the Warren family, the owners of Apex Financial. His last visit to this city of light was very dark – a time of betrayal. Franck had betrayed Ben and in turn, Ben betrayed the Warrens. The fallout began when Franck and his consortium in Brussels called in their loans and sold them to a California bank, Jefferson Countrywide. When the banking crises erupted, it brought Ben's world crashing down around him, leading to his ultimate betrayal of Nena, the most important person in his world.

Ben had to exorcise his demons alone, in order to truly put the past behind him. He suggested to Becky that she take Buddy on a grand tour of Paris. She jumped at the opportunity, remembering how she had played tour guide for her mother the first time she, herself, had visited Paris with her own parents, years before.

"I'm going to show you Paris, Uncle Buddy, the way I first saw it. And you're going to fall in love with this city, the same way I did." Becky's enthusiasm was contagious.

Buddy could not help worrying about Ben, and before leaving, he cautioned him to go easy on himself. Buddy knew this day was going to be anything but easy for his nephew. Ben mustered a faint smile.

As Ben watched Becky and Buddy leave the hotel, he wished he was going with them, but he knew in order to move forward he had to deal with his past, and what happened in Paris topped the list. This is where it all began. This was the scene of the crime, and like any crime, there were clues, and he suspected clues were here.

Ben wanted to remember how he felt during the evening he and Nena dined at the Ritz with Franck and his wife. It was sometime during the mid-seventies, when he had taken Nena and Becky with him on a business trip to celebrate his promotion to Vice President of finance with Apex.

Ben started by sitting at the bar, like he had that night with Franck. Ben recalled:

Franck was not pleased with particular financials in their deal, and he requested that Ben alter certain individual entries, justifying that the changes would be rectified as the business grew. At the time, their business relationship was developing, and the request seemed innocent enough, if not odd. Nena walked into the bar and overheard their conversation – a conversation that years later, would come back to haunt both of them.

When Ben returned to New York, he did what Franck had requested. For a brief moment, he questioned his actions and what was really behind Franck's request. What he was doing was not illegal; walking a fine line perhaps, but not illegal. And Ben was in too deep in his race to the top to consider the alternatives.

These memories were helping him, but Ben realized he would not find what he was searching for sitting at the bar. He needed to get into the rooms where the events of that fateful day in 1986 took place. Ben asked the concierge if the rooms in question were vacant. They were, and the concierge handed him the two room keys. But which room to enter first?

He decided to revisit the meeting room where he met with Franck and, to his surprise, Franck's boss, a man he had never previously met. Entering the room, he sat down at the same table they had used over six years ago. Ben looked across the table and around the room, trying to assess the way he had felt that day. This is where he learned that working with Franck and the consortium had all been for naught. The consortium sold the business they had developed to a California bank, leaving Ben holding real estate debt against Apex's profitability. The consortium had duped him. Closing his eyes, he could hear Franck's and his boss's laughter as they walked out of the room. His chest tightened. He stood up and walked around the room. His walk turned into a pace, and as he paced, the full force of his wrongful actions, the ones he had masked, came to the forefront. He could barely control the feelings roiling inside his gut. He rushed out of the room toward the elevator. He could not wait for the elevator and headed to the stairwell. He raced up the stairs to the fourth floor, put the key in the door of the room, and entered the room where he had stayed on that ill-fated trip. He was determined he would not leave the room this time asking, "Now what?"

Ben walked into the bathroom and looked in the mirror. There was no place else to hide. The remaining justifications and rationalizations that he held onto in order not to fall apart were laid bare. Like the clues at a murder scene that point to the suspect, Ben stared at that man in the mirror. No longer could he blame Franck, his boss or the consortium. The decisions to overlook what Franck had asked and promoted fell squarely on him. Ben surrendered to the heavy weight and burden he carried because of his unethical choices. He went back into the room, sat on the bed, and cried. These were not tears of pity for himself, but honest tears for those he had deceived. Weeping he realized and accepted the full responsibility of his actions without any excuses. He did not know how long he sat there, but when he arose, no longer did he fear and shrink from the dark place where he had descended. Coming to Paris, freed him from his demons. He walked out of the room and closed the door –and the past – behind him.

Ben went back to his own room and showered. The water streaming over his body completed his cleansing. He dressed and went to the lobby to return the keys.

"Did you find what you were looking for, Sir?" the concierge politely inquired.

"Yes, I did. Merci."

He sat at the bar, lost in his thoughts until Buddy and Becky returned, exhausted, from their grand tour of Paris.

"What a wonderful day!" Becky exclaimed.

"What a wonderful city!" Buddy added.

"You're both right; it was a wonderful day, and it is a wonderful city!" Ben added, the weight of his past actions finally beginning to drain away.

**

When their visit to Paris came to a close, Ben was ready to go home with Buddy, and Becky was ready to return to Oxford; both father and daughter looked forward to what lie ahead.

Chapter 3

Entering her apartment Becky picked up the mail. Sorting through the pile of advertisements and bills, she noticed an engraved invitation. Ever since she became a member of the Oxford faculty, albeit as an adjunct professor, she received invitations to one event or another. She usually discarded these invitations without much thought, but the elegant envelope caught her attention. "Okay let's see what this invite is for," she thought, sliding the thin letter opener across the gold embossed flap. Before taking out the card, Becky poured herself a glass of wine. Sitting on the couch she kicked off her shoes and read the details of the event:

> *The trustees of the British Museum cordially invite you to attend an evening of cocktails and dinner to discuss the future of the eleven fragments from the tomb of Nebamun.*

Nebamun was a scribe and accountant who lived at the time of the New Kingdom during the 14th century BCE in Egypt. Instead of a sealed burial chamber, his tomb was a chapel similar to present-day mausoleums, with an entrance at ground level, unlike the burial sites of the pharaohs. This meant that Nebamun's friends and family could easily pay their respects, pray, and make offerings. The wall paintings in his tomb depicted daily living, dress, agriculture, hunting, and fishing scenes, and family life: a rare find.

In the nineteenth century, there was a renewed interest in ancient Egypt following Napoleon's campaigns, which had facilitated scientific studies of the ancient culture. While a preponderance of the research and study centered on the Egyptians' beliefs in the afterlife, Becky was fascinated with how Egyptians lived their everyday lives. This invitation offered her the opportunity to spend an entire evening with decision makers of the museum as they discussed, over a relaxing dinner, the future housing of these remarkable artifacts.

No thought was required. She knew she was going to attend, and began counting down the days to the event.

~~~~~~~~~~~~~~~

Becky's excitement was palpable when the night of the dinner arrived. She had always loved art and wandering through museums, which she had done ever since she was a child. She valued times sharing pictures in art books with her mother, and admiring paintings on a gallery wall, or objects d'art filling a room.

Becky's favorite museum was The Metropolitan Museum of Art in New York City. She loved climbing the grand staircase on Fifth Avenue where people met to eat, talk, and people watch. She would bound up the stairs – eight steps, a landing; another eight steps, another landing; another eight steps, a landing – until she reached the entrance.

If she had to answer as to what eventually drew her to the work she loved, in retrospect she knew it began in 1978, the evening her parents took her to the Met to attend the opening of the Temple of Dendur. A gift from the Egyptian government, the temple was reassembled at the Met, surrounded by a reflecting pool, and illuminated by a wall of windows that opened onto Central Park. The evening of the event, candles filled the room, reflecting off the water. Men in black-tie attire and women in their finest dresses stood transfixed, gazing at the temple — the sanctuary of the goddess Isis. Although only thirteen, the experience that evening shaped her future career path.

Alighting from the taxi on Great Russell Street, in front of the British Museum, Becky walked across the open courtyard toward the museum's entrance. She could not help admire the building's forty-four stately ionic fluted columns and the Greek Revival façade. The pediment over the main entrance carved with sculptures depicting *The Progress of Civilization* reminded Becky of what awaited her inside. Anticipation grew as she climbed the twelve steps toward the museum doors.

Inside, Becky took a moment to appreciate the silence. She could hear the echo of her footsteps. Passing the colossal bust of Ramesses II, she could not wait for the evening to begin.

In the dining room, the sound of British accents filled the air. This sound always made Becky smile. Picking up a glass of wine off a passing serving tray, she began to mingle. Becky approached a group where she heard a distinctly American voice.

"I thought I would rescue the lone American. Who claims the accent?" She searched the faces in the party.

A young man in the circle raised his hand. "I confess! It's me."

"You haven't met?" a colleague inquired, and then introduced the young American man as J.R. Stark.

As they shook hands, their eyes locked. J.R. was utterly gobsmacked, as the Brits would say; she took his breath away.

Their prolonged look at one another was soon interrupted by the sound of the bell signaling dinner was served.

"Here, let me help you with your chair," he offered as Becky approached a table.

"Thank you." Becky's heart raced as J.R. pulled out her chair.

Becky had dated, but nothing serious. There never seemed to be the right time to be in a committed relationship. Besides, she enjoyed playing the field. But this was the first time in a long time someone made her feel like a schoolgirl, and within just moments of meeting.

Dinner completed, the trustees presented their thoughts for the painted fragments. Lively discussion erupted as the invited guests exchanged ideas, from fund-raising – the reason J.R. was attending – to archaeological concerns.

The evening ended with a plan to meet in six months to assess progress.

Outside the museum saying their good-byes, J.R. knew he did not want to wait six months to see this young lady again. "If you're available, I'd like to take you to dinner."

"It happens I am available, and dinner sounds lovely." Her heart was still beating at warp speed as she accepted his invitation.

"Would this weekend work for you? I can drive up to Oxford."

The smile on Becky's face told him everything he needed to know.

They exchanged contact information. Becky hailed a cab and headed to her friend's flat, where she was staying the night. She replayed J.R.'s invitation over and over in her head.

~~~~~~~~~~~~~

"I'll be right there." Becky glanced at herself in the mirror, her heart fluttering. She turned the knob and opened the door. On the other side of the threshold stood J.R., holding a bouquet of flowers and a box of chocolates.

"I didn't know your preference, so I bought you both."

"I love flowers, and who doesn't crave chocolate." They were staring at each other.

"Is it all right if I come in?"

"Oh, forgive my manners, please — please come in."

Becky went to get a vase for the flowers while J.R. surveyed her apartment.

"Nice place you have here," he said, trying to make small talk. His palms were sweating, and he could not remember the last time when he had been this nervous on a date.

"Yes, it is quite nice. I was lucky to find it. I needed something furnished, and furnished apartments in this city within walking distance of the college are hard to find. I have no intention of buying a car while living here. I can't seem to get used to driving on the wrong side of the road."

She commented on the irises that he had brought, one of her very favorite flowers.

"You reminded me of the Greek goddess Iris." He congratulated himself for picking out flowers she liked.

But Becky quickly countered his remark, saying, "Oh really, that's a smooth line. Use it often?"

"No." He rolled his eyes. "Before I put my other foot in my mouth, perhaps we should leave for dinner."

"Perhaps you're right."

**

As he drove into the car park of the restaurant, Becky was aghast. "This is where we're having dinner?" she asked.

"Why, do you want to go somewhere else?" For a moment J.R. was nervous about his choice.

"No — I've never been here. I've only read about the food, and I read it is Haute cuisine at its finest."

They were dining at Le Manoir aux Quant' Saisons. Stories of the manor can be traced to the year 1225 AD, but there are no descriptions of the house until Sir Thomas Camoys, a favorite of Richard II, took residence sometime in the late 1300s or early 1400s. From then on, the house was brought to life with each passing owner. Raymond Blanc, the present proprietor, continued to reform and transform the historical property into Le Manoir aux Quant' Saisons, one of the most desirable dining destinations in England.

Becky and J.R. were warmly greeted at the door and escorted to their table. The dining room was elegant but unpretentious.

A breadbasket of warm freshly baked rolls — buttery portions of focaccia, herb ciabatta (the Italian answer to a French baguette), and thick slices of rustic, crunchy sourdough, arrived at the table. Shortly afterward an Amuse Bouche – just a little bite to invigorate the palate, in the form of the tiniest goat cheese–stuffed mushrooms — was served with cocktails.

J.R. sat observing Becky as she sipped her French 45, a summery gin-champagne concoction. "You're awfully quiet young lady."

"I'm a bit overwhelmed. I feel I'm in a scene from a Disney movie, either *Cinderella* or *Sleeping Beauty*. This place is a cross between a castle and a house in an enchanted forest."

"I felt the same way the first time I came here."

"You've been here before?"

"Yes, my boss had a party here for his wife's fortieth birthday."

"I bet your date was impressed." Becky was fishing, wanting to know more about J.R.'s dating life.

"I didn't bring a date."

"Oh..." Becky then felt silly for asking, and thankful the waiter came just at that moment to take their order.

The waiter explained the offerings, from a five to nine-course menu, or ordering a la carte. They settled on the five-course menu. When the waiter left, Becky told J.R. she hoped she had made the right choice. Five courses seemed a bit intimidating.

Small glasses of chilled gazpacho with a faint kiss of cucumber and pepper, as to not overpower the soup's luscious tomato essence, was served for a first course.

"This looks divine, J.R. You might have guessed I enjoy food. I love to cook it, I love when someone else cooks it, and I love to eat it."

Most of his dates over the years had eaten like birds, and this girl's appetite impressed him. "I'm glad," he responded. "I hate seeing food go to waste." They both burst into laughter as the waiter removed the empty breadbasket from the table. The tension between them had broken, and getting to know each other had begun.

"Tell me the story behind your name. Why initials?"

Before he could answer, the table was cleared and their palates were treated to soft, light pillows of Devonshire crab ravioli plated on a sauce only described as heavenly.

"My full name is Jason Robertson Stark III." J.R. went on to explain, "My grandfather was called Jason, my dad, Jay. When I came along, a boy, and as their luck would have it an only child, my father wanted the name to be carried on. My mother thought there were enough Js in the family and insisted I was called Robbie."

"How did you get from Robbie to J.R.?"

"That happened when I went to boarding school in Massachusetts. A housemate of mine called me J.R. Others did as well, and the rest, as they say, is history."

J.R. went on to explain his parents never made an issue of him being referred to as J.R., except his parents and people that knew him before Deerfield Academy continued to call him Robbie.

During dinner, Becky learned that J.R. had grown up on the Upper East Side of Manhattan. His father ran the family business, a land development company started by his great-great-grandfather. After Deerfield, J.R. went to Amherst College, worked in the business before going to Harvard University for an MBA, and then joined Salomon Brothers in New York City in 1990. Almost immediately Salomon gave him a job in London. J.R. was happy to be there during those turbulent years of the early nineties when Salomon was caught up in what became known as the Treasury bond scandal.

"We have something in common. My Uncle Josh went to Deerfield, and so did his son Danny, my cousin, and my father went to Amherst and got his MBA from Harvard. What a small world!"

Becky would soon learn exactly how small. As J.R. was telling Becky about his parent's summer home in Ogunquit, Maine, overlooking the Marginal Way, the conversation stopped in mid-sentence. Their main entrée of free-range duck breast, served with clementine sauce perfumed the air. Accompanied by a medley of steamed summer vegetables with a wild herb pesto and caramelized chipollini onions, the dish surpassed their expectations. A Rhone wine poured, J.R. proposed a toast.

"I can't thank my boss enough for having me represent the company at the museum dinner. He was supposed to go, but something came up at the last minute. My good fortune!"

Becky countered, "I'm glad I didn't toss the invitation in the basket. I sometimes do."

"My good fortune," she thought, "the invitation came in such an eye-catching envelope."

The rims of their glasses touched as they smiled at this turn of fate.

"Are you going to eat?" J.R. asked as Becky seemed reluctant to touch her food.

"I need to admire the plates. Look at the artistry that went into this meal. The presentation of this food leaves me speechless." Tasting, Becky exclaimed, "Oh my goodness J.R., you have spoiled me. What will I do for dinner tomorrow?"

As they continued to talk, Becky realized she had lived in Boston the same time J.R. had been in nearby Cambridge, studying at Harvard. "I wonder how come we never bumped into each other. My family used to spend summers in Ogunquit. I might have even seen you on your lawn while walking the Marginal Way. I can't believe our paths have never crossed until now. When I say it's a small world, it really is."

J.R. sat totally captivated with his dinner companion.

When their entrées and salads were finished, the meal ended with a selection of cheeses and a delectable dessert of raspberry sorbet served with petit fours and mini French macarons.

Before leaving, J.R. had arranged with Chef Blanc's gardener for a tour of the restaurant's renowned vegetable and herb gardens. The gardener explained the various varieties of herbs and vegetables that filled each row of the meticulously well-maintained garden that would eventually become culinary delights on diner's plates. Becky's interest in the garden delighted J.R. and he had no doubts Becky was a keeper.

On the ride back to Oxford, Becky thanked J.R., telling him that from the meal, to the garden tour, to the company, the evening was special.

He had no words to express his feelings. When they reached her apartment, he stammered, "I had a wonderful evening." Hesitating, he asked her out again.

She did not hesitate to answer yes. Of course she would see him again.

Standing at her door, he took her hand, kissed her on the check, and left.

**

The first thing Becky did when she closed the door was telephone her mother. Like most girls, she could not wait to tell Nena about J.R., how they met, and their dinner date. Nena, unaware of this new man in her daughter's life, listened intently to the details, including that he was born on the Fourth of July and how he got the nickname J.R. from the lofty name of Jason Robertson Stark III. The conversation evoked a memory for Nena of many years ago, walking home from an evening at Harvard when Ben announced he no longer wanted to be referred to as Benny.

What should have been a simple conversation regarding a name turned into something more, and at the time it left Nena emotionally uncertain in her role as a young wife. If only their exchange had been as adult as her daughter's and her date's. If only their relationship had been on a different level, they might still be together. Quickly she dismissed the past, refocusing her attention to the present moment as she listened to Becky chatter away about this young man who had entered her life.

"He wants to go out again, and so do I," Becky told Nena.

"Remember when we both thought you would be charmed by some gallant Englishman, but it seems an American accent has caught you by surprise. I'll be interested to hear about date number two."

Shoptalk about work and family ended the conversation.

Sharing J.R. with her mother kept the evening alive, and the next morning Becky headed to the university on cloud nine.

Chapter 4

A year had passed since Becky's graduation. The trip to London and Paris brought Ben a sense of resolution as he continued his journey coming to terms with the devastation he had created seven years beforehand. The oil business was flourishing. Ben sold his mother Helen's house, his boyhood home, where he had found refuge when everything fell apart. But the house held other memories: ones he did not want to live with any longer. Corporations were moving into the county, and New Canaan, Connecticut, was beginning to change. Real estate was developing at a rapid pace, with large homes springing up on the outskirts, and condos being built in town. Ben purchased a townhouse on God's Acre, within walking distance to everything, including the office. This change was exactly what he needed.

He had just signed the papers on the townhouse when he walked into the office that morning and immediately told Buddy he had an idea.

"Now what?" Buddy asked.

"Why do you say that?"

"Because every time those words come out of your mouth, my life is somehow involved."

"You're right," Ben countered. "I wanted you to know the condo has three bedrooms, a bedroom for me, a bedroom for guests, and a bedroom for you."

Buddy looked puzzled, wondering why he would need a bedroom at Ben's place when he had a home of his own in town.

"Maybe it's about time you sold your house and come live with me, Buddy. Time you downsized — no more yard work, upkeep, close the door, and take off without any worries; what'd you say?"

"You can't spring this on me before my second cup of coffee," Buddy replied jokingly. Then in a more serious tone, he added, "Let me mull it over."

"Well, don't mull too long. I might rent the room out to somebody else."

Buddy shot his nephew a look and shook his head.

In the end, it was an offer he could not refuse. Buddy sold his house and moved in with Ben, telling anyone who would listen it was his idea.

~~~~~~~~~~~~~~~~~

Not being able to face any more changes in her life since her divorce, Nena remained in her apartment on Charles Street in Boston. Returning from Becky's graduation and spending time in Ben's presence, Nena felt she could take another step forward and bought a two-bedroom townhouse on the waterfront in the north end. The old wharves were being converted into living spaces. The area was going through a rebirth, as was she. Nena loved living in the city. She could walk to Government Center and work, stop in her favorite markets to shop on her way home, or if she were inclined, dine in the cozy, friendly restaurants in her neighborhood. She was moving forward — one day at a time.

~~~~~~~~~~~~~~~~~

At the end of each day, Nena would check in with her mother. Ruth and Peter were getting older, and Nena cherished the fact her parents were alive, healthy, and full of life. Peter had recently retired from MIT, and he and Ruth were enjoying their "senior" years. The term made Ruth bristle, as she never thought of herself or Peter as that old. She often would say to her friends, "I won't be labeled a senior until I can't get up from a chair."

Call waiting interrupted their nightly conversation. "Mum, it's Becky on the other line. I'll call you back."

Nena clicked to the incoming call. "Becky, I didn't expect we'd talk until the weekend. Everything all right?"

"I'm fine, but there's some sad news. J.R.'s mother passed away."

"I'm sorry to hear that Becky. I enjoyed the few times I spent with Trudi. Please offer

J.R. my condolences."

Becky let her mother know she would be returning with J.R. for the memorial service.

"I'll let your father know; I doubt Jay is up to making calls."

"That would be great; do you mind? J.R. spoke with him and he's devastated."

"Not at all. By the way, did you know your father sold the house?"

"Yes, and Uncle Buddy sold his. It's wonderful news they're living together, and Dad sounds the best I've heard him sound in a long time."

"I think the trip to England and Paris last year did him the world of good."

"Yes it did. Thanks for letting Dad know about Trudi, and I'll call you when the plans are made. Luv you, Mum."

"Luv you back."

Hanging up the phone, Nena sat quietly reflecting. Only a few years older than Nena, Trudi was too young to die. She had battled breast cancer, even making it through the five-year cancer-free mark, but shortly thereafter what was thought a bronchial infection turned into a malignant lump in her lung. She had fought valiantly for two years until her body finally gave up.

Nena remembered the first time they met, when J.R. and Becky flew home during the 1992 Christmas holiday. They had been dating for six months, and it was especially important to J.R. that Trudi and Becky meet, knowing his mother would not be able to visit them in England. He rarely introduced his dates to his parents, especially his mother, but this young lady was different. An evening in the city was arranged. Everyone got along, and although Trudi never told her son, J.R. hoped his mother approved of Becky.

J.R. and Trudi had had an interesting relationship. He wondered why his parents never had another child. He never asked, but this did not stop him from wondering. Boarding school gave him the chance to become independent because there were times he felt smothered by his mother. Maybe if there had been another sibling, she would not have been as overprotective. He could not put into words their dynamic. J.R. loved Trudi dearly, and he knew she loved him. She had definite ideas concerning the direction of her son's life. She did not send this message to him overtly, but covertly. He and his father were close, but Jay left J.R.'s rearing to Trudi. He was not the disciplinarian, but the guy who showed his son the good times. But in the end Trudi let him go. J.R. knew this could not have been easy, and admired his mother's ability to do right by him.

In early 1993, Trudi invited Nena to a Wednesday matinee, and during the summer, she, Nena, Buddy, Ben, and J.R.'s father Jay enjoyed a night out at the ballpark. Nena and Trudi met the last time, for tea at the Plaza. Nena found her engaging, but like some mothers with sons, especially an only son, Nena wondered if Trudi had an opinion about their children dating. Now that question would never be answered.

Nena picked up the phone to call Ben.

"Nice to hear from you. How's everything in Boston?" he asked. He loved to hear her voice.

"Everything is going well, but I have something else to speak with you about. Becky called to let me know Trudi passed away."

"Nena, I'm truly sorry to hear that. She put up quite a fight, and I enjoyed meeting her. That was a fun evening we spent with her and Jay at their box at Yankee Stadium this summer. How's J.R. holding up?"

"As well as can be expected. We didn't talk much. Becky will let us know when the funeral arrangements are made."

Ben thanked Nena for calling, and turned to tell Buddy what had happened. Still shaken by the news, Nena redialed her mother.

~~~~~~~~~~~~~~

The following week, J.R. and Becky arrived in New York. The service was held at Saint John the Divine on the Upper West Side. The magnificent Gothic structure had been the family's church for generations, Jay's great-great-grandfather having something to do with the purchasing of the land. The service was held in the Chapels of the Tongues, a fitting place, since Trudi enjoyed the art of conversation. There were serious moments and moments of levity. Jay spoke about the first time he met his wife, when she was not shy in telling him never to call her Gertrude. She had emphasized how her nickname was spelled: Trudi with an i and not a y.

Afterward there was a reception, and later that evening, the family went to dinner. At dinner, Jay asked his son how long he was staying in town.

"I'm not sure Dad. Why?"

"I thought since the fall weather is cooperating and you're here, we could take your mother's ashes to Ogunquit. That's what she wanted, Robbie."

"I can make that work. I'm going into the office in the morning and I'll call my boss from there and let him know."

Jay turned to Becky and asked her if she had made plans.

"I'm spending a few days with my family. I'm going to New Canaan tonight with Dad and Uncle Buddy, then on to Boston."

"Would you care to join Robbie and myself in Ogunquit? Be nice to have some female companionship."

"If I won't be an intrusion, I'd be honored," she told Jay.

"Then it's settled."

~~~~~~~~~~

Saying good-bye to the family, Nena met a few former classmates from Columbia for drinks, something she often did when she stayed in town. This evening held a surprise. At the restaurant an old acquaintance walked through the door: Professor Katz — the same professor Nena had spent time with the summer she attended graduate school. The summer she knew her marriage was in trouble. The same person she could have given herself to, but chose not to, living with the hope her love for Ben would save them.

Looking at him standing by the bar, Nena caught her breath. It had been seventeen years since she attended grad school and he had not changed — he was tall, fair-haired, and handsome, looking every bit a college professor with his glasses and tweed jacket. She had not seen him since graduation, or spoken to him on a personal level since the evening they talked before she caught the train home to Fairfield, Connecticut — home to her husband.

The professor joined his former students. "Please, call me Sam," he insisted. You've been out of graduate school long enough. I can't wait to hear what everyone has been doing since Columbia."

The night flew by, this time with the professor listening and the students talking. When the evening ended, Sam asked Nena where she was staying. She told him the Waldorf.

"Mind if I walk with you?" He lived on the Upper West Side, the opposite direction from the hotel, but he was not about to let spending time with her slip away.

She accepted his offer. As they walked, Nena shared what happened to her marriage with Ben. She did not go into every detail, only the ones she was comfortable with.

When she finished, Sam casually said, "I read something in *The Wall Street Journal* about Ben leaving Apex, but I had no idea. You were clear you wanted things to work out between the two of you. I know you thought being in grad school, giving Ben space, would help take some of the pressure off his schedule between work and home. I'm sorry things didn't work out the way you wanted."

"It's true what they say about not knowing what's around the corner. If we did, we might not take the turn," she replied, trying to make the conversation more light hearted.

It was the first time she had spoken to anyone outside her intimate circle about the situation and was pleased that she could speak of her misfortune without rancor. With a small laugh, she continued, "I guess if I can say that, I really am making progress."

"Good for you, Nena."

They reached the hotel. As Nena began to walk up the steps Sam suggested that perhaps he could call her, and maybe get-together the next time he was in Boston.

She did not say no, but smiled. She took his hand and kissed his cheek just as she had done years ago, when she told him she was going home to Ben.

Alone, Nena thought about that day on the platform in Harlem, when she turned her back on him. And now as if a movie had paused, it seemed to have started again where it left off.

~~~~~~~~~~~~~~

Becky's short but enjoyable visit to New Canaan was coming to a close. One day the new owners of Ben's childhood home gave them a tour. It was the first time Ben had been in the house since he moved.

"I couldn't believe the changes, Dad, could you?" Becky commented as she waited for the train to Boston with Ben and Buddy.

"It was about time," Ben replied. "The house needed some good old-fashioned TLC."

"Don't we all, Dad, at one time or another?"

Ben nodded his head in agreement.

Becky could read the look of regret on her father's face and realized his need for TLC, especially since the divorce. She wished she could be more supportive, but she had an internal struggle of her own. Becky still had unresolved issues regarding the breakup of her family, which she kept to herself. Not addressing these repressed feelings protected her from taking sides. Becky knew at some point she would have to deal with her parent's divorce — not today — instead she thanked Uncle Buddy for taking her sailing. "I can't remember the last time I was out on the sound. That old boat of yours certainly qualifies for antique status."

"Be careful how you talk about her, young lady. That's one gal who never gave me an ounce of trouble."

The blow of a whistle, alerted them to the train rounding the bend into the station. Becky kissed two very important men in her life and climbed aboard.

When the train pulled away, and out of view, Ben and Buddy stood quietly on the platform for some time before walking back to the office. How many times were good-byes waved and kisses blown on that platform? In the office, the silence continued until the telephone rang. It was Nena calling Ben, wanting to know if Becky had made the train on time.

"She should make the Amtrak connection with time to spare."

"How did things go?" Nena queried.

"Wonderful! We had a wonderful time."

"That's a lot of wonderful," Buddy noted when Ben hung up the phone, "but I have to admit, it was a wonderful visit. Becky has turned out to be quite a girl, Ben. In spite of everything, you and Nena did a good job."

Those words were music to Ben's ears, because for all his faults and failures, Becky was his true success. She was everything to him.

**

As the train rumbled along on the tracks toward Boston, Becky intently watched for her hometown of Fairfield to approach. There was not much to see other than the station, but her recollections of growing up in the town flooded her and filled her with nostalgia of an idealistic childhood. Regardless of how life had been altered, no one could ever take that away from her.

Whenever Nena went to South Station to meet someone, she would think of Peter and the time he met her train, after her first visit to Ben's home in New Canaan. They had just begun to date, and she could not wait to tell her father about the trip. There was an innocence to those times and her world seemed full of promise. But there were signs left unheeded, which Nena could see clearly now. Back then, she had been young and falling in love.

As Becky stepped from the train, Nena wondered what her daughter would have to say about her visit in New Canaan. It was the first time Becky had been to Connecticut since leaving for Oxford. On her few visits home, she had stayed in Boston and would meet her father in New York, neutral territory for Ben while he dealt with the divorce. The city, familiar ground, held happy memories for both father and daughter.

Since Becky was not volunteering any information, Nena finally asked about her visit.

"There have been a lot of changes, but all in all I had a great visit. I like Dad's new place. We walked by Grandma's house and the new owners invited us in for a tour. They've done a great job of bringing the old place into the 1990s."

Becky talked about her and Ben's trip to Fairfield, to see the home where she had grown up. Going to Fairfield was a complex of tangled emotions for Becky. "I didn't want to go inside," she told her mother. "Dad didn't either. We drove by slowly. I think the house had been painted, but other than that nothing has changed. Mum, you kept that house in such great condition."

"I remember the new owners telling me what they were going to do," Nena reflected, "but I didn't pay attention as to what."

Becky noticed her mother looked a bit distracted and saddened. "If it hurts to talk about this, we don't have to."

"No, I have some fond memories I want to hold onto."

"Anyway, Dad and Buddy are like the odd couple. Uncle Buddy's role is Felix. He's always puttering around, picking up, keeping the place tidy."

"I can picture that; your father always was a bit of an Oscar," Nena said, softening a bit.

"I know Daddy rues what he did, and wants to make amends. Is there any possibility you could ever be…friends, Mum?" Becky was thinking about her conversation on the platform in New Canaan, and the look on her father's face. Rarely did Becky speak to either Ben or Nena about their relationship. Maybe this question was more about her than them. She had J.R. in her life and did not want the past intruding on the present. Becky had emotionally buried the situation and tucked it away…or so she thought.

"I'm working on it. It might be possible. They say time heals all wounds."

Hailing a cab back to Nena's townhouse, mother and daughter pondered this age-old adage.

**

Becky savored her mother-daughter time in Boston, but was looking forward to J.R.'s arrival. Whenever he called, Nena would study Becky's face. She knew that look all too well.

The doorbell rang. Nena opened the door; J.R. stood on the other side. Tall, wavy sandy-colored hair, brown eyed — he was a good-looking young man with a slender athletic build of a runner.

"Love your place, Mrs. Hicks. I noticed the pool when I came in. I was on the swim team at Amherst."

She had guessed wrong — he was not a runner.

"The pool was a huge selling point in buying this place," she told him. "A pool in the middle of the city on a hot summer day is sheer heaven."

Becky stood listening to their conversation. Nena turned and looked at her daughter, reminded of how her little girl had matured into an accomplished young woman.

Becky approached J.R. and gave him a hug.

"Are you ready?" he asked.

"Ready!"

"Come again, J.R. The door is open whenever you're in town," Nena said as Becky readied to venture off once more, this time with J.R. by her side.

"I'll hold you to the invitation, Mrs. H."

"Call me Nena, please. Say hello to your father, J.R. Tell him he's in our thoughts."

Nena felt empty as she watched them leave, and hoped they would stop by before they returned to England. Becky told her they would try.

~~~~~~~~~~~~~

Crossing the state line into Maine, they drove historic Route 1, a quintessential New England experience. The drive took them through quaint towns and seaports, along the rocky coastline. They stopped for fried clams and onion rings at a roadside stand. A flock of seagulls entertained them as the birds vied for their lunch.

Driving into Ogunquit, J.R. turned off Shore Road onto a long, gravel driveway. Ahead of them, on a knoll, was a turn-of-the-century cottage. Yet it was anything but a cottage, with its weathered wood siding, wrap around veranda and commanding presence. The manicured grounds of the large piece of property seemed to stretch to the ocean — an optical illusion. Gnarled shrubs and thick bush covered the remaining property, cascading to the Marginal Way: a mile-long footpath that meanders along the ocean's granite cliffs from Perkins Cove, a fishing village, artist colony and tourists area to the Ogunquit Beach in town. With a view of the ocean in the distance, the setting was magnificent.

"What a breathtaking location, Mr. Stark," Becky exclaimed to J.R.'s father. "I can see why Mrs. Stark wanted to come here for her final resting place."

"Please call me Jay. Yes, Trudi loved it here. I hear you spent summers in Ogunquit."

"I did and walked the Marginal Way more times than I can count."

"Come on you two, let's go in, cocktail time. It's five o'clock somewhere."

"You sound like my dad," Becky said.

"Good man, your father." Becky wondered if Jay knew anything about what really happened with her father. Word travels fast in New York. If he did know something, he certainly wore a good poker face, and this was not the time to bring up the whole messy situation.

J.R. suggested they take a walk along the cliff as the sun set.

"You kids go along; I'll sit with my cocktail and read for a while."

J.R. suspected his father wanted to be alone with his thoughts before they spread his mother's ashes the following day. Leaving Jay to his solitude, they walked to the Marginal Way, sat on a bench and watched as day turned into night.

"Did you know Ogunquit means a beautiful place by the sea?" Becky asked him.

"I didn't know that, but it sure is. I love this place. I hope my father doesn't sell it. He and my mother came here often, but I wonder how often he will come without her."

"He needs time. He's been through a lot. Let him know how much this place means to you, too. It's a big decision."

They sat on the bench listening to the ocean crash against the craggy shoreline. Under a sliver of moon, remnants of pastel colors from the setting sun filled the evening sky, completing a scene worthy of an artist's brush. There was nowhere else on earth they would rather be, and no one else they would rather be with.

Overwhelmed by the location and his feelings, J.R. thought his heart would burst before he said the words, "I want to tell you that I love you."

They had been dating for a year, but the word *love* had never been mentioned in any serious way between them, and he had wanted to tell her this for some time.

There was no hesitation on Becky's part; the words fell from her lips. "I love you too J.R."

"I was almost afraid to say the words, because I really didn't know how you felt." He stared intently into her eyes.

"You didn't have any idea — none?"

"None, you're such a career girl, and I didn't know if love was in your plan," trying to explain why it took him so long to say the words.

"Well, it is, and you are the one. The joke between my mother and I was that I would marry an Englishman with one of those lovely British accents, but..." Before she could finish, he placed his fingers on her lips.

"I can cultivate one if you wish." And in this romantic setting, he took her in his arms. They could feel their hearts beating as one, as they lingered in a kiss.

Looking deeply into Becky's eyes as they walked back to the house at twilight, the blue of her hazel eyes reflecting the evening light, he told her, "I don't know how you could be more beautiful."

She told him he flattered her, but he should not stop.

**

Early the next morning, Becky prepared a country breakfast. In the city, Jay and Trudi dined out frequently, but here in Maine Trudi ruled the kitchen. Knowing that, Becky felt slightly stressed as she prepared freshly brewed coffee, rashers of bacon, farm-fresh eggs with thick slices of toast, and golden hash browns.

Jay asked Becky where she learned to cook. He thought her hash browns were some of the best he had ever eaten, and hoped Trudi was not listening. This was the first time since the funeral J.R. had seen his father smile when he mentioned his wife.

"Everyone said my great-grandmother was a fantastic cook. She taught my grandmother, my grandmother taught my mother, and my mother taught me. Guess it's in the gene pool."

"She's a catch Robbie; don't let her get away." Jay's comment caused Becky to blush.

**

Jay held the urn with Trudi's ashes lovingly cradled in his arms as they walked to the edge of the rocks lining the Marginal Way. When they reached a small tidal pool in the rocks overlooking the ocean, a favorite spot of Trudi's, Jay opened the jar. Father and son read messages they had written. When they finished, they bent down to catch the wind and let Trudi take flight.

"Mother would have loved this, Dad."

There was not a dry eye between them as they walked back to the house.

**

The next day J.R. and Becky left for Boston, allowing enough time to visit with Nena before their early evening flight to England.

Before leaving, Becky confided in her mother, "Mum, J.R. told me he loved me. It was beyond romantic. He said the color of my eyes reflected the evening light. I guess being in love brought out the poet in him."

J.R.'s words reminded her of Ben's words when they first kissed. Nena could feel the blood drain from her face. Rather than seeing a ghost, she heard a ghost.

"Are you okay? Mum?"

"I'm fine; your news took my breath away for a minute," she said, still a bit rattled by the memory.

Her heart was heavy as she watched them leave for a second time. Nena wanted to tell them to stay but instead wished them a safe trip.

When J.R. and Becky were gone, Nena had to sit down. Hearing her daughter tell her how J.R. spoke about her eyes was too surreal. She had almost forgotten how in love she and Ben were back then, and how the possibilities of that love seemed endless.

~~~~~~~~~~~~~~

The newly declared in-love couple's return flight to England was a blur.

J.R. hailed a cab outside of Heathrow. At the train station, the cabbie put her suitcase on the sidewalk.

"See you Friday night, Darling," she said.

"Can't wait." He held her close as they kissed good-bye.

**

Thank heaven for classes, meetings, and a busy schedule. Becky would count the hours until nine when he faithfully called her every night.

"I'll meet you tomorrow at Paddington Station. Do you think you can catch the five o'clock?"

"I'll make sure I catch the five."

**

J.R. paced, waiting for the train to arrive. At first he did not see her. He turned as the train began to pull out of the station and saw her walk toward him. Becky's graceful gait and broad smile put him at ease, and he scooped her into his arms.

"I hope you don't mind, but I've arranged dinner with a few friends I want you to meet."

Becky had met some of his friends, but not all of them. J.R. traveled in a rather large circle.

"Special people?" she asked.

"People I really want to meet you."

They arrived at his three-bedroom flat in Belgravia on Chester Square. He was leasing it from a family on assignment in Hong Kong. It was more spacious than he really needed, but he could not refuse the price he negotiated, or the location. Because of the three bedrooms, he had an endless parade of visitors. He never minded until now, not until Becky came into his life. He had never been in love like this before. For months he knew he was mad for her, but afraid to tell her. If he had known she felt the same, he would have spoken sooner. Trudi's death made J.R. realize life was not forever.

"Our flats are so different. Every time I come here I feel sophisticated," Becky told him, making small talk. Tonight everything seemed different to her.

"I'd describe your place as cozy. This place is shall I say 'citified,' for grownups with children; that's why I prefer spending our time together in Oxford."

"You're right about the grownup part," she said, in a playful manner, tilting her head, batting her eyes, giving him a come-hither look.

**

"How does Chinese sound? We're going to Tiger Lee," he said hailing a cab.

"Wonderful."

By the time they reached the restaurant, their party was already seated.

"Late again," a single male voice chided.

"Give a guy a break," J.R. countered. Becky could tell this was the usual banter between these two.

Introductions were made. There were two married couples, and one single man, all expats.

"Bill and Daisy Hobart, Chuck and Shelly Logan, Marc Silver, I want you to meet Becky Hicks."

Daisy spoke first, telling Becky how much they had heard about her from J.R. and how it was nice to finally meet. "We were beginning to think you were a figment of his imagination," she added with a sly smile. This broke the ice. Dinner ordered, Daisy spoke up again with a question for the guest of honor. "Tell us Becky, what exactly do you do? Our dear friend has developed a passionate interest in museums since meeting you."

Becky explained her work and love of ancient Egyptian antiquities.

"I also teach three undergraduate courses, and we are in the planning stages for a dig trip to Egypt next year," Becky told the group. "It's a long process for permits and all the red tape, but the thoughts of going back to Egypt are very exciting."

"You mean you've already been on a dig?" Marc was impressed.

"Yes, I went during my graduate program. I can't tell you the feeling you get when you discover something even a small shard from a vessel."

"How do you know J.R., Marc?" Becky asked.

"A mutual friend from Harvard put us in touch."

"And who do you work for?"

"American Express; you know AMEX?"

"Oh yes, I wouldn't leave home without my green card. What do you do at American Express?"

"I work for card servicing, that little green thing you can't leave home without!"

Becky found Marc interesting; she already knew she was going to like him. During the course of their conversation, they found they had much in common. Marc revealed he grew up in Bronxville, New York, across the street from a classmate of Becky's from boarding school, and his parents were presently living in Florida near where her parents had their home in Palm Beach.

The evening was a success and schedules were checked for getting together again, soon.

**

"I'll pour the wine, and you open this present." J.R. said before heading to the kitchen. He handed Becky a box tied with a beautiful bow. Until now his gifts were flowers, confections, and a book to commemorate Becky's attendance at the opening of the Temple of Dendur at the Met — a first-edition book — depicting the removal of the Temple from Luxor and the building of the Aswam High Dam.

The box he gave her was not too large but heavy. Carefully, she untied the bow and lifted the top. Tissue paper floated through her hands as she reached in to lift up the most exquisite vase she had ever seen. He walked into the room in time to see the look on her face.

"Oh my, I don't know what to say. This is gorgeous."

"How about, 'I love you madly for buying me such an incredible gift,'" he said with a smile.

Becky read the card describing the piece. The vase was by René Lalique, noted for his Art Deco style. The company became known for its amazing creations, and now one belonged to her. When she noticed the etching of three iris flowers on the vase, she exclaimed, "This is stunning; irises, the first flowers you brought me. How on earth did you ever find this?"

"I have my ways."

She set the work of art on the coffee table, turned to J.R., and kissed him passionately.

"If I knew this would be my thanks, I'd have bought two!"

It had been a long day. In bed, exhausted, they fell asleep in one another's arms.

In the morning when they awoke, J.R. drew her close. She was wearing a T-shirt of his.

"You look good in this." He ogled Becky. "But you would look even better with it off."

Gently he pulled the shirt over her head, her chestnut brown hair falling onto the pillow. Tenderly he caressed her face and neck. A stirring of anticipation went through his body as he let his hands run the length of her torso. Everything about Becky seemed different to him. This would not be the first time they had sex, but having expressed their love to one another made this time different.

"You're incredible…" he murmured.

"We were always good, but this was… What can I say? I just died and went to heaven." She cuddled in his arms in utter bliss.

**

While he made coffee, she sat and admired the vase.

"How can I ever thank you for this gift?"

"Oh, I'll think of something."

"One track mind, I see," she joked and then asked if he had any plans away from the bedroom that day.

"Nothing really, but I do have tickets for the theatre tonight. Have you seen *Starlight Light Express*?"

"No, but I hear, as the English would say, it's brilliant. There is something else I'd like to do today."

"And what's that?"

"Visit Kew Gardens."

"Any particular reason?"

How could she explain to J.R. what was going on inside her? Since falling in love with him, suppressed feelings involving her parent's divorce were rising to the surface. His gift of the Lalique vase, depicting the etched Irises, flowers he gave her on their first date, triggered thoughts of the story when her father and mother were falling in love. Ben gave Nena — a crystal figurine of a butterfly — a gift to celebrate the day Nena caught a glimpse of a Peacock butterfly in Kew Gardens, the summer before she and Ben met. Becky wanted to visit this place that factored into her parent's blossoming love. She had accepted the fact her parents would never reunite, but what happened to her family left her with a constant struggle of divided loyalties. Being in love with J.R., Becky realized it was time to face and address these issues. She did not want anything to negatively affect their relationship. Maybe a visit to Kew Gardens would help her begin this journey.

Becky and J.R. spent the afternoon at Kew Gardens, and while they did not see a Peacock butterfly, spending time there satisfied something inside her. A clarity washed through Becky regarding what had happened to her family. She would never question if it was the visit to the gardens, or the fact she was ready to acknowledge her parents were not the people she had put on a pedestal her entire life; but human beings with all that encumbers. Becky's journey had begun.

Chapter 5

1994 would be a year Becky would never forget. In February accompanied by the head of the archaeology department, she and ten of her students were leaving for Egypt. It had taken nearly six months to procure the proper work documents from the various Egyptian governmental departments for two months on the dig site and the rest of the time attending lectures and visiting other locations. The group would not know which site they were assigned to until they arrived, yet this did not diminish Becky's enthusiasm.

~~~~~~~~~~~~~~

"Bags packed?" he asked.

"Almost…but I'm going to miss you terribly," she told J.R. on the phone one night.

"I'll see you Friday. We'll have the weekend, and I plan on making the most of it."

"Can't wait."

**

Most of their weekends were spent in Oxford. To stretch out their time together, J.R. stayed until Monday mornings. Becky would walk him to the train station where they would stand locked in an embrace until the conductor called "All aboard" for the final time.

"I'll call you tonight!" he shouted.

"I'll be waiting," she said, knowing this good-bye was different. Walking back to campus, Becky could not believe how much she would miss J.R. She never dreamt she would ever feel this way about any man, but she did feel this way for him.

Her mother had married right out of college, and Becky vowed she would never do that. She wanted a career. The longer time went on, with no special man in her life, Becky began to believe she would remain single. Then that wonderful, unanticipated night at the museum happened. And there he was. He had been there all the time; she only had to meet him. He was totally unexpected, but totally welcomed. Every part of her came alive whenever she thought of him. Except for J.R.'s short business trips to New York in the nearly two years they had been dating, they had never been apart. Now she was going away for three months. She had to remind herself the importance of this trip and how fortunate she was to be leading the group. She could get through this — she knew it.

~~~~~~~~~~~~

After a five-hour flight from London, the plane touched down in Cairo. A representative from the Ministry of State for Antiquities met the group at the airport. They were taken to the hotel to await their assignment and itinerary for the duration of their stay.

While they waited, Becky took the students to Kahan el-Khalili, a maze of bazaars unlike anything they had ever seen. The souk, a Medieval-styled market, dating to the fourteenth century was built on the site of an historical tomb, part of a great palace and the burial place for the founders of the city of Cairo.

Walking through the narrow streets, they were bombarded by vendors each wanting them to step inside their shop. There was everything to purchase, from shishas (the traditional Middle Eastern water pipe) to crafts, rich leather goods, and hand-worked gold. The fragrant, exotic, and intoxicating aromas from the herb and spice stalls filled the air, adding to their immersion into this culturally diverse country. The group stopped at a café for a cup of the traditional drink of Egypt: tea, served black and sweet in a glass. To complement the tea, they ordered an array of desserts: apple cake, something that looked and tasted similar to Greek baklava, and a sweet considered a national dish of Egypt, a raisin cake soaked in milk and served hot. The entire experience was a great introduction for what was to come.

**

Before leaving for the dig site, the group flew to Abu Simbel and Aswan to tour both the temple of Ramesses II and the Aswan Dam. The dam particularly interested Becky because this was the location from which the Temple of Dendur was removed — the very temple that now resided at the Met in New York City. Her connection to this temple began as a thirteen-year-old girl, the evening her parents took her to the opening of the exhibit. And now she would experience the temple's place of origin. The region held other nearby monuments and a granite quarry containing an unfinished obelisk — each captured the imagination of a long ago civilization.

They returned to their hotel in Luxor on the east bank of the Nile. The desk clerk handed Becky a package from the ministry with their assignment. The group would spend its dig time at the el-Deir temple complex. This complex contained the beautiful temple KV60 of Queen Hatshepsut. Hatshepsut became the fifth pharaoh of Egypt in 1478 BC and ruled for twenty-one years. She was among a handful of woman rulers in ancient Egypt. Oftentimes, even female rulers of ancient Egypt were depicted by wearing a false beard, akin to the beard originally attached to the Sphinx. The tomb where Becky's group would dig was recently discovered, in 1990, on the west bank of the Nile in the Valley of the Kings.

The team was ready to get to work. Gasps were audible when the temple came into view. The beauty and scope of Hatshepsut's mortuary temple, guarding the entrance to the valley, appeared to grow out of the very rock and steep cliffs in the background. Becky had seen the temple on her last visit, but the vastness of the site yet again caught her by surprise.

**

Days turned into weeks, weeks into a month, and before anyone realized, the two months at the dig were over. Becky was ecstatic the first day her students unearthed a pottery shard. The thrill of watching the sifter yield ancient artifacts from the earth could not be put into words. Other shards were found, including some she unearthed herself. Each find was like a first discovery.

The remainder of the time in Egypt the group spent attending lectures captivated by the talks of Dr. Zahi Hawass, who later would become the Minister of Antiquities, and the American Dr. Donald Ryan, the archaeologist and Egyptologist who rediscovered the tomb where they worked for two months. Hours flew by in the Egyptian Museum, viewing and studying the vast collection, and a final trip to the Pyramids of Giza, the last remaining intact seventh wonder of the world, rounded out the excursions.

**

The pyramids loomed over Mena House. Built in the late eighteen hundreds for an Egyptian king as a hunting lodge, and nicknamed the "Mud Hut," Mena House was purchased as a private residence by a couple on their honeymoon. Eventually, the property was sold to an English couple and turned into a hotel, which would become world renowned for its beauty and location. The name came from the founding father of the first Egyptian dynasty, King Menes. The hotel with towers, minarets, and colonnades occupied space within forty acres of jasmine-scented gardens. The luxurious interior was filled with exquisite antiques, handcrafted furniture, and rich textiles. The Mena House consisted of the palatial hotel and a separate accommodation called the Garden Wing. The guest rooms were decorated with traditional details, but no decorations could compete with the view from the windows — the pyramids.

Besides playing host to famous visitors from across the globe, from royalty to world leaders and celebrities, the hotel was the location in 1997 where peace was forged between Egypt and Israel that resulted in the Camp David Agreement.

**

Each day brought another new discovery. One day a guide from the ministry met the group at the opening to the Great Pyramid of Khufu. They ascended the pyramid to the Grand Gallery and the King's Chamber. Khufu, twenty years old when he began the construction of his pyramid, took an additional twenty years to complete his "Stairway to Heaven." To reach the King's Chamber, visitors walk, stooped down, holding onto two ropes on either side of a narrow passageway through the Grand Gallery. Lit only by dim lights, scant fresh air filled the dark passageway. Becky would not count her steps on this walk, like she had climbing the steps of the Met as a young girl. When they finally reached the king's burial chamber, they were amazed. In the small, rectangular flat-roofed chamber was a chocolate-colored sarcophagus, carved from a solid block of granite over four thousand years ago. Because of the size of the coffer it is believed it was placed in the chamber before the workers closed the chamber and sealed the passageway. Walking out of the pyramid into the fresh air, looking up at the dizzying heights of this ancient structure, they all knew there could be no better way to end their months in Egypt. Tonight they would attend the sound and light show at the Great Sphinx, followed by a few days of free time, and then home to Oxford.

**

Becky had mixed emotions when she walked into the lobby of the hotel and asked the desk clerk for her room key. The dig had come to an end. Three days left in Egypt but in three days, she would be back in J.R.'s arms.

"I'm sorry Miss Hicks, your room has been changed," the desk clerk informed her.

"Changed? How come?"

"I'm really not certain Miss, but you have been moved to a Garden Room. It's a lovely room, and the view of the pyramids is one of the best. I hope you will enjoy the remainder of your stay with us."

Puzzled, Becky walked toward the room, past the pool, when someone called her name. She thought she recognized the voice, but could not believe her ears. Sitting on a chaise lounge was J.R.

"Oh my God, it's really you?" Becky ran toward him and threw herself into his arms.

"None other. Get your suit on and come join me."

She hurried and changed, dashing back to the pool.

"My darling *you* have some explaining to do," she scolded him.

"First, tell me how did everything go?"

"Fantastic, but you still need to explain yourself, Mister."

"Before you left I knew I had to come. I spoke with your department, they helped me make the arrangements, and here I am. I wanted to share at least a tiny bit of this experience with you."

"We're going to the sound and light show tonight after dinner. You must come."

"I wouldn't miss it for the world."

"Good! And tomorrow I'd like to take you to the pyramids. Anything else you wanted to see or do?"

"No, just be with you."

**

Sitting in front of the illuminated Sphinx, watching the sound and light show, listening to secrets about the history of the pyramids and the men who built them, and holding J.R.'s hand, eclipsed Becky's wildest dreams.

**

The next morning Becky could not wait to get started. "My time here has been tightly organized and scheduled; it's going to be wonderful to be a tourist. And to think yesterday I thought I would be sight-seeing alone." She told him.

They walked to the pyramids from the hotel. On the way, a barrage of men vied for their attention to buy trinkets or ride a camel.

A driver approached Becky. "Ride, take a ride to the pyramids, Miss?"

"Shall we?" J.R. asked her.

She agreed, and they hailed two camel drivers. As they were mounting the camels, a group of her students walked by.

"Want a picture, Miss Hicks?" the student asked.

Becky thought of her father's request for photographs. "How about a couple, in case we fall off," she joked.

Swinging their legs over the saddle as the camel sat on the ground, J.R. and Becky thought they were figuring out this camel-riding experience just fine. But as their camels rose upward, they rocked backwards, then lurched and jerked forward, giving them the sensation they were about to tumble forward, face first to the ground.

"I hope getting off is going to be a little less rocky," Becky said, trying to smile for the camera.

The second time inside Khufu's burial chamber still thrilled Becky and left J.R. in awe. Outside, along The Great Pyramid a small museum housed an intact solar boat built for the pharaoh. The boat captivated their imaginations. Built out of cedar probably brought to Egypt from Lebanon, and constructed in the shape of a sailing boat; in all probability, it served as a funerary barge to carry the pharaoh across the heavens. When the boat was discovered in a nearby pit at the base of the pyramid, preservationists built a museum over the site, for public viewing. J.R. listened intently while Becky fascinated him with her knowledge of ancient Egypt.

When they returned to the hotel J.R. told Becky to pack an overnight bag, along with a heavy sweater, and to ask no questions. They climbed into a waiting jeep. The driver headed into the desert.

**

"We have arrived, madam." J.R. helped Becky out of the jeep. "Welcome to your overnight safari." The aroma of lamb barbequing wafted through the air as she stepped onto the soft grains of sand.

A Bedouin tent greeted her. The floor of the tent had been covered with exquisite multicolored oriental rugs. On the carpets piled high were tasseled pillows in vibrant shades of yellows, reds, and blues. A bed sat low to the ground, draped with white netting flowing from the top of the tent and covered with luscious Egyptian bedding.

Turning to J.R., she asked, "This is for me?"

"For you, my love."

While they waited for dinner, chairs were brought outside where they were served champagne as they watched the sun begin to set in the west, casting golden rays that rested atop the dunes and the flat desert horizon.

"I knew this trip was going to be amazing J.R., but I never could have imagined this is the way it would end. This is the stuff of novels."

J.R. had even outdone himself. He wanted this night to be perfect. Once the sun set, dinner was served. Tall torches illuminated the tent, as they sat on the carpets in front of a low wooden table set with mezzes, Egyptian appetizers. A pile of freshly made pita bread on a hand-hammered silver plate accompanied hummus made of chickpeas, olive oil, Tahini, lemon juice, and lots of garlic, and falafel, the Egyptian-style deep fried ball of mashed broad beans, filled colorful clay bowls and their senses with the smells of the Middle East. The salads were made from aubergines and tomatoes, and Becky's favorite garlicky lemon tabouleh — the most famous Middle East salad of parsley, tomatoes, cucumbers, garlic, bulghar wheat, and lemon juice — completed the spread.

While eating the mezzes, Becky described in detail the Valley of the Kings and King Tutankhamun's tomb and wished he could have been there with her.

"Tomorrow afternoon we'll have time to visit the museum in Cairo. I want you to see Tut's collection and exhibit. I'm excited to take you there."

She had not finished regaling J.R. when the entrée arrived. The same aroma that greeted her on arrival: barbequed lamb on skewers served with zabadi, a cool yogurt dip mixed with pungent mint and cucumber and a big bowl of fluffy rice. A light white wine was poured, and they drank, and ate, and ate.

When they finished their tea, J.R. suggested they go outside. He took her hand as they looked up at the desert sky. There was no ambient light to disturb their view of the heavens.

"Look there's the Milky Way," she said in amazement. "I have never seen this many stars, ever."

"It is beautiful, but not as beautiful as what I am looking at."

Becky turned to see he was looking at her. They were face to face — he got down on one knee. J.R. had not been this nervous since their first date.

"I know this approach may seem old fashioned," he began, "but I can't wait any longer. Becky you make me complete. When we aren't together, I have all I can do to contain myself until I see you. You're smart, loving, kind, enthusiastic about life, and, might I say, always the most beautiful girl in the room. There is nobody else in the world I would rather spend the remainder of my life with — will you become my wife?"

Becky bent down. Taking her hands and placing them on his face, she gave her answer. "I never thought you were going to ask. Yes! Yes! Yes!"

He reached into his pocket and presented her with a magnificent antique ring.

"It was my mother's engagement ring, and my grandmother's before that. Now it's yours."

As he slipped the ring on her finger, they toppled onto the sand. Lying on their backs staring up at the stars, the same stars that the ancient Egyptians believed held the secrets to life beyond what they knew on earth, they both felt the same wonderment the ancients must have experienced, those thousands of years ago.

"You know you're more beautiful tonight than you were the night in Ogunquit, when I told you I loved you for the first time."

"Oh I bet you say that to all the girls you propose to."

Only the special ones, he said, as they walked to the tent. Inside the tent, the dinner table had mysteriously disappeared. The bed was turned down, and a tray with glasses and a bottle of champagne was placed on the rug. J.R. filled the glasses for a toast. "To my wife to be; how lucky can a guy get?"

They drank champagne and made love on the carpets until the fire outside the tent became smoldering embers; then they climbed into the bed while the soothing sounds of the cool desert breeze rocked them into a deep sleep.

The following morning, when they awoke, the table reappeared, set for breakfast. Egyptian omelets, called eggah, were served. They finished breakfast and as if on cue the jeep arrived for their journey back to the hotel. At Mena House, Becky gathered her colleagues and students. She could not wait to show off her ring. Champagne was ordered to celebrate before they left for Cairo and the flight back to Oxford.

Chapter 6

The minute Becky returned to her flat she phoned her mother.

"You're back. Everyone's anxious to hear about your trip," Nena said. "Tell me was it as exciting as you thought?"

"Mummy, it was that and more. Where do I begin?" Becky could hardly contain herself. "But first I have some really big news. J.R. asked me to marry him, and he asked me in the most romantic place I could ever imagine."

"Slow down; when did this happen?"

Becky went on to tell her mother in minute detail how J.R. proposed. When she finished, Nena was speechless.

"Mum?"

"Yes, I'm here. Give me a minute. I'm surprised. You must have been surprised."

"Surprised! How about stunned, astonished, blown away, deliriously happy."

"I guess I should ask the obvious question: When and where is the wedding?"

Becky told her mother that she and J.R. planned to marry over the holidays and wanted to get married in England, if their family members were okay with that. She emphasized that she and J.R. preferred a small wedding, with just family and very close friends.

"I know this is short notice, but we don't want to wait any longer. Do you think you could come to England this summer to help me with the plans?" Becky did not want to hear no. "Please..."

"No need for a please," her mother replied. "Absolutely, I'll come. I'll arrange my work schedule and get back to you. Let's tentatively plan on July."

"Mum, would you do me another favor and be the bearer of our good news? Call Daddy first. I've gotta run. I'm late for class, and behind at work. I can't wait for you to get here. Bye Mum, see you in July."

As soon as Nena said good-bye to her daughter, she called Ben at the office. He, too, was flabbergasted at J.R.'s ability to pull off such a feat, especially in a foreign land.

Hanging up the phone, he turned to Buddy. "Well old man, we're heading to England, and you'll never guess why?"

~~~~~~~~~~~~~~~~~~~~~~~~~~~~~~~~~~~~~~~

Walking into Christ's Church Cathedral, Nena was reflecting on her visit there with her brother Josh and mother, the summer her father, Peter taught at Oxford. Now here she was about to enter the cathedral with Becky to plan her daughter's wedding day. Nena vividly remembered sitting in the nave, with her mother and Josh, admiring the Norman architecture and the majestic rose window, listening to the choir rehearse, mesmerized by their angelic voices. She understood why Becky wanted to be married here.

"Let's ask if the choir can sing at your wedding," Nena suggested as they walked inside the cathedral. "With your Granddad's affiliation, and now you teaching here, maybe we can have some influence. The worst they can say is no."

Entering Dean Drury's office, Becky made the introductions. The dean greeted them with a warm smile, however, his body language was formal, causing Becky to be more tense than she already was. He motioned them to sit down.

"Becky, I hear you're getting married. Congratulations!"

"Thank you. J.R. flew to Egypt at the end of our dig and proposed. I couldn't have been more shocked," she told him, trying to instantly make the exchange more personal.

"How do you feel about your future son-in-law, Mrs. Hicks?" the dean asked.

Nena was unprepared and taken aback by his question. It took her a moment to collect her thoughts, before she answered. "He's a wonderful young man who has been through a lot lately with the loss of his mother.

Since he and Becky live in England, we haven't had the opportunity to spend a great deal of time with J.R., but we hope we'll have more occasions to get together in the future.

The dean studied Nena as she spoke, curious as to why she used the word *we* rather than *I* when referencing J.R., since he asked for her feelings regarding this young man. He was correct in wondering. Nena had one child: Becky. She knew she could not protect Becky from life, but she did not want her daughter to enter into a marriage, any marriage, and in the end go through the heartache she did. Nena shuddered at the thought she had become somewhat cynical, and constantly reminded herself that Becky was a grown woman and knew her own heart.

"I'm always glad to see you Becky, but I get the feeling this is not a social call," the dean continued.

"You're right. I want to reserve a date and time for our wedding ceremony. J.R. and I have two dates in mind, but they're during the Christmas season. We have our fingers crossed the church can accommodate us."

A tentative wedding date was set for December 17, 1994, and the dean gave consent for the choir to perform. Rehearsal times were booked, but before the wedding site was secured, a few strings would need to be pulled. Neither Becky nor J.R. were members of the cathedral, which presented a slight problem. It was not Peter but Jay to the rescue, asking the Bishop of New York, the head of The Cathedral of Saint John the Divine (where he and his family belonged for generations) to intercede with Dean Drury for a special license. With the granting of the license, the wedding became official.

Before Nena arrived in England, Becky and J.R. had booked Le Manoir for the wedding reception. This is where she and J.R. had their first date, and celebrated their engagement after they returned from Egypt. Even so, Becky wanted her mother's approval. The moment Nena walked inside the building she recognized why Becky and J.R. were taken with this venue for the reception. Sitting with Chef Blanc's sous chef and the restaurant's event planner, they selected the menu, which room to use, every detail to make this a memorable day.

The following day an excursion into London was planned to find the perfect wedding dress.

Trying on what felt like hundreds of dresses, Becky could not find one that gave her that aha moment.

"I'm really disappointed," she told her mother. "None of the gowns felt like me."

"I feel the same. I thought for certain we would find a dress, today. I have a thought, and you don't have to answer right away." Pausing, Nena continued, "Would you consider wearing my wedding dress?"

Her mother's offer brought back childhood memories. When she was little, Becky would peek in Nena's closet at the big box on the shelf. "I would beg you to take Cinderella's gown out of the box. Remember?"

"I remember, but you do realize it's not a Cinderella ball gown."

"I know Mum, but what did I know then?!?"

"I can ship it to you when I get home."

"If it's not too much trouble, I think I can make it work. Would you mind if I removed those crystals at the neckline? They might be a little outdated."

"If you decide to wear the dress, I want you to feel free to make it your own," Nena told her daughter.

Decision made, they left the bridal shop and hailed a cab to the Ritz for tea and a trip down memory lane.

Later that day, not wanting her daughter to see her crying, Nena looked out the window of the train on the return ride to Oxford. Becky was no longer a little girl, but she would always be her little girl.

**

The box arrived. Standing in front of a mirror holding the gown against her body, picturing the changes she would make, in that moment Becky saw herself as a bride and could not wait to walk down the aisle on the arm of her father, into the waiting arms of J.R..

Nena had not seen Dr. Katz since the evening in New York City with her classmates from Columbia, after Trudi's funeral. It had been an unexpected surprise to meet him again, but she found starting where they left off when she attended Columbia more difficult than she thought. The wounds from her divorce were still raw and on the surface. They had spoken often on the phone since that night in the city. She liked the idea of telephone talk. His calls were nonthreatening, avoiding personal matters. A kindhearted voice on the other end of the phone suited Nena just fine.

**

"How nice to hear your voice, Sam." Nena never knew when he would call, but when he did, she looked forward to their conversations.

"Do you have any plans for tonight?" he asked. "If not, I'd like to see you."

Nena was confused, believing Sam was in New York.

"Sorry for the confusion; I'm here in Boston. Took a while, but I'm in town for a two-day seminar at Harvard. I thought I'd try to entice you into having dinner with me. Sorry for the short notice, but I decided to attend the conference on the spur of the moment."

Nena was a planner. She needed her life organized – dates made in advance — especially since her divorce. She rarely did things on the spur of the moment. She had not done anything spontaneous since she and Ben went to Venice, before her world collapsed. She remembered Sam saying he would call her the next time he was in Boston, but he had given her no warning. Talking on the telephone had a safe element — distance. Sitting across a table in a restaurant, gave her no place to hide. His call had totally caught her off guard. Nena needed time to think.

Before she could say a word, Sam sensed her hesitation and tried to lighten the conversation, "It's only dinner. I hope you don't regard me as an unpleasant dinner companion."

Now she felt slightly ridiculous, and he was right; it was just dinner.

"Of course I'll have dinner with you. Where?"

"Since you live near the North End, pick a spot, and I'll meet you there."

"Actually, I'd rather have seafood, if you don't mind. I'd suggest Anthony's Pier Four if you can get a reservation." The reality was that Nena did not want to have dinner in her neighborhood – she needed a neutral place – and besides she did love seafood.

"I'm staying at the Ritz-Carlton. I'll see if the concierge can pull some strings."

**

Anthony's Pier Four was a fixture in Boston, and over the years it had played host to the world's elite, from presidents and celebrities, to the titans of industry. No patron ever left the premises without feeling special and singing its praises.

The restaurant sported a nautical theme with its ship's wheels, captain's chairs, and crisp white linen tablecloths. Nena and Sam were seated at a table by the window, looking out over the lights of Boston Harbor.

"Are you ready to order?" their waiter inquired.

With their orders placed, sipping cocktails, and nibbling on Anthony's famous popovers, Nena told Sam about her recent trip to England. She felt comfortable talking with Sam and found herself telling him about her concern when it came to Becky and J.R., wondering aloud if she was projecting her own fears onto her daughter.

"Nena you shouldn't be this harsh on yourself." Sam did not know if he should say anything else, rather predicting she was inheriting a rather romantic son-in-law.

Dinner was New England to the bone. Bowls of creamy New England clam chowder brimming with potatoes and clams, smelling of the ocean, steamers with drawn butter and briny broth, and boiled lobster, served in its shell because half the fun of eating lobster was the work needed to get to the meat. Anthony's creamed spinach, a garden salad, a divine chocolate soufflé with zabaglione sauce for dessert, and a bottle of French Burgundy rounded out the meal. Between each bite, they talked and talked, just as they had when Nena was his student.

"Would you like to have dinner with me tomorrow night?" Sam asked as they left Anthony's.

"I'd enjoy that. I'll make the arrangement. Call me tomorrow; I'll tell you where and when."

He leaned over to kiss her on the lips before she entered the cab, but she turned her head, and his kiss fell on her cheek.

**

The previous evening had gone better than Nena could have expected. She was ready to share her corner of Boston with Sam and invited him to her favorite place to dine in the North End, L'Osteria.

The restaurant had recently moved across the street and sat on the corner of Salem and Cooper Streets. There were many small Italian restaurants in the North End, but the minute she first walked through the door of L'Osteria, a Latin word meaning guest, entered the hallway, walked to the reception desk, and was greeted by the owner, she felt at home.

The dining space was small with a Tuscan old-world feel. With its large windows facing the streets, charming decorative lighting, and brick wall, at the end of a busy workday Nena felt transported to another place and time. A corner table tucked into the front of the dining room by a window looking out onto Salem Street had become her special place to dine and watch as people strolled by. She ate here at least once a week and had become a regular.

Once inside this warm cozy restaurant, Lina and Nicky, the proprietors, asked Nena where she had been.

"Our girl is getting married. I was in England helping her make plans."

"Please send her our congratulations," said Nicky. "I see you are not dining alone tonight. Are you going to introduce us?"

Nena introduced Sam as a former professor she had in graduate school, not knowing what else to say. Usually Nena dined alone or with family and friends, and had never brought a dinner companion to the restaurant.

Nicky took their orders. As he walked to the kitchen he could be heard humming, *That's Amore.*

"Nena, this reminds me of the neighborhood Trattorias in Italy. No wonder you come here often."

"I love this place. Lina and Nicky treat me like family. And the food will transport you to Italy. Well, wait until you taste it."

Two starters arrived at the table, Mussels Marinara steamed in a marinara sauce with just the right hint of acid in the tomatoes, and Calamari fried to perfection. For main dishes Nena ordered veal Marsala, medallions of veal swimming in sweet Marsala wine with mushrooms and with a house salad, while Sam chose his favorite, Eggplant Parmigiana with Linguini. Chianti Classico from Tuscany complimented the food. They passed on dessert, instead ordering a glass of Limoncello, a syrupy lemon liqueur from southern Italy referred to as sunshine in a glass.

Leaving the restaurant, they walked along Hanover Street and passed Mike's bakery. "Let's go in," Sam suggested. "I want to buy you something."

"Only if you'll come for coffee."

"Deal!" he replied, hoping she would extend the invitation and the evening.

They stood at the glass cases eyeing the excess of pastries, leaving the bakery with a box filled with Italian deserts of tiramisu, rum cake, lobster tails, and biscotti.

**

"I can't remember the last time I spent two wonderful evenings like this back to back," he said, as they sat in Nena's living room drinking espresso and eating the bakery treats.

"I've had a great time too, Sam; I'm glad you called me."

Standing in her doorway, this time Nena let him kiss her good-bye on the lips. She did not feel the way she felt the first time Ben kissed her that night at Smith. There was not the fiery excitement of youth, but she did feel something.

Sam had never gotten her out of his system. No matter how many women he dated after that summer at Columbia, not one woman measured up to Nena. He could not tell her this; it was too soon. He could sense she was not ready, and he would not push, but her kiss gave him hope. He could wait.

Clearing the dishes, Nena tried to assess her feelings. Could she begin a relationship with another man? She did not know. Undressing, she looked at herself in the mirror. At almost fifty-four, she did not have a gray hair, and her body still had youthful curves. She guessed she was sexually attractive, although thoughts of this nature rarely crossed her mind since her marriage dissolved. Thinking of being with another man made her slightly uncomfortable. She knew herself well enough to know, although they were divorced, Ben was not in her past. Would it be fair to either herself or Sam to see him again? But kissing Sam stirred something deep inside her. That night in bed she questioned her willingness to explore this new feeling.

~~~~~~~~~~~~~~~~~~~~~~~~~~~~~~~~~~~~

"I see your mother's wedding gown arrived. Going to show me?" J.R. asked Becky one night he was visiting her.

"No!" she answered emphatically. "And it isn't my mother's wedding gown any longer; it's mine. Well, it will be mine once the alterations are done."

"You are sure about the dress?" J.R. had reservations about the gown. He was not a superstitious person, but after all her parents' marriage did not last.

"I am," she admitted. "I know what you're thinking…this is the dress my mother wore when she married Daddy, but the dress is not the reason they divorced. The day my mother wore this gown she was full of hope, and besides I like it more than any dress I tried on." Becky wanted to change the subject. She was making strides putting her parents' divorce behind her, and did not want to tarnish the moment by looking back. "Okay let's stay focused. The wedding details are taken care of. Let's talk honeymoon."

"I was going to surprise you."

"No more surprises. Your surprise in Egypt was enough to last me a few lifetimes. Let's plan this together. There are some brochures on the table, or we can each make a list, and see what we have in common."

Drinking wine and comparing their lists, they spent the evening narrowing down the choices until they made a decision.

"Happy with our decision?"

"I'm thrilled!" she answered, flinging her arms around him.

~~~~~~

"Been a while since we've caught up." J.R. and Marc were sitting in a pub having lunch, enjoying traditional fish and chips and a pint. They had met at the Ye Olde Cheshire Cheese on Fleet Street. The building dated to the great fire of 1666.

"I heard you've put the rest of us bachelors on notice when it comes to proposing. How in hell did you pull that off?" Marc asked.

"Had some help from Becky's department at Oxford. Believe me, it wasn't easy, but it was worth it."

"Becky's a fantastic girl." When J.R. did not respond, Marc noticed his friend seemed lost in his own thoughts. "Okay, what's on your mind?"

"I want to talk about Salomon. Oh, I forgot to tell you that on my last trip to the States I met Warren Buffett. He gave a talk at headquarters. He said something interesting: 'if we lose a shred of reputation for the firm, he'll be ruthless.'" These words stuck with J.R.

"Whoa! You shook the hand of the man. Wow! No wonder he said what he said; Salomon really screwed up. Bet you were glad to be over here when the you-know-what hit the fan."

"Yeah, I was," J.R. told him. "I don't envy the guys who had to go through that mess. Here's the deal, Marc. I've been offered a new position and I want your opinion."

The two men discussed the offer, weighing the pros and cons. In the end, with Marc's input, J.R. decided taking a position in the banking sector of Salomon might be a good move, maybe not for the present, but for the future.

"Thanks Marc, you're a good sounding board my friend."

"Glad I could help. Say, let's get together soon. Tell Becky to fix me up. About time I got serious and settled down, seeing how it agrees with you." Laughing he added, "And I thought you'd be the last to go."

The two men walked out of the pub into a sunny July summer afternoon in London, a welcome change in weather from the cool, damp spring.

**

Even though J.R. accepted the new position, it was the first time in his career he was second-guessing himself. Salomon had gone through a lot of changes over the past few years. The Oracle of Omaha himself, Warren Buffett, had come in earlier to save the day and keep them afloat, but that did not stop the scandal from happening. The worst seemed to be behind the company, yet in spite of the optimistic outlook, J.R. wished he could shake his nagging doubt.

Chapter 7

The remainder of the year leading up to the wedding was a whirlwind for the young couple. Nena made another trip to Oxford to oversee last-minute details. She burst into tears when Becky walked out of the dressing room at the seamstress's shop, and stood in front of the mirror, a vision directly from the pages of a bridal magazine. The seamstress had converted the dress into a sweetheart neckline becoming to Becky. Nena bought her daughter a short fur jacket, to match the muff she would carry, in deference to Becky's winter versus her summer wedding, and Becky chose a pearl headband to match her great-grandmother's pearl necklace, for her something old. The seamstress shortened the veil to chapel length, bringing the dress from the sixties into the nineties.

"Mum, do those tears mean 'I like what you did to the dress,' or 'I hate what you did to the dress?'"

"I couldn't picture how the gown was going to look. It's absolutely gorgeous. You look lovely Becky, and the changes are modern and suit you to a T. And you were right about removing the crystals. Your father and grandparents are going to be over the moon."

"This is becoming very real, and a little scary," Becky confessed.

"Yes, my dear, this is one of the biggest steps you'll make in life. You are certain he's the one?" The minute the words came out of her mouth, Nena cringed, but she could not take them back.

"What would make you say that? Of course he's the one. The one and only."

Before Becky could comment further, as if on cue, the seamstress arrived to make the final adjustments, saving Nena from having to explain herself. She did not want to answer the question because her concerns were born out of what happened to her marriage. She had to stop projecting her issues onto Becky, and she promised herself there would be no more seeds of doubt regarding her daughter and her wedding day.

"Seems we have everything under control." Nena sighed with relief, as they left the shop, the two of them walking side-by-side. "I can go home knowing your day is going to be as special as you."

"Thanks Mum, I couldn't have done this without you."

"Well darling daughter, my single-minded career girl, the next time I see you, you'll be getting married. I never thought the day would come."

Out of the corner of her eye, Becky observed tears streaming down Nena's cheeks.

"You know what I think the two of us need Mum?"

"I'm reading your mind. Tea at the Ritz."

A mirror of many cities and towns across England, Oxford in December was no exception to the spirit of Christmas. Lights were festooned in abundance on Queen and Cornmarket Streets, and this year the entertainer Bonnie Langford turned on the lights in the city center. There was a carol service in Gloucester Green featuring one hundred young musicians and singers, which was broadcast on the local radio station. Christmas trees and nativity scenes were scattered throughout the entire city. Oxford took on a magical quality.

The week of the wedding had finally arrived. Guests from the States began to congregate in Oxford. Blocks of rooms were booked at the Randolph Hotel. A week of festivities had been planned. Trips into London for shopping and the theatre, a private tour of the university and Ashmolean Museum led by a student of Becky's, and a visit to Blenheim Palace, Winston Churchill's birthplace, were arranged. There was something for everyone.

On the night of the rehearsal dinner, spirits were high. The dinner was held in the Worcester Room of the hotel. The traditional yule log blazed in the grand fireplace, and a dazzling decorated Christmas tree occupied the large bay window. A mahogany dining table filled the center of the room, set for the occasion with crystal, china, and silverware. The space was traditional but not stuffy. A champagne toast preceded dinner. Throughout the evening meal, wine and conversation flowed. Later the party congregated at Inspector Morse's Bar for a final drink before morning arrived.

**

Christ's Church might have the reputation of being the smallest cathedral in England, but the sixty-foot-long nave seemed daunting for a walk down the aisle. The more intimate Lady Chapel suited them both for the ceremony, rather than the main sanctuary.

Arriving at the church for the four o'clock ceremony, Becky felt the butterflies everyone warned her about. Her unsteady legs were confirmation enough that choosing Lady Chapel had been the right decision. Holding onto her father's arm for dear life, Becky began what seemed the longest walk of her life.

J.R. was standing at the alter looking more handsome than she had ever seen him. He had chosen his father as his best man. Not just because they shared a close relationship, but he did not want to offend any of the many friends he had made over the years. Becky followed suit by not offending any one of her friends, choosing her cousin Rachael, Uncle Josh's daughter, to be her maid of honor. The local rabbi was invited to participate in the ceremony. Becky wanted to honor her Jewish heritage with this gesture as well as honor her grandfather and Uncle Josh.

The women of the church had outdone themselves with their floral decorations. Becky requested a green and silver theme, using ivy and white orchids to match her bouquet. They festooned the alter with an abundance of ivy, white irises, and orchards, and fashioned green satin tulle with silver lace ribbon into large showy bows on the backs of the chairs.

The angelic voices of the boys' choir sang the Twenty-Third Psalm and Wesley's "Love Divine" as guests filed into the chapel. A trumpet heralded the arrival of the wedding party. Rachael led the processional in a dusty gray tea-length taffeta dress. A bouquet of white freesia and orchids entwined with ivy tied with silver ribbon finished her look. As the music wafted through the cathedral, winding its way around the mighty columns of the nave into the chapel, a radiant Becky floated toward J.R. Nena watched as her daughter walked past, remembering her wedding day to Ben, hoping better for her daughter. Peter and Ruth watched Becky, remembering their daughter on her wedding day to Ben. They also hoped better for their granddaughter.

Ben lifted Becky's veil and turned to walk away, pausing to give his daughter, his little girl, a gentle kiss on the forehead.

Standing in front of the dean, J.R. and Becky became man and wife. The rabbi recited the seven Blessings in both Hebrew and English. When they went to sign the register, the organ played Pachelbel's "Canon in D" and Bach's "Jesu, Joy of Man's Desiring," and to the delight of the attendees, a bagpiper played Handel's "Hornpipe" as the wedding party left the cathedral. Bystanders on the street cheered, while the piper played until the last guests had left the church and boarded the buses to Le Manoir.

**

Decorated for the holidays, the hotel was fairytale-esque. Hors d'oeuvres consisting of tempting trays of caviar on tiny Russian pancakes called blini, thin slices of filet mignon atop flaky pastry rounds, mini crab cakes, and endive boats with smoked trout, were passed amongst the guests. A table laden with fresh oysters, bowls of chilled shrimp and Maine lobster completed the cocktail hour.

Dinner was announced. In the dining room, candles dotted the tables, complementing the freesia and iris floral arrangements, set upon silver gray cloths. Once the guests were seated, a first course of delicate salmon mouse on golden toast points accompanied a curried butternut squash soup with a squiggle of sour cream sprinkled with toasted squash seeds and crisped, smoked bacon. The entrée of roasted goose breast with spiced figs in a red wine reduction, wild rice, and pureed cauliflower piped to resemble an iris brought oohs and ahhs as plates were set on the table. A cheese tray followed a colorful winter salad of apple, cranberry, and pear on a bed of baby bib lettuce. A selection of fine wines complimented each course. The meal ended with petites fours, hand-dipped chocolates, and after-dinner drinks. The showstopper of the feast was the three-tiered wedding cake crowned with a pyramid for the newlyweds to freeze for their first anniversary.

The last toasts made, the guests climbed into the buses for the ride back to the Randolph where Becky and J.R. would meet them in the morning for a going-away brunch. Tonight belonged to the newlyweds. An antique four-poster bed awaited them in their suite.

"Alone at last my love," J.R. said when he finally whisked his bride away for the night. He was already undressing Becky with his eyes.

"As many times as we've made love, this seems like the first."

"It is our first time as husband and wife. Come here wife."

They made love with newlywed passion. The intensity of these feelings and emotions exploded into a dizzying thirst of sexual fervor that lasted until the moon began to sink and the sun began to rise.

**

There was a clink of glasses as more toasts were made the next morning. Guests were commenting that this had been one of the best weddings they had ever attended. Then someone spoke up above the din of voices.

"Okay, where's the honeymoon going to be?"

"What do you say? Should we tell them where we're going?" J.R. whispered to his wife.

"I think we should. On the count of three. One — two — three."

"Ogunquit," they said in unison.

"Of all the places in the world you could have gone!" Jay was elated by their choice. "Well, you know where the key is."

"Thanks, Dad."

**

Shortly, suitcases began to fill the lobby as the guests and family members prepared to leave.

"The week couldn't have been more perfect," Nena commented as the festivities came to a close. "Is there any chance we'll see you over the holidays since you'll be in Maine?"

"We were thinking it would be special if everyone could join us for Christmas in Ogunquit," J.R. told her, then added, "on *one* condition — you'll have to take rooms at the Cliff House. We're not sharing the house with anyone; *it is* our honeymoon, but we'll share the kitchen for the day."

"We'll see you on the twenty-fifth," Becky said as their family — except for her father and great uncle, who were remaining in England — boarded the shuttle to the airport.

**

Renting a car, Ben and Buddy were driving to Beeston, where Jack, Ben's father and Buddy's brother, had spent his service during World War II, and where he died. Both men felt this might be their last opportunity to visit the place where Jack gave his life for his country. On the drive through the Norfolk countryside, heading to the site where Wendling Air Base was once located, the two men talked about their trip across the pond in 1960 with Jackie and Helen, to bring Jack's body home to rest in his own country. They reminisced about the pilots they met that day from the 392nd Bombardment Group, who regaled them with stories of Jack, his antics and his bravery. This was a visit full of memories. Ben and Buddy wanted to remember this spot where a father and brother left them far too soon. They stayed until dusk before returning to London and their trip home.

**

Becky and J.R. were staying at her apartment before leaving for Maine the following day. He scooped his bride in his arms and carried her over the threshold.

Lying in bed after making love, J.R. brought up the subject of where they would live now that they were married. "I think we should consider living together."

"Gee, it would cut down on expenses, but do we have to decide right this minute?"

"Someone in this bed is going to commute. Should we flip a coin?" he suggested.

No coin was flipped and no decision was made this night, where they were to live became the furthest thing from their minds.

Ogunquit in the winter is quiet. Gone are the tourists of summer and fall, and the traffic congestion along Route 1. This is a season of reflection. No longer can myriad voices be heard along the Marginal Way; only the sound of the ocean fills the air as it roars into the rocks along the shore. They walked amid the calm to Harbor Candy Shop for her favorites, the coconut dainties, and to Perkins Cove, devoid of the endless cars circling to find a parking space to buy lobster fresh from the sea. Unlike in summer, no reservations were required at the handful of restaurants that remained open in winter, but most nights they preferred to shop at the Village Food Market and dine in. The mild December weather allowed for long walks on the beach that rivaled any on the French Riviera or the coast of Florida. It truly was a beautiful place by the sea, as the Abenaki Indians had named it, and Becky and J.R. congratulated themselves for picking the perfect spot to begin their life together.

**

"How are the newlyweds?" Ben called out as he entered the house.

The families had arrived. Nena brought a rib roast, the new traditional holiday meal, which was immediately put in the oven. They had given up Ruth's mother's Christmas goose in favor of their version of an English Christmas dinner, which Nena and Becky had adopted from years of living in the UK. Ruth brought the vegetables; Gabby, Josh's wife made the pies; while Rachael and Danny contributed the colorful English Cracker party favors. Once the crackers were popped and the contents of the tube revealed, the paper crowns were donned and Christmas dinner would began. Ben and Buddy brought the wine, and Jay had Zabar's overnight a huge gift box filled with an assortment of foods, a New York food lover's dream — smoked salmon, cream cheese, bagels, whitefish, dried fruit, a variety of sausages, sour rye and pumpernickel breads, preserves, an assortment of rugelach, and black and white cookies.

"I see Jay outdid himself," Nena commented, peeking into the box. "Are we invited for breakfast tomorrow, J.R.?"

"I don't think Becky and I can do all this food justice. You can come back in the morning, but not too early," J.R. warned with a sly smile.

They sat down to dinner around three, with Peter and Jay offering prayers of thanksgiving. After dessert, and with the dishes put away, Becky and J.R. stood at the door and waved as the cars headed down the drive to Bald Head Cliff and the Cliff House for the night. It was a different, but wonderful Christmas day.

Sitting by a roaring fire drinking wine, the young couple toasted to their first holiday success. "Not bad for mixing two families on a holiday. Seems we avoided the horror stories you hear," J.R. said.

"I take this as a good sign, don't you?"

"Going to make our lives a whole lot easier," he mumbled, holding Becky close. As flames flickered from the hearth, their silhouettes danced on the ceiling, and the newlyweds savored the remains of the day.

**

The following morning, they awoke to the chatter of voices outside. "Are you decent; is brunch ready?" someone asked.

Becky left J.R. in the shower as she ran to the door. "Ready or not we're here!" Danny called, with a big grin on his face.

"Well, we're almost ready; come on in." Becky motioned to the crowd standing on the porch.

Coffee brewed, eggs scrambled, the table laid with Zabar's delicacies, Ben opened the champagne, made mimosas, and brunch was served. Conversation filled the room until Josh pointed out the time, not wanting to travel home in the dark. Ben and Buddy would drive Jay to the train in Stamford. As it turned out, it was late when they arrived in Connecticut, and Ben invited Jay to spend the night. The three men were becoming good friends. This new relationship brought a sense of relief to Becky knowing that her father was moving out of the past and beginning to form friendships and a new social circle.

J.R. and Becky spent another week in Ogunquit before leaving for England. They wanted to spend New Year's Eve together in this place of tranquility, surrounded by the crashing waves, rushing tidal waters, seagulls cawing overhead, and sitting under the stars on the Marginal Way in the serenity of nature's beauty, as they celebrated the beginning of their new journey together.

**

Returning to England, Becky and J.R. were confronted with the question they left behind: Where were they going to live now that they were married? The distance between Oxford and London was about sixty miles by car, nearly an hour and a half drive, and give or take an hour by train. Either way, someone was going to commute.

"Should we flip a coin?" he asked.

"That again? How is a coin flip going to solve our dilemma?"

There were upsides and downsides to both their schedules of where to live, but in the end they opted for Becky's apartment. Although the quarters were small, they did not need the space of J.R.'s flat. They could save money, and in a year's time, they would reassess the situation.

PART II

1995–1999

Chapter 8

Living in Oxford turned out to be the right decision. "Is it time again to flip a coin?" he asked Becky one evening. It was over a year since their wedding, and the lease on the flat would be coming up for renewal.

"No coin flipping needed. Sit down, there's something I want to discuss with you." J.R. could not read his wife.

"Do we need wine for this discussion?"

"Yes, wine would be lovely," she told him.

Now J.R. was curious as he poured the wine, handing her a glass. "Okay, what's going on; you aren't pregnant are you?"

They had never had a serious talk about having children. Neither was in a rush. From time to time, they talked about raising a family, but only in the context of what it was like to grow up without siblings. They enjoyed the freedom they had, their careers, and the fact they had no other obligations. During their first year of marriage, they wined and dined with their friends; skied in the French Alps with the Hobarts, Logans, and Marc; spent a week on the Amalfi Coast; and jetted off to Morocco to celebrate their first anniversary, taking along their frozen wedding cake topper. Having babies was not on the agenda, at least not at this time in their marriage.

"No," Becky said somewhat dismissive. "It's a job offer I really can't refuse.

"Well, this calls for another glass of wine. Continue."

"You remember the night we met at the museum dinner?"

"How could I forget?!"

"Since then I've been in regular contact with the committee members, one in particular, and I've been offered a position on staff as they move forward with the Nebamun fragments. I nearly fainted when he offered me a job, but I remained cool — well as cool as I could. I told him I was flattered, but I needed a few days to digest the offer and could do nothing until the term at Oxford ends. Honey, the timing of this offer couldn't be more perfect. The lease is up here soon, we could find a place in London, and you would no longer have to commute when you are around." She was chiding him, but it was not lost on either of them how demanding his job was. "This solves the issue of where we live without flipping a coin. No more staying in town; you can come home and sleep in your own bed…right next to me."

J.R. could feel her excitement. "One question."

"One?"

"Yes, is this a career change you really want to make? Have you weighed the pros and cons?"

"I really have J.R., I really have. My first love is working in a museum. I loved what I did in Boston. I've felt very privileged to be involved in the archaeology department here at Oxford, and teaching, but I'm hands-on. This position is presenting an opportunity I didn't think possible, and the project is so me."

"Okay then, let's celebrate."

He called the Manoir, made a reservation and within no time, they had showered, dressed, and were out the door.

They dined on another one of Chef Blanc's fabulous meals. J.R. toasted his wife. "To you, and your new position."

"I can't believe my good fortune. I have to be the luckiest girl in the world. And to share this with you J.R. is more than I could ever have dreamt."

"We make our own good fortune," he replied. "Of course with a little luck along the way, but most of the time our destiny lies within our own hands."

"Do you really believe that?" she asked him.

"I seriously do."

**

They found an apartment in Eaton Square, not far from J.R.'s first London residence. The owners were on assignment in Washington D.C. with the British Embassy. It was not as large and grand as his former space, but this location was the perfect place for them. A few steps from their address was 54 Eaton Square, flat D, where Vivien Leigh and Laurence Olivier once lived, and she continued to live there after her divorce from Olivier, until she died in 1967. Becky loved pointing this out whenever anyone came to visit, since *Gone with the Wind* was one of her favorite movies.

**

The move to the city changed J.R. and Becky's lifestyle. No longer did they have to juggle commuting and travel schedules. Their lives became more predictable. There were events at the museum, work-related evenings they could both attend, nights out with friends, and their favorite: entertaining at home, and another year flew by.

Their annual New Year's Eve party had become a must attend affair. Becky planned for weeks, and hired a caterer. Enjoying this night was too important to be in the kitchen — no matter how much people enjoyed her cooking.

"Where did 1996 go?" Becky asked J.R. She was dressing when he walked into the room. Leaning against the bed admiring this woman he loved beyond words, J.R. reflected on their two years of marriage. She teased him that they were the best two years of his life. He could not argue. Before answering the doorbell, he told her he had made his wish for the New Year. "You are incorrigible," she told him, "and I bet I can guess what you're wishing." He smiled and left the room.

The evening was another huge success. Toasts were made at midnight; 1997 began on the highest of hopes. Once the last guest left, J.R.'s New Year's wish came true.

1997 was a year of upheaval and change and Salomon Brothers was no exception. For some time, there had been talk in the halls about a buyout, or a takeover, but it was the usual water-cooler talk fueled by baseless innuendo in London and New York. Since 1991, when the firm almost collapsed around the swirl of false bids in treasury actions, to 1994, when the company lost nearly a billion dollars before taxes, rumors were easy to come by.

In 1992, Deryck Maughan had been brought back to the States to be the company's savior. Maughan had been working in the Tokyo office, where he took the operation to a major profit source. He then became the chairman and chief executive of Salomon Brothers, and the right-hand man of Warren Buffett. Salomon seemed to be coming back since then. Presently, there was nothing to back up the gossip of a buyout or takeover. But the company was known to have a cutthroat culture, and there seemed to be the smell of disarray, once again, within the organization.

Where there is smoke, generally there is fire, and in the fall of 1997 the whiff of smoke turned into a blaze when the announcement was made that Travelers Group would acquire Salomon for nine billion dollars and would be known as Salomon Smith Barney. Along with the announcement, it was noted that as many as two thousand employees could be laid off. This made the water cooler talk very real.

**

"Did you have any idea?" Drinking her morning coffee, Becky read aloud the article in *The Financial Times*.

"No! You know that office, a rumor a minute, but this announcement blindsided us. Beck, would you mind if I called Marc to come over for dinner? I need to bounce this off someone I can trust."

"Tell him if he's willing to bring the wine he can get a good home-cooked meal."

When J.R. called Marc, he quickly accepted the invitation. Marc loved being asked for dinner. He tired of ordering in or cooking just for himself. He had grown close to Becky, taking her out for dinner when J.R. was not in town, and in return she would reciprocate by taking him to museum events, being his private guide and expanding his horizons.

The day had been raw and rainy. Becky thought comfort food was in order for dinner and served a hearty beef stew with homemade cornbread. Over glasses of wine in the living room, the conversation began in earnest.

"That's how you found out? *The Financial Times!* No advanced notice, no nothing?" Marc asked J.R.

"That's it! Isn't it funny? The entire office suspected something wasn't right, yet we were clueless. My question for you, brother, is do I sit tight, wait for the other shoe to drop, or start looking for something else now?"

Being the ever-analytical Marc, he responded, "Well let's look at this from all angles. You know they're going to let people go, but it seems to me the odds are in your favor of being kept on. They might move you to a different location, but that was a wise move on your part when you moved into the banking sector. If I were you, I would hang in there. This way you can quietly begin to look around, put out feelers, test the waters, and if that time comes, you'd be ready. Besides if they do let you go, you know you'll get a sweet severance."

Marc's advice was heeded. In the best-case scenario he would be kept on or be relocated. Hopefully being terminated was not in his future, but if it was, he had the time to prepare.

J.R. went to bed that night feeling more confident than he had been since hearing the announcement.

When the axe fell, J.R.'s position was spared, although uncertainty remained as to where he would be working. The museum proved to be the right career move for Becky, and they were enjoying life in London. Another new year — 1998 — was off to a good start.

**

The calm of the New Year did not last. In April a major shock wave hit with another announcement that Citicorp acquired the newly formed company between Salomon Brothers and Travelers Group. Things were changing at such a rapid pace it was difficult to keep up.

The fall of 1998, J.R. was called into his boss's office.

His boss, an older man who had been through other acquisitions – and had become hardened to the realities of the corporate world – wore a poker face. He motioned to J.R. saying, "Sit down J.R.; we need to talk." J.R. respected his boss more than liked him. A stern but fair man, a stiff upper lip sort, J.R. could never quite read him. He was hoping this was not an "it's been a pleasure having you work for us" conversation, but those were the first words he heard.

"It's been a pleasure having you work with us here is London," his boss said.

"Oh no," J.R. thought. "Here it comes. I didn't dodge the bullet this time!"

"We're beginning to get a handle on the new direction of the company; we think the best place for you would be in New York. How does that sound to you?" J.R.'s boss asked.

First, he could hardly believe his ears, and secondly, he realized that this was the first time his boss had ever asked him his opinion.

"If that's where I'm best suited within the new structure, I'm fine with that." What else could J.R. say? He knew an alternative to saying anything else regarding the merged companies would be career suicide. But what he wanted to say was: "Shit; I'm not ready to go back. My wife has a great job, we have fantastic friends, and I love my life here." Should he stomp his feet, have a temper tantrum? The only words that came forth were:

"When will the relocation take place?"

"The merger will be complete in October. We have a lot of details to work out, and there will be a transition period. We plan on having you settled in New York around this time next year."

J.R. noticed his boss never used the word I. It was always the proverbial royal *we*, as if passing along orders from some mysterious puppet master, and his boss had played no role or part in any of this decision. J.R. left the office and closed the door behind him.

Waiting for the elevator, he thought, "Who knows, maybe he is the messenger; maybe he's as controlled by those above him, as I am by him." On the way home, he stopped to buy flowers for Becky, hoping to ease the shock when he broke the news.

**

When Becky opened the door, she immediately noticed the bouquet of irises on the table in the living room (or lounge as the British called it). She had a strong suspicion something was not right.

"Uh-oh, what's going on?"

"Does something have to be going on for me to buy your favorite flowers?" J.R. answered.

"No, but you have to admit in the middle of the week, your gesture is a little bit unusual."

When he offered to take her out to dinner, she became suspicious.

"We don't keep secrets or play games, and I think that's what's going on here, but I'll play along until dinner is over," she said, accepting his invitation.

Their relationship was an open book. They had not even had their first real quarrel, a minor disagreement now and then, but not that so-called donnybrook. She would let the night unfold.

They dined at their favorite London pub, the over two hundred year old Churchill Arms in Notting Hill. Winston Churchill's grandparents were regulars in the 1800s, and after World War II, the pub changed its' name in his honor. Outside, the corner building was adorned with colorful hanging flower baskets from the street level to the roof, and inside the place radiated with the charm of aged wood paneling, heavy doors, leaded windows, and, of course, the fantastic collection of Churchill memorabilia. Recently, the restaurant had begun serving Thai food, which was receiving rave reviews. They ordered two noodle and two stir-fry dishes. Drinking their beer while waiting to be served, the manager Gerry O'Brien stopped by to greet them.

"Fancy seeing the two of you here in the middle of the week. What brings you by?" he asked.

"I'm not sure Gerry," Becky answered. "J.R.'s keeping a secret, but after another pint or two, I'll pry it out of him."

Gerry winked at her. "I bet you will girl; I bet you will!"

"Okay, are you ready to spill the beans, yet?" Becky asked J.R. as the meal was being served.

"All right, I wanted to come to our favorite pub tonight because I don't know how many more times we'll be coming here." J.R. had not been this nervous since he proposed.

Becky put down her folk. "Why, what's going on?"

J.R. went on to tell her about the afternoon meeting with his boss, and the decision that was made about his career with Salomon.

"You know if you aren't ready to go back, because I'm not certain if I am, I can find something else here. I know I can."

"Before you go and make a hasty decision, let me tell you something I haven't shared with you for good reason."

"I'd ask if you're pregnant, but I did that the last time."

"And I'd answer the same, no. Disappointed?"

"No, the timing isn't right, but maybe it's never right."

"You know I have been collaborating with the Egyptology department at the Met in New York regarding the Nebamun fragments, and some other finds. A few weeks ago the head of the department was here and took me to lunch. During lunch there was a door opener for a position in New York."

"You never said anything about it."

"Timing is everything. I told him it would be a dream of mine to work at the Met. He understood your work is here, but I said if anything ever changed, he would be the first person I'd call. I'm confident if I called him and explained the situation, they'd hold the position or hopefully find me another spot."

J.R. sat stunned. He never could have imagined this turn of events. "You wouldn't be unhappy if we went back?"

"Sure part of me would. Gee honey, this is where we met, where our life together began. My memories of us are here. However, I've learned nothing in life stays the same forever. Things change, and we have to change with them or we get left behind. The good news is we're not moving right away, and the rest of the good news is we're going home to a new adventure. What do you say — is it time to write another chapter in our story?"

"How the hell did I ever get so lucky to find you?" J.R. sat looking at his wife across the table in amazement.

They left the Churchill hand-in-hand, full of expectation.

**

For the time being, they were going to keep this information to themselves. The move was almost a year away. Becky contacted the Met to let the museum know she would be available for the position, if they could hold it for her, and told her department head at the museum to prepare for a new hire. They waited until spring, when J.R.'s transfer was confirmed by headquarters, before they announced to family and friends they were leaving for the States.

When the announcement was made, there were tears mingled with congratulations on the London side of the Atlantic, while joy and celebration reigned among their stateside family and friends. At last, Becky and J.R. were coming home.

A whirlwind of activities filled 1999. The farewell parties seemed endless. With the Hobarts, Logans, and, of course, Marc, they indulged in a two-week wine tour through France and spent a week by themselves in Tuscany. Becky and J.R. dealt with a rollercoaster of emotions as the time to leave England drew closer, but they knew they had made the right decision.

**

Lying in bed at the Manoir, Becky wondered if they would return next year to celebrate their sixth anniversary.

"I hope going home doesn't change the tradition we've started," she told J.R.

"I'd like to say yes…" His words hung in the air. "We're here now; let's not waste another second thinking about the future and what we can't control. Let's celebrate what we have right now."

They filled the night making love with wild abandon. They had been married for five years and their insatiable thirst for each other had not abated. They were in total sync, as if destiny and fate had brought them together for these moments to express the deep love they shared.

**

Chef Blanc stopped by their table while they were having breakfast the next morning.

"I heard from the staff you're leaving for the States and wanted to make sure I wished you well, but remember: don't forget us."

"How could we ever," Becky said. "You and this wonderful place have played such an important part in our lives. I hope we can continue to come back."

"You will," he assured them. "We'll be seeing you again." He gave them his personal contact information, telling them to stay in touch.

On the ride back to London, for the first time, the reality hit them both. They were leaving a place they had grown to love, a home away from home they would dearly miss.

Chapter 9

New York, New York! The plane touched down at JFK and taxied to the gate.

"Hard to believe a few days ago we were celebrating our fifth anniversary at the Manoir. Are you ready Mrs. Stark?"

"As I'll ever be Mr. Stark."

In late spring, they had made a trip to New York to house hunt. They bought a condominium on the Upper East Side on Park Avenue between Eighty-First and Eighty-Second Streets. A widowed friend of J.R.'s parents had decided to sell to be near her children. She had owned the apartment for nearly forty years. It was the smallest unit in the prewar building, and J.R. and Becky purchased it before it went on the market. The space needed work but the location was a dream — a few blocks walk for Becky to the museum and three subway lines nearby for J.R. He liked the idea of having a commute to the World Trade Center, giving him a chance to prepare for the day, and unwind at the end of the day.

For their homecoming, Jay had the apartment renovated to suit a young couple. Through his vast connections, Jay replaced old fixtures and appliances, had the electrical updated, and the bathrooms refitted, except for the claw foot tub in the master bath that Becky insisted remain. The floors were refinished to their original condition, and the cabbage patch wallpaper that had Becky in hysterics when she first saw it was taken down. Jay enlisted Nena's help with the decorating. With a good idea of their taste, she purchased the basic furniture to start a home. The high ceiling apartment had two bedrooms, a study, a nice-sized living room, a formal dining space, a good-sized kitchen, and two and a half baths — a nearly two thousand square-foot living space, a grand size for a place in New York. Nena bought a bed for the guest room for them to use until they furnished the master, a room Nena considered a couple's sanctuary. She did not feel comfortable decorating their private space. The few belongings they had in England had already arrived. Nena unpacked the boxes and put the items away. One of the boxes contained the beautiful Lalique vase etched with three iris blooms. Nena carefully placed the vase on the fireplace mantle.

**

When they opened the door to the condo, Jay and Nena greeted their children with warm welcome home embraces.

Stepping into the apartment, Becky was dumb struck. "Oh my goodness, I can't believe this! We were talking in the cab that we would probably be sleeping on the floor for a while."

"We thought that might be the case. We hoped you weren't going to mind — this is your first place — but we left you the master bedroom to do yourself. However, you need to thank Jay." Nena pointed in his direction. "It was his idea; I'm just his partner in crime."

"I can get used to this sort of crime." J.R. turned and hugged Nena.

"Come, let's take the tour." Jay explained the structural changes, and what it took to bring the apartment to code in the approaching millennium. "It'll be a long time before you'll have to have any work done, and it's quality."

"Dad, I wouldn't expect anything less from you. And Nena, you outdid yourself; this is so us."

Becky concurred. "Both of you got it just right."

In the elevator Jay and Nena congratulated themselves on a job well done. Jay asked Nena to join him for dinner.

"I'd love to Jay; drinks are on me!"

**

"This is surreal," Becky said as she kicked off her shoes, plunking herself down on the new sofa. "I can't believe they did this for us. Oh look honey, the vase has found the perfect home on the mantle. Whenever I look at it, it reminds me of the night you gave it to me. It's a night I'll never forget."

"Speaking of nights, what shall we do tonight?"

"We could grocery shop, order in, or go out for dinner." Becky went to the refrigerator. "Can you believe this? They even stocked the fridge! Boy, we're going to owe them big time. Let's take a walk, check out our neighborhood, find a restaurant, and have a nice leisurely dinner in our new town."

"Before we do that, let's christen our new home. I want to see if you feel the same in my arms here as you did across the pond, the night I gave you the vase." Lucky for J.R., she did.

**

At the last minute, Nena decided to stay in the city another night. Jay offered his place again, but there was someone else on her mind.

Leaving Nena in the lobby of the Waldorf Hotel, Jay reminded her he would see her in Maine for Christmas in a few days. Both Becky and J.R. did not have to begin their jobs until the New Year, giving them a few weeks to settle in. Becky suggested the two families celebrate Christmas and ring in the new millennium in Ogunquit.

~~~~~~~~~~~~

Settled in her hotel room, Nena made a call.

"Hi, I'm staying the night in town. Can we meet in the lobby by the clock?" she suggested.

He would have met her anywhere. He answered, "By the clock."

**

It had been six years since Nena and Sam met after Trudi's funeral. They had stayed in touch on a regular basis since his first trip to Boston. They often talked for hours on the phone and had dinner whenever he was in Boston and on occasions when Nena was in New York. The relationship had remained as good friends. Sam knew he had to move slowly, understanding Nena's divorce had devastated her, and her trust in men, and Sam was a patient man. He had waited seventeen years from the time she told him she wanted to save her marriage, to when he met her again in 1993. But the last few times they were together, he sensed a change in her.

**

Sitting in the lobby of the Waldorf, admiring the Art Deco design, in sight of the famous bronze clock, Nena watched Sam as he walked up the steps. Her heart skipped a beat when she noticed him. He was beginning to arouse feelings in her she had not acknowledged or felt in years.

Entering the Bull and Bear, a landmark bar within a landmark hotel, they took seats at the legendary mahogany bar. Many a mover and shaker of Wall Street actually did business or traded tales at this bar. It was a man's room, but Nena felt comfortable in the warm, clubby atmosphere. Drinks ordered, they found a table in the corner of the room.

"I would have called you earlier, but the past few days with Jay were non-stop. Lord that man doesn't seem to come up for air. I've never known anyone with that level of energy. Even Ben in his day was no match."

Nena could finally mention Ben in conversation without becoming emotionally unhinged.

"I figured you were busy. Did Becky and J.R. find the apartment to their liking?" Sam asked.

"They loved it. Let me tell you, we were a little concerned before they arrived. This is their first real home. I don't know if I would have cared for my parents fixing up and decorating the first home Ben and I owned. But they were genuinely ecstatic. We left the master bedroom for them to do; that room is too personal. We did the essentials. They need to buy a few things to put their stamp on the place…make it theirs."

"I'd say that was very considerate of the two of you."

"Secretly Jay and I enjoyed doing it as much as the kids enjoyed having us do it."

Sam was studying Nena as she talked and finally asked, "How long will you be in town?"

"Why do you ask?"

"I was hoping you didn't have to leave tomorrow."

A rush came over Nena. She could feel herself stepping into unknown territory. Until this moment she had kept a tight rein on her emotions, although lately when she saw Sam, she began to feel those reins slip. Her first instinct was to say she had to go home the next morning, but something stopped her, and she said she could stay.

"Let's finish our drinks and take a walk to Rockefeller Center. When was the last time you went ice skating?" Sam asked.

"At this hour?"

"Why not?"

"You're right; why not?"

When they reached Rockefeller Center, they were greeted by rows of brightly lit wire-sculptured angles holding brass trumpets. The sparkling white angels decorated the Channel Gardens along the promenade. Under the gilded bronze statue of Prometheus stood the spectacular festooned Christmas tree covered with thousands of colored lights, and below this incredible scene skaters spun and twirled across The Rink.

Neither had been on skates in years. Holding hands, they gingerly took to the ice as skaters whizzed by. A dozen spins around the rink left them rather pleased with the fact they had not fallen.

"I'm rather proud of us," he said, bending down to help her with her skates. As he stood up, his face met hers. He could not resist kissing her. Nena did not resist.

Crossing Fifth Avenue Nena suggested, "Let's stop and look at the decoration in Saks' windows."

Admiring the windows, Sam put his arm around her waist, drawing her to his side. She did not pull away. Instead she nuzzled close, putting her head on his shoulder.

When they reached the hotel, Nena unexpectedly found herself asking, "Would you like to come in for a drink?"

"What would you say if I suggested we go to your room for a nightcap?"

Words tumbled forth before Nena could filter them, and she agreed it would be a lovely way to end the evening.

As they rode the elevator to the forty-second floor of the tower, what had been easy-going conversation during the evening turned socially uncomfortable. When the elevator door opened, Nena greeted the guard on duty. There was a guard's presence on the forty-second floor since the Waldorf became home to the U.N. ambassador in 1946. He smiled at them as they exited the elevator. The guard's acknowledgement caused Nena to question her decision to end the evening in her room. Sam had been a safe fantasy. She found him attractive on many different levels, but had kept him at arm's length. Nena was not a schoolgirl, and knew what he wanted. Entering room 42H3 the question was if she did too.

Sam answered the knock on the door. The waiter rolled in a cart covered with a white cloth, a vase with a single yellow rose, a bottle of wine, two glasses, and a plate with cookies and chocolate-covered strawberries, which he placed on a coffee table by a loveseat in the corner of the room. The waiter opened the bottle and poured the wine; Sam tipped the man, thanked him, and closed the door.

"You thought of more than a nightcap," she said.

Sam handed Nena a glass of wine. "You were such a great skating partner; I thought you deserved a special end to the night."

"Thank you. I hope you had a good time, too." Nena searched for words, as she took a sip of wine and hoped her nervousness was not showing. Never having been in this situation before, she did not know what to do or say next. Again, Nena questioned if she was ready for more than what they had.

She did not have to speculate for long when Sam dimmed the lights in the room. Sitting next to her, he kissed her neck. She was as soft as he fantasized. His touch sent shivers through her body. Without a word spoken, he placed their glasses on the table and led her to the bed. When he began to undress her, Nena could not remember when she felt this apprehensive and excited, at the same time. Climbing into the king-sized bed, the silky Egyptian cotton sheets felt cool against the heat of their skin. Lying next to each other, each wondered who would make the first move. Slowly he reached for her hand and brought it to his lips, gently kissing her fingers. They were on their backs as she turned her face toward his. He could sense her gaze. He raised himself on his elbow and looked intently at her. He pulled her close to him, his movements slow and deliberate. The lines of her body under the sheets aroused him; she moved her body closer to his. She could feel her heart begin to race. Every synapse in her body was on fire. The years of Sam not forcing their relationship, allowing her to come to him on her terms, were now past. Nena could not hold back. No longer did she fear only having one other lover. Sam was gentle, taking his time as they made love, leaving her fulfilled beyond what she could have imagined or expected.

Nena got out of bed, put on the luxurious robe the Waldorf supplied, and walked to the window. The room on the corner of the building faced northeast. Below was Lexington Avenue, full of twinkling red and white lights from the flowing traffic below. She could see the Queensboro Bridge (also known as the Fifty-Ninth Street Bridge) that spanned the East River from the borough of Queens to Manhattan. Against the night sky, the imposing lit cantilever truss bridge resembled a work of art. Nena thought about Simon and Garfunkel's "The 59th Street Bridge Song" (Feeling Groovy)," and at this very instant, this was exactly how she felt — groovy. As she marveled at the view from the window and reflected on what had just happened, Nena felt Sam wrap his arms around her waist.

"What a sight! No wonder you love to stay here," he said, looking at the bridge.

"I do love it here, Sam. This room has always been my haven when I come to the city; now I've made a new memory."

"I hope not just one memory." He stepped in front of her, but not to block the window, and her view. "Look out the window Nena; we have a chance to have all that is out there. There is nothing to stop us any longer."

His words were overwhelming her. Her head was spinning. Looking over Sam's shoulder into the New York City night, she could only think of the moment, feeling his breath on her neck and the awareness of his body beneath his robe.

With the Simon and Garfunkel song running through her head, they brought the rest of the wine back to bed and Sam spent the night.

The following morning, Sam invited Nena to join him in the shower. He washed her body tenderly — the awkward silence vanished. "Okay I have twenty-four more hours until I leave. What do you want to do today?" she asked.

"First, I need to go home and change. I didn't bring an overnight bag in case you didn't notice and I want you to see where I live. How about catching the Rockettes' Christmas Spectacular? We'll call this our Rockefeller Center rendezvous."

His ideas sounded marvelous to Nena.

**

The weather was cold, crisp, and clear, a great winter day for walking in the city. They walked to Sam's apartment on the Upper West Side. The one bedroom, one bath, with a large sunny kitchen / living /dining room combination, and walls lined with bookshelves filled with books lived up to Nena's expectations of a college professor's home. Nena browsed through his books while he changed and filled a small backpack with a change of clothes. It was understood he would spend tonight with her. They spent the remainder of the day wandering in and out of shops along Broadway, while grazing at vendor carts, on the way to Radio City.

**

"The Rockettes never disappoint," Nena told Sam, while they walked to the Waldorf where Sam dropped off his bag. From the hotel, they took the subway to the Canal Street stop. Chinatown, until recently, consisted of a few block area, but it was growing and beginning to encroach its way ever so slowly into popular Little Italy. The streets of Chinatown were crowded with shoppers speaking every language imaginable. Sights, sounds, and smells were otherworldly, transporting the visitor to another place.

The sign above the restaurant on Mott Street in Chinatown read Peking Duck House. Sam wanted to share one of his favorite Chinese restaurants in the city with Nena. He could not have been more delighted to find out this was one of her favorite places to dine, too.

Sitting at a table drinking oolong tea, surrounded by Chinese families speaking an array of Chinese dialects, they watched as the waiter masterfully carved the tawny brown duck. When he finished, they put the slices of duck onto delicate pancakes with rich hoisin sauce, along with strips of thinly sliced scallion and cucumber — a taste of heaven on a plate.

A walk to Little Italy followed dinner. At America's first espresso bar, Ferrara on Grand Street, each had their favorites: she tiramisu, a little Italian pick-me-up, and a mocha espresso, and he a chocolate-dipped, sweet ricotta-filled cannoli and a café latte.

The last stop was a trip to Lung Moon Bakery on Mulberry Street, a well-known Chinese bakery where Nena bought the family's favorite pastries to bring to Ogunquit for the holiday. Sitting on the subway, each eating a delectable sponge cake, they felt like teenagers on a first date.

Over a drink in the hotel's bar, Nena commented, "This has been such a lovely day, Sam; thank you."

"It's not over," he reminded her, as they left Peacock Alley and went to her room.

They made love with ease, as if they had been together for years. Any reservations she had over whether opening up to Sam was the right thing to do were gone. It was the right thing to do. He made her feel special. As for Sam, he was living his dream. A dream he had for years, ever since he met her in class that summer long ago.

At Penn Station the following morning, they lingered over a kiss before she boarded her train.

"I wish we were spending New Year's Eve together," he said. "I'm going to miss you."

"I'm going to miss you, too." She kissed him for the last time before walking toward the train. There was no plan as to when they would meet again. They both hoped it would be soon.

On an impulse, she turned and whistled in his direction.

"Remember that day on the platform at 125th Street? You reminded me what Bacall said, about just whistle if I ever needed you!" she shouted, referencing the classic movie *To Have and Have Not*.

"I remember!" Sam did not say more; her whistle had said it all.

~~~~~~~~~~

The phone was ringing as Nena entered her house. She set down her bag and picked up the receiver before the call went to voicemail. She could hear her daughter on the other end. "For heaven sakes Mum, where have you been? I've been calling and calling."

"Honestly Becky, I'm a grown woman," Nena bristled. "I stayed in the city an extra day. I didn't know I had to check in." She never mentioned Sam. In fact, no one in the family knew Sam existed, not even her mother.

"If we had known you were still in the city, you could have stayed with us or Jay and not at the Waldorf."

"I didn't know I was going to stay until after I had dinner with Jay — although she knew this was not quite true — and besides at your place where would I have slept, on the floor?"

Her mother's brusqueness bewildered Becky, but she let the subject drop, returning to the reason for her call: the plans for Maine. "J.R. is renting a van, and we'll pick you up tomorrow afternoon. I'll phone Grandpa and Grandma when we're leaving Dad's; then you'll have an idea when we'll arrive in Boston." Becky hung up the phone totally mystified by the conversation with her mother.

Nena could not have the conversation with Becky end fast enough. She was floating on air, and did not want to come back to earth. The last thing on her mind was going to Ogunquit tomorrow. She probably should shop, but the rib roast was ordered; plus she had the pastries from Lung Moon. Anything missing could be bought in Maine. This was not like her. Organization was Nena's middle name. She convinced herself everything would work out; no one would go hungry.

Before she did anything else, Nena called Sam. This conversation was the only conversation she wanted to have. "Hi, Sam, I'm back, safe and sound."

"I was going to call you in an hour to make certain. I'm missing you already."

"I miss you too. When I left, we never said when we would get together again."

"I'll be in Boston the middle of January for a meeting. I'll let you know the exact dates, but I was thinking of taking some extra time before classes begin. Would you consider taking a break and come away with me? Someplace quiet, off season."

"I'm pretty sure I can arrange a few days. Let me know the dates. Happy New Year Sam, and I can't wait to see you."

"Happy New Year, Nena." He wanted to tell her he loved her, but he would wait.

**

Becky burst in the door. "Ready or not Mum, here we come," she said. Nena hugged her daughter, wishing the curt conversation of yesterday had not happened. Within moments, eight people crammed into the van and left for Ogunquit.

"This is going to be interesting," Becky told everyone as they crossed the Massachusetts border into New Hampshire. "All of us staying under the same roof."

"There's plenty of space, and room to spare," Jay assured. "It'll be like old times when you were a boy, Robbie, the house full to the rafters with company — except this time it's family, and I couldn't be happier."

Since Trudi's death, except for Becky and J.R.'s honeymoon and Christmas with the family, the house was seldom used. Jay wondered if he should sell it, but he could not bring himself to have the talk with his son.

"Josh, Gabby, and the kids are going to be missed," Becky said. "I know they wanted to come; maybe next year."

Rachael, now married, had given birth to a little girl in November, and Gabby wanted to spend the holidays with her new granddaughter.

"And by the way J.R.," Peter interjected. "Danny wanted me to thank you again for making the introduction through Marc with American Express. He loves his job. He tells me you'll be working in the same building.

"Yes, I'll make a point of getting together for lunch, and we plan on having him over for dinner soon."

Chatter filled the van as they continued north. The talk turned to food. Did they bring enough? Would they have enough? Reaching Ogunquit, the women made a list of the other must-haves and set off to shop in town, while the men brought in wood, readied a fire, and set up the drinks before walking to the cove to buy lobsters and clams for dinner.

The entire world was consumed with Y2K, as the new millennium approached. The conversation at the dinner table this evening was no exception. Everyone wondered if the prediction of a Y2K computer system meltdown would be a real factor. Would both nondigital and data storage be affected by a four-digit year being abbreviated into a two-year digit?

Should the New Year be recognized as a leap year? A complex issue programmers and scientists around the world struggled with.

When the last clam and bits of lobster were eaten, Nena brought in dessert. She set a platter laden with her purchases from Lung Moon on the table: rice cakes, delectable sponge cakes with cream and apricot filling cut into triangle shapes wrapped in colorful paper, chocolate and yellow sponge cakes rolled and filled with cream and lemon-flavored fillings, custard egg tarts, almond cakes, and cookies.

"When did you find time to go to Chinatown, Mum?" Becky asked. "Uncle Josh will be sorry he isn't here."

Relieved Y2K dominated the topic of conversation as she poured coffee, Nena had no desire to share why she was in Chinatown or whom she was with.

**

Early Christmas morning the entire household took a walk along the Marginal Way. They were the only souls on the scenic pathway, drinking in the salt air, and the grandeur of the ocean as waves collided with the rocky shoreline hanging from the cliffs while gulls flew silently overhead. Giving thanks and being grateful in these glorious surroundings of nature was akin to any spiritual experience they could envision.

Returning to the house, the smell of the standing rib roasting in the oven greeted them.

"Don't fill up on too many snacks," Nena announced. "Dinner is at two."

The perfectly roasted beef was presented on a large antique stone platter, surrounded by baby Brussels sprouts sautéed in garlic, butter and white wine. On another tray Yorkshire pudding, puffy and light, accompanied a bowl of deep, rich gravy made from the roast's pan drippings. Rhone wine filled the glasses, and at two the families sat down for dinner.

Before they began to eat, snaps were heard from the English crackers that were placed above each plate. It was a custom that Nena brought forward from her childhood. Everyone enjoyed finding their prizes and putting on their paper crowns when the crackers popped open. Jay said grace, and only compliments to the chefs were heard.

Dessert was an elegant English trifle: layers of sherry-soaked sponge cake, custard and raspberries, topped with whipped cream and toasted almonds presented in a glass pedestal bowl. With dinner over, and the table cleared, the cribbage board moved front and center.

"Wait!" Becky pointed out there were only three girls and five boys. "If we're doing teams, we need a boy. Who wants to join the winning team?" For a moment there were no takers until Ben gave in. "Way to go Dad, you won't be sorry."

The room became full of boos and cheers as the two teams pegged their way around the board. In the end, the ladies and Ben won by one game.

After a light supper and Jay's usual box of treats from Zabar's, J.R. coaxed Becky into taking a walk to Perkins Cove.

They sat on the dock at the cove, dangling their feet over the side. Water slapped the hulls on the moored lobster boats. J.R. pulled Becky close. "I love our families, but it's nice to be alone," he told her.

Becky reminded him, "Better get used to it; we're going to be together for another week."

"No one here...want to sneak behind the shack and make wild, crazy love?"

"I'm game if you are."

Behind the shack with the moon casting shadows on the cove, they made love. The feeling of doing something forbidden brought a heightened sense to the act; they were enjoying what they were doing more than they should have. Walking back to the house, they felt like naughty kids and wondered if their faces would give them away.

**

An unfortunate incident broke up the holiday festivities when Ben received an urgent call; a mainline water pipe had broken and flooded his office in New Canaan. Ben needed to leave. Jay offered to stay in New Canaan and help Ben and Buddy with the cleanup; Ben quickly accepted.

Being together with family celebrating Christmas was wonderful; nevertheless, it was time to go home. Ben's misfortune offered a pretext for most of them to leave, except for J.R. and Becky who would stay through the new year, to close up the house

"Didn't think the week would end this way," Becky said, as they waved good-bye.

"Me either. I told the gods I wanted to be alone with you, and here we are. Sorry it happened this way. I hope the office isn't as bad as your father believes."

When the van drove out of sight, Becky asked J.R., "Did you notice anything different about my father?" Becky hoped J.R. would say no, but instead he too noticed Ben did not seem his usual self.

"I asked Daddy if he was okay."

"What did he say?"

"He mentioned being a little tired, but said work had been busier than usual. I suggested he and Buddy take a nice long vacation in the spring — get away and relax. But I don't know…I think there's more to it."

"Maybe you're right, Becky. Let's keep an eye on him…but now what should we do with this big house all to ourselves, my darling wife? The usual?" he asked facetiously.

"The usual, my darling husband," she responded, mimicking his tone.

~~~~~~~~~~~~~

When Ben opened the door to the office, the scene was enough to make a grown man cry, and his constant fatigue did not help. Recently he had a persistent unexplained feeling of exhaustion, and was grateful Buddy and Jay were there to keep him steady.

Assessing the damage, Jay went into action mode and made a few calls. His contacts in the construction business reached far and wide. Within a few hours, a team of men streamed into the office. Before the day ended, the water was completely drained from the office. A container arrived to house the business files and furniture, while large industrial-sized fans were installed to dry the space. The water lines and pipes were inspected and fixed the following day, assuring the office would be up and running before the end of the week.

Thanking the men, Ben turned to Jay, "What would I have done without you? You've been a life saver."

Jay could see what his help meant to Ben, but he could also see something was not quite right. When Buddy left the office, Jay took Ben aside and asked, "What else is going on with you? We have gotten to know each other pretty well over the years, and I consider you my friend, not just Becky's father. I'm not prying, but I sense there's something else going on with you. You know you can tell me anything."

Touched by Jay's genuine concern, Ben confided in him. "I don't know. I don't seem to have any energy, and no matter how well I sleep, I'm still tired."

"Have you seen a doctor?"

"No."

"Listen, why don't you let me make an appointment for you in the city with my doctor? He's the best. You can make an excuse to Buddy; tell him I want to discuss some business with you. This way you don't have to worry anyone, and if it's nothing, then it's nothing. If it's something, we'll take it from there."

"What the heck are you Jay, my guardian angel?" The two men embraced before resuming cleaning the office.

~~~~~~~~~~

Nena could not get inside her house fast enough before she picked up the phone and called Sam.

"Have you made any plans for New Year's Eve?"

"No! Where are you?"

"Home — Ben got an emergency call, his office flooded, and he had to come back early. I got a ride with him and the others. We of the older generation had our fill. Please don't get me wrong, it was a lovely Christmas and a very nice few days, but time to go home to the comfort of our own beds. Do you think there's any chance we can get together New Year's Eve?"

"I'm on the next train. Don't bother coming to the station. I'll come to you."

Sam caught the last train for Boston from Penn Station. As the train headed north he mused, "Four hours — four hours — and she'll be in my arms."

While Sam sat impatiently on the train heading to Boston, Nena put her belongings away, hurriedly cleaned the house, and walked to the North End to shop. In her favorite stores she bought everything she could think of to stock her cupboards.

**

His footsteps outside her door made her heart race. She opened the door to welcome him. Sam dropped his bag on the walkway and took her in his arms. After a long embrace and a lingering kiss, she whispered, "You know you're invited in."

Picking up his bag, he walked into her living room. "I see you added a new table."

"Aren't you observant?" Nena confessed she did not need more furniture, but most of the pieces she had were from her marriage with Ben, and she wanted her home to reflect her new life. "It's rather lovely, don't you think? A table for two."

Small talk about the Christmas holiday filled their conversation until Sam said, "I couldn't stop thinking about being with you on the entire trip here."

"Want to know what I did after we spoke? I went shopping and practically bought out the shops, in case we never left the house."

They barely made it into the bedroom, the intensity of their desires leaving them breathless, making love until they satisfied their cravings for one another.

Nena did not know how many lovers Sam had before her, but Ben was her only comparison. Lying in bed, in the wee hours of the morning, appropriate or not, she opened the subject.

"I'm rather new at this," she said mustering the courage to say something. "I've only made love with one other man besides you, Sam. I suppose you've had a number of women in your life." Totally out of her comfort zone there was no turning back.

"What guy who's been single his entire life ever keeps count?" he thought. But he sensed Nena needed to know.

"No serious romances in high school, the usual college flings, a serious relationship in England, and a couple of affairs at Columbia, but I can honestly tell you since I met you at Columbia, every woman I met or dated I compared to you," he told her. "That night on the platform I knew it was going to take one heck of a woman to stir any feelings in me the way you did that summer."

"Are you serious? I had that much of an effect on you?"

"Yes, you did. When we made love at the Waldorf, I knew you were well worth the wait. Whatever went on in your marriage with Ben, you're a fantastic lover, Nena. You make me feel the way no other woman ever has."

Without going into details, Sam told Nena what she wanted and needed to hear. She drifted off to sleep with a different question floating through her thoughts. Was he her lover, or was he more?

The next two days, they shut out the world. She cooked, they talked and talked, and made love. On New Year's Eve, they left the nest they had created and walked to the Hatch Memorial Shell on the Charles River Esplanade. They tried to get as close as they could to hear the Boston Pops Orchestra perform for Boston's annual Fourth of July celebration, and watch the fireworks.

Sam drew Nena's face to his and kissed her, as the sky exploded with color. Though her face was cold to the touch, her response sent a rush of heat throughout his body. While fireworks shot toward the sky in sync to the music, home is where they wanted to begin this new year and new millennium.

**

The next morning, Nena made brunch while Sam packed his bag. He was catching an afternoon train to the city. "I wish I didn't have to work on Monday," she said. "Otherwise you could stay longer."

"I wish I could too. Unfortunately, I have a few meetings next week I must attend. I don't know how I'll ever concentrate."

"When will I see you again?" Nena asked.

"I have that meeting in Boston in a few weeks. If you can get a few days off, I'll rent a car and we can get away…someplace special."

"I'll make certain I get the time off, and I approve of a special place. Our special place."

South Station was full of holiday travelers saying their good-byes.

"Hurry back, Sam."

"It's going to be a long two weeks," he replied as the train began to fill.

"I love you, Nena." Her heart raced when she heard the words. It was too late to respond. He had already turned his back to walk away. In a way she was grateful, because when she said those words to him, she wanted to be 100 percent sure.

Part III

2000–2001

Chapter 10

Ben got off the train at Grand Central Terminal for his appointment with Jay's doctor, not exactly the way he thought he would begin the year 2000. Another thought struck him as he walked through the terminal. He remembered the first trip to New York with Nena, shortly after they began to date. He and his brother Jackie were introducing Nena to the New York they loved. The memory still made him happy, and a happy thought is what he needed to keep his mind off tomorrow.

When Ben reached Jay's apartment on Sutton Place, Jay wasted no time telling Ben his appointment was the following day at eleven. "I know you're going to like Dr. Harris. He's excellent." Jay noticed the look of anxiety on Ben's face and changed the subject. "Is the office back to normal?"

"Yes. Hard to believe there was a flood. Everything is back to normal. How am I ever going to repay you? The flood — now this."

"No repayment necessary...Ben, I think it's about time I told you something. I imagine you have wondered what I know about you and Apex, if anything. Well, I know everything that happened to you when you worked there. I haven't wanted to say anything until now, but I don't want any secrets between us. New York is a small place, and I've known the Warrens for years. We were on a few boards together, and Trudi always had us attending some social event or another where we would see them. When we found out about the kids, Trudi vowed we were not going to mention anything, even to them. I know people thought Trudi would have a hard time letting go of Robbie, but she wanted him to find happiness. When Robbie and Becky were falling in love, and she knew she was dying, she didn't want anything to spoil their chances. She would say, 'It's in the past. Let sleeping dogs lie.' Ben, Trudi really liked you and your family, and we have become damn good friends — and there isn't anything I won't do for my friends. There I've said my peace."

If Nena had heard Jay's conversation, the answer to her question regarding Trudi's feelings toward Becky would have been answered. Ben sat speechless. Tears of relief welled in his eyes. Over a drink, he poured out his heart to Jay. He covered all of his downfall and more — right up to his last visit in Paris at the Ritz — unburdening his past to this man who had become more than a friend.

~~~~~~~~~~~~~~~~

Sitting in Dr. Harris's office the following morning, Ben had a feeling of foreboding. Jay patted him on the knee when his name was called. Nearly forty-five minutes later, the nurse came to the waiting room door and asked Jay if he would please come in.

"Morning Jay, how are things with you?" Dr. Harris asked as Jay joined Ben in the examination room.

"Doing well Ted, how about you?" Dr. Harris had been the Starks's doctor and family friend for years.

"No complaints," the doctor said. "I hear from Ben that Robbie and Becky are back in the city. I bet that pleases you. Who knows; maybe you'll get him into that company of yours yet."

"It's his decision." Secretly that is exactly what Jay wanted.

Small talk ended when the doctor told Ben while his blood samples had not shown anything out of the ordinary, his fatigue was a concern, and he wanted Ben to have a more in-depth workup, including a bone marrow test, telling him, "I want you to check into Mount Sinai tomorrow morning."

"That's such short notice," Ben replied. "I have a business to run."

"If this is what Ted thinks you should do, let's do it." Jay became the voice of reason. "We'll figure out something to tell Buddy. I know you don't want anyone to know what's going on with you, which may be nothing, but I strongly suggest we take the kids to dinner tonight and tell them. Don't you agree, Ted?"

"I do, Jay." Then turning to Ben, he sternly told him to be at the hospital by ten.

Leaving Dr. Harris's office, Ben was in turmoil. From Jay's apartment, he called Buddy, making a flimsy excuse that he needed to stay in the city another night. He told his uncle that he and Jay had a frank talk about what happened at Apex, relieved the past was no longer unspoken. Buddy could not have been more pleased. Jay had turned into a hell of a friend, and there were no more secrets.

**

When they arrived at the restaurant, they were escorted to their table by the owner, Nino, wearing his customary pinstripe suit and welcoming smile. "Wonderful to see you Jay — and Robbie, this must be your wife. I've heard a great deal about you from Jay. Welcome back to New York, and welcome to Nino's."

"Thanks Nino, yes this is Becky. It's nice being back in town."

Nino ordered for them. Over plates of pasta and salad, Becky asked her dad why he was in the city.

Jay jumped in telling J.R. and Becky that Ben had been experiencing bouts of exhaustion, and he had suggested Ben come into the city to see Dr. Harris.

"I knew it, I knew it!" Becky exclaimed. "Didn't I tell you J.R., Daddy didn't seem like himself when we were in Ogunquit?"

"Yes, you did honey," he responded, trying to keep his wife calm.

"Okay you two," Ben interjected. "We don't know anything yet. Dr. Harris said my blood test was normal. He wants more tests he can't do at the office." Becky wanted to know what kind of tests. When Ben mentioned blood tests, she did not react, but when she heard bone marrow, her voice became agitated.

"Bone marrow? What does your bone marrow have to do with your being tired?" She could barely remain calm.

Wanting to deflect Becky from more probing, Jay stepped in. "Ted is the type of doctor who needs to test everything. It's routine."

The explanation seemed to appease Becky, but not her questions. "Does Mum know?"

"No, nobody knows but us, and I want to keep it that way until there is something to know." Ben gave his daughter a look that meant she was to respect his wishes.

"Well, can I at least come to the hospital with you tomorrow?"

"Jay is coming with me. He will call you when he knows anything, and then we'll see what happens next," Ben replied. "No jumping the gun, promise?"

"Promise."

"Now let's enjoy this fantastic-looking meal." Ben did not know if he could, but he would try.

**

The following morning, Ben checked into the hospital. Jay could not shake from his mind the last months he spent at Mount Sinai in the cancer ward with Trudi. Waiting for Ben, Jay went to the chapel and prayed.

When the tests were finished Dr. Harris stopped by Ben's Room. "There's nothing conclusive to tell you yet, Ben. I want you to go home. I'll go over the tests with some of my colleagues to make certain I haven't missed anything. I'll call you as soon as I have the results."

"Thanks, Dr. Harris. Would I be out of line if I asked you for your professional opinion?" Ben asked. "Should I be worried about being this tired?"

"It's Ted, please," the doctor answered. "Fatigue is a funny thing. Sometimes it's a warning sign, and sometimes it means you need a vacation. I don't want you to worry. I'll be in touch."

Jay had known the doctor a long time, and he saw a certain something in his face and manner that did cause him to worry, but he decided that he would not mention it to Ben.

Ben and Jay left the hospital. "Ready for a drink?" Jay asked on the way out.

"More than ready."

Before leaving the hospital, Ben called Becky to tell her the tests were still being evaluated, and asked her, again, not to tell anyone other than J.R. about the hospital visit.

"These past few weeks seemed like a year," Nena told her new love.

"For me too. Bags packed?"

"Yes, sir, I'm ready. Nantucket here we come."

They stepped aboard the ferry in Hyannis, spending the three-hour ride to Nantucket on the deck, watching and waiting for the island to appear on the horizon.

"My last trip to the island, I vowed to come back. I wished I wouldn't be coming alone," Sam said, holding her tightly as a winter wind blew off the water. "But I never could have predicted coming with you."

"It's all so surreal." Nena too could not believe her good fortune.

Once the ferry docked, they were taken to the White Elephant, a waterfront institution on the island. Their room had a sitting room with a fireplace and a deck overlooking the harbor, plus a king-sized bed in the bedroom.

"Let's go into town and do what couples do when they go away," Nena proposed. "There are some lovely art galleries and boutiques I want to browse."

"Is that what couples do when they go away?" Sam asked.

"Are you poking fun at me? Yes, browsing is *one* thing they do," she hinted as they left the hotel to explore the town.

Nena's browsing satisfied, they returned to the hotel and dressed for dinner.

When they finished dining, the day, the sea air, and the sheer pleasure of being away with Sam, on this island far from land, had its effect on Nena and she suggested they go back to their room.

When they opened the door to their room, the staff had the fireplace lit, and champagne chilled in a bucket.

Sipping champagne, they sat by the fire recounting the day until he could no longer hold back his desire for her. In front of a crackling fire, they made love.

Nena was as content as she ever felt; the time had come to tell Sam what was in her heart.

"I never thought I would ever fall in love again," she began, "certainly not at this stage in life." Sam wanted to interrupt her — to ask her to repeat what she had just said, but he held back. "How many people do you know get a second chance? And you know what? The song is true. Love is more beautiful the second time around; it really is. With what happened to Ben and me, I wondered if I could ever trust a man again. I loved Ben with all my heart. He was my first love, the only man in my life until you."

The night in New York when they first made love, she wanted to reveal everything. She was not ready then, but she was ready now. Her words came faster than she could control them. She could not stop herself, nor did she want to.

"From the beginning we had our problems, usually about family, his family, his mother. At first I thought it was me, and the fact I wasn't Catholic, but I learned Helen wouldn't have approved of any girl Ben married even if she had been Catholic. Helen just couldn't let go of her son. When she came to stay with us in England, and we found out she didn't have long to live, that's when things began to change. That's when she realized she had lost control, even of herself. Dying does one of two things: you either realize the folly of your life, or you keep connected to the sins of your past. Helen chose the former, and it was a blessing. By the time she died, we found a peaceful coexistence. In the end I admired her for being able to take responsibility for her actions, and leave Ben without the burden she had placed on him from the time his father died. At last she realized it wasn't my intention to take her place, and we made peace. This is why I couldn't comprehend how Ben did what he did. It took me a long time to understand he hadn't come to terms with his past, or the root cause of what motivated him. He had demons. He hid them well. But eventually they surfaced. And when they did, Ben took the wrong path and made the wrong choices. I struggled for years with what happened. I questioned my self-worth. In order to survive I played a role for the outside world, and myself. I believed my responsibility was to be the good mother, the good daughter, friend, sister, and, maybe someday, mother-in-law and grandmother."

"And how were you being good to Nena?"

"I wasn't. I didn't have any expectations."

"But can you see what you did? You closed yourself off to life. When you were at Columbia, I saw you as a woman who lived life to the fullest, almost fearless." Hearing what Nena had been through touched Sam profoundly. He knew she had been deeply wounded by the events in her life; he did not know how deeply.

"I know, but when something devastating happens in your life, even though you don't give up, you try to protect yourself consciously or subconsciously. I believed as long as I kept serious relationships at bay — no involvements — I could protect myself from being hurt again. I wasn't willing to take a risk with my heart. I created a good life, Sam. I really did. I like my work; I found a place I made into my home, and…"

He interrupted her. "You don't have to explain anymore, Nena. You don't have to justify to me how you coped. You've been to hell and back, and I'm honored you've shared your feelings with me; this could not have been easy." Tenderly he turned her head toward him. "I want to ask you something. I need to know if I heard you correctly earlier."

"About what? What did I say?"

"You started by saying you never thought you would fall in love again. Are you saying what I think you're saying?" he asked.

In telling Sam her story she failed to realize what she had said. This is not the way she planned to tell him.

"Yes, I did, and I do love you Sam. I never thought this would happen for me, but this is not the way I planned on telling you."

"It doesn't matter how you told me. I have longed to hear those words. You have just made me the happiest man alive." Under his breath, Sam was thanking his lucky stars.

He took her hand and led her into the bedroom. He brushed away the tears that had settled in the corner of her eyes and gently placed her on the bed and lay next to her. As the flames from the fire danced in the hearth, the fire of her love stirred throughout her body and she completely surrendered to Sam, both physically and emotionally; their bond forever sealed.

They spent the remainder of their get-away taking advantage of what Nantucket offered in the off-season. One day they rented a jeep and toured the island, another day they visited the Whaling Museum. In town Nena bought a glass bowl to fill with the scallop shells she collected at the harbor shore, and on their last day the hotel prepared a picnic lunch they took to Great Point Beach. With not another person in sight they dined and were entertained by a colony of gray seals frolicking on the edge of the water. Nantucket in the winter — peaceful, romantic, quiet — proved to be more than Sam and Nena ever expected.

**

When he dropped her off in Boston, neither wanted to say good-bye. "Call me the minute you get home," she reminded him as she kissed him again. He started the car. "And drive carefully."

"I will; I'll call you the second I get back, and I'll drive like a little old lady!"

She smiled and blew him a kiss as he drove away.

It had been over a week since Ben had seen Dr. Harris when the phone rang in the office. Ben hoped this call was about the results of his tests. His palms began to sweat as he picked up phone.

"Hello Ben, its Ted Harris. Sorry I'm a few days late getting back to you. I know how nerve-wracking waiting can be," the doctor said. "My colleagues have had a chance to look at your test results, and I want to see you in my office tomorrow."

"What time?"

"Tomorrow at two."

"I'll be there at two, and thanks Ted."

He hung up the phone, not sure what he was thanking the doctor for.

"Going somewhere?" Buddy inquired.

"I have to run into the city tomorrow for a few hours. Can you hold down the fort?"

"I can take care of things here, but I wish you'd tell me what's really going on with you because I know something is. I've known you your entire life Ben; secrets never get us anywhere. I think we should know that by now."

"I promise when I get back tomorrow, I'll tell you everything." Ben hoped he would have nothing to tell.

Ben knew he should confide in his uncle, but why worry Buddy unnecessarily? He needed another twenty-four hours.

**

"Positive thoughts, only positive thoughts allowed." Ben repeated this mantra as the train crossed the line from Connecticut into New York, but something nagged at him. Ben had called Jay to meet him at the doctor's office. Good news or bad news, he needed a friend by his side.

"Sit down, Ben." Ted beckoned him to a chair opposite his desk. Ben looked around the room. A wall of diplomas caught his eye. He tried to read where they were from, but he could not focus. He searched Ted's face but could not read him either.

Telling a patient they were facing a battle for their life is never easy for any physician. Dr. Harris remembered the day Jay heard Trudi had cancer. With Jay sitting by Ben's side he would hear those same words about his son's father-in-law, and the doctor knew this would not be easy for Jay.

"When I read the results of your first blood test, I was confused. Everything appeared normal, but your symptoms of fatigue were worrisome to me. I needed to get to the bottom of your fatigue, especially since your white count tested normal," Dr. Harris began.

"Did you find out?" Gripping the arms of the chair, Ben had a sinking feeling he did not want to hear what Ted had to say.

"Yes we did, Ben. The second blood test showed the same results, but we were able to determine from the bone marrow results you have adult leukemia." The doctor braced himself for his patient's response.

"Leukemia, I thought only young people got leukemia." Ben wanted to heave. His stomach was in a knot. His mouth went dry while his hands were dripping wet. His ears were ringing. He could barely comprehend Ted's words.

"There are forms of leukemia that attack adults. You have a form of acute myeloid leukemia. Your type is called acute promyelocytic leukemia or APL for short. What's happened is your bone marrow that helps your body fight infections has stopped working," Ted explained.

The doctor could see the look of bewilderment on Ben's face. He reached behind his desk and held up a chart showing Ben a picture of healthy and abnormal bone marrow cells.

"The cancer grows from cells that would normally become white blood cells. Your healthy blood cells are being crowded out in your bone marrow. This form of leukemia is usually an older person's disease, and mainly in men. I know this is a lot to take in Ben, and you must have a hundred questions for me."

Questions? Ben felt he had been run over by one of his oil trucks. He wanted to run from the room, but instead he heard the words echo in his head as he spoke. "What can be done; how much time do I have?"

"Let's take this a step at a time. First I need to reassure you, you're going to have the finest team there is with you every step of your treatment. We'll get you into the hospital and give you transfusions to build up your system, and then we will begin chemotherapy. We're going to keep a close eye on you. The chemo could be enough, or we may need some help with a bone marrow transplant. But Ben, this is jumping the gun."

"I know, but I don't want you holding back. I want to know exactly what to expect."

"I hear you, Ben. However, what I want you to do right now is get your family involved. You're going to need their support because this is something you can't win on your own. Go home, put your business in order, talk to your family, and I will see you back here at the hospital at the end of the week."

Ben hoped his legs would hold him up as he walked to the elevator. He was trying to digest it all. Jay put his arm around Ben's shoulder. "You're going to beat this Ben, and we're going to help you," Jay reassured him. "I'm going to phone J.R., and hire a car to take us to New Canaan. We can tell the kids together, and Buddy has to know. Leave this to me."

Ben would leave it to Jay. He was too tired to do otherwise. In the car, when Ben revealed the doctor's report, Becky began to cry.

"Don't cry sweetheart." Ben tried to comfort his daughter. "The doctor assured me the odds are in my favor; we can beat this into remission. I'm going to need you to be strong." Unfortunately he was feeling anything but strong.

"Can I call Mum?" she asked.

"Let's wait until we talk to Buddy, get the arrangements set, and then we can tell her."

**

As Buddy listened to Ben and Jay tell him what had been going on, what the trips into the city had been for, Buddy wondered what else life could throw at them. How many times in his life had he thought, "Hasn't this family been through enough? Just when life seemed to be going smoothly, another curve ball comes our way."

"Ben, I don't want you to worry about the business," Buddy told him. "You've done wonders — the company practically runs itself. We'll all pitch in."

In his mid-eighties Buddy never envisioned he would have to step back into the business full time. He felt confidant when Ben had returned that the legacy of the company his father had begun would live on for years. When Buddy was alone he pondered what would become of the business if anything happened to Ben.

"I'll be arriving on the last off-peak train. Miss me?" she asked Sam, feeling like a young co-ed in love.

"What do you think? More than you know. I thought we'd have an early dinner before the philharmonic. Or would you rather eat later?"

"Let's eat early, and afterwards go somewhere for coffee and dessert."

"Dessert sounds good to me," he responded in a slightly devious tone — their back-and-forth conversation full of double entendres.

**

Waiting for the concert to begin and listening to the musicians tune their instruments, Nena reflected on the many times she and Ben had sat in this very hall. She especially remembered the evening when Leonard Bernstein conducted. His performance left a lasting impression on her. That night seemed like a lifetime ago.

Leaving the concert, they walked passed the reflecting pool and down the steps. A light snow had begun to fall. Nena did not want to sit in a restaurant across from Sam when he could be sitting beside her. "Let's go home." No longer did Nena stay at the Waldorf when she came into the city. They stopped into Zabar's and bought pastries and bagels for breakfast then walked to Sam's apartment as the snow began to cling to their coats and crunch underfoot.

**

He awoke first, watching her as she slowly began to stir. "Do you know how much I love you, sleepyhead?"

"Oh those words are music to my ears, exactly what I like to hear first thing in the morning; the feeling is mutual. I can't imagine my life without you. Sam, we're going to have to come clean. I can't keep us a secret any longer. Otherwise I'm going to burst. I want to share what is happening to me, to us, with Becky. I want her to meet you. I want you to meet my entire family. I'm going to call Becky to see if we can get together for dinner tonight." Nena reached across Sam and picked up the phone.

Becky did not expect a call from Nena. She had planned on calling her mother that very day to relay the news about Ben. They exchanged hellos. Becky told her mother there was something she needed to talk to her about too.

"Mind if I go first," Nena could not contain herself.

"Okay Mum, what is it, because what I have to tell you is important."

"Can you and J.R. meet us for dinner tonight?"

"Us, who's us?" Becky asked.

"Someone special I want you to meet. Someone very important to me."

When Becky hung up the phone, she called J.R. at work to tell him they were meeting her mother for dinner that night at 7 p.m. "Under any other circumstance, I would be happy to meet my mother's someone special, but these aren't any other circumstances." Not happy about the turn of events, she implored J.R. about what to do.

"I don't know what to say," he replied. "Best bet is to wait until tonight; play it by ear."

**

Both couples arrived at the restaurant not knowing what to expect. J.R. and Becky arrived first.

When Becky saw her mother beaming as she walked in the door with another man, not her father, she understood more about this special someone. Her parents were divorced, her mother had the right to date, even fall in love, have a second chance, but she was not ready, especially knowing her father's condition.

Introductions were made. Waiting for their aperitifs, Nena explained that Sam had been her professor at Columbia, and they met again the night after Trudi's memorial service at a get-together with a group of friends from graduate school.

"Welcome aboard, Sam!" J.R. lifted his glass.

"Thanks, J.R. I was another lonely bachelor floating around New York. Truly I had given up on relationships. And then Nena walked into my life, literally." He turned to Nena and kissed her on her cheek.

Nena could not contain her smile as she looked at Sam. "I think you walked into my life; I was already in the restaurant."

Becky's heart melted enough to say. "I'm really happy for you Mum, and you too Sam." Although her words were sincerely spoken, there was a tinge of sadness, watching her mother build a new life as her father was facing the fight of his life.

"Okay I've shared my news; what's yours?" Nena asked.

Becky could not bring herself to tell her about Ben, at least not tonight, and certainly not in front of Sam.

"We can talk tomorrow. Let's have lunch."

Nena accepted Becky's offer for lunch.

The remainder of the night they learned more about Sam — about his life and his experiences living in Washington and in England. They talked about their trip to Nantucket a few weeks ago and suggested Becky and J.R. would enjoy the island in the off-season.

**

Walking home, Becky began to think more about tomorrow and her lunch date with her mother, which she was already dreading.

"Mummy is really happy. I haven't seen her this happy since before the divorce. Do you think the two of them are in love?"

"It's pretty obvious to me they're in love. I wish my dad would find someone, but he never will. Your mother is lucky to be having this second chance."

"I know, but how am I going to tell her about Dad? My father was once the love of her life."

"I'm not going to tell you tomorrow isn't going to be a rough day for the both of you. Honey, I know you; you'll find the right words." Knowing in his heart a problem loomed on the horizon, he held Becky's hand tightly as they walked home.

**

"I hope you don't mind, but I made reservations at the Carlyle Hotel for lunch. I wanted to go someplace quiet to talk," Becky told her mother.

A block from the museum, the Carlyle, a venerable New York City establishment was once known as the New York White House when John F. Kennedy was president.

Becky attempted to keep the conversation light, as they dined on two Caesar salads with blackened chicken and Pinot Grigio. Eventually, she could not contain herself any longer.

"Mum, there's something I need to tell you."

"That's what you said yesterday on the phone, but then at dinner you didn't say anything."

Becky told her mother that she did not want to spoil the evening, considering how happy Nena seemed, and decided what she had to say could wait until today.

"Well, we're here now," Nena replied, "what is it?"

"It's about Dad."

"What about your father?"

"Dad's sick." Becky knew of no other way to tell Nena.

"What do you mean your father's sick?" Nena put her fork down and stared at her daughter.

"I mean he is really sick Mum. There's no easy way to tell you this: Dad has leukemia."

"He has what?" She had heard the words spoken by her daughter, but they were not registering. Thoughts of her grandfather flooded over her, when she learned he had leukemia, and how valiantly he had fought to live right to the end. Is this what was in store for Ben?

When Nena composed herself, she wanted to know how long Becky had known about Ben's condition.

She said a few days, then asked Nena, "Didn't you notice he seemed different at Christmas?"

"No, he seemed fine to me." Becky's comments were beginning to irritate Nena. "Maybe a little quiet, but I didn't take that as anything serious."

"Well, I did." Becky told her mother. "When I asked him if he was alright, he attributed being a little tired to a heavy work schedule. I found the way he looked worrisome, and I told J.R. I thought something was wrong with Dad. We decided to wait until the next time we saw him before suggesting he see a doctor. Now, I wish we hadn't waited."

"Why didn't you say anything to me?" Nena had no idea where Becky was going with all of this.

"Mum, wait a minute. What would I have said to you? The two of you are divorced. Should I have called you and said, "Hey Mum I've got this sense something isn't quite right with Daddy?" What would you have done about it?"

Becky had a visceral response to her mother's reaction. When her parent's divorced, she never addressed her own feelings. She buried the impact and toll the divorce had taken on her in order to remain impartial. But Ben had cancer, and Becky wanted to protect him, no matter what. She loved her father dearly, and her mother was not cooperating.

Wanting to divert her daughter's building irritation with her, Nena asked, "How did he find out?"

Becky told her mother, Ben had confided in Jay that he was not feeling well during the flood cleanup at his office. She added that Jay suggested Ben see his doctor in the city.

"They've become good buddies, and Jay is this amazing person when someone he cares about is in trouble; he's the first one there."

How ironic Nena thought — while Ben dealt with cleaning up a flood in his office and then finding out he had cancer, she was falling in love with Sam, spending New Year's Eve in his arms, going to Nantucket with him, and opening herself to him, emotionally and every other way. She had the promise of a life with Sam, a second chance, and now this.

"What do you want me to do?" Nena seemed puzzled by her daughter's demeanor.

"What kind of a question is that? Mum, what's going on with you? You always know what to do."

Anger welled inside Becky. Her emotions were getting the best of her. She wanted her mother to take charge, regardless of the fact her parents were divorced. Until now, she had prided herself on not taking sides in her parents' lives. Last night her mother's happiness mattered, but today she could not separate her mother's happiness with the fact her father had cancer. After many years of staying neutral, she took a side.

Yes, Nena did know the right thing to do, but not this time. This time things were different. Her heart went out to Ben — she had been married to the man for more than twenty-five years. He was the father of her daughter. They grew into adulthood together. But she had moved on. Sam had come into her life and offered her love and a new beginning. She had opened up her heart to Sam, and she did not want to look back or get involved. A chill went through her. She could not rescue Ben. This was his journey. Nena feared that her daughter wanted her to step back into Ben's life — a walk Nena dreaded.

"In this case, there's nothing I can do, Becky. From what you say, your father is under the care of a great team. The important thing for him is getting the best medical treatment, and that is something I have no knowledge of. It seems your father is already in good hands."

"And you don't think you can be part of that support system?" Becky asked, more than agitated with the conversation.

"Becky, please. Stop." Nena felt backed into a corner. "I will call your father, but frankly other than visiting him when he's in the hospital, I don't see what else I can do."

Becky had never seen this side of her mother. Nena even surprised herself by her reaction to the situation. Maybe others would consider her behavior self-absorbed. But she, too, was fighting for her life, a new life with Sam. She could imagine this new life slipping away with this turn of events.

"Mum, you need to try and figure out why you're disconnected from this situation," Becky huffed. "One would suppose we were discussing a perfect stranger."

"I'm sorry you see me this way. You know I would never wish this on your father. I only wanted him to put his life back together. I know he's been trying to make amends, and this is unfair, when he has been making such progress. I'll call him," Nena relented, "but I don't know what else you expect me to do."

"Good, call him; I know he'll expect to hear from you," Becky answered, calming herself.

Nena felt beaten. Becky had boxed her into a corner, giving her no escape. She did not think her daughter had the right to make her feel guilty, but that is exactly what she had done. Nena ended lunch and asked for the check. Outside the Carlyle, their good-bye was strained. She walked to Sam's apartment and let herself in. When Sam came home, she told him about lunch with Becky.

"Honestly Nena, I don't know what to say. This is terrible news. How do you want to handle this?" Sam asked.

"I don't know; I don't know." Taking deep breaths, she sighed, "Just hold me; please hold me." He cradled her in his arms — she sobbed.

Leaving the city and Sam, Nena wondered if her life would ever be the same. She wanted to stay with Sam. He made her feel safe. Their love was too new to have something come between them. She wanted her world to be isolated from the outside, but knew this was not possible. She had lived a full life with Ben before Sam came along, and that life could not be wished away — no matter how much she desired her world to revolve around the two of them. Sam reassured her he would never leave her side. He told her they had waited this long to be together and he would be there for her no matter how long it took to resolve her family issues. Nothing could change the way he felt about her, and them having a life together. Sam said what Nena needed to hear, and she needed to hold on to that.

Chapter 11

Nena had a difficult time willing herself to call Ben. She picked up the phone a half dozen times before dialing. When she finally did, he told her the doctors were optimistic about his chances to beat the cancer. Nena felt encouraged by his diagnosis.

"When will they begin your treatments?" Despite the fact they had a marriage that lasted a quarter of a century, she was uncomfortable speaking with Ben about personal matters, and was not certain what to ask or say.

"I have to be physically stronger before beginning chemo. Ted…"

"Who's Ted?" Nena asked.

"Oh Ted is Dr. Harris, my doctor. Jay introduced us; he treated Trudi. Ted and the other doctors on the team have put me on a strict regime." During this conversation, they collectively realized their lives had separated. There were things she did not know about his life, and there were certainly things he had no idea about hers.

Ben told her Buddy had turned into a drill sergeant, watching him like a hawk, to make sure he took his pills, ate the right foods, and got enough rest.

"He might be worse than Nurse Ratched from *One Flew Over the Cuckoo's Nest*, but I'm damn lucky to have him."

"You are lucky, Ben. The person this family can always count on is Buddy. He's a blessing." Nena meant every word. "I'm glad he's there for you. If there's anything I can do, let me know." What could she do? Nena had no idea, but felt she should say the words.

"There's nothing really, Nena. I'm being taken care of…a phone call now and then would be nice." Ben could tell by the tone of the conversation Nena was not going to volunteer more than she already had.

"Done, I'll keep in touch."

Hanging up the phone, relief washed over Nena.

Conversely, when Ben hung up the phone, remorse overcame him. The actions of his past had dire consequences; the latest for him was not having Nena by his side when he needed her most.

~~~~~~~~~~~~~~

Arriving with Jay and Buddy at Mount Sinai for his first chemotherapy treatment, Ben admitted to himself he was afraid. He had put up a good front containing his fear, trying to protect those he loved. Jay lived through cancer treatments with Trudi and understood the consequences of chemo, and insisted Ben stay with him a few days after his treatments. From his own experience with his wife, he was aware that side effects could be debilitating, and Ben being close to his medical team and hospital is where he needed to be. Ben accepted Jay's offer. This brought comfort to both Becky and Buddy.

**

For months, Ben traveled back and forth between New Canaan and the city for treatments and tests. Weeks of treatment followed by weeks of allowing his system to rebuild until one day he received the news from Dr. Harris he longed to hear: there were no leukemia cells present in his blood or bone marrow.

"I can't thank you enough, Ted," Ben said when he received the good news.

"These are the days that make my job as a doctor worthwhile. However, you've not seen the last of me. We're going to set up a schedule for a short course of chemo. I call this a minor tune-up."

"Is this necessary?" Ben was not looking forward to additional rounds of chemo.

"Unfortunately yes, Ben. Think of this next step as maintenance to reduce the risk of the disease recurring. This is the best possible news I could give any patient, but it's not over. You're in remission. We need five years of positive test results before I can say you are out of the woods. We will become the best of friends through this."

"I couldn't have a better friend in my corner," Ben replied, shaking the doctor's hand.

Dinner tonight at Nino's would be different than months ago when Ben had to tell his daughter he needed to go to the hospital for tests. Over plates of pasta and glasses of Sangiovese wine, spirits were high when the family heard Ben was in remission.

Leaving the restaurant, Becky turned to her father and asked if he wanted her to call Nena and tell her the good news.

"I'd rather call her, if you don't mind," he told her.

Becky questioned why, because, although Nena did visit Ben in the hospital, she had not been an active partner in his treatments. She doubted if her mother had not come into the city to spend time with Sam if she would have even seen Ben. Becky still held a grievance towards her mother since their conversation at lunch, and something else occupied Becky's mind when it came to her mother — Sam. She had not said a word to Ben regarding the new man in Nena's life, wondering how much longer she could keep this information to herself. J.R. had advised his wife to let it go, her parents were divorced, they were adults, and they were the people who needed to work out their relationship.

"Beck, don't be hard on your mother. I know she's been worried about me. I don't want you to let this come between the two of you, and the wonderful relationship you've always had." Ben hoped his daughter would heed his advice.

"But Dad, Mum could be a little more involved."

"Beck, let it go."

Where had she heard that before? His words made her squirm.

"Your mother is involved as much as we both want…that's all that's important."

Reluctantly Becky told her father if this is what he wanted she would not argue. However, she was not convinced this is what her father needed or wanted, but dropped the subject, grateful for his remission.

**

Ben called Nena the next day to tell her the treatments were successful.

"Remission, what a lovely word. This truly is the best news you could have given me."

Now she was free to tell Ben about Sam. The worst thing would be for him to hear about them from someone else, especially Becky, but when to tell him?

Whenever Nena needed to talk, she could count on Josh as a sounding board.

"I'm free today," he said when she called him. "Faneuil Hall?"

"See you there." Nena hung up the phone, wondering what her brother would think about what she was about to tell him.

~~~~~~~~~~~~~~

"I'm glad you could come." Nena was sitting outside, across from Josh at Joe's American Bar and Grill. The sun sparkled off Boston Harbor on this warm spring day. "I never tire of this setting," she added, as they ate their burgers and caught up on family news.

Eventually, Josh asked Nena the reason she had set up this luncheon; it had to be something more than just to hear the latest about Gabby and the kids.

"I wanted to tell you I heard from Ben, and he's in remission."

"That's fantastic news. Regardless of the past, we care about Ben, and we were devastated when we heard he had cancer. I was with Mum when she found out, and she cried like a baby, but you could have told me this over the phone. What else is on your mind, sister dear?" Josh probed.

Apprehensive she blurted out, "I've met someone special. I'll tell you about him, but first I need your advice. I have to tell Ben."

Nothing ever shocked Josh. "Whom have you told?" he asked.

"Only Becky and J.R."

"Oh that must have been interesting; how did Beck take it?"

"As you can imagine, she wants to be happy for me, but when she factors in her father, and his feelings for me..." Nena was trying to put a good face on what happened. "It's the way it all came out. I asked them to dinner to meet Sam — the same day Becky found out about Ben's cancer."

"Ouch!" Josh responded.

"Yes – ouch! She knew, and I didn't. The following day at lunch, is when I learned Ben had cancer, and things haven't gone well since. I had no idea what she wanted from me regarding her father. I'm handling the situation as best I can." Nena needed to hear her brother say everything would be okay.

When Josh told Nena he thought things would change now that Ben was in remission, his words put her mind at ease. Josh had the ability to do this since they were children.

"You two are too close for Becky not to be glad you're moving on. It'll all work out."

"You think so?"

"I know so! Now...who is this new person in your life?" Josh being Josh, he could not help but probe — what was his name, what did he do. He wanted the details. When he found out Nena had first met him in graduate school, he asked her if they had an affair. Nena was aghast.

"Josh, what kind of a question is that!" she exclaimed. "Of course not. I was 100 percent committed to Ben and our marriage, even if Ben wasn't. What he did at Apex, and not being present in the marriage destroyed us. I truly believed being in grad school would take some of the pressure off the home front with each of us busy in our own worlds. Little did I know...but no...no, no. I did not have an affair."

"I wouldn't have judged you if you had, but I had to ask."

"His name is Sam Katz, and he is a professor."

"Ah...a nice Jewish boy?"

Nena shook her head. "Josh, you're incorrigible. Yes he's Jewish. I love him, Josh. He's wonderful. When Sinatra sings love is lovelier and more comfortable the second time around, it's true. I've been dying to share Sam with you, but I hope you can understand why I kept my relationship with him private — I needed time to be certain of my feelings."

"Of course I understand. When do I get to meet this Sam?"

"He's coming to Boston in a few weeks. I'm planning on having the family for dinner. You can't spill the beans, though. I want to be the one to tell Mum and Dad, but I dread telling Ben."

"I won't say a word. They're going to be happy for you, Sis; however, I strongly suggest you tell Ben…and soon…before someone else does, and we both know who that someone is."

"I know you're right. And I do know who. Josh, Ben was my first love, my first everything, but in Sam's eyes I'm his equal — he makes me feel special in a way Ben never did."

"Well, I can't wait to meet the professor," Josh admitted.

Confiding in Josh made her relationship with Sam real. She coveted her secret, her time alone with Sam, nonetheless the time had come to be open, to share this newfound love with those she loved.

**

When Nena told Peter and Ruth about Sam, they reacted exactly as Josh had said they would. They were happy for their daughter that she had moved beyond the heartache with the breakup of her marriage to Ben, and had found love and a new life. But they, too, realized Nena had a daunting task ahead of her — telling Ben.

Normally Nena took the train from Boston to New York City, but this trip she would drive. She stopped by the Parker House on the way out of Boston to purchase their house rolls and a Boston cream pie. The drive to Connecticut would give her time to prepare her speech, and steel herself to Ben's reaction.

When Buddy opened the door, he could not help but smile at Nena with her arms full of boxes. He opened the boxes while Ben looked on. "You never forget anything, Nena," he said. Nena's offerings brought up the trip Buddy and Ben made through New England when Ben was a junior in high school looking at colleges. Buddy reminded Ben how he enjoyed the rolls and the cream pie for dessert when they stayed at the Parker House. That Nena remembered this story, touched both men. Buddy tousled Ben's hair, dark and thick in spite of his chemotherapy treatments, as he reflected on their road trip.

Ben's eyes began to water, fondly remembering the trip. There was no better stand-in for a father than Buddy. Sensing how reminiscing affected Ben, Buddy quickly changed the subject.

Small talk and catching up exhausted, Buddy left realizing Nena had not come just to deliver baked goods from Boston. "Nena, please stop by the office to say good-bye before you leave," he reminded her on his way out the door. She assured Buddy she would.

Alone with Ben, Nena unburdened herself. She tried to gauge Ben's reaction when he heard Sam's name mentioned, but his eyes were downcast as she spoke. When she finished telling him about her and Sam, Ben sat silently on the couch for some time.

"I guess deep down I knew this day was inevitable. I guess I wished — no I did wish and hope, that we could somehow work things out, get back together, but I know what I did and what I destroyed. Regardless of what I want, it's only fair you move on, build a life, and be happy." Pausing, he continued, "Nena, do you think there's any possibility we could be friends — if not friends at least something more than just Becky's parents? I don't want to be cut out of your life entirely." What had been eyes swimming in a pool of water from remembering the college road trip with his uncle became tears streaming down his face.

Ben's words touched a place in Nena's heart she had closed off from him. "We've come a long way, Ben...we're making progress. I think we can both try to keep working on leaving the past in the past."

"If you knew how much I regret what I did, how I hurt you." His tears turned to sobs. "Nena, you were and are the love of my life." He knew he should not be saying these words, but he could not help himself.

Nena went to the couch and put her arms around Ben. She had hugged him before, but had not been able to bring herself to embrace him, and softly kissed him on the cheek as she did years ago when they finished therapy. They cried, for what was, but was no longer. Neither spoke a word, merely a silent acknowledgement of the hurt, the pain, the disappointment of their last years together.

On the way to say good-bye to Buddy, they talked about happier times. When the door to the office opened, Buddy knew something indescribable had happened. He did not know what, nor did he care; he was just happy it did.

~~~~~~~~~~~~~~

Walking down Broadway holding Sam's hand, Nena felt free. Now that Becky and Ben knew about Sam, it was time to introduce him to her family. A part of Nena had appreciated the anonymity of their relationship. Those years allowed her to heal, and to fall in love without prying eyes. She thought about the Bible quote: *"To everything there is a season, and a time to every purpose under the heaven."* Nena learned things do have a season and a purpose. Together she and Ben had lived a season, and that season had passed.

"I can't wait for you to come to Boston next week. The family is coming for dinner to meet you, and I'm so excited. You've been a patient man, Sam Katz, thank you! Keeping our relationship private hasn't always been easy, but having this time with you has allowed me to find myself, and in finding myself, I found you. I wouldn't change the way we handled this."

"Good, because neither would I."

They crossed Broadway at Lincoln Center and were seated outside at Café Fiorello, as twilight set on New York — the time of day when the sun lowered behind the buildings, and the city began to unwind from the daily bustle. He ordered Bellinis, a wonderful refreshing cocktail traditionally made with peach puree and sparkling wine, but these were made with champagne.

"To us," he toasted, looking at her, "I love you Nena. You've made my world complete."

"To us...I love you too, Sam. My world had fallen apart. You helped put it back together again."

"It's our time...our season," he replied. She felt as if he had read her mind.

They dined on seafood risotto, salad, and a chilled white wine. "We could have eaten at that French restaurant you like, but I thought Italian was more appropriate."

She looked at him puzzled, trying to figure out what he meant.

Not giving her time to ask any more questions, he pulled an envelope out of his jacket. "For you, madam."

Nena took the envelope in her hands and opened it to find two first-class tickets to Venice.

"My goodness. When did you plan this?"

"I've been planning this ever since we started seeing each other. I knew I wanted to take you there, but I had to wait until you were ready, and now that you have come clean about us," he said, "It's time."

She told him she would have to check her schedule, but Sam told her, "Nena if there's anything I've learned from life, from your life, my life, even Ben's life, life is to be lived to the fullest. We don't know what tomorrow is going to bring. Schedules be damned. Let's just do it."

For a brief moment she thought about the trip to Venice with Ben, when caution was thrown to the wind, and what happened to them when they returned. In moments like this Nena reminded herself to leave her past in the past. She leaned across the table, kissed him, and told him she'd figure it out. They ordered their dessert to go, and headed back to Sam's apartment to plan their trip.

~~~~~~~~~~~~~~~~~~~~~~~~~~~~~~~~~~

While Becky found her work at the museum exciting and challenging, J.R. continued to have concerns regarding Salomon's viability. With the dizzying changes Salomon had been through in recent years, the fact the company existed in any form was a miracle. The latest merger with Citibank went as smoothly as any merger could, but jobs were lost, people fired, and J.R. felt lucky he had dodged another bullet. He decided to talk with his father about the situation at Salomon. Jay had inherited Stark Land Development from his father and grandfathers before him, but he took what he inherited and grew the company into one of the largest commercial real estate companies in the city, and J.R. respected his father's business acumen and knowledge. When father and son finally sat down to talk about

Salomon's future, Jay told J.R. to keep his ears to the ground and his options open.

"You work in a world that's a crap shoot, Robbie. It's always been that way. You're astute. Don't burn any bridges." Then Jay told his son that he was always welcome to join the family business. "Remember, the door is always open. The offer has been there since you went to grad school. I understood your need to make it on your own. Well, you have proven that and more. How you've been able to navigate that financial jungle amazes me."

"Thanks Dad. I'll keep your offer in mind. Don't be surprised if someday I come knocking on your door." Jay hoped he would.

J.R. returned to 7 World Trade Center feeling more in control than he had in some time. In light of the uncertainty at Salomon, he was going to give the family business serious consideration. He planned on talking to Becky about it in the near future.

~~~~~~

Sam had met Nena's family, and was welcomed with open arms.

"You won them over Sam. I never had any doubts. I only wish Becky had come," she told him during one of their nightly talks.

Nena had concerns regarding her daughter. She understood Becky's outburst that day at lunch, and even sympathized with her. She recognized Becky, too, had withdrawn following the divorce. With no siblings to confide in, to help share the pain, Becky buried herself in school and then work. Once J.R. came into her life, she continued to play the part of the good and devoted daughter to both parents. When Ben became ill, it was easier for Becky to take out her unresolved feelings, which had been bottled up for years, on her mother. Nena wanted to restore her relationship with Becky to what it had been before Ben's cancer, but she wondered if their relationship might be entering a new season, and hoped her daughter could accept this new beginning.

~~~~~~~~~~~~~~~~~~~~~~~~~~

It had been a number of years since Nena had been to the European mainland. Flying to Venice with Sam, Nena thought about the last time she travelled to The Floating City with Ben on that fateful trip.

"Care to share your thoughts?" Sam asked Nena as the stewardess served the two of them drinks. He could tell Nena was lost in her own world.

"I know it's a little late to be bringing this up, but I've been second-guessing the choice of Venice." She had been moving forward and did not want this trip to be a step backward.

Almost reading her mind, Sam asked, "Why, because the last time you were there you were with Ben?" Even above the noise of the plane, Nena's silence was deafening. "Nena, you had no idea your life was going to fall apart then, did you?"

No, she had no idea then, but had she made a mistake agreeing on this trip to Venice? Her stomach was churning. Sam sensed her doubt and wanted more than anything to reassure this woman he loved.

"Nena, Venice is a fascinating, historic, romantic place to visit. I want to change your memory of Venice. I want you to see this glorious place through my eyes. I want to wash away your bad memories of this wonderful city. I want to do this for you and for me. I want us to begin where you ended."

Resting her head against the back of the seat, Nena tried to rein in her fears. This man sitting next to her was not Ben. Sam had become her rock. She stared at his profile. Her heart swelled knowing how he had changed her life. She turned and tenderly touched his cheek. "Sam, you're right; we will make Venice ours. I promise!" And at that moment any second-guesses vanished.

**

Arriving at Marco Polo airport in Venice, they were escorted to Plaza San Marco, where they caught the launch to Giudecca Island and the Hotel Cipriani. This venerable hotel would be their home away from home for the next ten days. Nena did not know how desperately she needed this vacation until she stepped off the launch. The tranquility of the setting engulfed her.

No sooner had they entered their room, a suite overlooking the lagoon, when there was a knock on the door. A waiter wheeled a tray laden with biscotti, rolls, butter, jams, and the traditional Venetian apple and raisin strudel onto the balcony. He poured Nena a cappuccino and a caffè latte for Sam. Looking out over the lagoon, neither spoke, savoring the moment.

They planned to spend the rest of the day at the pool and later explore the hotel grounds. Although the September weather was slightly warmer than normal, Nena appreciated the heated pool to temper the cool breeze off the lagoon as she swam. Climbing out of the pool, she curled up on a poolside lounge and fell asleep. Sam loved to watch her sleeping. Today she looked particularly peaceful, which filled his heart.

"Staring at me again?" She stirred and opened one eye, looking at Sam sitting across from her.

"You know I can't take my eyes off of you whether you're awake or asleep. I hope you don't mind, but I ordered lunch."

"I never mind when you take charge." Nena meant those words. She liked having Sam fuss over her, look out for her.

Eating a lunch of triangle-shaped sandwiches with fillings of prosciutto or shrimp, accompanied with cheese and wine, Nena asked Sam, "How spoiled am I going to be when this trip is over?"

"That's the point, I want you to be spoiled, pampered, and any other adjective you can conjure up."

They lingered in the sun, finishing lunch. Turning to her, he did not have to say a word. He took her hand and led her back to their suite. Once the door to the room closed behind them, Sam pulled Nena close. She could feel his heart beating against hers. She took off her bathing suit, letting it fall to the floor. The heat from his body radiated into her every fiber. He pulled her onto the bed. Neither wanted to move.

"Any chance we'll explore the grounds today?" she whispered in his ear.

"Sooner or later," he whispered in hers.

**

Before dinner they walked through the very gardens where Casanova had a tryst and wooed his lovers. "Sam, the brochures didn't do this place justice. It's extraordinary! And the pastel colors of the buildings are more charming than any picture. This is paradise."

"Glad you came?"

"Uh-huh!"

Cip's Club at the hotel was informal but fashionable, perfectly fitting their mood for dinner. They ordered à la carte, a Venetian Island salad of roots, leaves, and flowers that were artistically presented to resemble a still-life painting; creamy risotto with beans and mussels; and spaghetti con frutta del mare, perfectly cooked pasta surrounded by an appetizing selection of local seafood, shared over fruity glasses of a regional Soave.

Sitting outside on the terrace after dinner, admiring the spectacular view of St. Mark's Square as night fell, completed their first day in Venice.

"How could anyone be remotely blasé coming here? You would have to be the most jaded person in the world," Nena said. "I know I wasn't completely certain this was one of your better ideas, but Sam, it is. I couldn't be happier."

"If you are this happy on our first day, how happy are you going to be tomorrow and all of our tomorrows to come?"

"Happy, very happy, my love! Tomorrow let's do the tourist thing and get a Bellini at Harry's Bar," Nena suggested.

"It's a plan, but tonight will you allow me to be your Casanova. I'm asking you for a rendezvous."

"I thought you'd never ask."

**

The following morning crossing the canal the launch passed by the Hotel Danieli, the magnificent lacy stone structure that appears to rise out of the water, Nena felt apprehensive for the first time since her arrival. She had stayed with Ben at the Hotel Danieli her last trip to Venice. She took a deep breath and reminded herself she was here with Sam, and she would not allow anything to spoil the new memories they were about to make.

Stepping off the launch and walking to the Piazza, she turned to Sam and said, "To be perfectly honest with you and myself, my stomach was in a bit of a knot as we approached the Danieli. That's where Ben and I stayed." All sorts of thoughts ran through Nena's head. Pushing them aside, she looked around her at happy faces, people enjoying themselves. She embraced the moment and said, "This is a wonderful place, and I'm fortunate to be here with you, Sam. Whenever I do something with you I've done before, it's as if I'm doing it for the first time. Seeing Venice with you is *our* first time." In a gesture out of the ordinary for Nena, not being a person for public displays of affection, she cupped his face in her hands and kissed him.

"I like your thinking, Girl. Let's do the tourist thing!"

She loved it when he called her "Girl." It made her feel young. She could pretend it was just the two of them starting out, even though they both had full lives beforehand. This was their life and time together, and she would make every second count.

With guidebook in hand, they filled the day feeding pigeons at the Piazza San Marco, referred to by Napoleon as the drawing room of Europe, and meandered through the streets, weaving in and out of shops where local crafts were on display and a few items caught their fancy. They stopped to sample gelato as they walked the narrow passageways in the old artisan quarters, passing bars the local merchants frequented and where once the famous Venetian courtesans lived. They took a gondola ride and later climbed to the top of Saint Mark's bell tower, and he kissed her for all of Venice to witness.

In the fading light of day, they sat in Harry's Bar and drank Bellini's, then dined at a neighborhood restaurant that served spider crab, sea snails, and mantis shrimp, local marine curios prepared as only the Venetian can prepare seafood. Before returning to the launch, Sam suggested they walk to the Rialto Bridge. Standing on the bridge looking onto the Grand Canal, he turned to Nena.

"Never in my wildest dreams did I ever imagine you would come back into my life. These past years have been the happiest I've ever had. I had two reasons for wanting to come to Venice: the first to bury the past and the second to begin a future. I always thought if I ever proposed to anyone, it would be here, right here on this bridge. Nena, you are the love of my life, and I am asking you to be my wife. I want to share my life with you for the rest of our days."

Nena gasped. She had no idea he had this planned. Her pulse was racing; her heart was pounding. A few seconds seemed like an eternity, until she regained her voice and said yes, without hesitation, she wanted to be married to this man.

"Yes!" she repeated again, overflowing with happiness.

"You will? You will?" He could hardly believe his ears. He really did not know what to expect. He hoped she would say yes, but he was not sure. He reached into his pocket and opened a velvet box containing a pearl ring surrounded by diamonds.

"Sam, this is magnificent. What an exquisite ring. I adore pearls."

"I know you love pearls, and I didn't want the traditional diamond, but I wanted diamonds in there somewhere. A colleague of mine has a friend in the diamond district, and we designed the ring together."

He slid the ring onto her finger.

"It fits perfectly, Sam, just like us." Nena beamed.

"Yes we are a perfect fit. I don't know how I got so lucky at this stage in life, but I did, and I'm not tempting fate."

"Me either darling, me either."

On the portico of this ancient bridge, Sam tenderly kissed Nena and said, "Until death do us part."

On the ride back to the hotel across the Grand Canal, with the lights of the city shimmering on the water, Nena turned to Sam, "Pinch me. I'm beyond happy, and if this isn't for real, I'm not sure I want to know."

"This is for real; we are for real," Sam said reassuringly.

Under the star-studded night sky, Nena rested her head on Sam's shoulder, treasuring the feelings that filled her entire being. "Darling, no one should be this happy. Please never let this moment end."

By the time they arrived at the hotel, the dinner crowd had dispersed to the bar where the pianist was playing a medley of Dean Martin songs in the background. Finding a table Sam ordered champagne.

"A special occasion, Sir?" the waiter inquired.

"As a matter of fact it is. We're engaged."

"Congratulations," he said, looking at Nena and her ring.

"Sweetheart, do you know you're blushing?"

The waiter returned with a bottle of their best champagne and a tray of delicate desserts: chocolate truffles, tiny Tiramisu cookies, fresh raspberries, and the most divine miniature chocolates rolled in hazelnuts and pistachios.

"Compliments of the hotel's general manager Mr. Rusconi and Chef Piccolotto," the waiter said. "A small way of the Cipriani sharing in your happiness."

Thanking him, Sam proposed a toast as they listened to *Memories Are Made of This* being played on the piano and wanting this evening to be frozen in time.

**

The following day they rented a car and drove the Prosecco wine route, stopping to visit wineries along the way. Another day they took the train to Verona, where tourists flock to the balcony and courtyard of the thirteenth-century palazzo, the scene immortalized by Shakespeare in his play of the ill fated lovers, Romeo and Juliet, and stood in line to rub the breast of Juliet's bronze statue for luck. Sam did not want to leave Italy without a visit to the island of Murano, where world-renowned glassmakers have kept alive their art since 1291. At one glassmaker's shop, the owner presented Sam with a box.

"Open it." He gestured to Nena.

Nena opened the box. Inside was a glass figurine of a seal in vivid shades of blue. Sam had the piece commissioned for Nena as an engagement gift, to celebrate the time they spent on Nantucket. It was on this trip Nena gave herself completely to Sam, and both knew their love had bound them together.

"So this is why you wanted to come here. Sam, what a thoughtful present. I will cherish it forever. You were this certain about us?"

"Well, I did have my fingers crossed when I placed the order," he told her, holding up his hand with crossed fingers.

The rest of their trip was spent lingering at the hotel pool, walking the grounds, and dining on the most fantastic of culinary delights. Before leaving, they booked the same room for their honeymoon.

Checking out of the hotel, Mr. Rusconi congratulated them again on their engagement, inquiring if they had enjoyed their stay.

Nena gushed, "It was a trip of dreams, thank you."

Mr. Rusconi told them he and the staff looked forward to seeing them next year. "We will make your honeymoon special."

"We can't wait to come back — there is no place else we would want to celebrate our marriage," she said beaming. "Arrivederci!"

"Arrivederci!"

**

On the plane ride home from Italy, Nena and Sam made a decision to keep their engagement private. For the same reason Nena waited to tell her family about her relationship with Sam, they wanted to wait until the right occasion to make their announcement. They chose December, when Nena would celebrate her sixtieth birthday.

**

When Josh heard, he wondered why they were waiting until the following fall to get married. "Why wait?" he asked.

Sam had accepted a teaching position at Harvard for the fall of 2001, and with the move from the city, and planning a wedding, even though small, practicality won out over impetuosity. In the autumn of 2001, Nena would marry Sam.

"Your decision, but I wouldn't put off 'til tomorrow," Josh advised them, as only he in his straight talking way could.

Chapter 12

The beginning of a new year always brings a sense of hope, and 2001was no exception. Even after a bitter presidential political election, the nation wanted to believe the year ahead could be full of promise.

~~~~~~~~~~~~~~~

J.R. had been wanting to talk to Becky about leaving Salomon to join the family business, but busy work schedules kept the conversation from happening. Sitting in the Crystal Room at Tavern on the Green New Year's Day, waiting to have brunch with Marc, J.R. finally found the right moment.

"Honey, I've been thinking it might be time to seriously consider leaving Salomon," he began. "The last time I had lunch with Dad, he told me his offer still stands. With the constant uncertainty at work, the timing might be right. I wanted to get your input."

Becky listened intently to her husband "I was under the impression you were happy with the changes since Salomon was now part of Citigroup. I don't know what to say; it's a big decision. Have you talked to Marc?"

"Not yet, I wanted to run it by you first. It's a thought that creeps in every once in a while, because I don't know how many more changes I can survive before I'm terminated."

Just then Marc walked into the celebrated glass enclosed room with its massive windows and ornate chandeliers overlooking the restaurant's gardens in Central Park. The restaurant was the quintessential New York destination for celebrities, the elite of New York, and tourists, hosting special occasions from birthdays to weddings.

"A mimosa for the young man." J.R. motioned to the waiter as Marc sat down.

When his mimosa was served and eggs benedict were ordered, J.R. proposed a toast to a new year and the fact Marc had recently been transferred from London to American Express headquarters in the city. Marc responded, "To being back in the Big Apple. To the new year, and to friendships."

"It's great having you in town, Marc — Mr. Vice President — congratulations," Becky said. "We're going to have to get together on a regular basis. Don't know if I should ask, but I'm dying to know. Is there a special woman in your life yet?"

"Not yet, Becky; J.R. snatched her up before I had a chance."

"Come on, Marc, you always say that, and besides you're a heck of a catch. I'm going to have to look around the museum."

"Okay — as long as it's not one of those mummy friends of yours!"

"Enough you two," J.R. interjected. "Tell us, how are the Hobarts and Logans doing? We hear from them, but not often enough."

While waiting for their meal, Marc told them the Hobarts were being transferred to Paris, and the Logans would soon be moving to Belgium. It seemed the old group was going in different directions.

Their food arrived, and while they were eating, J.R. brought up his quandary, valuing Marc's opinion.

"Salomon has been in flux between their problems, the acquisitions, and changes in leadership, but right now they're holding steady and your section is beginning to make money. I hear your frustration, but if I were you, I'd wait things out," Marc advised. "Don't make any decisions in haste. Take your time. The family business will be there. Besides, going into a family business isn't always a sure thing. After Harvard, you chose to carve your own path. Stay on a while longer and see where it takes you. In the end, if you find you've had it with the corporate world, then take up Jay's offer. But before you do, you owe it to yourself to ride Salomon out. You've put a lot of blood and sweat into your career. I wouldn't throw in the towel just yet."

J.R. listened attentively to Marc. He had good business sense and could see issues with clarity. Marc could strip away the emotion.

"I hear you. You're right. I've worked my butt off for this company, and I need to see it through. But you've given me another idea. I'm going to talk with Dad, go into the office every once in a while, bring myself up to speed on the business, just to see if it's even a fit before I consider the company as an alternative to the corporate world."

"Now you're thinking ol' man. That's a brilliant idea."

They lingered over brunch, reliving their years spent in England.

Leaving the tavern, Becky offered, "Why not come for dinner some night next week?"

"Love it. Tell me when. Can't tell you how great it is to be back."

~~~~~~~~~~~~

"Thanks John, send them up. They're here," J.R. announced.

"Pour drinks and entertain them. I have to change."

"Okay boys what's your pleasure?"

"I'll have a scotch on the rocks," said Marc. "Make that two," Danny seconded.

Becky walked into the living room. "Good evening gentlemen. Glad you could come."

"Thanks for having us. Wouldn't miss one of your home-cooked meals, Beck," Danny said as he handed her a bottle of wine.

Presenting Becky with flowers, Marc commented, "What a great place you have here. It's not just the apartment, but the location is enviable."

"Well you know what they say about real estate, especially in this city, location is everything. J.R., show Marc around while I finish dinner."

With the table set and wine poured, they dined on a savory chicken pie filled with winter vegetables, a recipe handed down from her great-grandmother.

"Great meal, Becky." Marc patted his stomach.

"She learned from the best," Danny added. "And speaking of the best, Marc, I can't thank you enough for the door opener."

Danny was a late starter to the world of business. Inspired by his father, he had spent time in Israel during college, where he witnessed young men and woman serving in the military before beginning careers. Observing their dedication to country motivated him to join the Navy directly out of college, where he became a pilot and still served in the reserves. Following the Navy, he attended Harvard Business School, disappointing Josh who wanted his son to attend law school and join him as a partner. No one was surprised by Danny's choices. Since he was a boy, he was strong willed. On Marc's recommendation, he gained an interview with American Express in the company's Bank International Division located in the same building where J.R. worked at 7 World Trade Center.

"All I did was open the door. You had to get both feet in, and I hear through the grapevine you are doing good work over there." Marc gave Danny a thumbs up.

"Thanks again, but it never hurts to have connections."

"And speaking of work, how's everything over at Salomon?" Marc asked J.R. "Made any decisions since we talked?"

"I'm staying the course for the time being. But I started getting my feet wet at Stark. I don't want to give my father any false hopes, but as we discussed at brunch, I owed it to myself to get more involved."

"Wise decision. How's it going?"

"My father amazes me. Even at his age, he is sharp. Nothing gets by him."

"He isn't that old," Becky chimed in.

"You know what I mean. Most men his age are contemplating retirement, but not him. He says, 'What else would I do?' He loves this city, he loves making deals, and the business is really solid."

"Have you come across anything you would do differently?" Marc asked. "We are in the twenty-first century."

"There are a couple of areas he could move into, but it's too early for me to tell. I'm beginning to get the lay of the land, no pun intended, and I haven't made a decision yet. Besides I'm trying to keep emotion out of it."

"Good man, it only clouds the thinking, at least in business." Marc winked at Becky.

Danny listened attentively to these two young men talk. Although not quite a decade older than himself, their business acumen and knowledge awed him. They had lived abroad and had experiences he was yet to have, but hoped he would.

J.R. stood up. "Hate to kick you guys out, but tomorrow is a weekday."

"Before you go, I need the two of you to commit to tickets for the museum's gala in April. Black Tie, and I want you to bring dates. If you can't find any, I'll find them for you," Becky said. They told her to count both themselves in before they headed out the door.

~~~~~~~~~~~~~~~

The gala at the museum turned into a friends and family affair. The event celebrated the opening of a new Egyptian exhibit featuring pieces of fragments from Nebamun's tomb on loan from the British Museum. This was the first big event Becky organized, and her association with the fragments made the occasion especially important to her. Everyone came, including Sam and Ben. Ben knew it would be difficult seeing Nena with Sam, but he would not let anything spoil the night for his daughter. The evening was a huge success. Becky thanked everyone for coming, especially her grandfather who had not been feeling well recently.

"I wouldn't have missed this event for the world, Beck," Peter told his granddaughter, as they walked down the museum stairs out onto Fifth Avenue.

"Grandpa, you've always believed in me. Your love and support have meant the world to me." Becky hugged her grandfather tight, and watched the black limousine slowly disappear down the avenue.

~~~~~~~~~~~~~~~~~~~~~~

Peter had lived a good life. He was a beloved husband, wonderful father, grandfather, great-grandfather, exemplary professor and lecturer, a steady friend, a man of integrity; a man whose passing left a void amongst all who knew him.

Speaker after speaker stood at the lectern and honored Peter, his career, and his life. Then Becky spoke,

"As far back as I can remember, my grandfather was a man I admired. He came to this country tucked safely inside his mother's womb. He never forgot his parent's sacrifice, leaving their homeland, family, and friends, coming to a strange land with a different language and little money, to give their unborn son the opportunities they felt were slipping away from them in Germany," she read on. *"My grandfather loved and served his country both in wartime and in peacetime. He became a professor and married my grandmother. They brought two wonderful children into the world, Uncle Josh and my mother. They were given the same values his parents gave to him. He was a born teacher. He instilled in generations of students at MIT the love of learning, to question, to seek knowledge, and to be honest in the pursuit. Recently he was honored by nearly five hundred of his former students at a testimonial dinner, thanking him for the impact he had on their lives. Besides the professor, there was the father, grandfather, recently a great-grandfather, and friend. Grandpa led his life by example. He held steadfast to his Jewish roots and religion, teaching us tolerance when others were intolerant. He was kind and loving, a gentle man in the truest sense. He lived and loved life to its fullest. He was a man with a big heart, a heart that has now stopped beating. But the memory of him will never die as long as our hearts continue to beat. Rest in peace, Grandpa. You have moved on in your journey, but those of us that remain behind will continue to live the life you have taught us. Grandpa, your flame will burn within us, and we will celebrate you for a life well lived for as long as we live."*

The congregation sat rapt listening to Becky's words. When Becky finished, the rabbi offered prayers, and later the family held a reception at the Colonial Inn.

"We've had many wonderful times here. I know Peter would be pleased you've come to pay your respects, and he wouldn't want this to be a sad occasion. He would want us to remember the good times we've shared." Ruth encouraged the guests, "You must have stories to recount, and we would love to hear them."

Slowly, people began to relate experiences, funny and poignant. When the afternoon came to a close, Nena and Ruth walked to the house. The azaleas were in bloom, and nature was awakening after a long, hard winter.

"Rather sad to think your father won't be here to see the flowering bushes and trees this spring. He enjoyed it when the earth came alive," Ruth said to Nena as they opened the front gate.

"Dad would have found this spring particularly picturesque. That camera of his wouldn't have found a moment's peace. You'll have to take the pictures for him, Mum."

"We'll see, we'll see."

Her mother's response alarmed Nena. Ruth was an active woman. Not a person to sit idly. But with her husband's death, she seemed to have lost her spark.

"You and Daddy were planning another barge trip in France this fall. Any chance you're still planning to go?"

"Oh, it's too early to say. Now Nena, I don't want you worrying about me. You have a lot going on. Your wedding is coming up — Sam's moving to Boston," Ruth sighed. Her mind had wandered to Peter. "Your father was looking forward to you and Sam getting married, especially since it's going to be at his synagogue. He never said anything, but I always knew he wished he would have walked you down that aisle with Ben. Where was I...Oh yes, your wedding, planning a honeymoon, Sam moving to Boston, fall will be here before we know it."

"Mum, the wedding will be small. Sam is going to live at my place until we find something for the two of us, and who knows, he loves my place — maybe we'll stay there. We already know we're going to the Cipriani for our honeymoon. There really isn't that much to plan, but I do want you to come to New York with me to pick out a dress. We'll have a girl's weekend of shopping. How does that sound?"

"Sounds lovely, dear."

Unable to dismiss her mother's impassiveness, Nena suggested they take a walk to the bridge before she went home.

Sitting on the riverbank, next to the Old North Bridge, both women were awash in memories: Ruth engulfed with thoughts of growing up, marrying the love of her life, and raising her family all within the proximity of this beautiful spot; Nena thinking about the last summer spent with her grandmother, strolling to the river at dusk, while her grandmother recounted her life on the farm with her grandfather. Nena began humming the Andy Williams hit song of that summer, "*Moon River*." Ruth reached for her daughter's hand.

On the drive back to Boston, Nena wondered if what happened to her grandmothers would happen to her mother. Both her grandmothers passed away not long after their husbands died. Ruth was not ill like her own mother had been, but Nena was not used to seeing her mother dispirited. She did not want to contemplate losing another parent. "Come on, Girl," she admonished herself as she drove Route 2 to the city, "get a hold of yourself. Your mother is not your grandmother. She'll bounce back. She'll dance at your wedding."

The summer of 2001 was one of transition. On the national level, the country strove to recover from the constant talk of hanging chads resulting from Florida's recount of the presidential election between Al Gore and George W. Bush. Slowly life was returning to some sort of normalcy, lazy days at the beach and people trying to beat the dog days of August.

"I'm taking a week's vacation in August to work with Dad," J.R. told Becky one morning, as they were getting ready for work.

Until now he had been going into the office whenever he could find some extra time. He was hoping a week at the family business would help solidify his decision as he struggled making a choice regarding his career.

"Don't forget we're going to the Hamptons for a week the end of the month," Becky reminded him. "I wish we were going now. I can't wait to get away from this heat wave."

"I haven't forgotten; in fact Marc still owes me for his share."

They were renting a house for the summer with Marc. Becky had kept her promise and had introduced Marc to a coworker, hoping she and Marc would hit it off.

Nena and Ruth had taken the train from Boston. They were meeting Becky at Bergdorf Goodman, the venerable Manhattan store housed in what had been an elegant Vanderbilt mansion situated across from Central Park when mansions ruled Fifth Avenue. Nena was relieved her mother was beginning to gain some of her spark following Peter's death. Her fears that she might lose her were beginning to recede, as she watched her mother come alive.

"I'm excited to see what you find today," Ruth said. "I never thought I would help my daughter shop for a second wedding dress."

"I never thought I would be shopping a second time for a wedding dress with my mother and my daughter."

Any uncomfortable feelings that had existed between Nena and Becky had been resolved, mostly Nena suspected because Ben was in remission, and at least outwardly he accepted her relationship with Sam. But whatever the reason, Nena was grateful.

"Here she comes." Ruth's face lit up as she watched her granddaughter approach. "Are we ready?" she asked as she took the arms of Nena and Becky and walked inside the store.

"I want something with lace, but not fussy, perhaps tea length," Nena told the saleswoman.

The sales consultant returned with two dresses. A pale yellow lace dress, falling just below the knee, designed by Oscar de la Renta, and a long-sleeve, champagne-colored mid-calf silk dress overlaid with lace by Chanel. It was a difficult decision, but in the end Nena selected the Chanel for the wedding, and splurged by buying the de la Renta to take on her honeymoon. Expensive, but money well spent. Once she bought her shoes, the women were off to the Plaza for tea. The Palm Court with its fan-mirrored doors, gold décor, beautiful floral arrangements, and live palm trees was a haven in a busy city.

Tea consisted of tiny sandwiches — salmon, roast beef, and cucumber, while desserts were offered from the trolley. As cups of earl grey and jasmine tea were poured, the topic of conversation turned to the wedding. Originally the wedding was going to be held in Peter's synagogue, but since his passing, they opted for the rabbi's study. Nena could not bear the thought of Peter's absence. Dinner would be at the Colonial Inn, with a get-together at her parents' home afterward.

"Mum, J.R. and I are glad you chose October 7th. We're going to take advantage of the long weekend, add a few days and drive to Maine."

"Speaking of Maine, has Jay decided what he's going to do about the house?"

"No, he never talks about it. Maybe you can ask him tonight at dinner."

Nena and Ruth were guests at Jay's apartment while in the city, and they were meeting Sam, Jay, J.R., and Danny at Nino's later that night.

"We hope he keeps it. We go to Maine as often as we can, and Jay even went for a few weeks this summer. Did you know Dad and Uncle Buddy joined him for a week of fishing?"

"No, I didn't, but I'm pleased to hear it."

A visit to the museum followed tea. Becky had a treat in store for her mother and grandmother. Riding the elevator into the bowels of the museum where Becky worked, was another world of art where restorers were busy at work on everything from paintings to sculptures. There were rooms filled to the rafters with precious antiquities and works of art to equal the exhibitions, display cases and galleries that greeted visitors to the museum above ground.

"With the hours I've spent in this museum, I never would have imagined this exists below the street," Nena commented to her daughter in awe.

"I knew you would enjoy this," Becky replied, taking them to see the artifacts she was cataloging. They eventually made their way back to the museum's glorious entrance hall, with its massive archways opening to the grand staircase, all of these architectural features combining to give the museum an Old World feel, even now in the year 2001.

Proceeding to the impressionist gallery, standing in front of Pissarro's *The Garden of the Tuilerie on a Spring Morning*, Ruth reflected, "I remember last fall when your father and I visited Paris and sat on a bench in that very garden. We were planning another barge trip this fall. I'm glad we went when we did." Speaking directly to her daughter, she continued, "We don't understand or realize how short life really is, dear. I'm happy you've found love again, and you and Sam are going to have a second chance. Enjoy every minute of planning this wedding, and hold onto the fact a second chance has come your way."

"I'm happy too, Mum, but it's his first chance, and my second. And not too many people get either at this stage in life. Believe me, I'm counting my blessings." But Nena heard what her mother said, and realized Ruth would not be taking another barge trip now that Peter was gone.

~~~~~~~~~~~~~~

"Look who I brought home for dinner," J.R. announced as he walked in the door.

"I can't imagine," Becky said, knowing it was Marc.

At least once a week, Marc dined with them. He and J.R. had become close. Marc had one sibling, a sister, and J.R. was an only child. Over the years, a brotherly relationship developed between them.

"What's being served this evening?" Marc asked, placing a bottle of wine on the kitchen counter, peeking in the oven.

"You need to give a girl some notice. You're lucky I'm flexible mister, and I never really learned to cook for two," she chided him.

"How about setting Mondays aside?"

"On a regular basis? Don't you think that might be a little difficult with our schedules?"

This banter continued while Becky plated the roasted chicken and Marc helped J.R. set the table.

"I need to tell you two something, but you have to swear to secrecy," Marc announced as dinner was about to be served.

"Pinky swear," Becky assured him.

"I'm getting a promotion. Just call me Mr. President."

"Do we have any champagne?" J.R. turned to Becky.

"You know we always keep a bottle chilled. You get the champagne; I'll get the glasses."

"When did you find out?" J.R. asked.

"This morning…and you are the two people I wanted to celebrate with — well except for my parents, but they're in Florida. I'm not certain when the announcement will be made, so no spreading the word."

After dinner the celebration continued to the Café Carlyle where, on Monday nights, Woody Allen played his clarinet. More champagne was ordered, more toasts were made — life was good.

"Another month and you'll no longer be a free man." Josh needled his future brother-in-law as he tended the grill.

It was the annual Labor Day gathering at Josh's, a ritual he had taken over the last few years of Peter's life.

"I'm counting the days, Josh. I waited for your sister my entire life, and I can't wait for our life together to begin," Sam told him.

Nena approached. "Less talk and get grilling Josh. Mind if I steal Sam for a minute?"

"I wanted to talk with you about your trip to the city." Sam had moved in with Nena. He had sold his apartment in the city and was making a final trip to attend the closing. "Do you really have to go?" she asked.

"Well, if I don't go tomorrow, I have to go next week. I need to finish cleaning out the apartment, and then there is the closing. I want to have everything wrapped up before the wedding. I don't want to return from our honeymoon looking back. I want my past in the past, tied up with a nice ribbon and bow." He looked intently at Nena. She had the appearance of a woman younger than her age. His heart melted and he gave in. "Okay, you win, I'll rearrange my schedule, but I have to go next week; I can't put it off any longer."

"Okay, but that means I have you this week. Right?"

"Yes…have I told you lately how much I love you? Nena, I wish we were getting married tomorrow."

He took her hand in his. "Maybe we should have eloped, or I should have married you in Italy; this waiting is driving me crazy. When you're our age, every day counts."

~~~~~~~~~~~~

Nena had prepared Sam's favorite breakfast. The aroma of eggs and bacon, blueberry muffins and freshly brewed coffee filled the kitchen. "I heard a way to a man's heart is through his stomach," she told Sam.

"You already have my heart. What's really on your mind?"

"I don't want you to go." Pouring Sam a cup of coffee, Nena continued. "You know except for our honeymoon we aren't going to have a break until the holidays. I know I sound like a broken record, but you don't have to be at the closing."

Sam could not argue Nena's point, but he saw this trip as a rite of passage. He could have had his attorney send him the papers, however Sam was a man of ceremony and ritual. The sale of the apartment symbolized where he had spent his life as a bachelor and represented his past. He was closing the door on his past to open another door with the woman of his dreams. He hoped she could understand the importance of him being there.

"I hear you, honey, but it's something I want to do. I'm going to stay at the apartment tonight. The Salvation Army and cleaning people will come tomorrow. Tuesday morning is the closing, and then I'll be all yours. I've lived in the city a long time…I never thought I'd be leaving."

"Going to miss it?"

"Maybe a little." A yearning for her rushed through his body. "Mrs. Katz-to-be, I'm going to miss you more these next two days. Have you made the bed yet?"

"Would it make any difference if I had?"

"Not really." In the bedroom, he undressed. She untied her bathrobe revealing her figure through a sheer nightgown.

"I can't get enough of you. Sweetheart, you take my breath away." Sam took his time admiring Nena as his hands caressed her face and neck. He gently slipped off her robe unable to take his eyes off her. His hands moved to the straps on her nightgown. He slid the straps off her shoulders and he watched as the gown fell to the floor exposing her body, which was taut and firm for a woman her age. Their bodies' resembled magnets locked together with a force beyond their control. Nena's back was to the bed. Sam placed one arm around her waist and the other behind her neck. As he pulled her even closer, their passion erupted before they made it onto the bed.

"Darling do you really have to go?" she asked putting on her robe. "You can handle this over the phone and by fax. You don't need to be at the closing, and I bet your super would clean out the apartment, if you paid him enough. Please don't go." Sam was sitting on edge of the bed as she stood in front of him, looking deeply into his eyes. "I want you to stay here with me."

"Darling, I would love too, but I want to be there for the closing. Please try to understand. If I had gone last week, I'd be back," he reminded her, trying to make light of her concern.

Not wanting to hear his response, she pressed herself on top of Sam as he fell back onto the bed.

She murmured she loved him as they made love with an intensity neither one knew they were capable of.

Standing at the door, Nena spoke the familiar words. "And drive carefully."

Nena's words of concern tickled him. "I'll call, and I'll drive like a little old lady!" he called out."

~~~~~~

"Thanks for meeting me for lunch on such short notice."

Morton's The Steakhouse on 90 West Street with its purple awning and classic wooden door, decorated with the legendary gold-plated Morton's logo, was a favorite haunt of the Wall Street crowd. Marc had asked J.R. to meet him there for lunch.

Inside the main entrance wine lockers held private bottles of wine — *boire de la vigne* — for patrons. The dining room off to the right, with its dark mahogany walls covered with pictures of sports and entertainment figures, and the political elite, contrasted with the plain white tablecloths topped with wooden-handled utensils and Morton's signature pig lamps, giving the room an atmosphere of a private club. They approached the hostess table, situated in the narrow hall, and were shown to their table.

"Thanks for coming," Marc said.

"No problem," J.R. replied. "Lately it's been me using you for a sounding board. I'm glad I can return the favor. Let's order. I'm not up for steak today, how about shrimp cocktail, beefsteak tomatoes, and a juicy prime burger?"

"Sounds good to me!"

"Well my man, what's going on?" J.R. inquired.

Marc reminded J.R. he had planned a two-week vacation to Europe, but that morning he had been presented with a conundrum. He had been requested to attend a breakfast meeting at Windows on the World, at the top of One World Trade Center, the very day he was to leave. "There's a rumor it's about my promotion, but you know what I think about office cooler rumors. I've planned this trip for months. I'm not sure what to do at this point; any suggestions?"

"I think if it were about your promotion, you'd have been advised. Listen if I was you and my boss requested me to attend a breakfast meeting at Windows, I'd rearrange my schedule, toute de suite. If nothing else, you'll find out what's really going on. They could care less if you're leaving for Europe. Plane tickets can be changed."

Marc needed to hear what he already knew and what J.R. confirmed. He would change his itinerary when he returned to the office. J.R. was happy to accommodate his friend, considering all the advice he had received from Marc. Before leaving the restaurant, J.R. ordered a legendary Morton's hot chocolate cake.

Marc asked, "Why the cake?" J.R. told Marc that Danny was coming for dinner that night.

"Don't I get an invite?" Marc more than hinted.

"We thought you'd be packing. Beg some more and I'll call Becky and tell her to set another plate."

Marc poked J.R. in the ribs as they walked up West Street, outside the quietude of Morton's, and into the hustle and bustle of the financial district. The talk turned to the upcoming matchup that night between the New York Giants and the Denver Broncos on *Monday Night Football*, both of them wondering how the Giants would fare this season after losing the Super Bowl earlier in the year.

**

"I haven't been to Morton's for lunch yet." Danny was feeling his junior status in the group, as he and the others enjoyed the hot chocolate cake J.R. had bought at Morton's earlier.

Marc knew how it felt to be the junior member of a group. "You will in due time. Trust me, I'm not jaded, but there's nothing as good as Becky's home cooking."

Taking advantage of Marc's flattery, Becky asked him if he would bring her a few things from Europe if she promised him another home-cooked meal when he returned from London and the continent.

"Of course, your wish is my command."

With an impish grin, Becky handed Marc a prepared list, knowing he would not refuse her request.

At halftime of the football game, Marc got up to leave.

"I'd better get going, busy day tomorrow. I have breakfast at Windows and then packing for my vacation. Danny let's share a cab." He gave Danny a nod.

"Have a safe trip." Becky hugged Marc good night. "J.R. told me you're flying on the Concorde; lucky you. See you when you return, and we'll see *you* Danny on Saturday."

She and J.R. walked Marc and Danny to the elevator. Becky blew kisses as the elevator door closed.

~~~~~~

Sam thought about the first time Nena stayed with him at his apartment. Until his relationship with her, his apartment was lifeless — a place where he hung his hat, wrote, prepared lectures, and slept. Now this space he called home for years flooded him with happy memories because Nena had walked back into his life.

The Salvation Army arrived to pick up the few remaining pieces of furniture. The last piece to be carried out was the bed. As he watched the men lift the bed through the door into the hallway, he thought about the times he and Nena had made love in that bed, how she would stir and nuzzle her body into his before she fully awoke. Even when they did not make love, it was enough for him to have her close, but when they did make love, his world soared to heights he had never experienced with any other woman. He paid the cleaning company, locked the door behind him, and headed for the hotel. Tomorrow he would be back in her arms.

Spending his last night in the city a single man, Sam stayed at the Waldorf. He had reserved room 42H3 in the tower, where he and Nena had spent their first night together, and where their relationship began. When he entered the room, he wished she was there. He picked up the phone.

"Guess where I am Nena?"

"Don't tell me you're still at the apartment at this hour?"

"No, the move went well, and I can't wait for the closing tomorrow. I'm in 42H3 at the Waldorf. I wanted to feel close to you. This room is where we first made love — when I knew I was wildly in love with you, and if you didn't love me back, my life would never be the same."

"Reminiscing a little, are we?"

"I'm missing you terribly. I'm looking at the bed and I see you. The way you made me feel. I remember how the sheets felt when we first got into bed. I remember looking at you, touching you, feeling your body next to mine. I wanted to savor each moment, not rush a thing. I had fantasized about you for years, and my fantasy was coming true. How many people can say that? I thought my heart would jump out of my chest before we finally made love. And when we did, and did again, my fantasy became my reality come true."

Nena could feel the passion in his voice. "I can't wait for you to come home," she told him. "I understand you wanting to be present to close on the apartment, I got that, but I know the attorneys can handle the closing without you there. *Please* reconsider and come home to me tonight. I'll wait up."

"Perhaps you're right, but I'm here now. My appointment is at nine. I should be on the road by noon, and back by cocktail hour, barring traffic, and I know…I'll drive carefully — like a little old lady."

"Sam don't joke; be careful. I don't know what I'd do without you."

"Honey, I'm sorry. I don't mean to make light of your concern for me. In fact it's one of the things I love about you. I'll be home before you know it. I love you Nena; sweet dreams, sweetheart."

"Sweet dreams my love." Nena hung up the phone and began to weep. She did not know why she was crying, but she wished Sam was with her in Boston and not in New York.

Sam climbed into the king-sized bed. "Maybe this wasn't such a terrific idea," he thought. He missed Nena and wanted her by his side in this bed, where they once had made such passionate love that he could still taste her. He closed his eyes, drifting off to sleep and remembering that night.

Chapter 13

The cool weather of September was a welcome change in comparison to the heat of August. Tuesday, the ninth of September, was a beautiful late summer day in New York City.

Marc arose early, wishing he could have gotten out of the breakfast meeting at Windows. He would have preferred to be on a plane flying to London. He knew this meeting had nothing to do with his promotion, but he had no idea why the meeting had been called unexpectedly. As he sat drinking a cup of coffee, he pondered his life. He had been dating Becky's friend from the museum. He liked her well enough, but she was not that special someone. He sensed she cared for him more than he cared about her, and did not want to lead her on. When he returned from this trip he would tell her their relationship had no future. Perhaps they could be friends.

"Christ! How many times in my life have I done this? Too many," he thought. While talking to himself, he could no longer deny there was someone he wanted desperately. Not a friend of a friend, but someone he knew. There had never been another woman before like her. That morning over a cup of coffee, he admitted to himself he had fallen in love with his best friend's wife. From the day he met Becky, he was smitten. The years turned those feelings into a deep love, from which he could no longer hide. Shaken by this realization, his thoughts scared the hell out of him. Now, what to do about it?

"Maybe I should be having a stiff drink this morning instead of coffee," he said aloud as he paced around his condo. "Good God, man, how could you have let this happen? What the hell are you going to do now? How are you going to continue being around this woman without wanting to touch her, hold her, make love to her, tell her that you are crazy, madly in love with her?"

He admonished himself. He had to come up with a solution. He would approach this methodically. He did this every day when solving problems at work. As if lightning struck, he decided while abroad he would assess the situation in the London office and speak with his boss when he returned. He knew moving back to the UK would be a risk to his career, but his friendship with J.R. faced a greater risk. "I need to get out of here for Becky, J.R., and me," he told himself.

Marc realized the genie was out of the bottle, and he could not put it back. He continued to pace around his condo trying to concentrate on the day ahead, while thoughts of Becky filled his head. He wanted to hold her in his arms.

Walking to the North Tower, Building One at the World Trade Center, Marc tried to control his emotions. When he had a chance to calm down, he knew the UK idea was ridiculous. "What the heck is going on with you?" he thought. "You're being groomed to be president of your division. That's in the New York office, not London. If you turn it down, you might as well leave the company. You will be committing career suicide. They'll think you lost your mind."

Of course he had lost his mind, in a way, over a very special woman he could not have.

**

The ringing of the phone awakened Sam. It was his seven o'clock wakeup call. While shaving, he recalled the morning he showered with Nena. He committed to memory the smell of the soap as he washed her body. Now he wished he had gone home. He could have had the attorney send him the papers. She was right; he did not have to be at the closing. Why had he been obsessive about this? Should he call the attorney and go home, home to Nena?

"No, the plans are made," he told himself. "You wanted to be present; go and get it over with."

**

Marc looked at his watch — 7:45 a.m. Entering the lobby of Building One, he stepped into the elevator. The meeting was not until nine o'clock. He had time to spare. Instead of going directly to Windows, he got off at the 105th floor, and stopped at Cantor Fitzgerald to set up an appointment for when he returned from his trip, regarding their corporate business account with American Express. When he finished, he got back on the elevator and rode to the restaurant. The door opened on the 107th floor.

**

Sam dressed and grabbed a quick breakfast. He thought of calling Nena, but decided to call her when he got to the attorney's office. Leaving his car at the hotel, he took the subway to One World Trade Center. Inside the building, riding the packed elevator, he checked his watch. It was almost 8:45. He did not want to be late. The sooner he signed the papers, the sooner he could go home. His thoughts were consumed with Nena, their wedding, their honeymoon, and their new life together. He looked around the elevator, wondering if everyone was as happy as he.

**

Marc walked to a window. The skyline of Manhattan stretched before him. He admired the view. Still feeling totally off his game, he hoped his preoccupation would not be apparent during the meeting. Again he checked his watch — 8:46. He turned one last time to look out the window before walking toward his table, unable to shake Becky from his mind.

**

Sam's elevator began to climb. It made two stops. As it ascended upward without warning, the cage began to sway and then bounced up and down twice and came to an abrupt stop.

**

In the next instant a deafening roar of an airplane engine filled the air, followed by the noise of an explosion. Dishes flew off the tables along with the breaking of glass. The building swayed back and forth. Marc stumbled and fell to the floor. He stood up and looked around to see a room of faces that seemed as confused as he. When people were able to collect themselves, they realized something terrible had happened. It did not take them long to find out a plane had crashed into the building.

**

Sam looked up, they were on the 91st floor. His appointment was on the 94th floor. If he had to, he could get out and walk the three flights, but the door jammed when the elevator stopped. What he did not know, what no one in the elevator knew — a plane had just flown into the building between the 94th and 98th floors. A woman pressed the emergency button...nothing happened. "Christ!" someone shouted. "Late two days in a row; I'll have my ass fired."

"Ring the bell again," someone else called out. Still nothing.

"Here, I have a jack knife." A man worked his way to the front of the elevator. "Let me see if I can pry the door open." With his attempt, the door opened, and the passengers spilled out onto the floor.

"I smell smoke," a voice cried out. "There must be a fire." Everyone began to run to the exit.

Sam did not know what to do. "How bad can it be? This place must be fireproof," he thought. "Three flights, no problem."

"Hey Mister!" a young woman shouted at him. "You're going up; you should be going down!"

"I have an appointment at nine," he called back as he watched her walk down the stairwell.

By the time he climbed ten stairs, the smoke became thicker. He realized in an instant he had made the wrong choice. He started down the stairs. He could not see. The smoke became thicker and blacker. Voices echoed from floor to floor, bouncing off the walls while people called out for help or directions. He too called out, but through the confusion he could not understand what people were saying. The fog of smoke turned into a thick solid cloud until he could hardly breathe.

**

Frantically people began to make telephone calls for help. When the seriousness of the situation became evident, calls instead went to loved ones. Marc tried to call his parents, then J.R. and Becky, no response. He left messages on their phones. As the floors began to groan he and a group decided to go to the roof, but they could not get past the door. Fire erupted and the smoke became unbearable. Then the building began to twist and bend from the impact of the plane. In the space of an hour and a half the ceilings fell, the floors buckled, and the once glorious building and pride of New York City collapsed. Marc's world went dark.

**

"Why didn't I listen to Nena?" he thought. The words were swirling in his head. He tried to count what floor he might be on. Sam had one goal...to get outside and back to Boston. He reached a landing and stepped on something. He noticed the briefcase of the young woman who pointed out he was going the wrong direction, and saw her lying on the stairs nearly unconscious. Sam picked her up and carried her down the stairwell until he began to feel his legs buckle. He stopped to catch his breath, and when he did, he felt his lungs fill with the searing heat from the smoke. He fell, gripping his chest. With his last ounce of strength, Sam called out..."Nena."

~~~~~~~~~~~~~~~~~~~~

Danny had been living with three roommates since moving to New York. He had found an apartment with Jay's help, but he wanted another opinion before he signed on the dotted line and had called J.R. to meet him at the apartment before work. The apartment, a third-floor walkup in an old brownstone, was on 85th Street, off Broadway, in an up-and-coming area for young people. When Danny arrived, he sat on the stoop and waited for J.R.

~~~~~~~~~~~~~~~~~~~~

"Becky, would you please turn on *The Today Show* and catch the weather forecast for me?" J.R. asked as he dressed for work that morning.

"It's going to be a beautiful day, eighty degrees, and no mention of Hurricane Erin," she told him. "Maybe we could sneak out to the Hamptons while Marc is away. We'd have the place to ourselves. The weather is supposed to be great right through the weekend."

"That's an idea. What's on your agenda today, honey?"

Becky told him she was going to call her mother and talk wedding plans as she did not have to be at the museum until ten. J.R. commented Nena must be excited and bet she could hardly wait for the big day. Becky had accepted her mother's relationship with Sam. Still another part of her felt an overwhelming sadness for her father, knowing he had never stopped loving Nena.

"I knew you'd come around about Sam, Becky. Your mother is lucky to have this second chance, and we need to support her."

**

"You'd better sign the lease quick," J.R. advised Danny as he looked around the apartment. "The location is ideal. You made a good choice, my man." J.R. patted Danny on the shoulder. The lease signed, they walked a block to the 86th and Broadway subway station; it was 8 a.m.

Danny suggested they get off the train at Chambers Street, grab a cup of coffee, and walk the remainder of the way to Seven World Trade Center. With all the havoc at work, J.R. did not mind being a little late.

Coffee in hand, talking shop, they approached Vesey Street. For some reason, J.R. looked at his watch. It was 8:46. Suddenly, they heard the thunderous sound of an airplane overhead. Stopping, they looked up to see an airplane heading directly for One World Trade Center. Neither could move. Standing transfixed, as if their feet had been planted in cement, they watched the plane crash into the building. Neither man knew how long they stood there, immobilized, looking toward the sky, until a cacophony of unbearable ear-piercing alarms brought them back to the here and now. Horrified by what they had just witnessed, reality set in as pandemonium broke out — people were screaming and running in every direction.

When the aftershock began to settle in, Danny asked J.R. what time it was.

Before he could tell Danny it was 9:03, another loud roar came from the sky. They could not see what caused the noise, but it sounded like an explosion. They had no idea another building had been attacked by a plane.

J.R. grabbed Danny's arm and began to run up West Broadway. "Come on Kid, run; run like you've never run before," he yelled.

They had made their way from West Broadway onto Sixth Avenue, looking back as they ran. The plane they observed minutes before had disappeared. Smoke billowed from the upper floors of One World Trade Center. The sky appeared to rain confetti, which in reality was tons of paper falling from the blown out office windows, paperwork that had minutes earlier been waiting for offices to open and the workday to begin. While debris filled the air, the noise of metal twisting and bending reverberated everywhere, evoking the throes of a wounded animal. The building began to rupture followed by shattering blasts akin to violent cracks of lightning and ear-deafening explosions.

Instinctively, they kept running. As they ran, they could see flashes of red and orange behind them. The smell of smoke became intense, permeating everything around them. In these moments life seemed surreal, similar to being in a surround-sound movie, watching a film where the world was coming to an end, except they were unaware of the cause. Run is all they could do to survive.

Enormous gray-white clouds of pulverized concrete and gypsum rushed through the streets like a runaway train. The dust became three inches thick in places, raining a pyroclastic flow from the sky. The entire scene appeared akin to a volcanic eruption, but this was New York City. J.R. and Danny could see the dust cloud in the distance, mingled with debris from the buildings, turning day into night as they continued north. When J.R. checked his watch again, they had been on the move for over an hour. They did not stop moving until they reached Central Park and safety.

Sitting on the grass, catching their breath, Danny blurted, "What the hell happened J.R.?"

"I have no idea, but you're coming home with me. We need a shower and a change of clothes. We'll find out soon enough."

**

"Good morning. I don't have to be at the museum until ten. I thought I would check in on your last-minute wedding details," Becky told her mother.

Nena hoped to hear Sam's voice on the other end of the line, except it was her daughter. "I thought you might be Sam...he's closing on the apartment this morning."

"I forgot about Sam being in the city. We should have had him over for dinner."

"That's sweet of you, but he was exhausted by the time he got to the hotel last night. There'll be plenty of other times...wait a minute...there's some sort of breaking news on CNN. Oh my god...turn on your TV."

Becky changed the channel to CNN. There were graphics on the screen that read: "WORLD TRADE CENTER DISASTER." Carol Lin broke the news:

> *"This just in. You are looking at obviously a very disturbing live shot there. That is the World Trade Center, and we have unconfirmed reports this morning that a plane has crashed into one of the towers of the World Trade Center. CNN Center right now is just beginning to work on this story, obviously calling our sources and trying to figure out exactly what happened, but clearly something relatively devastating is happening this morning there on the south end of the island of Manhattan. That is, once again, a picture of one of the towers of the World Trade Center."*

A minute later, the vice president of finance for CNN, in an on-air phone call from his office in New York, reported a large commercial passenger jet crashed into the World Trade Center.

"Mum, J.R. is there," Becky said in pure disbelief. "Mum, are you there?" Becky tried to be calm, but she was barely holding it together.

In what seemed like forever, Nena's words stuck in her throat. "Sam's there too," she finally replied. "That's where he was meeting his attorney at nine."

Dead silence filled the line. Neither woman could speak. Their loved ones were in peril, and there was nothing they could do. Becky at last broke the silence, asking her mother if she thought the country was being attacked.

"I don't know, Beck. Can we please stay on the line?"

Shortly after nine, Becky and Nena watched as a second plane flew into Two World Trade Center.

"I don't believe what I'm seeing!" Becky shouted into the phone. "Mummy, I'm going to hang up. I need to see if I can reach anyone who knows where J.R. might be. You need to call Uncle Josh to see if he's heard from Danny. We can keep in touch by email, I don't want to tie up the lines. I will call the Waldorf and find out when Sam left, and if they have any information. I will let you know when I hear something, and you do the same. Mum, I love you; hang in there."

"I love you too, Beck; I'm trying."

Nena hung up the phone and began to pray. "Please Lord, don't let anything happen to Sam. Bring him home to me," she whispered. She was feeling selfish knowing what had happened meant scores of people would be missing a family member this night. The realization plagued her, especially because Sam had not contacted her that morning, not a single word. He would have if he were safe.

Becky went into high gear. First she called J.R.'s office — no answer; next his cell — a busy signal. Then she called Marc's cell, forgetting he was supposed to be at a breakfast meeting that morning. The call went straight to voicemail. The minute she heard the message she remembered he had a breakfast meeting at Windows on the World.

"Oh my god, Marc. Oh no!" Listening to the message and seeing the pictures on television, Becky knew there would have to be a miracle for him to have survived.

Suddenly, her concern for J.R. and Danny grew even stronger. She stayed glued to the television coverage while emailing everyone in her address book.

The news continued to worsen, if that was possible. The Trade Center buildings were on fire and collapsing. Another plane thought to have been hijacked went down in a field in Western Pennsylvania. Another flew into the Pentagon. The country *was* under attack.

Becky looked at the clock — 11 a.m., and still no contact with J.R. or Danny. She was frantic. She could not reach a single person. She called the museum, but the lines were busy. She thought of walking there, but knew she needed to stay home in case J.R. tried to reach her there. She called the Waldorf and then called her mother.

"Mum, it's me." Becky had no new information, but knew her mother was sitting by the phone. "The Waldorf said Sam left his car and took the subway downtown. They had the contact information for his lawyer's office, but nothing else."

Nena had been glued to the television, but the feeling of hope she had was now turning to despair.

"I called Josh, and they haven't heard a word from Danny. I'm scared. I'm worried Sam is in those buildings that were attacked."

"I'll call you as soon as I hear anything," Becky told her. "In the meantime don't give up hope, please. I know I gave you a hard time when I found out about you and Sam, but he's grown on me. He's a decent man, and I want the two of you to be happy. I really do, Mum. Please hold on."

Becky hung up the phone feeling weary. She went into the kitchen to make a cup of tea.

Tea always soothed her, but would it in this case? Regardless, it was all she could think to do.

Becky took her tea to the living room. As she listened intently to the latest updates on the television, the ringing of the phone startled her. She was afraid to answer. When she did, the teacup she had been holding fell from her hands and shattered into pieces on the floor. The voice on the other end caused her heart to stop. "Is that you J.R.?"

"What's that noise?" he asked.

"Nothing, nothing. Where are you?" she pleaded. "I tried to call you."

"I tried to call you too, but I lost my signal. Becky, Danny, and I..."

Relief overcame Becky. He and Danny were together.

"...are crossing Madison; we're almost home. I'll tell you about it when we get there."

Becky's hands were shaking as she hung up the phone. She told herself to calm down and immediately dialed Nena's number.

"Mum, I heard from J. R; Danny is with him. I don't have any details, but they're almost home. I'll call Jay. Please call Uncle Josh. He and Auntie Gabby must be worried sick."

"Oh thank the Lord. I'll call Josh right away. I don't suppose you've heard anything about Sam..."

"I'm sorry, Mum, I haven't, but I know as soon as J.R. gets here he'll try to find out something. He and Jay have a lot of contacts. Don't give up hope," Becky stressed. This was a mantra that would be repeated over and over across the city and the country in the coming days.

**

The door opened. She was never so glad to see anyone in her entire life as she was to see her husband standing there. Becky fell into J.R.'s arms, and then held Danny close. No words were spoken between them. What words could be spoken? A cataclysmic event had taken place, and their friends and loved ones had all been affected.

A million questions flooded Becky's mind. She could only say, "Look at the two of you. You look like you've run a marathon, and the smell, what's that smell?"

J.R.'s mind was a blur, and Danny appeared to have seen a ghost. "I think we need to shower," J.R. mumbled. He needed time to pull himself together before he talked about what he and Danny had witnessed.

"You must be hungry. I'll fix something while you shower." Her words sounded silly as she spoke them. She really did not know what else to say.

In the guest bedroom, Danny removed his clothes. He noticed the sickening smell Becky questioned; an acrid odor of smoke mixed with jet fuel. Looking in the mirror, he hardly recognized himself. In the shower as he washed the stench from his body, he could not stop thinking about watching that plane head toward Tower One. Would he ever get that image out of his head?

In his room, J.R. was having the same experience as he undressed. It was the first time since he looked up and saw the plane that he tried to digest what had happened. Nothing made any sense. He walked into the shower. Unable to turn on the faucet, he stood there naked, and trembling.

"Are you all right in there?" Becky went into the bathroom to check on him. "Here, let me help you with the water." She turned on the tap and stared at this man she loved to her bones. There he stood, staring blankly at the shower wall.

The phone rang in the bedroom. "Hello Jay, I was about to call you," Becky answered. "J.R. is home. He and Danny are here. They are taking showers, but honestly Jay, they are both in shock. They saw something that has deeply shaken them. Jay, would you please come over? I need you; we all need you. Oh and Jay, we haven't had any word on Sam...Yes, please keep trying...Love you too."

Becky went to the kitchen. She ladled two bowls of soup left from the night before, poured two glasses of wine, and set them on trays in the living room. She put a change of clothing in the guest room for Danny, checked on J.R., and went into the living room and poured herself a glass of wine. J.R. and Danny walked into the room outwardly looking fit, but what was going on inside of these two men was a different story.

"If the soup isn't warm enough, I'll reheat it." Becky usually knew what to say under most circumstances, but these were not most circumstances.

"No, this is fine Beck." She had never seen her husband this pensive.

"Do you mind if we watch the television for a few minutes?" Becky looked at J.R. for a reaction. She was beside herself wanting to know what they had been through, but understood they needed to process what they had seen. Maybe watching the news would help, because she did not know what else to do.

In no time, footage showed the first plane soaring into Tower One. Danny stood up. "Oh my god, oh my god, we saw the first plane, J.R. We actually saw that; it wasn't a hallucination. Who would do this? Oh my god, we saw this happen."

Holding his head in his hands, Danny began to pace around the room until he broke down and cried.

J.R. sat impassive on the couch. He was breathing heavily, afraid that if he spoke a word, just one word, he would fall apart. He felt the tears fill his eyes, and when he looked up at Danny, this young man so full of life a few hours earlier, getting his first apartment in the city, running with him for nearly five miles through utter chaos and terror, he broke down. Danny sat down and reached out to J.R., and in each other's arms they were bound together for life from this day forward.

Becky sat and watched. There were no words, only to be eternally grateful they were alive.

**

Days later a message came through on Becky and J.R.'s phones. It was the call from Marc. Hearing the calm in his voice, gave them hope. In the following weeks, Jay, J.R., Danny, and Becky scoured the city, showing photographs, asking everyone and anyone they could if they knew of the whereabouts of Marc and Sam. Eventually, Sam's body was recovered, but never Marc's. Becky would never know how much Marc loved her. He would live on in their memories, and in his recorded messages they saved.

Nena was devastated. She held a memorial service for Sam at Columbia, and hundreds turned out to eulogize this man, the love of her life. October 7, the day she and Sam had planned to get married, she left for Italy. She wanted to be alone in the place where Sam proposed, where they planned their future, and where they had planned to begin their new life together. She needed time to heal from her loss.

Chapter 14

A few weeks after the terrible tragedy of 9/11, Becky had another event rock her world. Jay invited her and J.R. for dinner; he had something important to discuss. Jay wanted to wait until they were finished with dinner, but halfway through the meal he could not wait and conveyed the news that Ben's leukemia had returned.

"He's not in remission? But it's only been a year." Becky sat stunned. "I thought…"

"We all thought," Jay said gently. He went on to tell her that he and Buddy were with Ben when he found out. "Dr. Harris explained about chemotherapy and a bone marrow transplant, but right now Ben needs to think about his options and make up his own mind."

"How did he take it when Dr. Harris told him?" she asked.

"He's having a bad time of it. I wanted to tell you so when you see him you're prepared. Becky, your father is going to need you, and need you to be strong. We've all been through a lot recently, but no one ever promised life would be easy." This was Jay's way of telling Becky not to fall apart.

"Why hasn't he told us? Is he going to call and tell me? What should I do?" Hearing all of this had Becky in turmoil.

"There's been so much suffering, he didn't want to burden anyone, but I think you need to call him. I know you Becky; you'll know what to say. But the two of you need to talk…soon. Ted has given him the medical facts, the data, the most recent literature, and once your father makes a decision, whatever that decision is, we'll all be there to support him."

Outside Jay's apartment, Becky broke down. "I don't know how much more I can take," she cried aloud in absolute frustration. "Losing Marc — watching Mummy go through the pain of losing Sam — and now this."

"We'll get through it," J.R. reassured her. "We have each other, and your father has the best medical team in the country." J.R. said the words, but he also realized how emotionally spent they already were.

In the weeks before she left for Italy, Nena could find no relief. Days ran into nights. She walked the streets of Boston hoping to lose herself in the crowded city, but it did not help. With every passing Tuesday, Nena could not get the memory of that horrible day out of her mind, and began to express her pain on paper.

TUESDAY
I try to fill the void.
It is a cold, windy day, and this causes me to feel more isolated.

In a restaurant I sit by a window at a table for one.
I people watch, especially couples.
I see them as they pass along the street, laughing, talking, sharing, touching,
But I am not a participant, I observe.
Memories of another time fill me.

I get on the T,
I sit next to a man with a female companion.
They are my age.
The man has his back to me;
They are engaged in conversation.
They hold hands; they sweetly and softly embrace.
Not so it offends, but so it touches the heart.
I feel the warmth of his body against mine; I feel his connection to love, to life.
I listen to them talk and sense their wonderment that I yearn to know again.
But beyond the surface musing, I have no other emotion.
The couple leaves and a woman sits in the man's seat, her body is cold — as mine must be to her.

My stop.
The ride mirrors my life, my existence.
Entering my house, no one is there to greet me, to ask about my day.
Tomorrow is Wednesday, but for me it is another Tuesday.

Spending what would have been her honeymoon in Venice at the Cipriani was the right thing to do. The staff welcomed Nena back and treated her like one of their own. She and Sam had reserved the same room they had last year when they became engaged. Nena wanted to keep the reservation. She needed to hold onto anything reminiscent of him.

Sam had left Nena his entire estate. She decided to use a portion of the money to buy a place in Venice. Making this gesture kept him close. Sitting on the hotel's terrace, after another day of house hunting, Nena ordered a Bellini.

"Can I get you anything else, Mrs. Hicks?" the waiter asked.

"Thank you, this is all for now."

She held the glass by the stem and looked at the peach-colored drink. "He should be here, Sam should be sitting right here, and my name should be Mrs. Katz. Mrs. Samuel Katz," she said to herself.

Nena looked at her hand, and fingered her black pearl and diamond engagement ring. She opened her bag and took out a small Tiffany box. Inside were two wedding bands: one was diamond and the other platinum. Opening the box, she took out the diamond band and slipped the band on the ring finger of her right hand. Tears welled in her eyes as she studied the ring, thinking that Sam would have put this ring on her left hand. Putting the box back in her bag, she stared at her finger. A man had been watching her. He had come to care for Nena and could feel her need to be comforted. He ordered a Bellini and walked to her table.

"May I join you?" It was Mr. Rusconi, the hotel's general manager.

"Please." She motioned for him to sit down.

"If you don't mind, I was watching you when you put the ring on your finger."

"I suppose you think that was a strange thing to do."

"No, no, no, it is a loving thing you did. You loved him and he loved you. In your heart, he is your husband. The ring should be worn. It is your way to honor him and your love. Love is all that is important." Nena began to cry. "It helps to cry — good for the soul," he added.

"Thank you for such kind words. They help; they really do."

"Let us toast. *Per il tuo*...to your love."

"*Al mio amore*...to my love, Sam."

Then Mr. Rusconi asked Nena about her day. "Did you find an apartment that suited you?" "I believe I have," she said.

"Ah then, let us have another Bellini, and you can tell me about it."

She told him she had narrowed her choices to two apartments: one on the island of Giudecca, and the other in Dorsoduro. He pressed her to tell him which one she liked best, and she told him the one in Dorsoduro. "I think Sam would have approved. I feel he is here with me, if that makes any sense," she added.

"Of course it does."

"In the end I wanted to be where I could walk, be nearer to the shops and restaurants. I can always take a taxi to have lunch at the Cipriani, sit on the terrace, and have a Bellini, if you'll let me."

"Nena, you are always welcome here."

Nena went on to describe the Dorsoduro apartment to Mr. Rusconi. It was in a seventeenth-century palazzo, on the second floor, right above a canal and across from the Accademia Bridge, a few minutes' walk from San Marco. "Sam probably would have bought a boat for us," Nena said with a smile.

"That's a wonderful location, Mrs. Hicks. And I can see Sam with a boat."

She pulled out some photos of the apartment she planned to purchase. She showed Mr. Rusconi its private entrance off a courtyard and told him it had a lift so when she got older, she could still access it.

"Look at this picture." She pointed to the views of the beautiful Campo from the front balcony as well as over the exquisite Palazzo Albrizzi garden across a canal at the rear. "The space is being refurbished, and it comes furnished. There is a large salon, as you call it, and a formal dining room that I really wanted. There are three bedrooms and bathrooms, which will be nice when the family comes."

"It sounds wonderful, Mrs. Hicks. I would like to see it someday."

"Please, I wish you would call me Nena."

"Only if you'll call me Natale."

She told Natale she planned to have a dinner party to celebrate her new apartment, and he and Chef Piccolotto would be invited. She wanted to repay them for all their kindness during this visit, when she was full of grief. "What happened last month changed my life," she said. "The Cipriani has been a haven for me, and this is the least I can do before I leave."

"When will you be leaving us?" he asked.

She thought sometime before Thanksgiving because her family wanted her home for the holidays. "But I plan on returning soon. You're going to be seeing a lot of me. We will become the best of friends."

"We are the best of friends, Nena."

Mr. Rusconi went back to work and left her sitting with her thoughts. Talking with Natale and sharing this new property, she had almost forgotten her pain, but left alone it came rushing back. The emptiness she felt. How she was cheated out of a life with Sam. What was the point of meeting him, falling in love, giving her heart away, only to have it broken and the dream of this new life stolen by these evil men, men whom did not even know Sam, men who he never did anything to? She had not been able to make sense out of any of the events of 9/11 and wondered if she ever would.

Walking into her room, she heard the phone ringing.

"Hello!"

"Hello Mum, how are you?" Becky asked.

"I'm doing okay Becky. I found a place I'm going to buy. Sam would have liked it. How are you, and how is everyone doing?"

"I'm all right, but J.R. and Danny are having nightmares. I can't imagine how it must have been to look up and see a plane heading into the World Trade Center, and not know what was going on until you see it repeated over and over again on television, and then to find out that Marc and Sam were in the building. I think it will be some time before either of them fully recovers. I doubt Marc's body will ever be found. The general consensus from the reports is anyone at Windows that morning died. J.R. has spoken with his parents, and they are going to have a memorial service, but there are no plans yet. They're living with hope, but then again, Mum, we're all living with hope."

Nena understood Becky's every word. She too lived with hope each day. Waking up she would pray the telephone would ring, and it would be Sam saying somehow he had crawled out of the rubble, and the body that had been found was not his. But she knew that was not true.

Although she had called on an entirely different matter, Becky could hardly stand the pain in her mother's voice. "I'm sorry Mum; I'm so sorry."

"I know; everybody is sorry."

"Mum, I need to ask you when you're coming home."

Nena had been gone a month. "I figured you would call sooner or later to ask," she continued. "I suppose I should come home for the holidays. I suppose this year more than ever we need to be together."

Her mother sounded distant, detached. Becky did not know whether to tell her about Ben or wait. The words blurted out, before she caught herself: "Daddy isn't in remission anymore."

Nena felt as if someone had thrown ice water on her face. "What, what did you say?"

"I said Daddy is no longer in remission."

"Oh God, how much more can we take?"

That is what Becky thought too.

"When did your father find out? When did you find out? Who else knows? What's he going to do? How's he handling this?" Nena rattled off.

"Slow down, Mum. Dad found out the week before 9/11. He was doing so well. I thought he would go the distance, the five years."

Becky then told her mother that Ben had not made up his mind regarding a course of treatment — further chemo or a bone marrow transplant.

"And as far as how he is handling this…he's worried," Becky added, "not for himself, but for us. He couldn't bring himself to say anything after the towers fell. He told Jay there was already too much suffering, and he didn't want to burden anyone. Besides myself and J.R., Uncle Buddy, and Jay, we're the only ones who know, and now you. This is part of why I want to make sure you come home for the holidays so we all can be together."

Nena told her daughter that she would speak to the real estate people and make arrangements to close on the Venice apartment long distance.

"Then you'll be home for Thanksgiving?" Becky asked.

"Yes, but please keep it simple. Maybe at your apartment, or we can go out. I'm not up for a big weekend in Maine. Talk to your grandmother and aunt and uncle about coming to New York. Let's keep it family."

Becky's next piece of news was not good either, telling her mother about another concern she had, this time regarding Uncle Buddy. She relayed that she had found some medication for him at his and Ben's condo and asked him about it, but he was not very forthcoming.

"When I confronted him, he made light of it, saying he had high blood pressure. He says it's nothing serious, but right now I'm not trusting either of them to be up front about their health." At this point in the conversation, Becky tired of being the bearer of bad news.

Although Buddy was in his eighties, he had never shown any signs of ill health. This shocked Nena. Buddy had been the rock of the family, and now for him to be having any health issues devastated her.

"Oh, not Buddy; nothing can happen to Buddy." The heartache that had befallen her these past months crashed down on Nena like a tsunami roaring onto land. Becky could hear her mother whimpering and moaning.

"Mummy, we're going to make it. We have to hold together. Please don't fall apart on me. I need you and your strength now," Becky pleaded.

Nena could hear her daughter's plea. "I'm trying, Becky. I'll call you as soon as my plans are firm. I love you, my darling daughter. We'll talk soon."

"I love you too, Mum. Call me as soon as you can."

Hanging up phones on both sides of the Atlantic, these two women joined by blood and love sat shrouded in grief.

Nena made arrangements with the real estate firm to close on the apartment while she was in the States. They took her on a last tour of the property, making notes and finalizing the asking price.

Leaving the Cipriani, Nena assured Mr. Rusconi she would have her dinner party when she returned, in the new year. He sent her off with a farewell dinner and a beautiful pin of a gondola as a memento, telling her to return soon.

~~~~~~~~~~~~~~

By the time Nena returned to Boston, the family had made their Thanksgiving plans. Dinner would be at Jay's apartment in New York, where Ben and Buddy were staying. Josh, Gabby, Rebecca, and her family would stay with Danny at a hotel, while Nena and Ruth would stay with Becky and J.R. The important thing this year was to be together.

At the last minute, Josh booked a suite at the Plaza. Thanksgiving eve he arranged a family dinner, the first time everyone had been together since the dreadful events of 9/11. They were all carrying scars from the uncertainty of waiting, hoping, and wondering about the safety of loved ones, and then facing the loss. And now they were afraid for Ben and what he was facing.

When Ben walked into the room, the first person he saw was Nena. He had not seen her since Sam's memorial service and then he really did not have time to talk with her about her loss.

"I can't tell you how sorry I am," he said to her when they had a moment alone. "I hear you went to Italy. Were you able to find any peace?"

"I don't know, Ben. I'm still in shock. That trip was supposed to be our honeymoon." She found it strange speaking with her ex-husband about the man she was to marry. "I miss him. Do you know he left me his entire estate? He had a brother, but he died when they were young, and his parents are both dead. I'm making donations in his name, and guess what I'm doing with the rest, or most of the rest?"

"I have no idea, but knowing you, it will be something sensible."

"I don't know how sensible…I bought an apartment in Venice."

"That's fantastic!"

"It's something that would've made Sam happy."

Ben told her he admired her strength and he was not surprised by it — because he had known all along she was a special person.

Ben's compliment made Nena uncomfortable. She wanted it to be Sam standing there saying those words. Nena needed to change the subject — quickly. "I heard from Becky Buddy is having heart issues. Looking at him holding court, he looks the picture of health."

"Looks are deceiving. I'm worried about him and the business especially since…"

"I know about the remission, Ben. I'd like to be of help; if there's anything I can do, please let me know." This time, without hesitation, Nena was sincere in offering her support.

"I'll keep that in mind, and I might take you up on it. Let's go see what the old man is saying that's so interesting."

The topic of 9/11 could not be avoided. The event still too fresh and consumed most of the evening's conversations. When the night ended, there was a solemnity to the expectations for the following day — Thanksgiving.

**

"Today is a difficult day." Jay's ribcage expanded with each breath as he tried to speak. "Before we eat this feast, and let me add thank heaven for excellent caterers who work on holidays, it would be appropriate for each person here to offer their own words of gratitude. Ben, let's begin with you."

"I am grateful to be sitting at this table today. There are no words to express my thanks to the Lord for sparing J.R. and Danny from what happened on 9/11. They were kept physically safe and out of harm's way, and I pray in time their memories of that dreadful day will heal. And my heart goes out to Marc's family, and for Nena's loss of Sam. I grieve for every family that sits around tables this Thanksgiving Day with a loved one missing."

Weak in his knees and drained, Ben sat down. Around the table, each person spoke, expressing similar thoughts as his.

~~~~~~~~~~~

Early Monday morning Ben had an appointment with Ted. Nena asked if she could go along. She had made a decision to help Ben through whatever procedures he would require. She no longer had a life with Sam, and needed to feel useful. She needed to feel something mattered in her life, and if that meant being a part of Ben's support system while he battled this cancer that is what she was going to do.

"It appears we're going to need extra chairs." Ted gestured to his nurse as Ben, Buddy, Becky, J.R., Jay, and Nena filed into his office. When seated, he asked Ben if he had made a decision about his next step for treatment.

Ben told him he wanted to give chemotherapy another chance, adding that he knew a bone marrow transplant was his last resort and he wanted to postpone one if he could.

"You do know that this round of chemotherapy will be more aggressive than the last, and the side effects might be stronger," Ted told him.

Ben said he understood and was preparing.

"This means I want you staying near the hospital after your treatments. I'll want to monitor you closely," Ted added.

"Don't worry about that, Dr. Harris."

All eyes in the room turned toward Nena. Nena knew a perfect place where Ben could stay. Sam's apartment had not been sold because Nena had not decided what she was going to do with the property. Now she knew. "I have an apartment on the Upper West Side, across the park from the hospital. Ben, you're welcome to stay there with me."

The room fell silent until Ben spoke. "Nena, are you certain you want to do this?"

"I have time on my hands right now, and you know what they say about idle hands."

Ted brought the room back to reality, saying, "I'll speak to the team, and call you when we're ready to begin the treatments."

"Can you give me an idea of what to expect?" Ben needed to know.

"Of course. Most likely there will be four rounds of treatments. Initially we're going to want you in the hospital for a week, thereabouts. Your port will be implanted and we will build up your white blood count. And if the treatments go well, and don't hold me to this, by the time the spring flowers are blooming, you'll be finished. But you know Ben, I need to discuss this with your team. We need a plan, and once that's in place, I'll be in touch." Then looking at each person in the room, he continued, "I want to thank you for coming today. Having a support system like the one you have Ben is half the battle. You're a lucky man."

"I know I am, luckier than most."

In the elevator, Ben turned to Nena. "How am I ever going to thank you Nena? Are you certain you want to do this?" he asked again. "I'll understand if you change your mind."

"I wouldn't have offered if I didn't want to."

Becky told her mother that she would help get the apartment ready for Ben's stay, and Nena let her know her help would be appreciated since the apartment was empty.

"Perhaps we could begin this afternoon when you finish work," Nena suggested. "And speaking of work, I had better call my office; maybe it's time for me to retire."

Becky was startled at her comment. She knew Nena loved her work and urged her mother not to make a hasty decision.

"I bet you can work something out with the office…give them a call," Becky told her.

Nena called her office later that morning. They did not want to lose her, and she knew she was not quite ready to retire either. So they reached a compromise. Nena would take a leave of absence until Ben's treatments were completed. Then she and her boss would talk again.

**

"It's going to be strange walking into Sam's apartment with new furniture; it won't seem the same," Nena told Becky as they browsed the furniture department at Bloomingdale's.

"I know Mum, but I can't tell you how grateful I am you're doing this, not only for Dad, but for me. I know he could have stayed with Jay again, but that would have been a lot to ask. Do you have any idea what this means for my peace of mind?"

This gesture towards Ben had more to do with Nena than him. There were days when she felt disconnected from life. Helping Ben would give her a purpose, a reason to get up every day. She could not nor did she want to explain this to Becky. However, she did tell her daughter when Ben's treatments were finished, she would sell the apartment. "I wonder what happened to the young couple who were going to buy it," she said. "Maybe I should try and contact them." What she was really trying to do was hold onto something, anything remotely connected to Sam, and Nena saw this unknown couple as some sort of a connection.

"Mum, you don't have to address any of that right now. Let's concentrate on furnishing the apartment and getting Dad through this next round of chemo. When the time comes and you want to sell, we'll all help."

Shopping continued to make the apartment feel homey while Ben convalesced, while Nena tried to fill the empty space Sam's absence left in her life.

**

The team confirmed the course of action for Ben's treatments. He would enter the hospital after the first of the year. In the meantime, what was to be done about the business? He knew another decision would have to be made and sought Jay for advice.

Sitting at Nino's, where Jay and Ben had become regulars, Jay ordered drinks while Ben verbalized his dilemma. "Even if these treatments work and I go into remission again, I need to seriously consider what to do about the company. I know Buddy's heart is not in the business any longer. He goes into the office every day, but his interest level isn't there, and hasn't been for some time. Lately he leaves by mid-afternoon. Believe me I can't blame him, not at his stage in life, but I can't run the business without Buddy having an interest even though we have dependable people. It isn't fair to expect them to have the same involvement as I do. I either need to hire someone on as a partner or sell. I don't have the stomach to bring any of this up to Buddy, and frankly Jay, I don't have the energy to take on any more right now."

"First things first — Ben. Get the chemo behind you and your strength back before you make any major decision," Jay suggested. "Your staff can keep things afloat, and I'll have my accountants keep an eye on the books since this is your busiest time of year. I'll begin to look around to see who might be interested in either partnering or buying a business of your size. This way some of the groundwork is done if you ever want to sell. How does this sound?"

"I'll tell you Jay, you have been a godsend in my life. A man couldn't have a better friend."

"Ben, it works both ways. You came into my life when I lost Trudi. Even with the business and my other activities, my life felt pretty empty."

"Oh I see, my friend, you needed a project!"

"I'll drink to that." Jay motioned to the waiter for a second round. "Seriously Ben, we'll figure this out."

~~~~~~~~~~~~

Between the week of Christmas and New Year's, another unexpected event tested the family's resilience: Buddy died. The autopsy revealed he had an enlarged heart. Ben learned the doctor had been treating Buddy for high blood pressure and a slight fibrillation of his heart, although he had no other outward signs of imminent risk. He refused a cardioverter-defibrillator implant the doctor suggested. But the family wondered if his refusal was just another way to neglect himself to focus on taking care of everyone else. Ben often had asked him about his shortness of breath when they walked to work. In true Buddy fashion, he would scoff it off as old age creeping in and wave his hand in a gesture of dismissal. "I'm nearly eighty-seven," he'd say. "You may get a little winded when you reach my age, young man!"

Once more the white steeple church on God's Acre held a funeral. It seemed the entire town attended. Buddy had become a fixture in a place that had grown from a sleepy village where he grew-up, playing with his brother Jack in the schoolyard on South Avenue, to one of the wealthiest communities in the country.

Ben rose to eulogize his uncle. He had written something on a piece of paper, but when he looked out over the sea of people sitting in the pews, each attendee knowing that with Buddy's passing a part of the old New Canaan went with him, he put the paper down and spoke from his heart.

> *"I'm not sure where to begin, so I guess I'll begin at the beginning. My grandfather started a company that has been in this town for three generations, but it was my father and my Uncle Buddy that had the vision to turn that company from coal to oil. When my father Jack died in the war, it was Uncle Buddy that stepped in and ran the company. At the same time he took on another responsibility much greater, that of being a father figure to my brother Jackie and myself. I never appreciated him and the sacrifices he made for us until I was a grown man, but during our entire childhoods he was the only father we ever knew. He didn't live under our roof, but he was there for us every day in every way. He took us to Yankee Stadium every summer; he taught us to play ball and sail. Boy, did he love to sail that old boat of his. He used to call it his one true love, saying she never let him down. He drove me to visit colleges and supported me even when he knew I was about to make a mistake, because he believed this is how we learned the lessons of life. He would have made someone a wonderful husband, but he never married. Jackie and I used to hope after Dad died, he would marry our mother, but he was content just the way his life was.*
>
> *"Uncle Buddy was one of the few people I knew who was happy in his own skin. I never heard him complain. He always had a solution to a problem; he was always there to lend a helping hand, not just to our family but to people in town as well. Many a winter he let bills slide when he knew*

someone was on hard times. He would always say people needed to eat and be warm. He took us to England to bring back our father so we could bury him at home. Now Buddy you will be right beside him. He gave me a second chance for a life when many doors had closed to me. My uncle Buddy lived a life of integrity and honesty, a kind and gentle soul with a fantastic sense of humor. He was the best friend anyone could ever have. Above all else he was a man with a big heart. As most of you know, he died of an enlarged heart, and maybe that was because so much of his life his heart carried the weight of others."

Ben stopped to collect himself, and in the silence of the sanctuary, soft sobs could be heard as they mingled with the shedding of tears.

"Dear sweet Uncle Buddy. It was so like you not to let any of us know you were not well. So like you to continue to care for everyone else to the end. Your passing leaves me with an empty space in my life and a hole in my heart. No boy could have asked for a better role model for a father. I count my blessings to have had you in my life."

When Ben finished, silence engulfed the church until the minister rose and offered a closing prayer. People gathered downstairs to share a meal and stories about a man who had become a fixture in this New England town where he had left his mark.

"Daddy, you honored Uncle Buddy just the way he would have wanted. I bet he's looking down and smiling," Becky told her father.

"Becky is right; your eulogy did Buddy and us proud." Nena approached Ben, seeing in his face the young man she first met those many years ago. "Buddy was one of the most wonderful people I have ever known. I'm going to miss him. I'm so sorry Ben." Tears rolled onto her face as she tried to comfort Ben with her words. This year had been too much — too much sorrow, too much loss, too many broken hearts and shattered lives.

Part IV

2002–2004

Chapter 15

Hardly a person in the country was sorry to see the calendar change from 2001 to 2002.

~~~~~~~~~~~~~

Since 9/11, Danny had not been able to come to terms with his life and what had happened. He could barely bring himself to go to work. He could not stop thinking about what he saw that day and the fact Marc died and his body never found. Marc had opened the door for him at American Express. Working for the company with him gone did not seem the same.

Midway through 2002, Danny traveled to Peru and took a train to Machu Picchu. It was the furthest place he could think of to find solace without the constant questioning of how he was coping. This ancient Inca community had been unnoticed to the world for centuries, until 1911 when explorer Hiram Bingham III, a professor from Yale University, discovered the site and spread the news of his finding to the world.

Walking through the ruins almost eight thousand feet above sea level allowed Danny to regain clarity of thought. Through the solitude offered by this sacred location, Danny came to understand he needed to make a change in his life. Retuning to New York, he shared his decision first with Becky and J.R. Then he went home to Boston to tell his parents.

**

Danny had decided to reenlist in the Navy, full time, which came as a surprise to both Gabby and Josh. Josh sat silently listening to his son. He knew Danny was not one to make rash decisions, and he also knew once his son made up his mind, it was made up.

"9/11 changed everything for me," Danny tried to explain to his parents. "We are at war, and I can't sit idly by doing nothing. I have a skill. I'm a damn good pilot. Everything is so uncertain and I need to do something."

Gabby wondered if her son had not witnessed that plane falling out of the sky and crashing into the World Trade Center, if he would be doing this, but she knew better than to ask.

"Have you already resigned at American Express?" Josh asked Danny.

"No, I wanted to tell you first. And I need to speak to my reserve commander to find out what they'll want to do with me or even if they want me. I realize I'm not a kid any longer, but I have a heck of a lot of experience, and I know they need that. Then I'll tell them at work."

Both Gabby and Josh were silently hoping the Navy would not want him, but never mentioned this to their son. Instead Gabby asked Danny what he would like for dinner. While he was pondering an answer, she stared at him intently. She could see he had aged since September 11. She wondered if he would ever be the same lighthearted, easygoing boy and young man she had raised.

"What else Mum…your pot roast."

"Pot roast, it is."

~~~~~~~~~~~~~~~~~~~~~~~~~~~~~~~~

Ben was in the hospital having his first round of chemo treatments, while Nena readied the apartment. Spending a few nights alone with her thoughts was difficult. The place had been newly painted. Sam's furniture and belongings were gone; however, his presence filled every corner. She asked the deliverymen to place the bed on the opposite wall from where Sam had his. She did not want to walk into the bedroom and constantly be reminded of the hours she spent in bed with him. She tried her best to make the rooms comfortable for herself and Ben. If she were honest about it, she dreaded Ben coming into Sam's place — their place — where she and Sam spent time together — made memories. She had to accept the fact things were different. Everything had changed with 9/11. Ben was fighting another battle with cancer. He needed to be taken care of, and she needed to be needed.

Each time Ben came from treatments he continued to express his deep appreciation for Nena's hospitality. "I can't thank you enough for letting me come here. I feel comfortable being close to the hospital, and now that Buddy is gone, I wasn't looking forward to being alone in the townhouse," he told her.

Buddy had been dead just a few weeks, and Ben was still mourning the loss of his uncle.

"I've been thinking since Buddy died how you'd feel about staying here at Sam's..." The minute she called the space Sam's she bit her tongue. "I'm sorry, Ben."

"There's nothing to be sorry about. This was Sam's apartment. I know you spent a lot of time here with him. I hope you know how deeply sorry I feel about the way he died. You were cheated out of a life with him Nena. I had my own feelings about the two of you, but you really deserved a second chance at happiness — what can I say other than I'm so so sorry?"

Setting the table she paused and turned to Ben. "Thank you for saying that. I know you were having a difficult time with my relationship with Sam, and you're right my times here with him were special. This has been a year of heartbreak, and tragedy. Sometimes when I wake up to the phone ringing, for a moment I think it's Sam. He was such a beautiful person, and he made me happy." Nena found herself talking to Ben about another man she loved. She knew she should stop. Since the bombing, Sam's death, Ben's cancer, and Buddy's death, Nena had controlled her emotions in order to keep herself from falling apart. She could hold it together no longer, and her grief came tumbling out onto Ben.

"I loved him so much; why was he taken from me? Why couldn't he have signed those damn papers some other way? Why did he feel the need to go to the lawyer's office?" Why? Why? Why?"

Nena's guttural sounds shook Ben to his core.

Ben walked to her and took her in his arms. "Oh Nena! You don't deserve any of what took place. I don't know why this happened. Why Sam was taken from you. I wish I could do something to help you through this. You can talk about Sam with me any time you want. I'll listen." He held her while she wailed to the universe, letting out the gut-wrenching cries of anguish and despair she had been holding in for far too long.

Ben's words soothed Nena, but it unnerved her to have confided in him about her feelings and life with Sam. Her outburst was a momentary lapse. Quickly she regained control of her emotions.

That evening, over dinner, Nena asked Ben, "Don't you find it ironic after all the twists and turns our lives have taken...here we sit?"

"I guess you could call it incongruous. If nothing else, life is a puzzle, unpredictable. I never would have predicted that after everything I did to you, to our marriage, you could turn around and support me through cancer. You're a remarkable person. When I say I don't deserve you in my life, I mean it with every fiber in me. I don't take what you are doing for granted — one iota."

Nena reiterated her offer. "Ben would you like to stay here until you finish your chemo treatments? Here, there will always be someone available 24/7. There won't be in New Canaan with Buddy gone."

"You mean stay here for the next few months?"

"I know originally it was only during chemo for a week or two, but yes for the duration. Becky, J.R., Jay, and Danny are nearby. When I need to go to Boston, you won't be alone. How do you feel about it?"

"I'm overwhelmed." Ben broke down.

"I take that for a yes."

Through tears of gratefulness, Ben nodded yes.

Becky felt relief when she heard her parent's decision. She had concerns about her father going home between treatments, being alone, working when he should be trying to regain his strength, eating properly; all the things a loving daughter would worry about.

~~~~~~~~~~~~~

Through months of chemotherapy treatments and Nena's attentive care, Ben heard the word he had waited for — remission.

In the months he and Nena had spent together, they had newfound respect and understanding for each other, which neither had expected. On his good days, they walked to the museum, picked out a gallery to explore, and had lunch with Becky. Nena would accompany him and Jay to Knick's games. Jay convinced them to attend Saint John the Divine on the Upper West Side and to avail themselves of its pastoral center. It helped Nena to be in a spiritual forum, where she could discuss and share feelings from the losses in her life. At first Ben was apprehensive. He quickly realized being with other people who had experienced loss, the death of a partner, a marriage, being a 9/11 survivor or a cancer survivor contributed to the healing process. It was here he and Nena honestly began to face their past together.

On his last day with Nena before going back to New Canaan and work, Ben had a gift for her.

"This is my way to thank you, Nena, for everything you have done for me, but I hope when you open the package you will know what I am trying to say."

Nena opened a box. Inside held a hand-carved wooden sign that read Sam's Place. Nena was touched and appreciative for his thoughtful gesture.

"Sam would have loved this. Thank you, Ben. Thank you so much."

In a way, Ben needed Nena to know he had accepted her love for Sam. This was his way.

Nena had requested an extension to her leave of absence from work, and while Ben packed his bags ready to leave for New Canaan, Nena packed hers, ready to return to Italy for the summer. She had not been back since buying her apartment and she could not wait.

"Before I go, I wanted to give you these." Nena handed Ben a set of keys. "I know you always stay with Jay when you come into the city, but I had a set of keys made for you in case you might need some quiet time. I want you to feel free to come here anytime you want."

It was the second time Ben was overwhelmed with Nena's generosity. Taking the keys, he kissed her on the cheek. "Please stay in touch. Send me a postcard, and call when you can."

When Ben left, Nena hung the Sam's Place sign over the door. "You'll never be forgotten Sam, not as long as I'm alive." Nena had to believe he was out there somewhere in the universe, listening.

~~~~~~

Looking back, 2001 had been a horrible year for J.R., both on a personal and professional level. Citigroup was involved in unscrupulous practices with Enron Corporation, WorldCom, and Global Crossings. All three companies eventually filed bankruptcy. These financial dealings ended in a national scandal, with Citigroup paying out billions of dollars to settle claims and lawsuits by the Securities and Exchange Commission and creditors.

On the heels of Citigroup's recent scandal, J.R. was constantly on alert. Since his promotion, he was in a position to know things he wished he did not know. The first of the year his division had begun recommending and selling shares of mutual funds, which he believed were in violation of regulatory rules, but he could never find solid proof to substantiate his belief. Now well into 2002, the work situation had not improved. At times like this J.R. would have picked up the phone and called Marc — Marc his indispensable sounding board. With his business acumen and vision, Marc's insights would have been invaluable. They spoke the same language. A day did not go by that he missed his friend.

J.R. needed to talk to someone about his situation. He took the train to New Canaan, under the pretense of visiting Ben, when in actuality, he wanted his father-in-law's opinion. Ben had been to hell and back in the '80s, the last time the country went through something similar to what was presently happening. He needed another point of view. He hoped Ben's perspective and experience with Apex would benefit him.

**

Ben motioned J.R. to sit down.

"How have you been doing, Ben?"

"Do you want the long or short version?" he asked his son-in-law.

"Whichever one you want to give me."

"Let's say I'm living in a state of grace. The last round of treatments has me in remission, I'm back at work, your father is keeping me on the go, and Nena has been a godsend."

"Speaking of my mother-in-law, I hear she's enjoying Venice."

"Yes, she calls me once a week to check in, but I don't think you came all the way out here to talk about Nena. So…what's the real reason for this visit? Certainly not to make small talk…"

"You're right. I need to run something by you." J.R. laid out his concerns at work, while Ben listened intently.

Ben was astonished at how bad things really were at Salomon. He asked if working for his father was still an option.

"Yes it is. Spending time with Dad has been an education; he's quite the businessman. I've learned a lot from him over the past year. The company is solid, yet I see potential for growth, which excites me. I was thinking about joining the company before 9/11, and with these new developments at work, it's probably time."

"Give yourself a few more months. Summer is always slow. If, let's say, by October you continue to have doubts, it might be time to cut the cord. The last thing you want is to become entangled in a mess, especially not of your making. Many a man has become a scapegoat. Don't become one of them. I'm not in the habit of giving advice J.R., especially the way I screwed up my career, but in your case I will. Please don't sign off on anything until you are 100 percent certain that all the t's are crossed and the i's are dotted. If something is bothering you, pick up the phone and call me. It's easy to overlook details thinking it's no big deal, when in reality it is."

J.R. took Ben's words of advice to heart.

Danny planned to exchange his business suit for a Navy uniform. Within the family his decision was received with mixed reactions. Next he had to approach his commander. Danny knew his age might be a factor against him, however, his experience and training were invaluable, and he was counting on this. The minute the Navy approved his request, he resigned his position at American Express. There was awe and pride amongst his coworkers, and some surprise, including from his boss who extended an offer that a job would be waiting for him if he ever returned to the corporate world. The office threw him a party to end all parties.

In July of 2002, Danny left for the Naval Air Station Oceana in Virginia Beach, Virginia for refresher training on the F/A-18 Hornet fighter aircraft. Following his training, the Navy assigned him to the VFA-37 "Raging Bulls" of Strike Fighter Squadron Thirty Seven, for its upcoming deployment aboard the carrier *USS Harry S. Truman*.

The past few months had drained Nena, and being back in Venice was the change she needed. She could not wait to see her new home. Walking into the beautifully tiled courtyard, she noticed the four-tiered fountain that was under repair when she left had been brought back to life. She watched as water splashed from tier to tier, filling the courtyard with soothing sounds that echoed off the walls of the building. The bronze seals she had requested had been installed at the base of the fountain; they were surrounded by containers filled with red, white, and pink roses. Nena climbed the staircase and entered the apartment. The first thing she did was draw back the curtains of the Palladian windows to let in light and sunshine. The views from the corner apartment's balcony exposed the canal on one side and a lovely garden on the other. She could also see the canal from the living room windows as the sun streamed into the rooms, shining on the classical architecture of the apartment with its high ceilings, carved moldings, and hand-painted scenes of Venice on the dining room walls.

Yet within the ambiance of formality and elegance of the past was the comfort of the present. The management company had filled the space with flowers that perfumed the rooms. Everything had been freshly painted, and the small but workable American kitchen had been fully stocked. The space was perfect. She entered the master bedroom last. This is where she and Sam would have spent hours making love, planning what they were going to do for the day, sleeping in each other's arms. Nena opened her suitcase and took out the last picture taken of her and Sam and placed it on the nightstand. The entire day had been bittersweet, but she knew Sam would want her to move on, to keep living until her time came, because that is what he had done.

**

"Pronto. Mr. Rusconi please."

"Nena, it is so good to hear your voice. Where are you?"

"I'm across the canal, sitting in my living room, enjoying the view."

"We've been expecting you. When did you arrive?"

"This morning."

"Wonderful to have you back."

"Yes, it's wonderful to be back, Natale. Could you find a table for me this evening?"

"We always have a table for you, Nena."

"Thank you! We need to make plans for my long overdue dinner party I promised you."

"We will make plans. See you at seven."

"Until seven," she said.

**

"Benvento, Nena, welcome." Mr. Rusconi greeted her as she embarked from the water taxi.

"I'm so glad to be back Natale. You will never know."

"Come, we have a table for you, and I will join you for dinner."

Nena was relieved she would not be dining alone. She had become used to being on her own after her divorce from Ben, but since Sam had come into her life, she had loved being a couple again. She found adjusting to the role of a single woman in a couple's world difficult. If she were of a different generation it would be easier, but in her world, being the lone woman in the crowd was often problematic.

"I heard from a little bird I have your kitchen staff to thank for stocking my pantry. You've been too kind Natale."

"We could not let you move in to an empty kitchen. Cooking is too important to us Italians, and besides the staff had fun doing this for you."

"But you have spoiled me. Speaking of cooking, when can you and Chef Piccolotto come to dinner?"

"Perhaps next week. I will call you. Tell me, how are you enjoying your new home?"

She told him she liked it very much, that the space and location were perfect. She then told him she had taken a leave of absence from work earlier this year to care for her ex-husband while he went through cancer treatments, and would soon have to decide if she would go back to work or retire.

"*La mia cara amica*, you are too young to retire," he told her.

"True!" Nena supposed, "Ah but I could live in Venice for half the year, and once I know the city better and the language, I would give walking tours to tourists from America." She had no idea where this idea came from; it was something she had never even contemplated before.

"Beautiful idea, beautiful. And you would be a superb ambassador for our beloved city. I will help you. You could bring people here for lunch."

"I wasn't serious, Natale. I was making a joke."

"No Nena, this is a wonderful idea for you. Not a joke!"

"Well what I do know is I need to change my life. Sam would want me to find something to make me happy again."

"Yes he would, Nena. Sam would not want you to be sad. You must remember him and the good times. That is what you need to concentrate on, not the sadness. Yes, we will help you find happiness again. Italy does that," Natale said, projecting his hope on her.

**

Reluctant to leave Venice, Nena finally returned to the States. She had come to a conclusion regarding her future and needed to talk to her family.

Nena was not the only person in the family who had made a life-changing decision. In October J.R. decided to leave Salomon. Salomon was found in violation of various sections within the Securities Exchange Act of 1934. Besides having to pay a major settlement, more regulations were put in place, and one of these regulations would impact J.R.'s department. It would insulate the banking and analysts departments to avoid conflicts of interests. These measures were taken to enforce and ensure proper trading took place regarding any sharing of insider information. Besides the settlement, there were substantial fines assessed in the billions of dollars. J.R. had been advised that in December this information would be made public. His department was going to be hit hard and go through, yet again, another reorganization. He had been able to maintain damage control within his department, but he had no stomach to live through another corporate upheaval and planned on turning in his resignation effective the first of the new year. Now all J.R. had to do was tell his father.

**

"What brings you by today?" Jay inquired of his son.

"Remember the offer you made me years ago, after I graduated from Harvard?"

"I believe my exact words were, 'Are you coming aboard?' And I remember what you said — you needed to get out on your own and prove yourself."

"Good memory. Is the offer still open?"

Jay let J.R. know the offer had never been off the table, and he hoped that his recent interest in the company had changed his mind about joining the family business.

Then J.R. spoke the words that Jay had been waiting years to hear — he told his father his days in the corporate world were numbered. J.R. sat across from his father and laid bare the situation at Salomon Smith Barney.

"Lord, what a mess. I'm relieved you didn't get your pants caught in that ringer. How in heavens name did you keep your nose clean?" Jay asked his son.

"You may not think I ever listened to you, but I did. Plus I went to Ben when things were beginning to get dicey. I figured with what he went through he must have learned a lesson or two that would benefit me."

"You know Robbie, listening to what someone has to tell you from their mistakes and then being able to use the advice wisely takes maturity, especially in the world you've been operating in. That's a pretty rarefied atmosphere." Jay got up from his chair and walked around his desk. "Come here Robbie," he said as he held open his arms. "Welcome aboard!"

Jay suggested they call Ben and ask him to catch the next train to the city; it was time to celebrate. Jay had waited a long time for this day. Tonight would be a boy's night out.

"Robbie, you just made your old man one happy fella."

**

"Let's toast to J.R.'s decision," Ben proposed, as they sat at Nino's bar waiting for their table. J.R. thanked Ben and told him the conversation they had helped him solidify what was important.

"Let's face it you were in a darn seductive business. I should know. It's not easy to walk away, but what you are walking into is going to be as exciting and a whole lot more rewarding." Thinking of his own life, Ben admired his son-in-law's decision. "I'm impressed J.R., how you were able to navigate Saloman's rough waters over the years. This says a lot about you, and your ability to keep your head about you. It couldn't have been easy."

It had not been easy for J.R. His boss never ordered him overtly to cross the line, but he could read the subtle covert messages, and had to admit there were times he had been tempted to exaggerate on research reports to support the department.

"How do you think your resignation is going to be accepted?" Ben inquired.

"You'd be surprised how much loyalty exists in my department. Since I'm going to be joining a pretty well-known family business, not too may feathers will be ruffled. I don't think I'll be viewed as a rat jumping ship. I'll get a decent sendoff."

Their table ready, another bottle of wine ordered — boy's night out was off to a good start.

**

"You look fantastic, Mum. Italy sure does agree with you." This was the first time mother and daughter had a chance to catch up since Nena had returned from Venice.

"Thank you dear, I can't wait for you to visit; you'll love my new place. I'm glad you suggested we dine here. It's nice some things don't change."

Becky had made reservations at Café Luxembourg, a long-standing favorite restaurant of Nena's.

"Your father tells me that J.R. is going to work for Jay. Is that true?"

"He's been struggling with this decision for some time. There's been a lot going on at Salomon. I don't think J.R. could handle another change in leadership, and finally came to the conclusion it was time to resign, but we can talk about all that later. I want to hear about your plans, Mum."

"Hmm, my plans, I wish I were as certain as my son-in-law about my plans. I'm struggling with a decision: retire or not to retire."

"Mum, you're too young," Becky countered.

Jolted by Becky's words, Nena realized this was the second time she recently heard herself described as too young to retire. Was she missing something? Could it be trying to let go of Sam, and the life they planned, clouded her perception of herself? But rather than reflect on her internal emotions and the uncertainties that still held her hostage to the events of 9/11, she responded to her present circumstance in a practical manner.

"The reality is I'll get a nice retirement if I stay on for another three years, and I do have a sense of fulfillment with my work"…Thinking out loud, she continued…"but since my leave of absence, I realized I don't want to work full time any longer either. I'm going to speak to the commissioner and try to arrange my work schedule so I can spend time in Venice. I need a more flexible schedule. If I tell him upfront I'm going to retire in 2005 and will be around to train my replacement. He might go for it."

Becky agreed the plan sounded reasonable, and told her mother how proud she was of her — of her bravery to face the future after all that had happened.

Finally Nena knew what she needed to do regarding her future. She still missed Sam every day. Nevertheless, she knew she had to move on. Living without a clear direction only created a false illusion that nothing had changed; when everything had.

"You've set a very high bar for me; you know that don't you?" Becky told her mother.

"Well let's hope I can continue to live up to your image. Now tell me about J.R. and what's going on in your lives."

**

Becky was already in bed waiting up for J.R., anxious to hear how his evening went. He told her that her father was thrilled to hear he would be joining the family business.

"Your father gave me a perspective of someone who had been there and done that. I don't think Marc could have advised me the way your father did. But boy, I miss my buddy."

"I know you do, honey; I do too. He became such a big part of our lives. There will always be an empty place in our hearts when it comes to Marc."

"Anyway, the new year will be a fresh start with Dad. I'm looking forward to the change – new challenges. I know the business has always been commercial real estate, but I'm thinking the time might be right to explore the residential marketplace."

Becky asked him if he had talked to his father about this idea.

"No, not yet, I want to wait until I actually climb aboard. Plus, I need to formulate a plan before I present him with anything. It's a thought I need to develop. But it does get my juices flowing. Now how was your dinner with Nena?"

"She misses Sam and still struggles with what happened. She's not going to sell the apartment, and she's going to keep working until 2005. I'm proud of her after all she's been through this past year," Becky added.

"That surprises me. I thought she would quit, and live between here and Italy. Chill out and enjoy her life."

"I thought so at first, but listening to her, I'm glad she's made this decision. She needs time to come to terms with Sam's death. I noticed she was wearing her wedding band on her right hand. I didn't say anything, but that tells me she is nowhere near accepting what happened. Having meaningful work and keeping busy with the apartment here in the city and the place in Venice to look forward to when she wants to get away is what she needs for now. Oh sweetheart, how this world has been turned upside down," Becky lamented.

J.R. crawled into bed and took Becky in his arms. He pulled her close and sweetly kissed her eyelids. "I love you," he told her, as he held her tightly.

And in the stillness of the night, the only sound heard was a cadence of breathing as their passion ran free.

~~~~~~~~~~~~~~~

Nena approached her boss at Human Services apropos her plan to edge toward retirement. After an exchange of her reasoning, he told her they would find a schedule that would work to everybody's satisfaction. Perhaps now she could settle in to a routine and come to terms with what life had handed her. She needed to hold on to the good times, as Natale reminded her at dinner, and let go of the sadness and what she could no longer control — a tall order.

~~~~~~~~~~~~~~~

The holidays this year were not as somber as the last. With time and distance, and Ben once again in remission, the season held more joy. The family decided to return to Ogunquit for Thanksgiving, but stay home to celebrate Christmas and usher in another year.

**

The serenity of Ogunquit at Thanksgiving was a welcome respite.

Talking with Nena and Ben on one of their afternoon walks along the Marginal Way, watching as the ocean waves bumped into the rocky shore, and smelling the clean salt air, Ruth agreed with Ben's perspective. "Yes, there is something intangible about this spot that has a soothing and calming effect on one's soul."

Nena wistfully commented, "It's almost healing," as if imploring her surroundings to take away her pain.

Ben turned and put his arm around Nena's shoulder. "I know exactly how you feel."

Nena gently removed Ben's arm. How could he or anyone else know exactly how she felt? These were her feelings. She did not expect anybody to understand her pain over the loss of Sam. Although a year had passed since 9/11, Nena clung to her love for him. She desperately wanted to move forward in every way, but not at the cost of losing her emotional tie to Sam, and in some strange way her heartache kept him real. Approaching a bench that looked out over the ocean, Nena sat down.

"Are you okay Mum?" Becky had been walking behind her parents when she saw her mother remove Ben's arm. She watched as Nena recoiled and knew instinctively her father had invaded her mother's space.

"I'm going to sit and enjoy the quiet and the view. Please go along; I'll catch up." What kept her from screaming was concentrating on the ocean melding into the far off horizon. Gulps of sea air drawn deeply into her lungs, and exhaled ever so slowly, stopped her otherwise uncontrollable tears.

When Becky joined the rest of the party, Ben inquired, "Is your mother okay?"

"No Dad. Losing Sam is still an open wound. It's going to take time. Mum needs space and some solitude. She'll join us when she's ready."

In a kind and gentle manner, Becky tried to tell her father, although they were making progress, not to push. She hoped he got the message.

~~~~~~~~~~~~

At Christmastime, Ruth stayed with Nena in the city. She told her daughter how much she liked what she had done to redecorate the apartment.

"I only wish I had a few more pieces of Sam's furniture," Nena said. "I'm grateful he brought some things to Boston, especially his books." Selling the apartment was no longer an option for Nena. "I needed the space to feel like him, but I also wanted to make it my own."

"Well, you have accomplished your goal. I can see the both of you here. Where did you get that?" Ruth asked, pointing to the Sam's Place sign.

"Oh that. Ben had it made as a thank you present when he stayed here during his treatments and for my excellent care giving." Nena could not hide or explain the irritation in the tone of her words and in her voice. "I know he's trying, Mum. He wants to be friends, and we've come a long way in how we relate, especially since his second bout with cancer — but sometimes I find his interest — I don't know how to explain it…" Nena could not put her feelings into words.

"Do you remember what seems a lifetime ago…the conversation we had regarding Ben's family when you were first starting to date?"

"We had so many, which one?"

"The talk where I tried to explain meaningful relationships and how complicated they can be? Relationships are not one-dimensional. You need to remember you and Ben have had a long history. Your relationship is anything but one-dimensional. He desperately wants to have you in his life, which causes him to be overzealous at times. I doubt he even realizes how he's coming across to you. I understand you feel smothered by his behavior."

"That's exactly how I feel, smothered. I don't want to hurt his feelings or make him feel I don't appreciate his concern, because I do. I just don't want Ben to misinterpret how things were between us during his treatments. I don't want him to confuse my concern for him with love. Mum, everything changed when I fell in love with Sam, and we can't go back to what we had years ago. Ben can't replace how I feel about Sam."

Ruth suggested that maybe someday Nena might want to share those feelings with Ben: talk to him about it.

"I guess, but I don't want to talk about my feelings with him — not now — I really don't, and the saving grace is we don't see each other that often. A lot of stuff came up for me over Thanksgiving. I'll be going back to Boston, back to work, and a routine. I need to keep busy."

Ruth did not want to push the subject further and asked, "Now what shall we do with this beautiful day before New Year's Eve?"

~~~~~~~~~~~~~~

Becky told J.R. she wanted to stay home New Year's Eve, watch the ball drop on TV, and not battle the masses in Times Square. J.R. suggested that they invite Ben, Jay, Nena, and Ruth for dinner.

"Thanksgiving and Christmas weren't enough? I mean I love our families, but don't you want to be alone with me to greet the new year?" she asked him.

"Honey, with the losses we've suffered and your dad's remission, it would be nice to be together to celebrate. As soon as midnight arrives, we can shoo them out the door and you can have me all to yourself."

Since 9/11 Becky had noticed that J.R. wanted to spend as much time with his family and friends as possible. She could not put herself in his place having been a bystander to the events of that day, while he was directly in the line of fire.

"Is that a promise?" she asked.

"It's a promise, my love."

**

With the family gathered around the television in Becky and J.R.'s living room, waiting for the ball to drop at midnight in Times Square, Nena expressed how glad she was that they were all together, in spite of her underlying unease about spending more time with Ben. The countdown began, the ball dropped, and the clinking of glasses ushered in a new year. Jay proposed a toast to 2003. "Let's hope and pray the worst is behind us." No one disagreed.

Everyone said their good-byes, and as the door closed Becky turned to J.R.

"Alone at last, I've been waiting for this moment all evening. Let's leave the dishes," she proposed, grabbing his hand and leading him to the bedroom.

"You're the one who always wants things put away before we go to bed. Are you saying the hell with the cleanup?" J.R. could not believe what his wife had suggested.

"That's exactly what I'm saying, the hell with the cleanup, and bring the champagne."

It was more than lust Becky was feeling. She drew J.R. to her as they lay in bed, and surrendered to these uncontrollable and primal urges that had overcome her. They spent the night making love until Becky no longer craved his touch.

The following morning J.R. commented. "That was some way to usher in a new year."

"Would you care to meet me in the shower?"

J.R. could not resist her offer. Standing in the shower, making love, Becky still could not get enough of her husband. She always felt passionately for him, but this was different, and she could not explain her desire, even to herself. Leaving the shower, she took his hand and led him to the bed. She knelt over him. He laid looking up at her, kissing her tenderly as her hair fell across her face. He sat up and pulled the curves of her body into his.

Lying on the bed, J.R. turned to Becky. "What has happened to you?"

"I don't know; all I know is I can't get enough of you."

"Don't get me wrong, I'm not complaining," he told her.

They cooked brunch, cleaned up the kitchen, and spend the remainder of the day in bed.

"I love the way you think, Mr. Stark!"

"I love whatever is going on with you, Mrs. Stark!"

~~~~~~

A new year and a new beginning, and J.R. felt a mix of emotions as he walked into the Stark Land Development offices on his first day. He knew in his gut he had made the right decision, but with change came a certain amount of apprehension. He was making a leap from the corporate world. Although he had worked at the family business before graduate school and had limited involvement in the company over the past year, this was jumping in with both feet — making a serious commitment. He knew his father had expectations, not just as his son, but as a full contributor to the business.

"Good morning, Robbie. Nice first impression. You're here before the rest of the staff."

"I'm trying Dad. I want to get off on the right foot, and send the boss the right message."

"I've set up a meeting in the conference room for 8:30. I want everyone to understand your role — teamwork is essential to this business."

"It's important for me the office staff understands I'm just another employee, even though I am your son. I take orders; I don't give them."

J.R. took a deep breath and then added, "I'm full of anxiety Dad, but this was the right move, and I'm really looking forward to working with you."

Jay told his son he understood his apprehension, that starting any new job was daunting, especially one in a family business. "But this is a company your great great-grandfather started. He wanted it for his son, just as my father wanted it for me, and I've always wanted it for you. So welcome aboard J.R. I can't put into words what this day means to me."

The staff began to arrive. By 8:30 a.m., the conference room was full, and the day began.

**

"Well, tell me…how did your day go?"

"Amazing! I couldn't have asked for a better beginning. Dad has put together an outstanding team. The atmosphere in the office is professional but relaxed. Might take me a little while to completely fit in, but I'm determined not to play the boss's son card."

"That's smart of you my darling husband."

Then she asked him if he had shared any of his ideas about expanding the business into residential real estate with his dad.

"It would mean taking the company in another direction, or at least adding another dimension to the business, and I want to know I'm not flying blind before I approach Dad."

Becky could see her husband was grappling with not only this new idea, but his role in the family business.

~~~~~~~~~~~

One morning in February after J.R. left the apartment for work, Becky sat on the bed wishing she could take the day off. She felt wretched. She did not feel herself. She constantly felt tired, but had difficulty sleeping, and had begun to experience bouts of nausea. The thought crossed her mind she needed to see her doctor. She picked up the phone and made the call.

"We have a cancellation at two. Can you come in then?" the receptionist inquired.

"Yes I can, thank you."

**

When the doctor eliminated the usual winter diseases, Becky asked if she could be menopausal. The doctor looked at her curiously.

"Menopausal! What makes you think that? You are rather young."

"I read somewhere that this can happen to women my age."

"Yes, it can, Becky, but rarely. Why don't you tell me what's going on with you?"

She told him that her breasts were sore, and she had been spending more time in the bathroom. Her internist recognized Becky's signs and called in the gynecologist.

The gynecologist examined Becky. When the doctor completed her exam, she told Becky she was not menopausal, and asked her if she ever considered she might be pregnant.

"Pregnant?"

The doctor asked for a urine sample and drew blood before telling Becky, "Why don't you get dressed and come into my office?" She could hear the disbelief in Becky's voice and knew this pregnancy was certainly not planned.

Fifteen minutes later, Becky, still speechless, walked into the gynecologist's office. The doctor told her that her urine test confirmed the pregnancy and that she thought Becky was about six weeks pregnant. "I want to write a prescription for vitamins and…"

"Wait, wait a minute," Becky interrupted. "I'm pregnant? How did this happen?"

"You tell me how it happened," the doctor said. "I wasn't there."

"But we've never planned; we really never talk about having a baby."

"Sometimes Mother Nature takes its course Becky. If you weren't using any protection, it can happen. Have you been wearing your diaphragm at *all* times?"

Then it dawned on her. She told the doctor that on New Year's Eve and New Year's Day she had not been wearing the diaphragm and was having wild, unadulterated sex with her husband. Becky and J.R. had never made a conscious decision to have or not have children, but as they grew older and their lives became more defined as the two of them, the thoughts of children became less important.

"Then there's your answer." The gynecologist smiled, having heard this story before. "Becky, sometimes these so-called accidents are subconscious. Perhaps somewhere deep inside you wanted to have a child, but on the surface you were not prepared or ready to address the need. Your body knows your biological clock is ticking. Your hormones took over and made the decision for you."

Becky's head was reeling.

"I'll do another pregnancy test…a double check. I'll call you later today with the results, but I'm pretty confident that I'll need to see you in another month. If you have any questions before your next appointment, please call. Congratulations again, Becky."

Becky went back to work. At the moment, it seemed the only thing that made any sense. Sitting at her desk, the phone rang. "I have reservations for tonight at Café des Artistes," J.R. told her. "It's Valentine's Day; have you forgotten?"

Actually she had forgotten but hoped he did not realize. "I was wondering what you were going to come up with this year."

Before Becky left the office, the doctor called and confirmed her diagnosis. Becky put down the phone and placed her hands on her stomach, thinking, "And I have a Valentine's surprise for you, my sweetheart."

**

Besides serving delicious food, Café des Artistes was perhaps one of the most romantic restaurants in the city. J.R. arrived first, holding a familiar blue box. When Becky saw him she realized she had not bought him a present.

"Do you want to open it before dinner?" Becky thought she had better open the box before he heard her news.

"Oh it's lovely, J.R." Inside the Tiffany box was a gold charm bracelet with a single heart.

"You've been hinting for a tennis bracelet, but I wanted to give you a bracelet that I can add onto on special occasions, anniversaries, birthdays, and holidays. I wish I had done this years earlier because it would be full of memories by now."

"This is probably the best timing you've ever had with any present you've given me."

"Really, you've never said that before."

"Sweetheart, I don't know how to tell you what I have to tell you, and it's something I've never said before."

"Now I'm really curious."

"I haven't been feeling myself lately."

"Why haven't you said anything to me? Please go see the doctor," he gently pleaded.

"I did, today."

"And…"

"…I'm pregnant." She relayed what the doctor had told her — that maybe she was subconsciously aware her biological clock was ticking, explaining why she became pregnant without intending to.

J.R. sat speechless, staring at Becky.

"Say something, please."

"I don't think I've loved you more than I do this minute. Beck, you're going to have a baby, our baby. I never thought it would happen. We hardly ever talked about having a baby. I figured what would be would be." He reached across the table and took her hand. "I love you so darn much, we have a wonderful life, and I didn't dare dream of more. I'm so happy I could burst."

She never knew how much he wanted children. For her, it was different. Having lost her twin at birth, and then with her parent's divorce, Becky had fears. Fear of what, she never quite knew, but here she was carrying his child, and to see the utter joy on his face wiped away her fears.

"You know when this happened don't you?" she asked.

"Is this a guessing game?"

"If it is...you only get one guess."

"Hmm...New Year's Eve?" They both laughed.

Then looking into his wife's eyes, he continued, "What a way to conceive! I don't think I'll ever tell our child about it, but I'll never forget this past New Year's Eve. Darling, this is the best Valentine's Day present you've ever given me." He let his hand fall onto Becky's stomach.

"Well Mister, this will have to do. Consider this baby your gift."

"Would you like to order?" their waiter interrupted them.

"Yes, I'll have a glass of champagne, and for my wife and mother-to-be a glass of something nonalcoholic."

"Congratulations!" the waiter said.

"Thank you, you're the first person we've told." J.R. was beaming.

On the way home a light rain began to fall. It was the front of a major snowstorm, heading towards the city on the beginning of a long holiday weekend. "Just think," J.R. said, still processing he was going to be a father, "we're going to be snowed in for three days, you me and our baby. I can't think of any place else on earth I would rather be."

Becky asked, "Who should we call first?"

"Your mother naturally. Let's call her tonight. I'll tell Dad in the morning, and you can call your father."

J.R. watched as Becky undressed. He studied her body and waited with anticipation until she got into bed. "Can we…?"

"Yes we can, and we should."

**

Good news could not have come at a better time, and what better kind than the announcement of a baby. Never thinking they would have grandchildren, the grandparents were both shocked and excited over the news. Now it was time to tell other family members, especially Danny, who was coming home on leave. While they could have called him, J.R. wanted to tell Danny in person.

~~~~~~~~~~~~~~~

"We need to hurry or we'll get caught in the Friday afternoon traffic," J.R. told Becky. They were going to Boston for the weekend.

"Don't rush a pregnant lady," she replied.

Whenever Becky used the "pregnant lady" card, all J.R. could do was shake his head and give in. In this case, he sat and waited patiently until she was ready — traffic be damned.

On the road and crossing the Willis Avenue Bridge leaving the city, J.R. talked about his favorite topic, the baby, wishing he knew if it was a boy or girl.

"Beck, sometimes I have to pinch myself. I never thought it would happen. I wish Marc were here…" His voice trailed off.

"I know, Love, I know. He would have been over the moon."

He squeezed her hand, and the car fell silent as it continued to speed along the Merritt Parkway toward Boston.

~~~~~~~~~~~~~~~

Danny had been in Virginia for briefings and was home on a weekend leave before joining his squadron. His squadron and the rest of CVW-3 (Carrier Airwing Three) had been stationed onboard the *USS Harry S. Truman* in the Mediterranean off the coast of Israel since the carrier deployed on the fifth of December 2002. There were rumblings of an intervention in Iraq. The Bush administration had been working at cobbling together a coalition of nations. The UN sent weapons inspectors into Iraq to determine if there were weapons of mass destruction, which in the end could never be verified. Realizing that the UN Security Council would not authorize the use of military force (because France and Germany opposed it), the United States prepared for war. A "coalition of the willing" was formed with more than twenty nations, including the UK and Australia, participating. It was the beginning of March. The country was again divided about entering a conflict. However, the hearts and minds of Americans had not healed from 9/11, and there was an overall feeling that someone or somebody needed to pay for that dark day.

~~~~~~~~~~~~~~

"We're glad you could all make it," Josh said as people congregated in the kitchen.

"Danny, you look handsome in your uniform," Ruth noted, wanting to say something positive, knowing her grandson was staunch in his choice.

"Thank you, Grandma. I know you love a man in uniform. I saw how handsome Grandpa was in his," Danny replied.

Ruth could only smile, thinking of Peter. "How long will you stay in the Navy this time?"

"Five years, or maybe I'll make it a career."

"If you do, you're going to have to promise me you'll get home every so often for some of my home cooking; otherwise no deal."

Danny laughed and promised his grandmother she had a deal.

Before dinner, J.R. took Danny aside. "There's something you need to know Danny." Then he broke the big news — that he and Becky were going to be parents.

"That's fantastic. Where's Becky?"

"Someone talking about me?"

"Congratulations Mama. I'm happy for you guys."

"Thanks Danny. We swore everyone to secrecy until J.R. could tell you in person," Becky explained.

Danny hugged and cried with J.R. These two men had transcended a family connection after 9/11, and were bound together in a way even they did not fully comprehend. "We'll let you know as soon as we know if it's a boy or girl," J.R. promised.

During dinner the table conversation centered on Becky finding out she was pregnant during the President's Day weekend snowstorm, now referred to as one of the biggest Megalopolis snowstorms in the northeast. Josh was thankful there was something else to talk about besides what seemed an inevitable war in Iraq. Danny had not divulged his upcoming assignment, but Josh expected his son would be sent to the Middle East.

~~~~~~~~~~~~~~~~~~~~~~~~~~~~~~~~~~

"Twins!!" Becky repeated as she looked up at J.R. from the table where she was lying, having an ultrasound.

"Twins!" he repeated, stunned. "Are you sure? Can you please look again?"

"Yes you're having twins. Two babies," the doctor repeated, and then she pointed out the images on the screen. "Here, let me show you. It won't be long before we'll know their sex. Maybe you'll have one of each."

Hearing the doctor mention twins, Becky's eyes filled with tears. Her thoughts turned to her twin who did not make it.

"I hope those are tears of joy," the doctor said.

Becky explained she was thinking about her twin brother who died at birth.

The doctor turned around on her stool. She took Becky's hand in hers. "Do you know what he died of?"

"I remember something about his lungs not being fully developed."

"Well, we've come a long way since your mother lost her baby. Today your brother most likely would have lived. We'll keep a close eye on you every step of the way. Nothing is going to happen to your babies. Now I'll let the two of you have a moment alone to soak in this wonderful surprise."

The doctor left the room, giving Becky and J.R. time alone to digest the news. In disbelief she wiped away her tears. "J.R., what are we going to do with two babies? I was just getting used to the idea of one."

"We're going to love them, that's what we're going to do. Our families are going to be thrilled. I know I am."

J.R. was taking this much better than his wife, and he hoped Becky would come around soon.

Lying in bed that night, J.R. could not take his hands off Becky. "Remember Valentine's Day when I said I could never love you more? Not true. Because if it's possible, I do this very minute."

~~~~~~~~~~~~~~~~~~~~~~~~~~~~~~~~~

Opening his mail on deck, Danny read the words: "We're having twins." "Twins — wow!" He nudged a buddy, sharing his news. The men on the carrier had become family. They knew one another's stories and joined in their joys and sorrows. He thought about phoning Becky and J.R. to offer his congratulations, but looked at his watch. Realizing the time difference, he instead sent an email: *"Congratulations to the both of you. I can't wait until you find out if they are boys, girls, or one of each. J.R., take care of Becky; she's carrying precious cargo. Waiting for the other shoe to drop over here. Stay safe. Miss you. Love Danny."* While at the computer he sent an email to his parents.

Later that evening the loud speaker announced all personnel were to stand by television monitors in an hour. The president of the United States would be speaking.

On March 17, 2003, president, George W. Bush, began his speech:

> *"My fellow citizens, events in Iraq have now reached the final days of decision. For more than a decade, the United States and other nations have pursued patient and honorable efforts to disarm the Iraqi regime without war. That regime pledged to reveal and destroy all its weapons of mass destruction as a condition for ending the Persian Gulf War in 1991."*

The president then went on to explain to the American public what led up to his decision to take action. Danny, along with the rest of his fellow pilots, listened intently to the president's words, knowing exactly what this meant for them.

Within two days, on March 19 at 10:16 p.m. EST, when Danny was flying a mission over Iraq, the president of The United States took to the airwaves again to address the American public:

> *"My fellow citizens, at this hour, American and coalition forces are in the early stages of military operations to disarm Iraq, to free its people and to defend the world from grave danger. On my orders, coalition forces have begun striking selected targets of military importance to undermine Saddam Hussein's ability to wage war. These are opening stages of what will be a broad and concerted campaign. More than thirty-five countries are giving crucial support — from the use of naval and air bases, to help with intelligence and logistics, to the deployment of combat units. Every nation in this coalition has chosen to bear the duty and share the honor of serving in our common defense. To all the men and women of the United States Armed Forces now in the Middle East, the peace of a troubled world and the hopes of an oppressed people now depend on you. That trust is well placed."*

And thus began the Iraq War.

**

Every pilot knows landing on a 500-foot flight deck is one of the most difficult landings they will ever make.

There was nothing unusual about the night of March 22, 2003. Mission accomplished, Danny reflected as he flew over Turkish airspace, on his way back to the carrier from an airstrike on Baghdad. Earlier there had been showers, but the sky was clear overhead: CAVU (ceiling and visibility unrestricted), in Navy speak. As he began to make his approach, he knew the drill, aim for the "3" wire. There were four parallel wires on the deck, about fifty feet apart, but the third wire was the optimum one to catch with the tailhook. This skill was critical to landing, and in order to move up the ranks, pilots needed to be able to catch the "3" wire on a consistent basis. Danny was consistent, an ace at this task.

Danny's plane had plenty of fuel and was designated the last plane to "stack up" in a flying pattern near the carrier. Waiting his turn, Danny began to ponder his life. "Do I really want to go back to American Express?" he wondered. "Maybe I should stay in the Navy. I love flying; I could become an instructor or a commercial pilot at some point…" While speculating about his future, crackle over his headset jolted him back to reality. It was the carrier's Air Traffic Control Center informing him to prepare for landing.

Danny headed toward the stern of the ship as the landing signals officers (LSOs) began to guide the plane through the darkness. Night landings were the most difficult landings for every pilot. The landings were not visual but controlled by instruments. As Danny made his approach, he heard a radio command from the LSO that he was not on the glidescope. They waved him off and sent him around for another try.

"Come on Danny, concentrate. You've done this hundreds of time. Pay attention to the ball. You'll be the squadron Bolter King if you have to make any more attempts to land." He said to himself as he gained control of his plane for a second try.

Danny concentrated on the Fresnel lens, a lighting system that provided additional guidance for landing planes at night. If a pilot were on target, he would see an amber light in line with a row of green lights dubbed by pilots as the "meatball," or "ball" for short. If the amber light was visible above the green lights, the pilot was flying too high, and if the plane was flying too low, the pilot would see red lights.

Coming in for his second attempt, Danny could distinguish by the red lights he was coming in too low. He knew he had to shoot for the "1" wire. However, the LSOs could see he was even too low for the "1" wire and signaled him to add power and wave off. Danny could feel his heart pounding in his chest. Sweat poured out of his pores, drenching his flight suit. Trying to remember every emergency-landing procedure he was taught, he prayed his tailhook would catch the "1" wire because he knew it was too late to pull up. Traveling at over 122 knots, he could see the stern of the carrier, a big hulk of steel, directly in front of him. The scene was akin to a Formula 1 racecar driver watching his car hurl into a concrete wall. The plane continued to dip lower and to the right, slamming with its full force into the carrier. The crew on deck watched helplessly as the nose of the Hornet crumbled into the stern like a piece of foil. Danny had no time to eject, and in the early morning on the 22nd of March, Danny sank into the Mediterranean Sea strapped in the seat of his plane. On deck a rescue truck rushed to the scene. A sense of helplessness permeated the crew.

The plane was hauled out of the water by a Navy salvage ship and put onto a barge. Danny's body was recovered and flown to Ramstein Air Force Base in Germany. From there Danny's remains were returned to Dover Air Force Base in Delaware, where a military escort prepared Danny for the trip home.

~~~~~~~~~~~~~

"Nena, can you come for dinner?" Gabby had a pleading quality to her voice.

"Is everything okay?"

"Yes, I'm a bundle of nerves with what's going on in Iraq. I can't stop worrying about Danny."

"I'll leave work early. Don't fuss; I'll stop and get dessert. Do you want me to pick up Mum?"

"That would be nice. I need the both of you right now."

Lately Gabby had been consumed with feelings of foreboding over Danny serving in Iraq…feelings she wished she could control.

Greeting her sister and mother-in-law Ruth asked, "Is there something going on we should know about?"

"Not that I know, but I have this feeling I can't shake."

When Josh arrived home, they sat down to dinner. No sooner had they began to eat than the phone rang. Josh jumped up to take the call, thinking it might be work-related.

"Hello…yes…" Josh could not believe what he was hearing. "Yes, when will this happen?" His hand shook so badly he could hardly hold onto the receiver. "I understand. I will wait for your call." Words were hard to articulate. Breathing heavily, his mouth dry and parched, he knew he needed to say something. "Thank you for calling." He hung up.

When Josh returned to the table, he was as white as a ghost. Gabby's worst fears were coming to the surface. She did not ask Josh who had called. At that moment, she did not want to know. The silence at the table was eerie.

Gabby at last spoke. "Josh, please tell us; did something happen at the office?"

"No. Something happened to Danny. Our Danny…my son…he's dead." Josh looked like he was in a daze.

Gabby slumped in her chair. Nena went to her side, pushed Gabby's chair from the table, and cradled her in her arms. Sobs filled around the room. Ruth held her son the same way she did when he was a child, wanting to make his hurt go away. It was some time before a word was spoken. Finally, Gabby spoke the obvious: "My boy, he survived 9/11, he survived, and now they tell me he's dead. I knew in my heart something horrible had happened. Danny's presence was with me all day. I feared if I spoke his name my world would shatter into so many pieces."

"What did the military tell you, Josh?" Nena asked.

"Danny's body is being flown home from Germany to Dover, Delaware, tomorrow. They want to know what we want to do about burial."

"When did he die?" Now Gabby wanted details. She needed something, anything, to stop this surreal trance she found herself in. She needed Danny to be real.

"Early Saturday morning. He was returning from an airstrike on Baghdad. There were no details only that his plane crashed before it could land on the deck. There will be an investigation. I don't know anything else except we lost our boy; our son Danny is gone." Josh could not control his emotions. He excused himself from the room. Then they heard the front door close, and moments later the engine of his car revved and he drove off.

Nena and Ruth cleared the table and adjourned to the family room where Nena poured three glasses of wine and raised her glass saying, "To our Danny, a son who loved his mother, and his mother who loved her son unconditionally, enough to let him go to war when in her heart she did not want to let go. To a grandson loved beyond words and to a nephew who was cherished." The three women sat in the room, as women over the ages have sat alone in rooms around the world when they received the news of a loved one lost in battle.

Nena went to the phone and called Rachael to come to the house, and then called Becky.

"I can't believe this; we just heard from him. Mum, how are Uncle Josh and Auntie Gabby doing?" Becky asked after she heard what happened.

"Not good, as you can expect. Your grandmother and I are here with Gabby, and I called Rachael to come over. Uncle Josh left the house; I hope he's okay."

"I don't know what to say…They must be beside themselves. Should we come up?"

"No, not now. The body is being flown back, and once the funeral arrangements are made, I will let you know. I need to go now; I hear Rachel's voice. Please take care of yourself and those babies."

When Rachael heard about her brother, she looked around the room. "Where's Daddy?" she asked in anguish.

Ruth could not bear to look at her granddaughter. Rachael's face captured the pain of the entire family. "Your father had to get some air; he went for a ride."

**

"Rabbi, thank you for seeing me. I know you're in the middle of dinner, but I didn't know where else to go." Then Josh broke down, telling the rabbi that Danny had been killed when his plane crashed.

"Josh, there is never any easy way to accept the death of a child. We are led to believe we should outlive our children. But Yahweh does not always work the way we expect or want." The rabbi continued, "I have known your children since they were born. Danny always had a mind of his own. He questioned, he listened, he was respectful, but he followed his own path. Do you remember the last time the both of you came to temple before he returned to active duty? I called fighting for his country brave. He said it wasn't brave, but right. Josh, Danny watched those towers go down, one of those three thousand souls could have been his. Your son is a hero; he was both brave and right. Where would we be without the Danny's of this world? Let us say a prayer for the dead, and then I want you to go home to Gabby, put your arms around her, and give thanks you had this young man as your son. You as parents have to share this loss, but you must never forget what a gift Danny was to everyone who knew him, and we share your loss too." They prayed and Josh went home.

**

Becky hung up the phone and ran to J.R. "What's the matter?" he asked. And in each other's arms, they wept for Danny and the loss of a young man who had become more than a family member but a friend, and for J.R., a best friend, the only person in his life who could relate to the day they almost died together. Not even Becky, the love of his life, could understand – only Danny, and now he was no longer.

**

When Josh returned from seeing the rabbi, he went into his study. He asked Gabby to join him. Danny had left a letter with his father before he left for the Mediterranean. He opened the letter and read:

> *Dad, I know Mum is not happy with my decision about the Navy, but I think you understand. It goes back to my time in Israel, and the young men and women and their devotion to the safety of the country they love. After the towers fell, I could not turn my back on my country and how I feel about this mission I am on.*
>
> *I am writing this note to tell you my wishes. If anything happens to me, I want to be buried in Israel. I want you and Mum, and whoever else wants to go, to bring me there to the place of our ancestors, who taught us to fight for our land. I have always felt I have two countries I love. Don't misunderstand; I love America. This is where I was born, and I am proud of what I am doing for my homeland. I believe in this fight, but I am also connected to Israel and want to rest there the remainder of my days. Plant a tree in my memory. I love you and Mum, Dad. I couldn't have asked for better parents. You let me fly in more ways than one. I will always be your faithful and loving son. Danny.*

Josh carefully laid the note on his desk, feeling the pride of a parent who had raised a child who became a man of such integrity — with such purity of heart. Gabby looked into Josh's eyes with the same pride.

"Gabby, we did a wonderful job, you and I. We raised the best of the best, and we will take him to Israel. Are you okay with that?"

"It's not about me, is it? It's what Danny wanted. Sometimes I wonder how we got so lucky with him. My regret is our time with him was too short. Go ahead; call the rabbi and make the arrangements."

As Gabby started to leave the study, Josh grabbed her arm. "I know this was your worst nightmare come true, but you've been solid and steady keeping us together. We'll make it through this. We're going to plant an entire forest of trees for our Danny, and we'll think of some other way to honor him."

"We have to Josh, because Danny's death can't be in vain. We're going to honor our son in such a way he will live on long after us." Tightly, they clung together.

**

The entire family flew to Israel. Besides Josh and Gabby, there was Rachael, her husband and children, Nena, Ruth, Becky, J.R., Ben, and Jay. At the gravesite, Josh thought about what the rabbi had said to him about Danny, about how he had followed his own path. They planted trees in his honor, and a few days were spent visiting the places that Danny grew to love. Everyone there made a vow he would never be forgotten.

The technician slid the transducer probe across Becky's stomach. She and J.R. were looking at the screen when the doctor came in to tell them the news.

"Boys, two boys. Double trouble."

J.R. had a different perspective.

"What do you mean double trouble?" he asked the doctor. "This is fantastic."

"I knew it, and it does mean double trouble." Becky turned her head toward her husband who was in seventh heaven.

The doctor smiled. "I know you were hoping for a boy and a girl, but the bright side is everything is looking excellent. Sometimes one twin is on top of the other, but these two are nearly side-by-side. You're doing fine Becky; I'll see you in a month."

Alone in the examining room, Becky asked J.R., "Are you certain those are the names?"

"I've never been more certain."

They had talked about names, names that would mean something. "Marc and Danny it is. They'll live on through our boys, J.R.; they will."

"Yes, they will, Beck. I keep saying this, and I'm probably sounding like a broken record, but I love you *more* than I thought I ever could love anyone." J.R. bent over and kissed her belly. "These boys are a gift my love, a gift."

"They are, and they will know the men whose names they carry."

Venice seemed a cure-all for Nena. Not exactly a magic potion, but a refuge for her weary soul. Before she left for her summer break, she suggested Ruth and Gabby come with her. At first Gabby resisted, until Josh and Rachael insisted she needed a change.

Neither of them had visited Nena's apartment, much less Venice. Walking past the fountain in the courtyard as the morning sunlight reflected in the water, Ruth wistfully expressed, "Peter would have loved it here." Upon entering the apartment, she continued, "How lovely Nena; I can see why you are attached to this place. This *is* an oasis in a world of turmoil."

"I knew you would understand why I'm comfortable here. Sam would have felt the same way." For a moment Nena was transported to what might have been. But she quickly remembered why they were here.

"Gabby, you've been awfully quiet." Nena did not want to probe, but asked, "Are you sorry you came?"

"On the contrary," she sighed. "This place is just what I need. Everyone but me knew I needed to get away. Thank you Nena, for everything —

everything you've done for me since Danny…" Her voice trailed off, and tears filled her eyes.

Nena turned to her sister-in-law, taking her hand. "We are always going to miss Danny, but Danny was about living, and that is what we are going to do, for him. Tonight I'm going to take you girls to the Cipriani for dinner. I'm calling my old friend Natale for a table. This family has had its share of heartache the past few years. Life has tried to push us down, but we keep getting up — and this time will be no different. We're going to live for those we have lost." These words had a hint of bravado on Nena's part, because she herself still mourned Sam.

Ruth looked at her daughter. This once happy-go-lucky child who had the rug pulled out from underneath her twice as an adult had not let her circumstances harden her. "You're right, Nena, we're going to take Venice by storm. Danny would be darn proud of you, Gabby. Come on girls. Nena make those reservations. Let's change our clothes and take a walk around Nena's neighborhood. I'm not too old to learn a little Italian, am I?"

Gabby hugged her mother-in-law. "No Mum and neither am I."

**

For the next month, the women explored the area, went on excursions to Florence and Verona, where Nena relived her trip there with Sam. Locally they shopped at the one-of-a-kind specialty food shops, cooked in, and ate out. Ruth and Gabby even learned a little Italian. They left Venice with a sense of renewal and arrived back in the States just in time for the arrival of the newest members of the family.

"Push!"

"What the hell do you think I'm doing?"

With a side-glance, the doctor looked at J.R. who was white as the sheets covering Becky. "Keep it together; please don't faint on me. Honestly J.R. your wife is holding up better than you. Someone give him a damp cloth." Turning back to her patient, she said, "You're doing fantastic Becky; push. We're almost there."

"What's this *we* crap? Becky thought. She's always saying we. We this…we that. I'm the person here doing all the work." She wanted to tell them what was on her mind, but she was too busy trying to give birth to these boys.

Within a minute, a loud wail filled the delivery room, followed by another seconds later.

The doctor announced, "Two beautiful baby boys. Good job, Becky."

She dared not ask, but she had to. Would both of her boys survive? Becky was afraid history would repeat itself. She remembered the doctor had told her that John would have lived if he had been born now, but Becky needed reassurance.

The doctor assured her, "There's nothing to worry about Becky; your sons are healthy and strong. Take a deep breath, and enjoy this moment."

"Did you hear that J. R? My babies are strong and healthy." Becky could feel the relief explode throughout her body.

"Yes, I did Beck. We have two tough boys. You did a beautiful job, Mama. I'm so proud of you."

On Tuesday October 7, a warm fall day in New York City, the twins were examined, dried, wrapped in two blue blankets, and placed in Becky's arms.

When the babies left for the nursery, J.R. and Becky started making telephone calls. The sounds over the phone from the grandparents filled the room with utter euphoria. Questions were asked about names. The new parents were evasive, waiting until the weekend, when they came home from the hospital to share their decision. Until then, they told people they were still considering names.

**

Monday, on Columbus Day, as oohs and ahhs filled their apartment, Becky and J.R. prepared to announce the boys' names to the family.

"This is a special day for us," J.R. began. "I never thought I would be a father, let alone a father of twins. I know Becky carried our boys with joy, but with concern, knowing her twin brother John did not survive when she did. However, here we are today, celebrating two healthy little boys. Now that they are here, I couldn't imagine our lives without them. Becky and I had so much love and that love has now doubled." He paused and looked at his sons, trying to grasp what act of providence had created this miracle.

"Now for the names. Drum roll please…In this bassinette is Marc John," J.R. announced, pointing to the baby wearing a yellow nightgown. "Of course he's named after our dear friend Marc and after Becky's brother John, her uncle, and grandfather. We're going to call him M. J. for short." Then J.R. turned to the other baby crying in his bassinet, "Now for this little fella, heaven help us if he stays this loud. He's getting three names: Daniel Peter Samuel, after Danny, Nena's father, and Sam, a man we all grew to love. Their names honor some very special people. People we have loved who are no longer with us. Their names are also a symbol for all those souls lost on 9/11, lest we shall never forget. We didn't think we needed a Jason Robertson Stark IV. I hope that's okay with you Dad." Jay gave his approval, and J.R. continued, "I'm afraid these tiny babies have no idea what big shoes they're going to have to fill. Family, we are proud, happy, and thrilled to introduce you to M. J. and Daniel!"

There are moments in life when the world falls silent. This was one of them.

Gabby was barely able to speak. "To honor our Danny in such a thoughtful way leaves me speechless. He would be bursting with pride, if he knew."

Becky looked at her aunt and uncle. "He does…I know he does.

"I don't know what to say," Ben began. "To name your son after my father, my brother Jackie, and the son Nena and I lost…I am lost for words. I don't know if…" Before he could finish, Ben broke down.

All eyes in the room turned toward Nena. She did not know if she was prepared to say anything, especially hearing Ben speak of their son. She feared she would give in to the heartache of their loss those many years ago. Regaining control of herself, she knew what needed to be said.

"I'm pleased you chose to honor Dad, but what can I say — to pay tribute to Sam is unexpected and affects me deeply in ways you will never know. I think I can speak for all of us when I say you have touched our hearts. You have helped this family take another step in our healing process. Besides bringing two new lives into the world, you have breathed new life into us. May the Lord continue to fill you with wisdom while you raise these two beautiful boys."

After the birth of the twins, Tuesdays would take on a new meaning for Nena. No longer would this day only represent the sorrow of 9/11 — but now the day would also represent gratitude for the gift of these two new lives.

~~~~~~

J.R. had been working at Stark Land Development for six months. Things were going well, and he felt it was time to make a presentation to his father. He arrived to work early one morning, telling his father he had something he wanted to talk with him about.

"Talk away Robbie.

"I'm wondering if you might want to add another dimension to the company."

"Another dimension, hmm? Want to elaborate? What's your idea?"

"Residential real estate."

"Honestly, I've never even thought about it. We've been successful with commercial real estate since the founding of the company. Give me your best argument. Convince me."

This is what J.R. had been waiting for, his chance to put his stamp on the family business. He had done his research, and he was ready.

"As you know, there are signs the housing market is on the rise. Prices are beginning to slowly climb. If we bought some land outside the city, depending on the size of the property, we could build a dozen houses in the high six figures, and see how it goes. If it doesn't go well, we can cut our losses, but at least we gave it a try."

Jay listened intently. "I need a day or two to weigh the pros and cons. I want to do a little homework, and we'll talk again."

"Thanks, Dad." While J.R. was not thrilled to wait for an answer, he was relieved his father did not close the door.

**

A few days later over lunch, Jay let J.R. know he had reservations about a residential real estate project. "I reread an editorial Robert Hunn wrote this past spring and he thought that unless real estate will outstrip other investments, you might want to rethink real estate."

"I hear you Dad, but there are other analysts who say Hunn is wrong."

"And I hear you, but I value Hunn's opinion. Our business is built on commercial investments, and we need to keep a close eye on them."

Jay studied his son's body language and could see how badly J.R. wanted his approval for this idea.

Pausing for what seemed to J.R. like an eternity, Jay relented, "Okay, let's do this. Take a trip to Westchester and look for a piece of property. We'll build the houses, but let's try to presell. If it goes well, we'll talk about the next step."

"Thanks, Dad. You'll see this is going to be a nice addition to our bottom line and company growth."

"A step at a time, Robbie, a step at a time, I want you to remember this company was built a step at a time." Jay observed the enthusiasm of youth in his son, wondering if he really heard his counsel.

J.R. returned to the office two feet off the ground. He immediately phoned a real estate agent in Westchester County. He set up appointments for the following week, more excited than he had been about anything since finding out he and Becky were having twins.

**

Driving to the suburbs north on the Hutchinson River Parkway to Interstate 684, J.R. began to second-guess himself. He knew his father had a different take on this project; Jay had been in this game a lot longer than he. Nevertheless, J.R. put any doubts aside as he drove from the highway onto a two-lane road leading to an old farm. The first property was in Bedford, a small well to-do town in the northeastern part of Westchester County. Established in the late seventeen hundreds, and known for its three-hundred-year-old oak planted by the original settlers, Bedford was within commuting distance from Manhattan and a safe place to raise a family: a desirable location. Getting out of the car, he was greeted by the agent.

An hour of walking the land, J.R. knew this was not what he had in mind and asked the agent to see another property.

"I have a place in Lewisboro, and another across the line in Ridgefield. Let's leave your car at my office, and I'll drive."

Lewisboro, New York, abutted the Connecticut line. Settled a few years after Bedford, the town had a rural feel and was noted for its gardens and graceful Colonial mansions. "Well what do you think?" the agent asked. J.R. made his assessment: "I feel the same about this property as I did about the last. It's close, but not quite what I'm looking for. Let's check out the Ridgefield property? Fingers crossed three's the charm!"

Driving across the state line into Connecticut, they reached Ridgefield. Ridgefield was further north in Fairfield County, just off the main line of the commuter rail. The housing prices were affordable for families needing to live within proximity of a commute to work in Stamford or Manhattan. Located in the foothills of the Berkshire Mountains, Ridgefield was formed around the same time as Bedford and Lewisboro and exuded New England charm. With a commuter rail nearby, great schools, and part of the town center on the National Register of Historic Places. Ridgefield appealed to J.R., and the minute he walked onto the property, less than a mile from downtown, making the location ideal, he knew this was the place to begin his dream. The land had been approved and subdivided for twelve houses, saving J.R. months of town meetings before he could begin to build.

"Well?" the agent asked him.

"We might have a deal." Not wanting to appear overly excited, J.R. played a poker face. "Get the negotiations underway, and make this happen to my benefit."

On the drive back to the city, J.R. was confident he had made the right decision and could not wait to tell his father.

~~~~~~

"Are you nervous, excited? How are you feeling?" Becky asked J.R.

"A little of each." The sale had gone through quickly. Fifteen acres of land had been divided for building use. Surveying completed, today was groundbreaking day on the project. "I wish you could be there."

"Oh, I don't think a construction site is the right place for a woman who has recently given birth to twins."

It was early November and the plan was to get the land cleared and install the utilities before winter and the ground froze. J.R. was in a time crunch. He wanted to be ready for building once spring arrived. The plans were drawn for twelve single-family homes, each on an acre around a cul-de-sac, with three acres of open space. The objective was to presell the houses as quickly as possible. J.R. set the completion date for 2005. If real estate continued to rise, he had no doubts he would meet his goal.

**

The year 2003 came to a close. In spite of the cold weather, the project was moving forward. The twins were thriving, Ben was in remission, Nena had come to an agreement at work where she would continue working, but on a part-time basis, allowing her to split her time between Boston, New York, and Venice. Josh and Gabby were holding their first fund-raiser after the holidays — an education fund for children of fallen heroes. This would be their way to honor Danny and his love of learning. And the house in Ogunquit would not be sold, now that Jay had M. J. and Daniel in his life. The new year, 2004, arrived on notes of hope.

Part V

2004–2009

Chapter 16

The winter of 2004 had not been kind. It was colder than normal, and a moderately severe flu season began earlier than usual. Although Ruth had a flu shot, she came down with what she referred to as a lingering cold.

"Honestly Nena, it's nothing, just a nasty cold. I don't need to see the doctor. The minute someone sneezes or has an ache you young people run to the doctor," she told her daughter in one of their frequent telephone calls.

"Mum, you know that's not true. Humor me, please. Let me make an appointment."

**

"See, I knew it was only a touch of the flu. You need to stop fussing over me." Ruth had gone to see the doctor at Nena's insistence.

"I'm just making sure you stay healthy. We're going to Venice in April, and I don't want an achy, coughing mother on my hands."

"Lord, I certainly hope I'm better by then."

"Let's go for tea at the Inn before I take you home."

"That would be lovely; we haven't done that in ages."

Sitting in the Colonial Inn, the fireplace ablaze, sipping their tea, both mother and daughter talked about the many memories this place held, and were comforted that some things did not change.

"Except for the unnecessary trip to the doctor, this has been a wonderful afternoon," Ruth said.

After they finished tea, Nena took Ruth home. Before leaving, she reminded her mother that they were going to Gabby's the following day to work on Danny's fund-raiser.

"Love you, Mum. See you at eleven."

"Love you back." Ruth watched her daughter leave and blew her a kiss.

**

The next morning when Nena arrived to pick up her mother, Ruth did not answer the door. Nena used her key to let herself in.

"Mum, are you ready?" There was no answer.

Nena walked into the bedroom to find her mother in bed. She stood paralyzed in the doorway. She flashed back to the day when she, Ben, and Becky were living in London, when she found her mother-in-law Helen in her bedroom lying in the bed cold as ice. Nena did not know how long she stood there, this time looking at her own mother. Finally she found the courage to walk to the bed. Taking her mother's hand in hers, she could still feel the warmth of her body.

"Mum, Mummy, can you hear me? Please say something, PLEASE." Ruth was staring at the ceiling. No words were forthcoming.

Nena picked up the phone and called Josh at his office. Nena was crying inconsolably. Josh could hardly make out what she was saying, but he knew something was terribly wrong. He stopped to pick up Gabby on the way, knowing he could not handle the situation alone. They ran into the house to find Nena sitting on the bed, holding Ruth to her bosom, rocking back and forth, like a mother rocks a child.

"Come…come with me, Nena," Gabby said gently. "Let's lay Mum down, and you come with me." Gabby and Nena left the room, while Josh closed his mother's eyes and covered her body.

After calling the undertaker and minister, Josh made the most difficult calls he had made since Danny died.

**

A simple memorial service was held in the family church, celebrating a woman who was not only a pillar to her family, but to the community where she lived her entire life. Nena gave thanks her mother did not suffer a horrible illness, instead dying peacefully in her sleep. But this was her mother, her rock, the steady hand that raised her, stood by her, became her dearest friend, and now she would have to face life without her. Nena had not prepared for this moment — this day. She felt lost.

Outside the church Nena heard a voice. "Mum," the voice startled her. "Mum, I'm here for you." Becky told her. "I know it won't be the same, but I'm here."

Nena looked at her daughter. This was one of the big passages in life. Nena had stepped into the role her mother had held her entire life. For the first time, she understood how Ruth felt when she lost her mother. She thought, "No one can understand until it's your turn." She knew Becky could not understand either, but to see her daughter standing beside her brought reassurance.

"I'm going to be okay, Becky. I will be all right."

**

Losing Ruth was the last straw. Josh wanted to sell the house right away, but Nena convinced him to wait until later in the year. She needed to bury herself in work, and plan her trip to Venice. The trip she thought she would be taking with Ruth.

Before leaving for Italy, Nena asked Becky to check on the apartment while she was away. Nena had owned the apartment for three years, but it would always be Sam's Place to her.

"You never have to ask; of course we will," her daughter replied. "I can imagine when the boys are older they'll love having your apartment to escape to."

"Older, much older, I hope." The thought of it, however, brought a lightness to her otherwise somber soul.

"How long will you be gone?" Becky asked.

"I'll be gone about a month. I told them at work I would be back by May. Are you planning on spending time in Ogunquit this summer?"

"Yes. J.R. and I have decided since he is consumed with the project the boys and I will spend July and August at the house. There's plenty of room. Why don't we plan on you coming for a visit when you get back?"

"Lovely idea. This will give me something to look forward to when I return."

Then Becky asked her mother what she was planning to do about her home in Boston.

"I don't know." Becky's question took Nena off guard. She had recently buried her mother; first her parents' home needed to be sold. Nena could not take on another thing. "I'll retire next year, and then I'll cross that bridge."

Becky pushed her agenda. "Perhaps you could start thinking about it when you're in Venice. I know Josh and Gabby and your friends are in Boston, but we want you near the boys as they grow up. Is that being too selfish?"

"No! I promise I'll think about what you've said." Underneath her thoughtful response, Nena realized she really needed space to assess her life for herself, and not for anyone else.

~~~~~~~~~~~~~

Nena looked out the airplane window, flying above the clouds heading east across the Atlantic. Venice had become her sanctuary. The city felt like home, and she was comfortable not only with her surroundings, but with the locals who acknowledged her presence whenever she walked through her neighborhood. Her anchor was the staff at the Cipriani, taking her yet again under their wing and offering her comfort and friendship.

~~~~~~~~~~~~~

"Pronto!"

"Mum?"

"Oh I couldn't help myself; I'm still on Italian time." Nena had arrived home from Venice that afternoon.

"I've been calling all morning. I thought you were flying in yesterday."

"Becky, you knew what day I was coming home, and you must stop this worrying. I know why you do, but you need to stop. I'm fine. The trip did me wonders. In fact I'm going to call Josh tonight and tell him we can begin to clean out your grandmother's house."

This was music to Becky's ears, hoping her mother would return the mother she knew.

"I remember cleaning out the farm after your great-grandmother died," Nena continued. "I was at Smith at the time and had just begun to date your father. He drove up from Connecticut. Lots of memories associated with cleaning out a family home, especially when the place has been in the family for a lifetime."

"Would you want me to come down to help?"

"Thanks honey, but I need to do this with your uncle. If we get into the weeds, we'll appreciate extra hands. Let's see how it goes."

Becky then asked her mother if it would be okay if Ben visited them in Maine while she was there too.

"Becky, you don't have to check with me. You know what might be nice though, let's include Jay."

"Great idea — two grandfathers, one for each boy."

That night Nena called her brother. They made plans to begin the task of clearing their parents' home. Nena was not looking forward to the process, but knew with Josh by her side, the lifetime of happy memories the house held would outweigh the sadness of selling it.

~~~~~~~~~~~~~~~~~~~~~~~~~~~~

The twelve houses in Ridgefield were presold. To complete the project on target for the summer of 2005, extra crews needed to be added. Not an easy undertaking, as the housing boom was in full gear, and high-level skilled craftsman were in demand. Jay called in a few favors, something he rarely ever did, to keep the project on target.

"I never would have guessed the housing market was going to experience such an explosion," Jay commented when they went over the books. "By the time you finish, your initial profit estimates will have tripled."

"I know this market has been unbelievable. Dad, I'd like to move ahead and make an offer on the property in New Canaan I mentioned to you. If we bought that property for the land, tore down the two houses presently there, we could approach the planning and zoning commission for maybe six housing permits." Again, J.R.'s enthusiasm was unbridled.

"Isn't that getting a bit ahead of ourselves? First we need to build and sell the remaining houses in Ridgefield. Robbie, let's focus on one project at a time," Jay reasoned.

"I hear you Dad, but the land in New Canaan is going to be bought by someone, and soon. You should see what's going on in that town. Builders are snapping up in-town houses almost daily, tearing them down, and building these huge houses."

"Just the same, I want us to tread carefully in this market," his father cautioned. "The market can come down as quickly as it goes up."

"Okay, I hear you, but would you do me a favor? Would you take a trip to New Canaan? Ben knows the town; he grew up there, and on the same street as the property. Get his opinion. That's all I'm asking. But if we're going to do this, we have to move quickly. Besides, by the time we bought the land and went through the red tape for the necessary permits, the houses in Ridgefield will be sold."

Reluctantly Jay gave in to his son.

"Thanks, Dad." J.R. felt confident that once Jay saw the property and talked with Ben, his father would be on board with the plan.

~~~~~~~~~~~~

Jay and Ben were leaving the following day for Maine. As long as he was in New Canaan, he took the opportunity to have Ben show him the land J.R. wanted for his next project.

The two men walked along Main Street until they came to the property — a corner lot on a slight embankment. Ben pointed to the land. "This is it. You'd have to tear down the big white house on Main Street and the little cottage around the corner."

"How much land do you figure is here?" Jay asked.

"I'd guess about two acres, give or take."

"Do you think the town will give permits for six houses?"

"If they were designed with a house on Main Street, another on the corner, and the other four on this side street where the cottage is, they might, as long as the sidelines and setbacks work. You can never guess how the board will rule."

"I wonder how many offers they've had."

"I haven't heard of any yet, but the market is getting hot. If you're serious, the only way to find out is to put in an offer," Ben suggested. "Let's go to the town hall and see what the records are showing. We can compare prices in town. I know the head of planning and zoning, perhaps he can give us an idea how many houses he thinks you could build. At least you'll know what you're up against."

Jay was a businessman who never made rash decisions and he would take a few days before talking to his son.

"Let me ask you something, Ben. You know this town. You've been around real estate, but I'm confounded with this market. What's your take?"

Ben admitted he was baffled by how much real estate prices in the area had been soaring.

"Are you concerned J.R.'s taking on more than he can handle?" Ben wondered aloud.

"Bingo! It almost seems like you can sell a dog house for a fortune and I find that worrisome."

"I hear you." Then Ben told Jay to consider looking at it from a different angle. "The worst that can happen would be you buy the land, and the market slows down for a while. Until now, land in New Canaan has held its value, and right now the in-town market is outstripping property further out. That would be the gamble, that the land prices hold on, but in the end, Jay it's your call. I'm glad I'm not you. This can't be an easy decision."

Jay continued to evaluate the options. Not the type of businessman to second-guess himself, he understood the real estate market was exploding and he knew how much J.R. wanted to ride the crest of this sudden expansion; nevertheless, he had serious reservations. He would wait until he returned from Maine to make his decision.

**

Talk of buying the property in New Canaan consumed their conversation on the trip to Maine.

"Made up your mind?" Ben queried.

"I'm still struggling, but I'm leaning toward giving J.R. the opportunity to tackle another residential project."

"Did you call to tell him?"

"No, I'll wait until I get home. Ben, real estate has changed into something I don't recognize. It seems to me it's taking the place of the stock market, and sometimes that's a crapshoot. I'm not convinced real estate is going to keep on this track, but those in the know seem to say there is no end in sight." Arriving at the house and before getting out of the car, Jay offered his last word on the subject, "Let's keep our fingers crossed it works out. And for now that's about all we can do. Oh look, there's Becky and Nena on the porch."

"Likely trying to find some quiet while the boys nap," Ben added, sensing Jay needed a break from the pressure of this land purchase decision.

"Welcome, welcome, we're so happy you're here." Becky bounded toward the car.

"The relief team has arrived." Ben put his arm around his daughter and walked to the house. "It's good to see you, Nena. Have you been enjoying your visit?"

"Who could not be having a lovely time here with Becky and the boys? We came to Maine for years, passed this house on Marginal Way walks, and never did I ever think I would be sitting on this porch with my daughter while my grandsons slept inside."

"Nena, we've learned by now life is full of the unexpected." Jay had a way of making a point. "All right Becky, what do you have planned for me and your father?"

Babysitting, Becky told the grandfathers. She and Nena were going shopping but promised to buy steamers and chowder for dinner.

"Sounds like a plan to me; how about you, Ben?"

"We can manage. Go and have fun."

At dinner that evening, the conversation eventually turned to the property in New Canaan. Jay wavered from wanting to share his concerns about buying the land when Ben spoke up.

"The last time I spoke with Ms. Danielson," Ben explained, "from what she told me, I thought she might sell the big house with some land and stay in the cottage." Ms. Danielson lived in the Hansel and Gretel cottage on the property and rented out the big white house. She was a lifelong resident of the town. "I know she hasn't been well, which is probably her reason for selling the entire property. She has a sister in Florida, and she hinted to me she might move there. I remember how my mother looked forward to her sister's visits when Jackie and I were kids. She would bring Mom a big box of grapefruit and oranges. What a treat."

Listening to the conversation, Becky seemed unaware her husband's interest in the property had taken a serious turn. He had only mentioned Ms. Danielson's land once in passing. She never thought he was considering another project this soon.

"Jay, where does this deal stand?" Becky wanted to know.

"After looking at the property yesterday, and speaking with the planning and zoning department, talking with your dad, and watching J.R. successfully handle the Ridgefield job, I'm going to give him the go ahead when I get back. But I have to be honest, I have my concerns."

"What are they?" she probed.

Jay told her he felt uncomfortable with the rate properties were increasing in price, the tearing down of older homes and building large houses being dubbed McMansions, and the growing popularity of flipping houses — buying run-down houses and fixing them up quickly for a big profit.

Nena was surprised when Jay put the situation in those terms. "We always thought of a house as a long-term investment," she said in mild disbelief. "A house was a goal, a place to raise a family; it signified stability. This world is changing too fast for me to keep up."

"I don't pretend to understand what's going on either, but this is the real estate climate at the moment, and as Ben pointed out in the worst-case scenario, the land should hold its value," Jay told her, trusting Ben was right.

Ben interrupted. He wanted Jay to avoid having any more anxiety regarding this deal. "No more business talk. We're here to enjoy ourselves and spoil those boys rotten. Time for these two grandpas to get a good night's sleep; we're going to need our energy for tomorrow."

When Ben and Jay left the room, Becky asked her mother, "Do you think I should be concerned about this? Maybe try to talk J.R. out of it? I don't get the feeling Jay is 100 percent behind this deal."

"My advice, if you want it, is you need to let it be. This is between Jay and his son. Let's take a walk to the ocean; we haven't been able to do this at night since I've been here. I love the ocean in the evening."

"Me too, let's go; the dishes can wait."

Walking out the door, Nena took her daughter's hand, hoping the concerns voiced at dinner were not an omen of things to come.

~~~~~~~~~~~~~

Jay invited J.R. to his apartment for dinner. The office was not the place to have this conversation. Ordering in Chinese he wanted the evening to be as casual as possible. He handed his son a glass of wine, gave them each a tray, and placed the containers of food on the coffee table.

J.R. could hardly contain himself wanting to know what his father was thinking, but instead asked, "How was Maine, Dad?"

"Wonderful as always, and the girls and my grandsons are enjoying themselves. I'm glad I didn't sell the house. If only Trudi could be here to see M. J. and Daniel crawling around the place. Your mother would have been in her glory." Jay paused. "Though I doubt this is what's on your mind, Robbie."

"Of course I want to hear about your trip, but you're right, I'm curious what you thought about New Canaan."

"What's not to like about that town? It has everything going for it: location, schools, and recreational facilities of all sorts. Ben was a big help. We checked out the property, and I had the opportunity to get an overall impression about what's going on downtown. The town seems a potential gold mine. I'm amazed at the houses that are being torn down and what's being built in their place. Ben took me to the town hall to look at the property's records. We had a brief talk with the planning and zoning manager. Nice guy by the way. As to my decision…" Jay took a second helping and poured more wine.

"Here comes the no," J.R. thought.

"I'm going to say yes, Robbie, with reservations. I'm still not convinced about this runaway real estate market. I've listened to your arguments, and here's your chance to take your idea and prove your old man wrong."

Jay was not an "I told you so" person, nor did he ever make his son prove himself to him. But in this instance there was a great deal at stake — a now multi-generational family business — and Jay did not take this lightly.

J.R. did not care about the reasons. He had his father's go-ahead, and told him that he would not regret this decision.

Knowing he had taken this leap of faith, not only in the real estate market, but his son, Jay raised his brows and shrugged his shoulders. "I ask one thing of you."

"What's that, Dad?"

"Proceed with caution. Negotiate tough for the land, and make certain you build a sound product, but keep a close eye on the costs."

"No problem, I won't let anything slip by me."

During the following weeks, J.R. negotiated tough for the property, while the Ridgefield project continued on time.

~~~~~~~~~~~~~~

"Hurry up J.R.; everyone will be here in half an hour." Becky was trying to get her husband away from his computer and the project to help her prepare for the boys' first birthday party. Besides the family, they were inviting parents and little ones from Becky's Baby and Me group. She wondered how their apartment was going to accommodate everyone, especially ten toddlers.

Four hours later, the last guest left, and J.R. closed the door. Surveying the apartment, he saw the living room in a shambles. He commented to Becky he never knew ten tiny people could make such a mess.

"Life would be easier if we had a bigger space. The children could spread out. Honey, I think we should move," Becky said.

"Move? Move to where? Why would you want to leave the city?"

"Because the boys are going to get bigger. They're going to want to have friends over to play and we don't have a yard. I'm just saying…"

J.R. pointed out they had a huge yard right around the corner called Central Park. Plus he reminded her that with overseeing the New Canaan project, he did not have time to consider moving and suggested they could revisit the subject again when the project was completed.

"How long is that going to take?"

"A few years, but with this market who knows."

"But the real estate market is hot right now; we could get a great price for this place. Apartments in this neighborhood are selling with multiple offers. We bought at the low; we can realize a handsome profit if we sell."

"I hear you Becky, but I predict the prices will continue to rise. Our profit has nowhere to go but up. Besides we have plenty of room until the boys get another year older. Most people would kill for an apartment of this size in Manhattan. Anyway, are you really ready to leave the city? Once we move to the 'burbs, it will be a while before we move back. Keep that in mind."

Becky realized this was not the time to push the subject any further. She could see the valid points to his reasons; even so J.R.'s resistance bothered her. True, their place was large by New York City standards, but everyday life in an apartment with two rambunctious toddlers had Becky yearning for a house. They could sell now, make a profit, move to the suburbs, and become part of a community. Becky did not tell him, but she was ready to move out of the city.

**

Nena was waiting for Becky and the twins on the steps of the Metropolitan Museum. They were taking the boys to see the Christmas tree, a holiday treat for visitors from all over the world. The 20-foot blue spruce and Neapolitan Baroque crèche were a long-standing yuletide tradition in New York. The museum's collection of eighteenth-century Neapolitan angels and cherubs hovered among the tree's boughs and the nativity scene sat at the base of the tree in the medieval sculpture hall, to the joy and delight of holiday visitors. Background music filled the hall and there was a daily lighting ceremony Nena wanted the boys to see. They planned to shop in the museum's store, have lunch, and before leaving they would take the twins to see Becky's former coworkers. Truth be known, she missed her job. Her coworkers adored the boys, and Becky relished being back in the environment she loved.

Once in the museum, their coats checked, the tree admired, and shopping finished, they were ready for lunch. Becky had not seen her mother since the boy's birthday party.

"Thumbs up or thumbs down on the success of the party?" Becky wanted her mother's approval.

"Thumbs up…your first birthday party, and with all those little ones in the apartment, you did a super job."

"Speaking of apartments, I had a talk with J .R. after the party about the apartment."

"Oh…"

"I asked him to consider selling the apartment and moving to the suburbs. I feel the time is right, but my husband and I are not exactly on the same page."

"Where would you move to? And why do you want to move?"

"I want a house for the boys to grow up in like I had. Where to…possibly New Canaan or Fairfield, either town would be an easy reverse commute for J.R. I loved growing up in Fairfield, and I know Daddy would love it if we were in New Canaan."

"Well, you can't move to a town because of a parent. Someday the parent might not be there. You have to live where it fits you and your family. Have you considered Greenwich or someplace in Westchester?"

"I don't know, Mum. It's all hypothetical anyway. J.R. isn't interested, so for the time being we are where we are."

Nena could sense her daughter's frustration with the situation, but she was not about to get in the middle. Besides, she enjoyed having her daughter and grandsons close by when she was in town.

"It will work itself out; it usually does," Nena told her daughter.

**

This would be the first Christmas that M. J. and Daniel would be dazzled by the decorations that adorned the city. They were mesmerized by the scenes in the store windows, the tree at Rockefeller Center, and unlike many one-year-olds, they loved their visit to Santa for picture taking.

"Now aren't you glad we're in town?" J.R. asked Becky leaving FAO Schwarz toy store. "The boys would never see any of this if we were living in the suburbs."

She had to concede, nothing could beat the cornucopia of attractions New York City offered.

**

The only thing he told her was to put on her best formal dress. When the cab pulled up to the curb outside 30 Rockefeller Plaza, Becky told J.R., "I hope this isn't a bribe."

The elevator opened on the sixty-fifth floor. Décor resplendent in hues of soft blues, reds and yellows greeted guests. In the center of the room couples floated on a revolving dance floor under a dazzling chandelier. Men in tuxedos and women in elegant evening dresses sat at tables draped in red cloths against a backdrop of floor-to-ceiling windows that overlooked breathtaking, sweeping views of the New York City skyline.

"Well if this is your idea of a bribe, you're off to a good start," Becky informed her husband.

The Rainbow Room was a coveted spot to usher in New Year's Eve. The restaurant did not bar any expense on the evening, and those that attended paid the price of $1,600 a person for the pleasure of being there.

"No, not a bribe, I'm making up for all the date nights we've missed, but you have to admit you can't find this in the 'burbs." J.R. said, still trying to convince Becky.

"Let's agree to disagree tonight. I want to enjoy every penny of what you've spent."

Absorbing the extravagance of the night, Becky savored each bite of dinner, from the toast points covered with caviar to the decadent lobster casserole swimming in a light butter sauce and a garden salad looking as if it were freshly picked that morning. An assortment of individual fruit tarts finished the meal, and vintage wines and champagne flowed throughout the evening.

At midnight, as the ball in Times Square dropped, J.R. led Becky onto the dance floor, unaware of the other revelers. He held her in his arms and kissed her as the year came to a close.

"It's going to be a year we'll never forget. Everything is coming together. Are you ready?"

Becky made an audible sigh. "I'm ready!"

~~~~~~~~~~~~~

By the end of 2004, families were beginning to move into their homes in Ridgefield. The workmanship and quality of homes J.R. delivered exceeded his own expectations, and because housing prices were on the rise, he delivered a generous profit to the bottom line of the company. Jay still had his doubts, but he could not argue with the numbers. Ms. Danielson had accepted his offer to buy her property, and the deal in New Canaan was sealed. Year's end brought the closing on the property, which took months. The planning and zoning board took longer than expected to approve the lot for subdivision. The housing plans were submitted, and the final planning and zoning meeting was scheduled after the first of the year, when the decision would be delivered regarding how many houses the town would allow to be built.

As for the rest of the family, the twins were healthy and had made it past the milestone of their first birthday, easing Becky's concerns. Ben felt the best he had in years, and if Nena had learned any lesson in life, it was that nothing stays the same. She seized these moments, holding onto them, letting the future take care of itself.

The year 2005 began with Iraq in the news when a gunman assassinated the governor of Baghdad. News of this sort caused Gabby and the rest of the family to hope Danny did not die in vain. Fighting in Afghanistan continued to escalate. Saddam Hussein may have been toppled, but the Middle East appeared as volatile as ever. Terrorism around the world was alive and well. George W. Bush was inaugurated for his second term as president, and in April, Pope John Paul II (the first non-Italian pope since the fifteen hundreds and the third-longest reigning pope) died. A champion of the poor and a major player in hastening the fall of communism in his native land of Poland, his passing was mourned by Catholics and non-Catholics alike.

"We're going to stay with your father tonight," J.R. mentioned to Becky as he packed an overnight bag. "I'll take the train back in the morning."

"Why don't you drive?"

"The train is Dad's idea. Could be a car is too close quarters. In the train, we are less apt to get into any deep conversation. He's not totally convinced yet. He'll come around when we start adding to the bottom line. All that matters is we get approved. I'm banking on it because I have a meeting set with the demolition company to have the houses torn down. Demolition completed, we can talk about the placement of the houses. There are a lot of details, surveyors, architects; my head is spinning."

"Do you think this is more than you bargained for?" Trying to get a sense for J.R.'s mindset, Becky asked the question somewhat trepidatiously.

"A tiny bit." J.R. cocked his head, and rolled his eyes. "Seriously Beck, how many people have the opportunity to watch their dream project unfold, and on the street where their father-in-law grew up?"

He kissed Becky and the boys good-bye. "Wish me luck."

"We do."

~~~~~~~~~~~~~

The chairman of the planning and zoning board announced the Stark Land Development Main Street property would be next on the docket. The secretary began: "The request to develop the property is accepted by this committee with one caveat."

Jay looked at J.R. He could see the blood drain from his son's face. What would the board say next? The secretary continued, "It is the board's decision to grant permission for five houses rather than the six requested. With this acceptance, the petition is granted for Stark Land Development to proceed."

When the secretary concluded, the blood returned to J.R.'s face, and the three men took a collective sigh of relief. With the meeting adjourned for the night, Jay and J.R. thanked the committee, assuring the members they would build houses both them and Ms. Danielson would be proud of.

Returning to Ben's townhouse, he broke out the champagne.

"You were this certain, Ben?"

"I figured we would need the champagne whichever way the vote went. I know this town, and the way people operate, but I was never certain about the six houses. I hope this doesn't play too much havoc with the bottom line."

"I'll go back to the drawing board with the architects and the surveyors, but I'm confident this is going to work." J.R. needed to hold onto this belief.

On the train ride home the following day, father and son were lost in thought, one thinking of the present and the other wondering about the future.

~~~~~~~~~~~~~~~~~~~~~~~~~~~

April brought the end to a long, cold winter in the northeast. J.R. was ready to get construction underway now that he owned the land. The following months consumed him. He lived and breathed the project. At least three to four days a week, he would walk to Grand Central Station and climb aboard the Metro North Train heading east. Most mornings, he would stop by Ben's and they would go for coffee; then he would walk down Main Street to the site in high spirits. This morning he was meeting with a salvage company and the demolition team that would tear down the houses. The team estimated three to four weeks to tear down both houses unless they came across some unforeseen complications. Today would be spent walking through the buildings with the salvage people to determine what could be saved and sold. At the end of each day, J.R. would walk back to Ben's, where he would sit and have a glass of wine before catching the Metro North back to the city, a routine he thoroughly enjoyed.

**

By late summer of 2005, the land had been cleared, the houses were torn down, the surveying completed, the architectural plans approved, the lots staked, and the first two basements were poured. J.R.'s plan to sell and complete the first house by spring of 2006 and be ready to build a second was in motion. Everything was going according to his plan. With the successful completion of the Ridgefield project on time, and the market in New Canaan continuing to soar, J.R. had no doubts he had made the right decision.

At least for the moment, any concerns Jay might have were set aside. People both in and out of the real estate business could not believe what was happening. Prices continued to rise to record highs. On both sides of the Atlantic, there seemed to be no stopping this phenomenon.

**

"I know what I see." Jay and Ben were sitting in Jay's box at Yankee Stadium watching the Yankees play the Red Sox. "But I believe in what goes up eventually comes down. You heard J.R. sold the first house."

"I did, and I hear the price made you smile."

"It's a little insane." Jay wanted confirmation that he was not the only one who thought this market was almost too good to believe.

"To tell you the truth Jay, I don't know what to believe," Ben replied. "The price on that house was ridiculous. I hope the market holds up until you get the property completely sold, pay off your loans, and make a profit."

"I'll drink to that," Jay said, holding up his cup of beer.

~~~~~~~~~~~~~~~~~~

The year seemed to be flying by. October arrived along with Daniel and M. J.'s second birthday. With J.R. working in New Canaan most of the week, and the boys in bed by the time he arrived home, this year's party birthday would be a family affair.

Becky also wanted to keep the holidays low-key for the same reason. However, at the Thanksgiving table Jay announced that a client of his had offered them his house in the Bahamas over Christmas and New Year's. Gasps filled the room.

"I'm as astonished as you, but then I thought these offers don't come along every day. All in favor raise your hand."

Everyone around the table did, including the twins, causing the room to erupt in laughter.

"Good! I'll have the office make the arrangements, and it's off to the Bahamas."

**

Christmas and New Year's was fun in the sun. Days were spent at the beach, playing tennis and golf, lazy suppers by the pool, and Jay arranged a sunset dinner cruise New Year's Eve to welcome in 2006. The family returned home, invigorated and looking forward to the promise of a new year.

Chapter 17

After Buddy's death and his second bout with cancer Ben knew he needed to sell the company. But letting go of the family oil business his grandfather started, and his father and uncle built, especially Buddy after Jack's death, left Ben without a purpose. He missed work even though he had an open-ended invitation to stop in whenever he wanted and did on occasion. But it was not the same. When the project came along and J.R. asked him to watch over the site, it gave Ben something to look forward to every day, and took his mind off waiting for that much hoped for fifth year of remission. Secretly, Ben was delighted to be a part of J.R.'s world.

"What do you think, Ben?" J.R. asked, on one of their early morning walks down Main Street to assess the property.

"J.R., you're going to transform this corner of town. It's going to be a showplace. One house already sold, a second under contract and in construction. I'm impressed."

"And there's serious interest in a lot; that leaves two to go. Ben, I was thinking if I gave you a checklist of the day's work, would you be willing to inspect the property after the men leave, and ensure the day's work is completed — then give me a call? This would be a great help — I suppose this would mean coffee for life."

"You said it; I didn't."

**

The day the first owners moved into their house, J.R. was floating on air.

"At this rate we'll be able to raise the price of the next house over 25 percent," he told Jay.

"That much?"

"Dad, depending how this market keeps climbing, it might be more. The first two buyers will have bought at bargain prices."

"I hear you Robbie, but first you need to get those other buyers," Jay reminded him.

"We will; I'm not the least bit worried."

~~~~~~

Retirement suited Nena. She did not know what to expect. Working had become her raison d'être, filling her life until Sam came into her world, and work rescued her when he died. Now her life had changed again. The big decision she faced was what to do about her living situation.

Over dinner one evening with Gabby and Josh, Nena solicited their opinions.

"My opinion is you should sell," Gabby volunteered. "Josh?"

"Look at it this way, Nena. Becky and her family are in the city. Most of your friends are moving away. We'll probably keep the house here because of Rachael and her family, but we have the place in Florida where we spend half the year, and I'm cutting down on my practice. In this marketplace, your home will sell and sell quickly, and for a considerable price. You'll have New York and Venice. Not a bad living situation at this stage in life for the granddaughter of a farmer."

Her brother's comment caused Nena to pause. "You're both right. Thanks, I never could have or would have made this decision without your approval. The both of you are my anchors."

"Nena, you've become the sister I never had. You mean the world to me. We may not be able to get together a few nights a week for dinner like we do now, but we'll be spending weeks at a time together."

"Gabby, I feel the same, and I do feel this is the right decision."

Josh added, "Okay let's get your place on the market, and on to Act III of life!"

**

The following weeks, Gabby helped Nena ready her townhouse for sale. Josh was right; the place sold in a few weeks, with a closing date of June 1, and as Josh predicted for a considerable price. The chore of packing began. Nena packed the blown glass seal figurine Sam bought her as an engagement gift in Venice when he proposed. The act of doing this brought up the memory of packing the crystal figurine of a butterfly when she moved from the house in Fairfield when her life with Ben ended. Both these gifts elicited very different memories.

**

June 1 — moving day arrived before Nena realized. Emotion filled her with a deep-seated sadness. She bought the townhouse in the aftermath of a life-altering divorce with Ben to make a new dream. Sam came along offering her a second chance at love; then through the cruelest of events, she lost him. Today was not the day to dwell on the past or the future. Nena wanted this day to be over, to close the door of her townhouse where for those brief years with Sam, she came alive again in ways she never could have imagined. She hung onto her belief that things happen for a reason, yet, at this moment in life, Nena was having difficulty understanding and accepting the reasons.

"Are you ready?" Gabby asked as she walked into the almost empty space.

"Just about." Nena turned to her sister-in-law, tears filling her eyes.

"I know Nena. I know." Her words said it all, as Gabby held her in her arms.

Nena paid the movers, locked the door behind her, and she and Gabby walked to meet Josh for dinner. She would stay with them until the closing and then begin another chapter in her life.

Sitting in L'Osteria on Salem Street, her favorite restaurant in the North End, Josh could see the depth of sorrow in Nena's eyes.

"Difficult day, Sis?"

"Difficult doesn't quite sum it up. I was given a second chance, and for whatever reason, which I might add I still don't understand, it was snatched away. But then I don't need to tell the two of you how it is — what happened on 9/11 took Danny from you, from us. I can't seem to make sense out of any of it."

"I don't think we ever will." Josh understood because he had difficulty accepting the death of his son.

"And maybe we're not supposed to." This was the only response Gabby could add to the conversation because if she did not believe those words she would not be able to go on.

"Will any of us ever come to terms with what has happened?" Nena searched the faces of the two people closest to her, who understood her emptiness.

Ever the philosopher even in these circumstances, Josh knew exactly what to say. "Today you had to close the door both psychologically and symbolically on a life you thought was your future, but I believe, and I say this because I know you, once you close on the townhouse and in a few days get on the train to New York, you will leave this station behind and head toward your new destination."

"How can I disagree with such a wonderful prognosis?" Josh's words touched Nena's heart. "I know you're right Josh, and I needed to be reminded. Now let's order."

Lina and Nicky came by the table.

"We're going to miss that beautiful face of yours." Nicky cupped Nena's face in his hands with his usual charming demeanor. "Let me order for you tonight, and it is on the house."

"You can order, but not on the house," Nena insisted.

"Yes on the house," Lina interjected. "You have been our faithful customer and have brought so many people to us. Let us treat you to a farewell dinner."

Nena looked out the window, as she had the first time she came to L'Osteria, watching people pass by, feeling in the fleeting moment what a safe haven this place had become.

"Thank you, but I don't want to say farewell. When I'm visiting, I'll be back; you can count on that."

"Buona Sera," Nena said in her best Italian. She hugged Lina and Nicky as they left the restaurant and walked to Hanover Street to Caffé Vittoria. They whiled away the rest of the evening drinking the best hot chocolate in town, eating chocolate-covered biscotti, and watching customers come and go while the same "Old Blue Eyes" and Dean Martin songs played in the background.

~~~~~~

It began as coffee and turned into breakfast, before they walked to the construction site.

"The usual?" the owner of The Back Street Café began to write on his pad as Ben and J.R. sat down.

"I'm going off the grid this morning." Ben felt the need to change up his routine. "Make mine eggs poached on wheat bread with a slice of ham."

"Make that two," J.R. chimed in.

"Now down to business…how did it go yesterday?" J.R. asked.

"Smoothly, very smoothly. A few minor kitchen issues, and the shrubs in the front are on order, otherwise, things are on schedule."

"I want to stop by the realty office after breakfast. We need to get the remaining lots sold," J.R. said as he finished his morning coffee.

**

Within days an interested party put money down on the third lot. J.R. could barely contain his excitement. And while defying real estate history, the housing market continued to climb. The business still owed on the initial investment, but the selling of the second house would begin to make a dent in the loans. In spite of J.R.'s continual enthusiasm, what little enthusiasm his father had about the project was waning.

Discussing the building of a third house, Jay mentioned to his son, "*The Wall Street Journal* is reporting this morning there are places around the country where the real estate market is slowing down…starting to show signs of what could be a slump."

"Prices are slipping in parts of the country — not all over, and not in New Canaan, Dad." J.R. tried to reassure his father. "Prices are soaring."

"We have sunk a pretty penny into this project. We need the other houses to sell to make this worthwhile, and right now I am not seeing this in black and white," Jay said, again the voice of caution.

"Is this a vote of no confidence?" J.R. smarted under his father's comment, sensing his deep concern.

"Not a vote of no confidence in you, but a vote of no confidence in the real estate market. You mentioned that only parts of the country are beginning to feel a crunch. I suspect you are referring to Florida and California. Well, look at what's going on there."

"You mean flipping, Dad?"

"Yes, this flipping is beginning to hurt the market. What can anyone expect? Houses are meant to be a sanctuary, a place to hang your hat. Real estate is not the stock market, and that is exactly what's been going on, and Greenspan, the head of the Federal Reserve Bank, hasn't gotten it right."

"I read the same reports, and hear what's going on, but I believe Fairfield County will hold on to its value. I'll get the houses finished, and we'll come out of this project with a nice profit and leave a mark in New Canaan this company can be proud of."

Jay did not push the conversation any further.

~~~~~~~~~~~~~~~

Once Nena made the transition from Boston to New York, she began in earnest to put the past few years behind her. It did not happen overnight and took all her fortitude. Through Becky's insistence, Nena volunteered one day a week in the gift shop at the Metropolitan Museum. Another day she took charge of the twins, giving Becky a day for herself, and she signed up to monitor a day class in the history of Italy at Columbia. Little by little, she began to make the city home.

**

"What are you going to do today?" Nena asked Becky, as Daniel and M. J. raced around the apartment. The twins had recently celebrated their third birthdays and had the energy of most three year olds — a lot.

"I'm meeting a friend in the Village for lunch. And what are you and the boys doing?"

"We're going to the Natural History Museum to see the dinosaurs for the hundredth time."

When discussing plans for the upcoming holidays, Becky asked Nena for a favor.

"There's a house across the street from the project, and J.R. thinks it might be perfect for us. The husband recently died and the wife is moving closer to her children. He wants to go to New Canaan the Friday after Thanksgiving to show me the property," Becky explained. "Will you watch the boys for the day?"

"Of course I'll mind the boys. I'm a little surprised, though. I thought J.R. didn't want to move until the project was finished."

"I didn't either. I'm not sure what's going on with my husband these days, but I'm willing to take a look."

After Becky left and before Nena took the boys to the museum, she called Jay.

**

"This is a pleasant surprise." Jay greeted Nena as they sat down in the museum's Starlight Café. "Boys, shall we order?"

While the boys were enjoying their chicken nuggets, yogurt, and homemade cookies, Jay glanced at Nena.

"I know you, Nena. I figured you had something important on your mind to call me."

"Is my face that much of a giveaway?" Nena realized they had come to know each other well. "I wanted to talk about the house in New Canaan Becky mentioned this morning. I sense the subject came out of the blue. What's your take on them moving at this time?"

"Frankly I don't know what's changed Robbie's mind. He mentioned the house yesterday. What I'm going to say cannot go beyond this table."

"It never will," Nena assured him.

"From the very beginning, I've never been completely behind this project. I understand in town property in New Canaan is a premium, and generally holds its value, but even Ben concurs real estate is never a sure thing. I must admit Robbie's decision to build in Ridgefield turned out highly successful, however, the New Canaan project is different, and I am watching the market rapidly changing. It's building these mega houses on small lots in what I believe is a false real estate market that is worrisome to me."

Nena asked what he would have done differently. He told her building townhouses on the property might have been a better option.

"You know sort of a brownstone look for in-town," he added.

"Ah yes, a Beacon Hill ambiance," Nena responded.

Jay concurred, then shared his other concern — banks freely lending large amounts of money for mortgages. "I can't see how this is going to continue, and the personal worry for me is we're not going to be built out before there is a collapse of some sort. If we're left with any unsold houses, the project is in trouble, and I'm on the hook."

"But J.R. has sold two. I don't understand."

"Sort of…the house under contract isn't sold until the closing and there are the remaining lots. Nothing is done until it's done. Even though J.R. negotiated well, that land didn't come cheap. The first house didn't pay back the initial investment. J.R. believes we'll turn a profit once the second house closes. I question his belief with the numbers I'm seeing, and that still leaves us with those unsold lots."

"How does this scenario fit into them looking at a house right now and selling Park Avenue?" Nena asked.

"Good question. They feel they need to move for the boys, although Trudi and I raised J.R. in the city and he turned out all right. They need to get a deal on the place they're looking at, but what are the chances of that happening in this market? I know they'll do okay with Park Avenue, because they bought that place at a steal, and before any of this silliness in the real estate market began."

Nena appreciated Jay's candor, but she watched him intently as he spoke, noticing his look of worry.

"I see…I guess all we can do, Jay, is support them, and hope for the best."

"You're right. Enough talk. Let's finish this fantastic lunch." Jay winked at the twins, adding, "And check out those dinosaurs, right boys?"

Devouring cookies and drinking chocolate milk, the boys nodded in agreement.

~~~~~~~~~~~~~~~~

"I love it J.R. I really love it," Becky said as they left the house. "Although the house needs a lot of updating, is there any possibility we could remodel the kitchen and bathrooms before we move in?"

"I don't think so, honey. I need to get the houses across the street built and closed first. We can get a cleaning company in, maybe take up the carpets, sand the floors, and we'll need a new refrigerator, dishwasher, and stove, but the remodeling will have to wait. Can you live with that?"

"If I have to, I love the house. It's so charming. There's a nice-sized yard for an in-town property, and I can see us raising the boys here. Can't you?"

"I can. Come across the street and I'll show you the house we're working on, before we stop by the realtor's office and put in an offer."

At the realty office, they found the house had another offer. Taking this into consideration, the realtor told them in order to have a chance, they would have to put in a bid for the full asking price.

"What?" Becky felt panic creeping in as she tried to digest the conversation. "I thought the market was slowing down?"

"Not in New Canaan," the realtor quipped. "Your husband can tell you that. He'll be closing on another house, and there is interest in the lots."

"Can we have a minute please?" Becky requested.

"Take your time, but not too much time; this house will sell quickly." The realtor left the room.

Becky had a knot in her stomach that was getting tighter as she considered what they were contemplating. J.R. originally resisted the idea of moving to the suburbs, but he had grown fond of the town, the fairly easy commute into the city, and saw it as a great place to raise the boys. Becky on the other hand had resigned herself to life in the city until he finished the project. J.R. had raised her hopes of moving, but hearing the price of the property made her cringe. Somewhere in his thought process J.R. knew Becky was right, timing was everything, but he deferred to location rather than timing. "Real estate is about location and you can't beat this location." He told her, but he also knew timing and location went hand in hand.

"So...does this mean we're putting in an offer for full price?" Becky studied J.R. waiting for a response.

"Yes!"

On the drive back to the city, Becky vacillated between the prospect of a house in the suburbs, and nagging apprehension of the monetary commitment.

"Have faith. It'll work out. You'll see," J.R. told her. His confidence level was at an all-time high.

Their offer of full price was accepted. They put their apartment in the city on the market. They were not in a hurry to sell and would wait for the best offer, since the house in New Canaan was an estate sale, and these sales took time to close. Setting aside her reservations, Becky began to contemplate a move to the suburbs.

~~~~~~

Then the first shock wave of the trouble in the real estate market hit home in the spring of 2007. The buyers backed out of the second house. The sale of their home fell through. The bank would not approve their buyer's mortgage, which meant they could not go forward with the house. They lost their down payment, but for them it was better than owning two houses with high mortgages. Adding to this, the party that had an interest in the third lot had silently walked away.

J.R. tried not to panic. The company would now hold the commercial development loan, the construction loan, costs on a nearly built house, plus three empty lots. Sooner or later, his father would have to hear this information, but before he did, J.R. would put the house back on the market. If the house sold, then the consequences would not be as dire.

When J.R. sat down with the realtor, the agent told him he would have to make a price reduction in order for the house to sell.

"Really, by how much?" J.R. asked.

"I'd say we start at 10 percent."

"What, 10 percent? Are you crazy? I paid full price for my house across the street a month ago, and now you're telling me to drop this property 10 percent?" J.R. was dumbfounded.

"I don't know what to tell you, J.R. We need the right buyer and buyers at this price are getting skittish. Our buyers are mostly from the banking world and Wall Street, and at the moment everyone in the banking world and on the Street are jumpy as hell."

"Okay drop the price, but get me a buyer and quick."

J.R. left the realtor's office and walked to Ben's.

"Cripes…you look like something the cat dragged in." Ben eyed J.R. as he sat down.

"I feel more like I got hit by a Mac truck," J.R. explained.

"What's going on?"

"Before I tell you, first I need to thank you for the advice you gave me about Salomon based on your own mistakes. That wasn't easy for you to do, but you had my best interests at heart by telling me, and I appreciated your openness. What I'm going to tell you is a result of my not fully listening to you, and my own ego."

"I guess we all know about ego, my boy."

"You aren't going to believe this, but the deal on the house fell through."

"You're kidding me."

"I wish I were, Ben. I wish I were. And if that isn't bad enough, I have to drop the price on the house by 10 percent before putting it back on the market."

Ben could not believe what he was hearing. "10 percent?!"

"You heard me right... 10 percent. I guess even New Canaan is finally not immune from this so-called housing bubble. I need to get this place sold and quick." He sighed. "I sure hope someone out there needs to get into a place as quickly as I need to sell, maybe a job transfer or something."

Ben could hardly stand to see the look of defeat on his son-in-law's face. "What about the other lots? Wasn't there recently an interested buyer in one?"

"Not any longer. They probably got scared off with the market sliding, figuring they'd wait it out. The indicators are those who bought at the high are in trouble, and those who don't need to move are going to stay put until the dust settles, and who knows when that will be. In the meantime, I'm left with a nearly finished house and three empty lots."

"What will you do about the place you and Becky bought?"

"I don't know. It's an estate sale and we're waiting. I'm glad the apartment hasn't sold. At this point, I wish we hadn't bought the house. Becky wasn't pushing. It was my idea. I take full responsibility. What I can't understand is how quickly this happened. In all probability we'll have to back out of the deal, like my buyers did."

"This bubble has been coming to New Canaan for a while, Son. The problem is no one wanted to acknowledge it. Look at the mess Florida, California, and Arizona are in. Fairfield County could not be immune forever. Would you want a word of advice from someone who was in a worse spot than you?"

"Please." J.R. hoped what Ben had to say would be magic.

"Don't get down on yourself. Don't go into denial. You're going to need your wits about you to figure out how you're going to keep the project from going under. You need to sit down with Jay and look at this in black and white. There's going to be a loss, but now the trick will be how to mitigate the loss. Tell you what, why don't you call Becky and tell her you're spending the night here? Then call your father and ask him to come out. He needs to know what's going on, and you need him and his experience to figure a way out of this fiasco. The office is no place to initially do this. Here you're on neutral territory where clear heads can prevail."

J.R. made the calls. When he hung up the phone with his father, Jay had a good idea his concerns were becoming a reality. Jay, no stranger to the vagaries of real estate, hoped the situation was not as bad as he anticipated.

That evening, the three men sat in Ben's living room while J.R. had the most difficult conversation he ever had with his father.

**

"Mum, are you busy? J.R. is staying overnight in New Canaan with Dad. It's something about the project. Please come over for dinner and stay the night. We can have an old-fashioned sleepover."

"That'll be a first in many a year," Nena laughed. "Let me check my calendar...Yes, I'm free this evening. Can I stop by Zabar's and pick up dinner?"

"I didn't mean to ask you to dinner and then have you bring it, but since you offered..."

"Done, see you in an hour."

Becky hung up the phone, remembering the sound of J.R.'s voice when they spoke. There was an uneasy tone in his speech that troubled her.

**

"This was thoughtful of you, Mum. M. J. and Daniel enjoyed the chicken pie, and you know how to please — black and white cookies do it every time. Come on boys, bath time. Mum, want to help?"

After the baths, they read the boys stories and tucked them in for the night. The kitchen cleaned, and toys put away, Becky opened a bottle of wine, and mother and daughter sat down to talk.

"I know you, Becky, something's on your mind; spill it."

After hearing about Becky's conversation with J.R., Nena advised her daughter that she was reading between the lines, which could be a good or bad thing.

"I know, but I know my husband, and he has never stayed over with Dad before, even in bad weather when I suggested he stay. Something happened today; I just know it."

"Okay then, what would be the worst thing to happen? Let's begin there and work backwards."

Becky was stumped even to what the worst-case scenario could be. Nena asked if she had been reading the papers, specifically articles about how the real estate market was collapsing across the country.

"Oh that, that's in Florida and California."

"Not true," Nena countered. "I recently spoke with a friend. Her son tried to sell their home to buy something larger. They couldn't sell the house. And guess where the house is?" Before Becky could answer, Nena interjected, "Westport, right there in Fairfield County. So in my humble opinion, today something went awry with the project."

"Mum, you think so?"

Taking a sip of wine, Nena stared into her glass. "Becky, we've never spoken much about what happened when your father lost his career over the savings and loan and real estate crisis, but I learned a lot from what happened then. I'm not remotely comparing what your father did to what is going on with J.R., but real estate has its ups and downs, and banks have their times of crises as well. It may be something unforeseen has happened with the project, and J.R. is trying to figure it out. If anyone can give him sage advice from his own hard lessons in life, it's your father."

"If J.R. is in trouble, what are we going to do?" Becky felt sick to her stomach.

Nena reminded her daughter that she did not have all the facts yet and was jumping ahead of herself. "A word of advice from my experience…I couldn't help your father. His mistakes were made in secret, and I doubt J.R. has done that. When he comes home tomorrow, you need to be prepared for whatever he tells you, and you need to be supportive. Jay is going to have a big say in whatever is going on. This is all about a family business. I have no doubts you're going to weather this storm, as long as you stay strong. Okay, we need more wine. I'll pour, and you pop some corn. I'll find a movie and we'll get this sleepover started — tomorrow will take care of itself." Nena looked for an upbeat movie, and picked a favorite, *Moonstruck*.

If there was a crisis facing her daughter, Nena thought how different the circumstances would be from what she faced with Ben. Becky and J.R. would be in this together — if only she and Ben had done the same.

~~~~~~~~~~~~

J.R. knew he had to tell his father, but where to begin? How could he blurt out the project was in dire trouble? There was no doubt in J. R's mind his father already knew what he was about to say. He looked at his father sitting across from him. A mea culpa seemed the best way to begin.

"Dad, the last thing I wanted to do was to fail, but I have. I wanted to grow this company, to make you proud of me. What a mess I've created. I'm so damn sorry, Dad. You have all the right in the world to say I told you so."

Jay appreciated his son's regret, but this was business, and if he let emotion enter into the equation, wrong decisions would be made.

"There will be plenty of time for Monday morning quarterbacking, Robbie. Right now I need the facts, and then we need to come up with a strategy to get us out of this situation with the least amount of loss. No more recriminations, not right now anyway." Jay's mission was to find a solution, and he needed his son to lay all the facts on the table.

J.R. knew his father wanted straight talk, and he owed him nothing less, "The house fell through; it goes back on the market tomorrow, reduced, along with the lots."

Jay interrupted him. "Slow down…Why reduced? And what about the lot that had some interest?"

"Because the real estate agent said putting the house back on at the current asking price won't fly, and I found out today the people are no longer interested in the lot."

"Hmmm, so it's a house, the three lots, and the loans. Give me a minute to think."

In his business career Jay had weathered difficult real estate markets in the past, albeit in commercial real estate, not residential. J.R. knew his father was one savvy businessman, and he would find an answer. But J.R. also knew his father would not speak until he had a solution.

Ben sat silently along with J.R. until Jay spoke. "Ben, let's get on the Internet and go to this site." Jay gave him a site that monitored towns, cities, and counties for each state and their latest real estate information. Looking at the site, Jay began to formulate a plan.

"From what I'm seeing, it's not going to be long before the bank recalls the loans. There's several million outstanding on the construction loan; they might begin with that loan first. I'm thinking we should find a buyer to take over the loans and let them hold onto the property. I'd rather cut our losses, give up any long-term profit, than take a chance the loans would go into default. And right now with the market so volatile, I'm not ready to take any more gambles. We need to sell the property and get out from under these loans. The trick is in this down market to find this buyer or buyers. Ben, you have contacts and you know this town. What I'd ask you to do is quietly begin to feel people out. Get your ear to the ground. There have to be people with money who are looking to invest. J.R., I want you to get in touch with some of your old buddies at Salomon; see what they can tell you from the inside. See what the talk on the Street is. We may have to go with a foreign investor. We're going to have to move quickly and smartly, if we want to come out of this without too big a loss, and the three of us can't let anyone see us sweat."

"Dad I thought the worst thing would be taking a tax loss…How bad is this loss going to be?" J.R. asked.

"Besides a tax loss, the bottom line to the company is going to take a hit. No doubt in my mind; our job is to mitigate the loss as much as we can. We'll have to be magicians."

J.R. had never considered the overall impact of what had happened today. He was caught up in his own angst over the loss of a sale, losing sight of the big picture.

"I believe we're finished for tonight." Jay stood up. "Let's have a drink, watch the news, and get a good night's sleep. We know what we have to do next."

J.R. marveled at his father. His cool demeanor, and how he sprang into action. His mind resembled the workings of a Swiss clock; each movement precise and with a purpose.

"I feel a little to blame, talking up land values in town." Ben wished he had kept his thoughts to himself.

"Ben you're not even close to being responsible for any of this. I could take the position and say we could hold on, but I see this downturn lasting for some time. This is not a little blip on the so-called radar screen. What the banks and the government have done is going to cause lasting repercussions, or at least for a long while. If that's the case, and I'm going with my gut, then we need to cut our losses and not put a drag on the overall business. Commercially we are hanging on, although the city is beginning to feel the pinch. But I know how to hold on in a commercial downturn. I know nothing about residential property. You know the old saying, you have to know when to hold them and know when to fold them, and I believe we need to fold them."

Then J.R. asked his dad about the house he and Becky bought in New Canaan. He wondered if they should back out of the deal before the closing, trying to cut their personal losses.

Jay knew what he really wanted to ask his son — why they did not think they could raise the boys in the city — but he bit his tongue. "I suppose you could try to stop the deal, but it's going to cost you, the same way it cost the people who pulled out of the house. You need to talk this over with Becky. Don't you agree, Ben?"

"I do. This is something only the two of you can decide. You need to sit down, look at the numbers, call your real estate agent, and your lawyer. I don't envy you, J.R."

**

"I'm sorry Becky; I'm so sorry" was all J.R. could say, and seemed to be saying lately. "It's not just the project, Beck; I'm afraid the house is going to have to go too."

"The house too? Aren't we too far along to withdraw our offer? Will we get our deposit back?" Becky implored J.R. for answers, not knowing if she really wanted to hear them.

"It's complicated because this is an estate sale. That's why it has been taking so long. If this were a straightforward sale, we would have closed months ago. What we need to do is call the realtor and our lawyer. We need professional advice on this."

Becky tried to remember what her mother said last night about being supportive, but she was finding this difficult at the moment. "If you had any inkling about this real estate bubble finally reaching New Canaan, why in heaven's name did you entertain the idea of moving?" she asked. "I had given up thinking about moving until you finished the project. I got my hopes up J.R. — and now this."

"I know, I know. I wish I hadn't brought it up, but I thought this place would be perfect for our future. Can you ever forgive me?"

What could she say? The present situation was not of his making or even in his control. What he could have controlled was his blind ambition — jumping onto a bandwagon heading for a cliff.

"I need a little time to digest what you've told me. I'm going for a walk."

Becky put on her coat and left, leaving J.R. alone, questioning his every decision since leaving Salomon.

**

"Coming!" Nena opened the door to see her daughter standing there in tears. She knew without asking the worst had happened. While Becky unburdened herself, Nena listened intently.

"This is a difficult state of affairs for everyone: you, J.R., and let's not forget Jay." Nena drew a deep breath. "This isn't just about your house. This is a generational family business that's going to be affected. I won't pretend to understand or know the consequences and ramifications, and I hope they will be minimized, but let's look at what is positive here. Thank goodness your place didn't sell. The four of you have a roof over your heads, and quite a lovely roof at that. I'm certain the business will survive, and J.R. will be employed, which means you and the boys will be fine."

"I know you're right Mum, but is this another case of ego…" Becky asked.

"Stop Becky, I know where you're going, but this is not history repeating itself." Becky's insinuation brought back Ben's betrayal. "Yes, J.R.'s ego led him to chase his dream to show his father he could walk in his shoes, but J.R. never deceived anyone. He went to Jay and came to you the minute he was in trouble and did not hide what happened. There is a big difference."

Becky was not quite ready to hear what her mother had to say. She needed to blame someone for the disappointment she felt. "Maybe I need a little time to accept what has happened," she said.

Nena was not letting her daughter off the hook. She wanted her to see her situation clearly before she made any wrong choices or decisions. "The situation is what it is. For your sake, the boys' sake, and your husband's sake, in other words Becky for your family's sake, you need to accept what has happened — now. You need to go home, put your arms around J.R., and be his partner. There will be another house, but your family is another matter."

As Becky was leaving, Nena handed her some money. "Stop by Zabar's and get the boys and yourselves a treat from me; your family can use a little something sweet this evening."

She hugged her daughter and watched her descend the stairs. Inside the apartment, Nena sat and wept remembering over twenty years ago when she faced a crisis, one her daughter would never be able to comprehend.

**

Walking past the fireplace mantle in the living room, Becky looked up and noticed the Lalique vase J.R. had given her in London the weekend he introduced her to his closest friends. She took the vase from the mantle and traced the outline of the engraved irises with her finger, pausing to remember how she felt towards him then, and knowing she felt the same even now.

J.R. was in the kitchen preparing dinner. She placed the box from Zabar's on the counter. "Treats from Grandma, boys, but not until you clean your plates."

Then she turned to her husband. "There's a treat is there for us, too. Mum thought we could use something sweet tonight." Putting her arms around J.R., she kissed him as he held her tight. He buried his head in her neck, crying and telling her he was sorry over and over again.

"It's okay, I know you are. We'll get through this; we will."

The following morning, they called the realtor to withdraw from the house and were informed it would be costly. Their attorney negotiated the best deal he could to minimize their loss. They had bought at the high of the market and now the prices were falling. The estate's argument was they too would suffer by selling in the current market. The deal, bitter to accept, released them from a house no longer worth its prior value. It was the only way Becky and J.R. could rationalize what happened.

~~~~~~~~~~~~~~~

The following weeks and months were spent working to financially salvage as much as possible. Through contacts and research with ex-Salomon coworkers, J.R. learned about the mortgage-backed securities that secured the loans. The irony for him was these securities were put into place in the 1980s by none other than Salomon Brothers, along with the government agency Ginnie Mae. Jay called a meeting at his office to talk about J.R.'s and Ben's latest finding.

"Can you believe this?" J.R. showed them article after article from his contacts. "Everything that has brought us to where we are today started years ago, and the banks and government have played a hell of a game with people's lives. Look at the pain and suffering they created."

Then it was Ben's turn to tell what he had uncovered. "I've been snooping around and it's almost as if the builders and most realtors in town are unwilling to say New Canaan is in trouble. Businesswise this bodes well for you trying to sell the property. The negative press is at bay. I have a friend at the club who has a couple of international acquaintances. He is willing to contact them if you are serious about selling."

"Serious? You bet I am. What's in it for him?" Jay was too sharp to think otherwise.

"He wants a finder's fee."

"He brings the buyer, he gets the fee." Jay was not about to play games; he wanted to unload the property. Fast.

"Let me give him a call, and move the ball forward."

**

By the end of the year, Ben brought two buyers to the table, a wealthy Brazilian, and a businessman from the UK. This made life easier for Jay. He was able to play the men against each other. In the end the buyer from the UK bought the remaining property for fifty percent of what J.R. had paid. He planned on renting out the unsold house for the time being. Stark Land Development paid off the construction loans, but the commercial loan was another issue. This would have to be absorbed as a loss into the company, sharply affecting the overall balance sheets and bottom line of the business, and eat into the company's net worth. A bitter pill, but better than the alternative.

**

No one else could have predicted the deceptions of the investment houses, the banks, and even the government with Fanny Mae and Freddie Mac. Greed on so many levels caused a total collapse of the real estate market, which eventually became worldwide.

**

A smile crept across his face at Christmas dinner as Jay looked around the room.

"Why are you smiling Grandpa J.?" Daniel asked.

"I was thinking this has been one heck of a year, but when I look around this room everyone I love is here — you Daniel, your brother, your mum and dad, Grandpa Ben, and Grandma Nena. I'm the luckiest man alive, and we have much to be thankful for."

With 2007 coming to a close, J.R. did not feel very festive, but at that moment he realized how lucky he was. He always thought of his father as an honorable man, a giant in the business world, but he never paid much attention to this man's heart.

"I'm the luckiest person in this room, Dad. You let me take a chance; I failed and then you rescued me. I was thinking there wasn't much to celebrate this year, but I was wrong."

"To us," Ben said. "To family," Nena added.

Chapter 18

In Central Park, the trees were covered with buds bursting forth, heralding the end of a long winter. The earth exploded with life welcoming spring, the season of rebirth. As Becky and the boys crossed Park Avenue on their way to meet Nena at Serendipity, she admired how the median overflowed with flowers, tulips in every shade of the rainbow spilling down the center of the avenue. Color was everywhere.

Serendipity, an iconic New York City sweet shop located on the Upper East Side in a cozy brownstone delighted both children and adults alike, and the twins were no exception. While the boys indulged in heaping bowls of ice cream, Nena commented as she watched Becky play with her spoon in her frozen hot chocolate, "You look lost in thought."

"No, just wondering how different 2008 would have been if we had been able to buy the house in New Canaan." Becky bemoaned.

"Goodness Becky, I thought you had let that go. From a financial perspective, you and J.R. did the right thing. You might have lost your upfront money, but look at how the housing prices have continued to fall. Do you know how many people bought houses over the past few years at the high and now their mortgages are worth more than their homes?"

"I hear you Mum. It's always the what-ifs in life; isn't it?"

"Seems to be sometimes, but we can't live with what-ifs. How is J.R. doing?"

"Continuing to beat himself up. Work is his salvation. Jay is counting on him right now because the commercial market in the city is beginning to soften."

"There's no doubt in my mind the two of you are going to come out of this stronger and in a better position. It might take you a couple of years to get your house in the suburbs, but you will. In the meantime take advantage of what's in your backyard. This city has so much to offer, and Daniel and M. J. are of an age to appreciate much of it."

Becky looked at her mother. " I can hear Grandpa now — *look at the glass half full, Becky* — think I needed to be reminded."

~~~~~~~~~~~~~~~~

Spring turned into summer. Jay opened the house in Ogunquit, and Maine became home for a few months. Becky made a decision to go back to work part-time when the twins started pre-school in the fall, and the boys celebrated their fifth birthdays with a surprise party at Serendipity. But like the seasons, everything was about to change again.

~~~~~~~~~~~~~~~~

Ben had been in remission for over six years. When he reached the five-year mark, he was relieved, feeling home free. Faithfully every six months, he made an appointment with Dr. Harris for a blood workup. Then he would have dinner with Jay, spend the night, and return on the train back to New Canaan the next morning, with a grateful heart for another day cancer free. But this trip to see Ted, following the twins' birthday party, was not like the others.

"How was the big party?" Ted inquired.

"Terrific; wish I had the energy of those boys."

"You look tired, Ben. Are you feeling okay?" Dr. Harris asked.

"Funny you should say that. I have been feeling tired lately."

"Anything different with your schedule?"

"No, maybe I'm not doing enough." Ben laughed a nervous laugh.

"Well, let's take some of your blood, the lab will take a look, and I'll call you in a few days."

**

"Mr. Hicks?" a voice on the other end asked.

"Speaking."

"Please hold the line; Dr. Harris wants to speak with you."

Ben's heart sank. Ted never called him. His nurse always gave him his tests results. He knew the test results were not positive.

"Ben, Ted here."

"You don't have to say it; it's not good news." By now Ben could read Ted's voice.

"I'm sorry Ben, it isn't. The tests show a recurrence."

"I'm not in remission…" Ben didn't know if he was asking a question or making a statement.

"You are not Ben; I'm sorry. We need to talk. When can you come into the office?"

"Can it wait until after Thanksgiving? I'm going to Maine. We're going to help Jay close the house."

"That's fine. I'll give you back to the front desk; make an appointment, and I'll see you after the holiday."

Both men hung up the phone — the healer feeling the weight of his profession being the bearer of dire news and the patient feeling the weight being the recipient of dire news. Neither man wished they had to fill these roles.

~~~~~~~~~~~~

"Another delicious Thanksgiving meal. I think we're making Ogunquit a tradition." Jay surveyed the room with a full heart as he spoke. "I trust we're all ready for tomorrow. I bought new rakes."

Blank faces were the only response.

"Hey…where's the enthusiasm?"

"I'm ready, Grandpa J.," said M. J.

"Me too," seconded Daniel.

"Well thank you boys. I'm glad I won't be out raking the lawn by myself."

"Poor Jay," the table said in unison, poking fun.

"Enough, who's ready to be beaten at cribbage?" Josh asked.

They adjourned to the living room in front of a roaring fire. Cards shuffled, the game began.

When everyone had gone to bed, Nena poured a glass of wine and went onto the porch. The evening was cool. She got up to get a sweater. Before Nena could open the door, Ben walked toward her with her sweater in hand.

"You forgot this."

"I thought you went to bed."

"I waited until you were alone. I need to talk to you, Nena."

"Anything special?"

"I don't know if you would call what I have to say special. I went for my biyearly checkup. I saw Ted last week, and I'm not in remission any longer."

For a moment Nena was not certain she heard Ben correctly. When the words penetrated, she heard herself repeat, "Oh no…oh no! Ben, I'm so sorry; what can I do? Who else knows?" she asked.

"You're the first person. I haven't had the heart to burden Jay and the kids when they are just beginning to recover from this past year. I didn't think it was fair," he told her.

"Fair! Ben, you made it past five years cancer free and it comes back. That's not fair."

"You know what I meant."

"No, actually I don't. Don't get me wrong. What the three of them went through was disastrous. It turned their lives upside down and put in jeopardy a family business, but they've come out the other end, alive and in one piece. That was not life or death; your situation is."

Ben was taken aback by Nena's forthcoming words. But Nena was not. This news brought back memories of losing Sam. She never knew what would trigger off her raw emotions when it came to Sam, but hearing about Ben's cancer opened her old wounds.

"Nena, I want you to hear what I am going to say. I've had time to think about this. I'm going to see Ted next week, and I'm going to tell him what I'm telling you. I'm not having any more chemotherapy, nor am I going to have a bone marrow transplant." Nena began to say something when he stopped her. "I need you to listen. I'm done with treatments of any kind."

"I'm looking at it this way. I screwed up my life. I had the best thing going and I threw it away because I had to prove I could make it to the top...top of the world, that's where I was headed. Well, we know how that worked out, and I know what I lost because I never understood what was really important until I didn't have it any longer. Jay came into my life and taught me you can change, and I did. Somehow I got lucky and life offered me a second chance to redeem myself with you, and with Becky. I was able to help J.R. — give him the guidance I never had in business and kept him from losing his family. I couldn't have stopped what happened in the real estate markets either time, but I could help J.R. walk through the minefield. And with you Nena, I watched you fall in love with Sam. I can't tell you how many times I wanted to be Sam. However, I had learned by then it wasn't about my happiness, but about you having a second chance at it."

"I don't know what to say, Ben. You have so much to live for, Becky, the boys..."

"Nena...Becky, J.R., and the rest of the family...they're all going to say the same thing, but my mind is made up. There is something else, though."

"What's that?"

"I'm going to ask something of you that is huge, especially after all we've been through, and I'll understand if you say no." Ben set himself up to hear "no" because he so badly wanted to hear a "yes."

"My wish is to go to England and retrace the steps of our youth. I want to revisit Beeston where my father died, and I would like you to come with me." Ben paused, gathering his courage before he continued. "Then I'd like to go to Venice where we took our last trip together, where I lied to you by not telling you the truth. I knew then I had ruined our lives. You love the city, and I don't want our last time there to be that terrible memory. My hope is after I'm gone Venice will hold only pleasant memories of you and Sam, and us as well. I know this is a lot to digest, and I'm not expecting an answer from you tonight, not until I see Ted and he tells me how much time I have left." His body was taunt; every fiber stiffened.

Overwhelmed by Ben's candor and hearing the way he wanted to spend his last days on earth, something came over Nena. She could see he had thought this through. There were no words. Instead she walked to Ben's chair and held out her hands. He rose. She put her arms around him and softly spoke. "If this is what you need Ben, I will go with you to England, and you can come to Venice." She lightly kissed his cheek and walked into the house. She went to her room and laid down on the bed the same way she laid on the bed in Fairfield when she found out her life with Ben had fallen apart and she thought her heart would break, but this time her heart was breaking for a very different reason.

After talking with Nena, the following morning Ben told the rest of the family. They sat in shock as he explained to them exactly what he told her the night before.

"Please Daddy, don't make up your mind until you talk to Ted," Becky implored.

"Yes," Jay added. "Wait until you see Ted next week."

J.R., Josh, and Gabby expressed the same feelings.

"I hear you, I really do, and I can't tell you how much I love you for loving me this much, but my mind's made up, and I'm not going to change it. What I really want is when I'm in Venice with Nena that you will come to visit," he told them.

Becky looked at her mother and then turned to her father. "Daddy, does that mean you're not coming back?"

"Yes, Beck that *is* what it means. You know what? None of us know how much time we have in this lifetime. Look at the losses we have suffered — Marc, Danny, Sam, lives cut short in their prime. We only have this day, and I want however many days I have left to be full and to live them the best way I know how. I have given this a lot of thought since I found out from Ted I was no longer in remission, and this is what I want and need to do for a lot of reasons, and I need you to accept this decision."

Josh spoke first. "It's been a long, hard road for you, my brother. You know Ben, I have never stopped thinking of you as my brother, and as we Jews say, you have atoned for your sins, and if this is the way you need to spend you final time on earth, you will see Gabby and me in Venice." Josh looked at his wife. "Right Gabby?"

Gabby did not speak, but went to Ben who was standing by the fireplace and buried her head in his neck. In turn each person in the room approached Ben and said they would see him in Venice.

~~~~~~~~~~~~~

Sitting in the doctor's office, Ben knew he had made the right decision regardless of what Ted was about to say. Ted walked in and closed the door.

"Trust Thanksgiving went well?" he asked.

"It was a wonderful weekend. Did you enjoy yours?"

"Yes, we flew to South Carolina to visit the kids. Played a little tennis, ate and drank too much. You know how it is. And how have you been feeling?" the doctor asked.

"About the same, a little tired, but otherwise I would still think I'm in remission."

"I couldn't believe your lab results. Let's get down to your options." Ben was relieved when Ted did not make small talk.

"I'm going to stop you right there, Doc. I'm not going to go have any treatments. Period. I don't have it in me, and besides can you give me any guarantees it's going to work this time around? Or what my quality of life will be?"

Ted took off his glasses and placed them on the desk. He looked straight at Ben. "These are words no physician wants to hear. Our job is to keep you alive as long as we can, and that's what I want to do for you, Ben. We can try the chemo treatments again, and then there is always the bone marrow transplant. But no, I can't guarantee you anything."

"Can you give me any kind of a medical determination as to how long I have if I walk out of this office today and never come back?"

Ben was serious and Ted could see this.

"I'm not God, Ben; you're forcing my hand...an educated medical opinion, I would say give or take a year."

"Good!"

"That's good?" Ted asked quizzically.

"Yes." Ben went on to tell Ted his plan.

"And when you announced this in Maine, what was the reaction? Remember I know these folks," Ted reminded Ben.

Shaking his head, Ben said the family had not been happy with his decision, but when he explained why, they accepted his choice. "Nena was the biggest surprise," he added. "You know our story. She had all the right in the world to turn me down, but she didn't. I'm going to be able to die, having made amends in a place where I took Nena once under dishonest circumstances, and now I can spend my last days with her, leaving the slate clean. How many people can say that? And how many people get a second chance, and make the most of it? I'm a damn fortunate man, Doc."

"This profession has taught me to never underestimate my patients, and you're amongst them. Ben, I'm here for you, even if you'll be across the ocean. I'm only a phone call away. I'll put you in touch with some colleagues of mine. You realize the end is going to be difficult, and you will need to be on pain medication. I'll keep in touch, and there is always Jay as a go-between."

Ted had one last order: "Seriously, Ben I want you to call me at least once a week and give me a progress report on how things are going in general. Your well-being is important to me."

"Promise, I will. It was a lucky day for me when Jay introduced us. You kept me alive these last six years. I've seen my grandsons born, and I've had the chance to live some quality time in spite of cancer. I think of you as a friend, not just my doctor."

"I feel the same, Ben. Take care, and say hello to Nena for me, please."

Ted walked Ben to the door. Ben turned and hugged Ted.

Back in his office, Ted was thankful Ben was his last patient. Before leaving, he had his secretary cancel his appointments for the following day.

"Something come up?" she asked.

"Yes, I'm going for a drive up the Hudson. I know a cozy inn where I've been wanting to take my wife for dinner, and I don't want to put it off any longer. Take the day off and enjoy yourself," he told her.

"Thank you, Doctor Harris; I will."

As Ted got on the elevator, he thanked Ben aloud for reminding him what was important in life.

~~~~~~~~~~~~~~~

Becky tried to keep the family Christmas dinner as normal as possible, however each person attending was painfully aware this would be the last family gathering with Ben. She served their traditional dinner: rib roast, Yorkshire pudding, Brussels sprouts, and trifle for dessert. Nena reveled in watching the boys delight when they popped the customary English Crackers, seeing how something that brought her so much joy would live on with another generation. Wine and champagne flowed, songs were sung, the boys opened presents, and the evening ended with a rousing game of cribbage. There were no long, drawn-out good-bye toasts, only pledges of, "We'll see you in Venice."

Chapter 19

February, of 2009, Becky, J.R., Jay, and the twins sat in a limousine with Nena and Ben on the way to JFK airport. Easy conversation filled the car, no different than any ride to the airport.

"Are we going to watch Grandpa and Grandma get on the big airplane?" Daniel asked.

"No silly," M. J. poked his brother. "We can't see the plane; it's dark out."

The boy's conversation amused Ben because with the new rules, regulations, and tight security since 9/11, even if it were daylight, they would not see the plane.

The driver took the bags to the check-in. Good-byes were shared as well as hugs, kisses, and tears as Nena and Ben got into line. "Call when you get to London." Becky could barely speak the words.

"We'll talk every day," her mother replied.

When Ben and Nena passed out of view through security, Jay motioned it was time for them to go. On the drive back into the city, silence, not easy banter, filled the limousine.

~~~~~~

They were staying at the Ritz Hotel. No other place seemed fitting. The two weeks they planned in London before leaving for Venice, turned into a month.

They visited their old apartment. Nena had been back with Becky the summer of Ben's business trip, the summer she met the banker and his wife in Paris, but Ben had never been back inside. The building looked the same, and the lift had not changed. It was exactly as he remembered — small.

"Remember our first ride in this thing?" Ben questioned Nena as she closed the gate, and they rode to the third floor.

"How could I ever forget? Suitcases falling out the door, laughing until we almost cried. It was a comfortable home, Ben, for those three years."

The current occupant let them in. Walking into the bedroom, Ben pictured making love to Nena in that room. It was the first day they arrived in London. The day she conceived the twins. He wondered if John had lived if things might have been different. Other thoughts crept into his mind: those of Helen, his mother, and her dying in the other bedroom. The flat was full of memories for the both of them.

Another day, they took the train to Oxford. Nena wanted to revisit where her father taught the summer she stayed in London with her family and where Becky married J.R. They sat in the chapel and reminisced about the wedding, fondly remembering those who were there that day, but were no longer with them.

The same summer Nena visited England with her family as a young girl, Ben came to England with his brother, mother, and Uncle Buddy to bring home his father's body. When they first met, they marveled at how they were both in London the summer of 1960. But their reasons for being there were very different, and perhaps in the end it was their differences that created what lay ahead for them.

The last excursion out of the city was to Beeston. Ben hired a car. He wanted to show Nena where his father spent the last days of his life and died during World War II. Nothing had changed since he was there as a teen or with Buddy on their last trip after Becky's wedding. They walked the grounds while he recalled meeting the veterans, the pilots from the 392nd. Ben repeated the stories they shared with him, Jackie, Buddy, and Helen. They knew his dad, and recalled Jack — the best mechanic that ever serviced their planes, Jack's beloved B-24 Liberator. For Ben, this seemed like yesterday.

"Ben, I hope when the boys come to Venice you'll tell them about your father being in WWII, how he died, and how proud of him you have always been," Nena encouraged him. "You need to tell them about Jackie and his dying in Vietnam. Your father and brother are heroes, and your grandsons need to know these stories."

They sat on a bench in the quiet of a lovely English afternoon, reflecting.

**

That night, sitting in the opulent dining room of the Ritz, under a halo of light from the chandeliers overhead, Nena looked stunning, reminding Ben of the young girl he met at a college dance. He ordered champagne. Lifting his glass, he toasted, "Thanks Nena, for accompanying me. It's my last journey, but we all have one to take. The beginning has more than met my expectations." Old wounds had finally healed; a peace between them had settled in. "Tomorrow's our last day before we leave for Venice. I want it to be your day."

"Let's make tomorrow our day. Let's do things neither of us has ever done in this town," Nena suggested, and her smile said it all.

Over after-dinner drinks, they planned tomorrow. Tracing the steps of Jack the Ripper topped the list, then lunch at one of the oldest pubs in London, the Ye Olde Mitre, established in 1546 and where it is said Henry VIII was married next door and his daughter, Queen Elizabeth I, danced around a cherry tree in front of the pub's door. After lunch, they planned a ride on the London Eye to view the city from the tallest Ferris wheel in Europe, and in the evening a visit to Wilton's Music Hall, a step back into the nineteenth century, have drinks at the Mahogany Bar pub, and watch a film in the tattered but charming main hall.

~~~~~~~~~~~~~~

"Your place is amazing, Nena; the pictures you showed me don't do it justice," Ben told her as she opened the door to her apartment in Venice.

"I do love it here. It brings me a serenity I can't seem to find anywhere else. I hope it does the same for you, Ben."

"I'm praying it will, Nena."

**

The following months, Nena and Ben walked the streets of Venice. Once a week, they took the boat to the Cipriani for dinner, where Mr. Rusconi and Chef Piccolotto treated them like royalty. J.R. came as often as he could; Josh and Gabby visited, as well as Rachael and her family. Becky and the twins spent two months in the summer, and when Becky and the boys left, Jay came and stayed through the fall.

As Nena suggested, Ben told Daniel and M. J. about their great-grandfather and great uncle and their war stories. The boys listened intently, having Ben repeat the stories over and over. He was just their age when he lost his father. His memory dim — he derived what he remembered from Uncle Buddy, and the curiosity the twins displayed filled his heart.

"I have something for both of you; come sit by me," he told them one afternoon. Ben was holding a box. When he opened the box, the boys' eyes widened.

"Can we touch them?" asked M. J.

"Can we, can we?" Daniel pleaded.

"Of course you can touch them. You can wear them. There is one for each of you."

Carefully, Ben took his father and brother's dog tags from the box and placed them around the necks of his grandsons. Nena was watching from the other room, thinking how pleased Jack and Jackie would be to see the memory of their lives living on in these two boys.

"Thanks, Grandpa Ben." Daniel and M. J. threw their arms around him.

"Boys, I have one more thing to show you."

Ben sat on the floor with his grandsons as he opened the sketchbook filled with the magnificent charcoal drawings and sketches of what Jackie had witnessed in Vietnam — beginning with the drawing of the countryside below, drawn from the vantage point of his window on the plane flying into Saigon, to the last drawing done on the day he was injured before he died.

"Now you will have to share this book and take very, very good care of it for your great-grandfather, your great uncle, and for me. Promise?"

"Pinky promise," they swore.

~~~~~~~~~~~~~

As the days turned into weeks and then into months, Ben's health began to fail. Before he became frail, Nena called Becky to let them know everyone should come to say their last good-byes. The decision was made the family would come to celebrate Daniel and M. J.'s sixth birthday in Venice. This would be Ben's last birthday with his grandsons. He wanted this more than anything. Mr. Rusconi hosted the party at the Cipriani, and decorated a room with streamers and ornaments depicting scenes of Venice. Nena hired a juggler and a magician, and each person left with a mask they made and painted. It was a day nobody would ever forget.

**

After Jay left, Ben's remaining days were spent sitting at St. Mark's Square in the warm late fall sun, drinking espresso, talking with people he had become acquainted with, and practicing his limited Italian. When he could no longer go to the square, he would sit in the window of Nena's living room and watch the gondoliers in their rowboats pass by. He would wave, and they would wave back.

On a mid-December afternoon, as Ben sat by the window, he called to Nena. "Nena, could you please help me to the bedroom? I need to lie down."

"Are you in pain? Do I need to call the doctor?" she asked.

"No, just tired; maybe you'd come and sit with me for a while."

"Of course, let me make some tea."

Before Nena made the tea, she called Ted. "Should I call the doctor and take him to the hospital? He seems so weak," she told him.

"No need, I talked to him last week. He's been in severe pain for some time now. I ordered a stronger medication. I hope it's helping. He told me in no uncertain terms absolutely *no* heroic measures. This is what he wants; it's his time. Please call anytime. You're both in my thoughts."

"Thank you Ted, I'll do that." Nena hung up the phone, made the tea, and went into the bedroom. Ben was already in bed. She held the cup for him to take a sip and then set the cup down on the table.

"Nena, could I hold your hand?" Nena put her hand in his.

"I need to tell you something. You have given me such a gift by coming with me first to England and now here to Venice, to your home. You not only opened your home to me, but your heart. You've given me the ability to end my days coming full circle with you. You gave me a second chance to make things right with us."

"Yes, these months here have been healing for the both of us. I thought I had come to terms with us when I met Sam, but there was always that something in the background never resolved, and here we did that together. You know Ben, I never had any expectations for myself when you asked me to take this journey with you. My goal was to make your last days as comfortable as I could. It has been quite a journey, you and I." Nena stopped to reflect on the life they had shared. "Ben, you were my first love, and you were the father of our twins. I felt this was the least I could do for you, for us, and for Becky, but I got more than I counted on. I found the peace I needed and wanted between us, so I'm thanking you Ben for asking me to come on this journey with you."

A beam of gratitude filled Ben's face. Would he have the courage to tell her what his heart ached to say? Knowing this was his last opportunity and looking directly into her eyes, he spoke his final words: "I still love you, Nena. I always have…I've never stopped."

Nena could not respond, and Ben did not expect her to, because as he smiled at her and closed his eyes, he knew she cared deeply for him. Yet she still loved Sam and he understood this. Holding his hand, she gently kissed it and brought it to her cheek.

Long after he took his last breath, she sat and held his hand, looking into the face of this man who had been in her life since she was a coed, in a different time and in a different place.

When she finally got up, she phoned Becky. "He's gone, isn't he, Mummy?" She knew.

"Yes, sweetheart, he is."

~~~~~~~~~~~~

Nena flew home with Ben's body. A service was held in New Canaan, and it seemed as if the entire town turned out, the same as when his father, brother, and uncle had died. Nena stayed through Christmas and then returned to Venice. She knew she would miss Becky and the boys, but she needed to go back to this place that allowed her to find herself like no other place seemed to.

Part VI

2010

The year 2010 began with an earthquake in Haiti of a catastrophic magnitude, 7.0. Then there was the BP oil spill in the Gulf of Mexico, the horrible economic situation, and the Julian Assange Wikileaks scandal of classified cables; the bad news went on and on.

For the family, the new year seemed to begin the way the last one ended, with a lingering feeling of loss; however, each member was determined that no matter how bad things were, they were going to make this year matter, and they did. By the time 2010 was coming to a close, Jay and J.R. were moving the family business back into the black. Becky and J.R. decided to stay in the city until the real estate market stabilized. They made the decision to keep Ben's townhouse, which Becky inherited. They used it on weekends and times they felt the need to have a break from the city. That summer, J.R. and Becky took a trip to England with the boys to show their children where their parents had met and fallen in love. They went to Le Manoir aux Quant' Saisons, where they had their first date and celebrated so many happy occasions, and were greeted by Raymond Blanc and the staff as long-lost guests. They promised they would not be strangers and would come back soon. Josh and Gabby spent a lot of time in Venice and had fallen in love with the city, selling their home in Florida and buying an apartment near Nena. In spite of all the bad news happening in the world, the family had beaten the odds on their terms.

Looking out the window in her living room, watching the gondoliers guide their gondolas deftly along the canal and lost in thought, Nena was flooded with memories of the two loves of her life.

She came to Venice with Ben, her first love, when he was trying to stem the tide of disaster as his business career and their worlds were about to collapse, and again when he was dying. His last wish was to come to this sliver of paradise so his final days and her last memories of them would be where the sunsets hold the promise of new beginnings.

And she came to Venice with Sam, her second love, a man who loved her unconditionally from the day he laid eyes on her. Her second chance for love was short-lived but full. Nena never thought something so amazing would ever happen to her — he taught her to love again, to open her heart. If only Sam had lived, he would be here with her now.

On the bookshelves in her living room standing next to each other were the two figurines: the butterfly and the seal. Nena had never discarded the figurine of the butterfly. Somewhere deep inside her she knew Venice was where they both belonged. These were gifts from two very different men and yet symbols and reminders of their love. Now both men were gone and their memories surrounded her.

**

The family would arrive shortly to celebrate her seventieth birthday.

The doorbell rang. When Nena opened the door, there stood the two new loves of her life, M. J. and Daniel. As she kneeled to greet her grandsons, they threw their arms around their grandmother. Joy filled her heart. Looking up at Becky, J.R., and Jay, she understood the reasons why things happened the way they did and felt a sense of purpose, even at this stage in life.

Recently, Nena had heard a quote author William Purkey ended his speeches with: "You've gotta dance like there's nobody watching, Love like you'll never be hurt, Sing like there's nobody listening, and live like it's heaven on earth." And Nena could not have agreed more.

www.ingramcontent.com/pod-product-compliance
Lightning Source LLC
Chambersburg PA
CBHW020559260626
47157CB00003B/782

* 9 7 8 0 9 8 6 1 2 6 4 0 6 *